I HADN'T UNDERSTOOD

Diego De Silva

I HADN'T UNDERSTOOD

*Translated from the Italian
by Antony Shugaar*

Europa
editions

Europa Editions
214 West 29th Street
New York, N.Y. 10001
www.europaeditions.com
info@europaeditions.com

Copyright © 2007 by Giulio Einaudi editore s.p.a. Torino
First Publication 2012 by Europa Editions

Translation by Antony Shugaar
Original title: *Non avevo capito niente*
Translation copyright © 2012 by Europa Editions

Library of Congress Cataloging-in-Publication Data is available
ISBN 978-1-60945-065-6

De Silva, Diego
I Hadn't Understood

Book design by Emanuele Ragnisco
www.mekkanografici.com

Cover photo © Fot Wide Group/Stone/Getty Images

Prepress by Grafica Punto Print – Rome

Printed in the USA

For Andrea Frazzi,
who knew how to laugh

I was 42 years old.
I categorically refute those who claim
that this is the best time of your life.
In part because who on earth
would ever say that?
——VINCENZO MALINCONICO

Why travel a thousand miles
when you can embrace failure
in the comfort of your home?
——GIANFRANCO MARZIANO

CONTENTS

I HADN'T
UNDERSTOOD

MISPLACED ALTRUISM

W hy you go for walks when a love affair ends:
a) Because you can't stay still.
b) So that, without wasting any time, you can crack
your head against the brick wall of reality.

c) To go buy a shirt, a grill lighter, or any other object that
you don't particularly need.

d) Because when you get new prescription lenses, it's best
to get used to them right away.

e) So you can fall in love.

f) So you can wallow in self-pity.

g) Because you're going to suffer anyway, so why wait
around at home for it to swing by and pick you up? (For
instance, depression tapped me on the shoulder in a shopping
mall, while I was pricing LCD TV sets.)

I don't know why it happens. It just does. Try getting
dumped by the person you love sometime, and tell me if you
don't get a sudden urge to step out for a little tour of the town
you live in—oh, just for half an hour or so. It's desperation
shopping, the impulse to invest in markets that don't exist.
Obviously, when you have no alternatives, you start distorting
the reality that's available to you.

Anyway, while we're on the subject, there was another thing
I wanted to say. When a woman leaves you, you might find
yourself going all high-minded, tossing your brain out the window and listening earnestly to monologues that often take the

form of a weird blank verse, like this: *I'm practically certain / that I'm making a horrible mistake / and I'll live to regret it / in fact, I regret it already / but now it's too late / to take it all back*, as if someone had spiked your coffee. As if your immune system had decided to sign a full admission-of-fault accident report, instead of just doing its job. And there you are, reacting like an idiot at one of the most critical moments of your life. Actually lending a hand, trying to make your own eviction as painless and convenient as possible for the woman who's kicking you out. Listening as she rattles on, instead of demanding that she show you the timetable that says it's too late. Too late? You were there, you have a watch, it didn't seem like that much time had flown by. Instead of telling her it's never too late for two people, and that it's always one person who decides what time it is.

You might choose to spare her this line of reasoning (and a line of reasoning is what it is, in contrast with hers; and normally, you'd already be veering into the familiar territory of one of those spats that so get your blood up: ah, the fine itch that only a verbal brawl can scratch, the words jail-breaking out of your mouth without an escape plan!), and in the blink of an eye, with the sweeping power of an epiphany, you're transformed into your own opposite, a virtuoso of variables, a custodian of failed relationships, as if you were diagnosing the issues of a colleague or acquaintance, as if you'd spent your life providing even-handed advice about divorces and their traumatic aftermaths, as if the avalanche that is even now thundering down upon you (moving into a new apartment, custody of the children, monthly alimony checks, trouble sleeping, jerking awake with night terrors when you finally do fall asleep, chronic depression, loss of professional momentum, generic embarrassment at being alive, social guilt complex, encroaching baldness, weight gain from poor nutrition, and the ingestion of medications that not long ago you'd never even heard of) were just a minor inconvenience compared with the exquisitely philosophical imperative of assessing the present state of affairs.

You might muster every ounce of determination and strive to aid the efforts of someone who's bent on wrecking your life; you could say, yes, I see her point of view, *deep down / we both / knew it was true* (I wonder if they're still paying royalties to the guy who came up with that last line), say your dignified final farewell, issue a full acquittal on all charges and add a kiss on each cheek, and forego entirely the red-faced shouting, the fuck-you's, the slamming of whatever comes to hand, the mean-spirited cross-examinations that verge on mental cruelty. You can respond to the crushing rejection with nothing more than an ironically raised eyebrow, while bestowing upon her the incalculable goodness of simply issuing an amnesty for all the outstanding grievances you'd been holding on to for a rainy day. You might find yourself rehearsing statements like: "Should I remind her of this one thing, or that other? Should I consider myself indemnified by this fistful of pennies?" knowing full well the whole time that the correct answer is: "*Yes, indeed!*" (But for the love of God, when you find yourself thinking back on this humiliating spectacle—which she, don't kid yourself, is the first to find less than entirely convincing—how will you face yourself in the mirror? And what will you do then? Pick up the phone and heap insults upon her that are not only out of place but long past their sell-by date?)

You may realize you're on autopilot, that you can no longer restrain yourself, that you're letting yourself slip into a pool of saccharine masochism where it seems eminently reasonable that your wife is fed up with you and is now free to go out into the world, as if she were a daughter who's turned twenty-one and has received a job offer in a big city to the north. You can offer to be the one man she'd want by her side when she needs someone who truly understands her (and she'll tell you, as she holds both your hands in hers, not to go too far: she needs you, not your I Told You So's). You can even have sex with her—why not?—every now and then (when it's right for her, of course), and you may decide that the milquetoast architect who took your place and now lives in your apartment isn't such a bad guy after all (why is it that ex-wives always seem to wind up with architects?); he's perfectly nice to your kids and he'd never dream of pulling the loathsome move of trying to compete with you in that sphere. You might talk yourself into believing that it's possible (and actually surprisingly easy) to resolve the conflict of interests, to construct a new relationship with your wife, certainly as meaningful—if not more so—as your previous one (so routine and contractual, after all), and finally learn to think of her as a human being, and not a possession, *a woman / with a world / that you had always / ignored.*

Sure, you could do all that.

It's just that, once you decide that this is the way to go, though it now seems like an amazingly simple thing to do (so simple that it's not worth thinking about), you will realize that spitting in your own face is an endeavor that better men than you have been unable to accomplish.

So how on earth are *you* going to be able to pull it off?

TANGLES

I started telling this story from too far back; no, that's not right, because far back is a distance. Telling a story from too far back would mean starting at a certain point and reaching a brink after which there is nothing, but still you stand there looking around you as if there were something you ought to have understood. Instead, I started by setting forth a theory. That in itself wouldn't be a problem, if only I knew where I was taking that theory.

It strikes me that this is my shortcoming: I lack conclusions, in the sense that I have the impression that nothing ever really comes to an end.

I only wish (really, I do wish) that the out-of-date disappointments, the wrong people, the answers I failed to give, the debts I incurred needlessly, the small cruelties that poisoned my soul, all the things I can't relegate to the past, love stories especially—would just vanish from my mind and never come back. But I'm filled with residue and aftereffects, specters with nothing better to do who just drop by to see me all the time. I blame it on memory, which freezes and thaws of its own volition, hindering the digestion of life and making you feel appallingly alone when you least expect it.

So, anyway, that's how I began . . . well, you'd hardly call it telling a story. A story should have a beginning, an end, and a fat juicy middle, with plenty of meat. Otherwise, inevitably, you lose your reader.

Why on earth—say the readers you're busy losing—should

we go to the trouble of understanding you? We don't want to do your work for you. Why don't you take us for an enjoyable ride someplace?

And you can't blame the distractible readers. Beginning, end, and juicy middle: that's what people want. Even if—truth be told—they're willing to turn a blind eye when it comes to the matter of the ending. Unless you decide to tack on the ending as a contractual clause, like at school, when you had no idea how to conclude an essay and you tried to fake it with one of those sentences cobbled together with spit and chicken wire, like: "To me, the Christmas spirit that fills the air is especially nice because it takes our mind off the problems of modern-day life." And when your middle school teacher handed back the graded papers, you found a squiggle in red ink next to that sentence, which wasn't a correction or a verdict, it was a genuine graphic shudder.

The fact is that I'm an inconsistent narrator. I'm not a narrator you can rely on. I'm too interested in incidental considerations that can take you off track. When I tell a story, it's like watching someone rummage through the drawer where they keep their receipts and records. First I feel around a little bit, to get familiar with the bulk and heft of the material, and then I delve in, pretty much at random, hoping to find what I'm looking for. Of course, I find nothing, and I start pawing through a little more frantically. I shuffle things into a jumble. I daydream, I get distracted. I make little piles of paper. I find receipts I wasn't looking for and stop to think about them. I look at the date embossed into the paper on a return receipt, recognize my own handwriting from when I was younger (have you ever noticed how people's handwriting shows the passage of time?), and I try to remember where I was and what I was doing when I mailed it. Was I better or worse off? Was my son already born? What our apartment smelled like. Who my friends were. I like to get a glimpse of myself in a delivery confirmation form. Somehow I find it more reliable than a photograph.

All this is just another way of saying my thoughts don't seem to grip the road, they tend to skid and drift. In fact, I think that my pathology is basically just an intermittent collapse of this natural tendency. I cheat on the topics I'm talking about, is what happens. And it's not really that I lose the thread of what I'm talking about. Even when the tangled does get more than a little thread.

There, I knew it.

The thing is, I suffer (but only now and then; in fact—did you notice?—it hadn't happened till just now) from a morphosyntactic impairment, a dysfunction of the structure of my phrasing. In practical terms, the nuts and bolts of my sentences come undone. My words go haywire, it's like herding cats. The words fail to yield the right-of-way. Like with the thread and the tangled—I can't even remember how that was supposed to go anymore.

The embarrassing part is that in my mind, I have the sentence set up correctly, and then it comes out all discombobulated. If I could tell it was about to happen, I'd just keep my mouth closed. But no: the mouth opens wide, and it ruins my reputation.

The first time it happened I was in court. It was around noon, Court of Appeals, the courtroom was packed (by the way, I'm a lawyer by profession), a civil procedural hearing assigning cases for deliberation and judgment. The kind of hearing where you do practically nothing at all, except to wait your turn and then formally request that the panel of appeals judges proceed to deliberate and issue a finding in your case. Here's how it works: when the judges call the case with the names of the parties (which is the legal title of the file) immediately followed by the names of the legal counselors, the only thing that you are required to do is rise (that is, if you were able to find a place to sit; if not, you can skip the part where you rise) and state: "The cause may be submitted for judgment."

Nine times out of ten, the appeals panel doesn't even dignify you with a glance, and simply moves on to the next case. Your work is done. So easy that the first time you perform a legal service of this kind, you think to yourself: "Ah, what an excellent degree I took." Choreography of the law: they should make that a subject in the curriculum of law schools everywhere.

So there I was, cheek by jowl in the crowd (already a humiliating experience in itself), poised to declare: "The cause may be submitted for judgment." But when it was my turn, I said: "The judgment may be submitted for cause."

Whereupon a pause filled the room that was deeply reminiscent of one of those extended *"Oooooh!"* moments that were so common in American movies from the forties when—in a courtroom, as it happens—someone who's completely above suspicion takes the stand and, without warning, breaks down and admits they did it. And then you'd hear that *"Oooooh!"* followed by the judge banging his gavel and threatening to have the bailiff clear the courtroom. After which the audience regains its composure (which is exactly what an audience is: a roomful of people who bought their ticket in the hopes of saying *"Oooooh!"*).

Now, if you stop to think about it, "The judgment may be submitted for cause," even if it's not really that bad—in the sense that you can kind of understand it—is decidedly odd, as sentences go. It smacks of a rank beginner, someone who doesn't quite know how to work the language, speaking Italian but with training wheels on. Say I had modified it just a little, said: "The judgment of the cause may be submitted," then it would have been an entirely different matter. Awkward but functional. Instead, I came out with that monstrosity, the sort of mild anomaly that immediately flags, however, out of a crowd of normal people, a victim of disorganized thinking.

For a moment, the courtroom went into a collective organizational state of systole, just long enough to calculate the exact duration of the subsequent diastole, and then once again lunged at the new object of its attention, namely me, as I stood there inspecting my surroundings, moving my head back and forth with odd little birdlike micro-jerks of the head. Really, a disgusting situation. As far as I knew, I might have been on the verge of Parkinson's, the incipient extinction of all cerebral functions, an early-onset dementia (I know one guy whose mother woke up one morning and she just wasn't hitting on all four cylinders, like for instance he said "Good morning, Mamma" and she looked at him and said well it's taken them long enough to send someone up to the fix the water heater), but I managed to tamp down my spiraling sense of panic, because what I was chiefly worried about was my reputation. What I wanted more than anything else on earth was to get out of there, to get myself and my name out of that courtroom and then, and only then, once I was out of range of the morbid fascination of that roomful of eyes, try to come to some conclusions about what malfunction had come over me in that unseemly fashion.

It's unbelievable how an emergency reveals the hierarchy of truly important things. For instance, your reputation.

Alberto Tritto, a specialized broker in traffic accident lawsuits, shot me a close-up stare at a distance that fell just short of a kiss. Ivo Frasca (a complete moron) looked at me with the scorn of someone who has just confirmed long-held beliefs (but has he taken a look at himself lately?); Gisella Della Calce, a Roman Catholic divorce lawyer, covered her mouth with one hand, probably a psychological transference of what she thought I ought to have done (so thoughtful of her).

Aside from these few examples that I was able to gather in the immediate vicinity, most of the onlookers were, I have to admit, nonplussed. You could hear them buzzing with dismay.

There was even an asshole or two who barely stifled a laugh, and I know their names.

The judges, who take great care not to look anyone in the face on general principle, raised their collective heads, making an unmistakable effort to remember my name (unsuccessfully, I imagine). They probably assumed that I was mocking them. Judges are always worried that lawyers are mocking them, basically because they can't wait for that day to come; then they'll show those lawyers who they're dealing with.

At that point, more upset at the bull's-eye I could feel on me than at the seriousness of the incident, I just managed to stammer out, "Excuse me: for judgment," and I made my way to the exit, as my colleagues fell back to open a passage for me, recoiling as if they were afraid they might catch whatever disease it was that I had contracted.

I went downstairs to wander aimlessly past the offices of the clerk of the civil court, just to get a better sense of how I was feeling, and a short while later Alessandra Persiano caught up with me. She had been present in the Court of Appeals when I'd blurted out the incriminating phrase.

"Are you feeling all right?" she asked me.

She seemed worried.

"Yeah, I think," I said.

She was wearing boots and a close-fitting T-shirt under her jacket and she wore her hair loose. Women who wear their hair loose—even if it seems like there's nothing odd about wearing your hair loose—are never the same when their hair is pulled back in a bun or a ponytail. It has something to do with the fact that they undo their hair when they have sex, because that way they can caress you with their hair too, spill it all over you, and most important of all, make sure that you find strands of their hair in your sheets after they've left, and so you, even though you don't realize it, whenever you see a woman with her hair down, you just immediately have that association of ideas.

At the end of the hallway, two fellow lawyers who were walking downstairs (and one of them was none other than Ivo Frasca, ha ha) froze in unison, slackjawed at the sight of me in the company of Alessandra Persiano.

Now it's not like there aren't plenty of cute women lawyers. But Alessandra Persiano is a celebrity. The whole courthouse pants and drools when she walks by, and she is well aware of it. She doesn't give any of them a hint of encouragement.

It must have been that long-range ballistic envy that made me feel better. I was swept with a frenzy, a desire to fight, to take back my wife and pack the car and load the kids in back and head for the beach—gangway!

"Are you sure you're all right?" Alessandra Persiano asked me once again.

Those two assholes were still at the far end of the corridor all agog.

"I'm fine," I told her, and at that very moment it occurred to me that maybe she liked me a little, because this singular thought popped into my head like a contact (in the sense of electricity, just like in a movie when a car thief touches the ignition wires together under the steering wheel and makes the engine turn over). And just to make the two guys at the end of the hallway eat their hearts out, I reached out and stroked her lovely hair, though in gratitude.

So then Alessandra Persiano told me that if I could wait she'd be happy to give me a ride, but I told her that I had something fairly urgent to do (in fact, I couldn't wait to do that one thing, the one thing that had just flashed into my mind) and so I thanked her for her concern and told her some other time, without a doubt.

So then she told me that she had to head back upstairs to the Court of Appeals, but that if I needed anything I just needed to let her know.

"That's very kind of you," I replied.

She turned around and walked away, but almost immediately turned on her heel.

"Do you have my cell phone?" was her question.

When I walked out of the court house, I was basically roller-skating.

And then, the way I do, I immediately tried to take advantage of the situation. Which is to say that I called up my wife and said to her, in the voice of someone who's just survived a plane crash, that I didn't know what the hell had just happened to me at the Court of Appeals, but that it was almost certainly her fault.

Whereupon she asked me what was wrong and why I was so worked up.

The last thing I felt like at that point was telling her the whole story (I'd called her up to make accusations, not for her professional advice), so I remained speechless on my end of the call.

"Hello?" she said.

"Eh," I replied.

"Well?" she asked, justifiably.

"Well what?" I replied.

So I handed her a silver platter on which she could serve up the little sermon that she immediately delivered with all the enthusiasm of a star student who has just been asked the exact question she was hoping for. That my aggression, whatever might have provoked it—though at this point the matter became a corollary (that's exactly what she said: corollary), since I had no intention of talking to her about it—was, in her point of view, quite easy to explain, because when something happens to you that you can't understand, the first thing you do is to seek the cause outside of yourself, and immediately afterward you seek out a mastermind (that's exactly what she said, a mastermind, that is to say, a "guilty party," but decaffeinated; she is always very careful to use words that involve the least possible risk of potential responsibility), and it was therefore absolutely consequential (that's exactly what she said: consequential, an adjective that should never be used between two people who have ever been a couple, as far as I'm concerned) that I would try to pick a fight with her, since we had only decided to separate (Ah! Not so, my dear: it was you who decided to leave me) less than two years ago. But that I shouldn't worry about it.

"Oh, thanks," I replied.

And I hung up on her, obviously coming off looking like an idiot.

The problem with my wife is that she takes everything down to the level of explanation. It's because she's a psychologist. Either she says nothing (a well-tested technique for inducing exasperation) or else she insists on telling you what you did, when you did it, and why. Let's be clear: without any authentic expectation of getting any of these things right (which is the diabolical initial pact that is underwritten by anyone who enters analysis).

Up to a certain point, the thing works pretty well. It's sort of like reading your horoscope. You listen because you have the impression that she's talking about you; then the narrative falters on an adjective, an adverb, or a transition that is so blatantly generic, contrived, and unisex that you wind up saying, "Okay, whatever."

And this is where the devil bursts onto the stage with a flash-bang and a cloud of brimstone, because even though every time my wife delivers one of her perorations (Oops, is that Freudian?), I wind up thinking, "Okay, whatever," but I can't seem to interrupt her. There's something in me (something I find profoundly disgusting) that drives me to act as her sidekick no matter how much I hate it.

It's not like I turn into a poodle, it's not like I give her the satisfaction that she's looking for. I might raise my voice, I might slam around, I might break something (something of mine, usually), but I remain thematically correct, I never put it in general terms, I'm not sure if you understand, while it's in general terms (not in personal terms) that you have to work when you're having a fight. If you really want to hit home, you can't talk in absolute terms, you have to focus on categories. What offends people is being common. If you call someone a crook, that's one thing. But if, say, you tell someone they're a crook just like all real estate agents are crooks, then watch them lose their temper. If you want to offend someone, then you have to make them look like a fool in front of their friends, in a certain sense. Try telling your wife that she's a bitch just like her mother was, and then just wait to see what she answers back.

For instance, I would very much like to tell my wife the following.

Sometimes, at home (in the early afternoon, ideally), I put on exhaustive rehearsals, fine-tuning the tone and diction of the harangue that sooner or later I will deliver to her.

I make her sit in the Tullsta armchair at the end of the hallway, so that I can walk up and down while I talk, and then I get started.

I tell her that she'd better not try to get up until I'm done.

And sure enough, she stays put.

I tell her to pay close attention, because I'm not going to do her the favor of saying this twice.

And even though by this point she really feels like saying, "You're scaring me," she keeps her mouth shut because she's afraid she'll only make things worse.

I tell her that for fifteen years now I've pretended to agree with everything she said.

That all this time I've been humoring her as if she were crazy.

I tell her that what she foists off on an unsuspecting audience as scientific introspection is just the kind of common sense you hear at an academic cocktail party.

I tell her that the professor who acted as her graduate adviser is a big fat zero, moreover with a weakness for horses (racehorses, that is, to bet on).

I tell her that she's been putting on airs as if she were a militant psychologist since the morning of the day after she passed her final exams, just like southerners who adopt the local accent—*Anvedi questo* and *Aoh, che stai a fà*—two days after they arrive in Rome.

I tell her that her intelligence is a feat of prestidigitation, an only moderately successful sleight of hand, and it's only because of her attractive appearance that her audience pretends they haven't seen through the illusion.

I tell her that she's overvalued, and so she hasn't got the slightest idea of what it is to really earn a living. That she's a mediocrity just like everyone else (including me). But while the rest of us are barely scraping by, she has a waiting room crowded with people, and she can earn all the money she wants.

And it just isn't right for her to get by that easy.

I tell her that her groundless professional success is nothing more than tangible evidence of how low we've all fallen.

I tell her that her patients, except for the bloodsuckers (my term for the ones who only want to get her into bed, and at least they have a reasonable motive), are just a bunch of nouveau-riche bumpkins who use analysis to take the place of all the books they've never read.

Because it's obviously much harder work to read a book than it is to be interviewed by a good-looking woman who listens to you speak in respectful silence; plus she even takes notes.

I tell her, just to remain on the general subject of privilege, that she has always enjoyed complete emotional immunity.

Whereupon she asks me what emotional immunity is.

And I explain that it's a prerogative accorded to certain bitches, allowing them to suck up the love of others while giving little more than nothing in exchange. And that we're fed up with seeing women like her surviving with impunity. That it's time for them to stop exploiting people, that it's time for them to get a real job.

And I tell her to wipe that expression off her face, like a mistreated dog, straight out of *Lady and the Tramp*. And it's useless for her to bite her upper lip and stroke her left elbow, because it's just not going to work on me anymore.

Whereupon she grips her knees together, brings both fists to her lips, and in a rasping voice tells me that I've never spoken to her like that before.

So I tell her that it was high time I started.

And she bursts into tears.

So at this point, quivering at the idea of delivering the final blow, I tell her that I don't give a damn if she starts crying, because sobbing isn't the way to win my respect (which is a completely bullshit line, I'll admit it, but I've just been waiting for so long to say it to her).

And she rubs her nose with the cuff of her sleeve and says nothing.

And as long as we're at it I take advantage of the opportunity to rebuke her for the macrobiotic phase she put us through from 1996 to 1998 (with a partial relapse in the second half of 1999), and I tell her that during all that time I was secretly taking the kids to McDonald's twice a week. That we had always lied to her about the spelt soup, the razor clams with shallots, and the tofu with a double helping of curses on the name of the guy who ever invented it.

Believe it or not, at this point, she even starts nodding her head a little.

And now, even though it has nothing to do with anything, I tell her that her mother is a locust. That for years I've put up with her walking into the apartment unannounced with the keys in her hand, and now that we've separated, I wish I could go back in time just for the satisfaction of walking out of the shower with my junk in plain view, so that I'd send her mother into a state of panic and break her of that bad habit once and for all.

And I keep hammering at her until, exhausted, she falls to her knees from the Tullsta in desperation and, crawling on all fours, she comes over to me and clutches at my trousers, and so we wind up fucking and getting back together forever.

Then I return to reality, the place I inhabit, the place where I'll never be able to do the things that pass through my mind.

And after all, who even knows if that's what I really think?

The truth is that there are people, and no one knows how it happens, but they have the gift of always catching you at your most insipid and inane, of bringing out the very least you have to offer. I mean to say: each of us has a behavioral standard, each of us relies upon a mass-produced series of platitudes, thinking and saying the things that everyone thinks and says. Then, at rare intervals, we come up with a funny line or a brilliant observation. That's how a normal relationship works. We consist of banality and intelligence, and we shuttle from one to the other quite calmly.

Yeah, that is, we shuttle from one shore to the other quite naturally.

But then there are relationships in which, oddly enough, this relaxation, this indifference to what you're going to say, the way that you walk, how you sit in a chair or what you do with your hands, just vanishes. Relationships in which, without even realizing it, you decide how to put yourself across. And the fact that you're putting yourself across begins to condition everything you say. And that's when truly unpleasant things start to happen, like losing your balance when standing still, or hearing phrases like this issue mysteriously from your mouth:

"My, what delicious frozen foods they sell at that supermarket across the street from your apartment."

It's a little bit like waiting for a camera shutter to click in the certainty that you're about to look like an idiot. The harder you try to relax, the more tightly you can feel the iron coils of insecurity wrapping around you.

These people that I'm talking about, the ones who, without even meaning to (because the incredible thing is that it comes naturally to them), hold their finger on the shutter release, regularly manage, through some incomprehensible magic, to catch you in the most embarrassing situation, a contingency that indicts you even if you're guiltless. The kind of situation in which appearance counts more than the truth. In the sense that the search for truth would necessarily entail a reverse reconstruction of the scene in order to uncover the mechanism that made you look like an idiot. The only problem is that in practical terms, this replay is impossible. You can never explain the way things really went. Because if you try to do it, you look like twice the idiot. Words lose their relevance as you utter them, they break away from the concept as if they were less convinced than anyone else of what they ought to be saying. You have to catch the truth red-handed.

Which is why in cases like this you start to just give in and fold your cards. Obviously, you have to limit the damages. It's just that you start racking up negative points. You run into debt. And the person who puts you into this disgraceful condition starts to accumulate an enormous privilege with respect to you. Every time you interact with her, she has this huge head start. You feel awkward and out of place; you perceive her as rock solid, unburdened by the obligation to prove anything. She is. Each time, you have to become.

The oiliest aspect of this matter is that it needn't even be someone you admire or like. It can be someone you despise personally or (what's worse) politically. Someone whose worst song-and-dance routines you know by heart. And still they may have this power over you. They might even have that power over many people.

It happens, it happens.

For instance, let's take the day my wife gave me the happy news. We were at the train station, but downstairs, on the subway platform (which, from the get-go, shows poor taste as a choice of a setting for a breakup).

The finale of the little sermon in verse ran like this: *We aren't bed sheets / that come clean / after a last laundry cycle* (in response to my understated attempt to recoup: it was clear that she'd prepared that line).

If I'd had even a smidgeon of self-respect left, at least in response to this shameful piece of hip-hop (which even now—like any bad piece of music—will surface in my mind ten times a day, renewing the humiliation every time), I should at the very least have issued a Bronx cheer. Instead, silence. As if I were experiencing a perverse enjoyment in sitting there seeing how far I would let her go on indulging in that ridiculous language stuffed with television metaphors that she popped into every second or third sentence, as if she were addressing a meeting of the Rotary Club, not me.

But I interrupted her before she could finish (I wonder what other masterpieces she had in store). I gave her a childish kiss on the cheek so I could whisper into her ear, in a cringe-inducing falsetto: "I'm leaving now. Ciao."

She was clearly disgruntled (which is probably the effect I was aiming to achieve), neutralized by that premature denouement, as if I'd interrupted the punch line, and she just stood there while I rode away up the escalator, a pathetic pantomime of a break-up, the conveyor belt of life carrying you away without the slightest personal involvement (she standing motionless, you moving off into the distance).

If I had turned around just then—truth be told—I would have burst into tears the way my own children did the day I left them with the teacher on the first day of school. But I toughed it out. I don't know who I was trying to impress with all this spiritual fortitude. There was nobody watching me. Not even my wife, who was definitively out of focal range.

I blame the movies. It's inconceivable that all the thousands of movies that we've seen have failed to influence our behavior, in ways we don't even realize. Over the course of a typical day, if you stop to think about it, more than once you'll find yourself doing things—usually related to sports or leisure activities, things with a vague aesthetic overtone—as if twenty feet away there was a full camera crew filming you. Things like deactivating your car alarm with a decisive thrust of the remote control and then darting into the driver's seat (maybe slipping off your jacket as you slide behind the steering wheel), or else staring intensely into the middle distance, as if you were being swept by some stirringly profound thought. This unasked-for performance, this illusion of an audience waiting to enjoy our finest moments while we pretend we don't know we're being watched, is our meager revenge for the mediocrity of the lives we lead, an opportunity that the popular arts have always provided (and the reason that, when all is said and done, we refuse to let the popular arts die).

So anyway, I walked up out of the subway station and it was a beautiful day outside, warm sunshine, sparkling air (sixth of October), people talking quietly, streets relatively uncrowded.

At that moment—truth be told—I felt strangely better, as if the clubbing I had just undergone didn't hurt nearly as bad as I'd thought it had when we were underground.

I started walking aimlessly, skirting the taxi queues and listening to the conversations of people waiting for a cab, leaning on their wheelie suitcases. The world struck me as reasonable, arranged in the only way possible, if you know what I mean. The taxicabs, the buses, the cell phones going off, the cars slowing down to avoid hitting anyone.

I'll be okay, I was telling myself; this is hardly going to kill me.

So I went on strolling, in the grip of a weird Zen sense of calm, until—once I wound up in the shopping mall, standing in front of that giant LCD television set—despair lunged out and wrapped its tendrils around me, like a carnivorous plant seizing you by the ankles.

I look around with that bewildered gaze that you get when you're trying to catch the flight attendant's eye right after liftoff and no one feels bad but you, so in a frenzy of panic I went and buried myself in the self-service cafeteria that luckily was on the same floor. I walked up to the pasta counter without even picking up a tray and ordered a dish of *bavette al pesto*.

The girl served me with an indifferent shrug, whereupon I thought to myself: "Why don't people mind their own fucking business?" That made me feel a little better.

I paid, I sat down at a formica table for two, and I twisted my fork in the pasta. While I was sitting there, I reflected that if this was one of those movies with a happy ending, my wife would show up unexpectedly right now (I'd recognize her from her clothing, and only then would I look up from my plate) and say nothing more than "What are you eating?"

And then we'd each have a forkful of noodles without saying a single word.

I swear on anything you care to name that for a couple of minutes at least I believed that might really be about to happen.

The Penguin on the Ledge

J ust as I'm starting to wake up, I instinctively reach out to
touch the other pillow and I discover—like a scene from
the corniest movie where there's some guy starting to wake
up and he instinctively reaches out to touch the other pillow—
that I'm alone.

I open my eyes wide as if I didn't already have a perfectly
clear idea of the way things are and I see her standing in front
of the Leksvik chest of drawers, already almost completely
dressed, brushing her hair and scrutinizing herself in the mirror with the gaze of a detective.

She isn't done getting dressed, but she's already out of the
house, already mentally returning to her own world. She's
already disavowing, it's obvious. She has to accelerate her return
to the role that she abandoned once again on my account: that's
why she put on that hostile expression, as if I'd just done something to her (and in fact I have just done something to her).

She dominates me unconsciously with her vertical indifference. She's no longer present, she's already out of here, I ought
to just accept it for what it so blatantly is.

But instead.

"Nives," I say to her.

It's not like I have anything to say. I just want to intone her
name, that's all.

"Mmm?" she asks as she fiddles with the catch of her left
earring. I knew she'd say "Mmm?" as she fiddled with the catch
of her left earring.

"Don't go," I whine.

Just listen to me. I'm a disgrace to my gender.

I'm a dishrag of a man.

She emits a barely perceptible nasal sigh (which I perceive all the same) and then answers without even turning around.

"Vincenzo, please."

That's exactly what I would do if I were in her place, and this convergence of views about the right way to treat someone in my condition is the detail that crushes me once and for all.

"Why don't you stay a little longer?" I add, just to gild the lily.

From my point of view, the right angle that we form is pure humiliation.

At last she gives me the benefit of a glance and turns around. At this instant in time, she couldn't be any more elegant, graceful, or unself-consciously majestic. The hour and a half of sex we've just had has conferred upon her movements the perfect degree of sleepiness, an aesthetic contrivance that as far as I'm concerned will never go out of style. Every individual element and feature, from her high cheekbones to the pair of Hogans (lying there on the floor, waiting obediently to be laced onto her delicate little bare feet), all conspire on behalf of her beauty. The dress she's wearing is her handmaiden. Her calves are breathtakingly perfect. Her hair, bountiful and chestnut brown, allows itself to be coiffed without the slightest resistance.

In the half-light, I detect a slight tan that up till then had eluded my notice, and I register the detail with a sting of resentment, as if I'd been deprived of something.

She lets my last line linger in the air for a few seconds and then she puts her hairbrush down on the counter of the Leksvik dresser, suspending the process of eliminating all evidence of the crime (this drastic interruption of her current task—as if it's something that can wait, whatever it might happen to be—is a typically feminine form of gallantry), and walks toward me.

I continue to look at her, in gratitude, as she sits down on the bed, invading my space and forcing me to move over a little.

I'm completely in her hands, a patient enduring the throes of an acute kidney stone attack as he glimpses the syringe full of painkiller in the hands of the nurse. She's good, though, she doesn't take advantage, that much I have to admit.

"You're not going to change my mind if I stay a little longer," she says, with impeccable simplicity. "All that'll happen is I'll be late getting back to work."

Which is the perfect answer in a case like this one.

I'm so completely in accord with her that I'd be willing to countersign the phrase.

As she extends her lovely legs to snag the Hogans with her toes and pull them toward her, I take a worm's refuge in the thought of Alessandra Persiano, fantasizing that I'd accepted the ride she offered me that time.

I'm in her apartment (which I've never seen, so I improvise on the spot a generic floor plan, since it's notoriously impossible to fantasize a sex scene without some modicum of set design), in a spacious entryway with a vintage coat rack, a handpainted Vietri majolica umbrella stand, and a late-eighteenth-century hall table that, if I'm not mistaken, she mentioned to me on one occasion. She no sooner gets the door closed than I'm on her; in fact, I embrace her from behind, I pull her to me and kiss her on the lips, obliging her to twist her body in an unnatural contortion that super-excites the hell out of us both right then and there, so we put off all foreplay to our second go-round. Halfway through the kiss, Alessandra Persiano turns, mischievously diabolical, shoves me back against the door, and starts to unbutton her blouse. She wants to drive but I don't give her the chance, I lunge at her hungrily and before she knows it I'm in her, I'm holding her in midair, my hands clamped firmly around her thighs, and I can hear her moaning into my ear: "The . . . con . . . dom . . . umm . . .

mmm," which means that we're fucking without one. And I think to myself who cares, and it's wonderful. I even lose my grip on her and she starts to fall, grabbing me by the shoulders and knocking me backward so I bang my head against the door we were braced against, whereupon she laughs and—truth be told—she keeps laughing just a little longer than she needed to (so she too is a member of the category of actors without a film crew) and at that point she asks if she can make me that cup of coffee that she invited me up for in the first place.

While the whole vignette evaporates from my retina, Nives stands back up triumphantly. I still have the fantastic moans of Alessandra Persiano in my right ear, but I feel like a complete piece of shit. Nives is leaving again. She's my wife, and she's about to go home to another man.

She walks back to the Leksvik, picks up her hairbrush to apply the finishing touches. A sudden wave of anger sweeps through me.

"Are you done with the disinfestation?" I say, while I fold a pillow in two and lodge it comfortably behind my back, another move straight out of cornball cinema.

She stiffens, but she won't do me the favor of looking at me.

"You're safe to go, no one will notice a thing," I add, fleshing out the concept.

Another silence.

"You took a shower, didn't you?" I add relentlessly.

At that point, I deserve a response. Which she doles out, barely turning her head in my direction.

"Okay. You need to make me feel guilty so you'll feel better. Go ahead, be my guest."

The hairbrush is poised in midair. Her hair, charged with static electricity, is eager for the next stroke.

"No fair. It's no good if you say it," I shoot back promptly.

"Excuse me?" she enunciates distinctly, accompanying each

syllable with a bat of her eyelashes, aristocratic and supercilious.

So I straighten my back a little, sitting upright and pursuing the intuition on which I've decided to stake everything.

"It's like asking me to tell you a joke, when you've just told me the punchline."

She reddens slightly. One point to me.

"Oh, really? And what do you expect me to do?"

"You tell me. You're the psychologist."

She dismisses my riposte with a sniff and goes back to brushing her hair. Her hand isn't as steady as it was, though.

I renew my attack.

"But if you need a hint, here it is. Explaining the explanation isn't all that noble on your part, is it? Maybe you should just keep it to yourself, if you're so convinced of it, and let me behave the way I see best, for example."

I'm hitting my stride now. And what's more, I haven't even inverted a sentence. But here comes the countermove.

"So you're saying that I should stand still so you can spit in my face, right?"

A couple of hours from now it'll occur to me that at this point I could have said: "Hold on there for a second, let's try to play fair. You're the one who brought up spitting in the face, not me. If you think you're clever enough to understand the reasons for my aggression, then you should let me express my aggression, and not throw it back in my face so you can use it for your own benefit. Why don't you learn to accept your own responsibilities instead of avoiding them, my good doctor."

But right then and there, I can't think of a single word to say.

Nives picks up her purse from the Poäng side table, slips her brush into it, and snaps it shut.

There, she's leaving, and now she's pissed.

I stand there counting the sheep of my own idiocy as I

watch her speed up the various maneuvers involved in getting out of the apartment, hesitate, stand on the threshold, bow her head in the throes of a sudden attack of misgivings or something approaching it, and speak to me again, without turning around.

"Why do we have to fight? I'm happy."

Don't say a word, kid. Not a single word. You've already caused enough trouble. You know the ledges that run around apartment buildings, the ones that, when the husband comes home early from the office and the lover backs along it, half an inch at a time, making his way to the first open window? Well, you just move like that. Move like a penguin on a ledge.

Still half incredulous at the amnesty that has been offered me, I stand up, slip on my vintage 2004 espadrilles and shuffle over to her with an attitude equably split between mortified and pathetic.

She lays her head in the hollow of my left shoulder (which, as surrenders go, is just as fake as a three-dollar bill, but as a consolation prize it must be worth something) and stands there, without saying a fucking word.

I wrap her in my arms, hoping for a reaction of some kind, of any kind.

I hunt for her lips, but she turns away. I try again, but she means it. She breaks the clinch when I give up.

I walk her to the door.

I stand in the doorway dressed in boxers, a Carisma T-shirt, and espadrilles while she walks to the elevator and presses the call button.

The bang of the elevator motor starting up, the noise of cables pulling the cab upstairs. I start awake out of my excruciating enchantment. And I remember something important.

"Nives wait, wait just a minute."

"Now what?"

I raise one hand in the universal symbol for halt and push

air toward her twice. Nives shrugs reluctantly. I rush back into my bedroom, open the third drawer of the Leksvik, pull out my checkbook, and come running back, panting. Nives immediately identifies the foreign object I'm clutching in my hand. She looks skyward, without arrogance.

"Oh come on, it doesn't matter."

She opens the door of the elevator, which has stopped at the floor in the meanwhile.

I step out on the landing, intractable.

"Oh, but it does. We signed an agreement, you and I, remember?"

Taking advantage of the short distance that separates us, she gives me the once-over with her eyes, halting briefly on the espadrilles. I imitate her reflexively and when I look down at the last thing she laid her eyes on, I discover the shameful state of my espadrilles, which look as if they barely survived the attack of a ravening horde of sewer rats.

Nives suppresses a laugh, but mine bursts forth. So now she starts laughing too. It's a nice moment.

"Couldn't we just forget about it, for this month?" she asks.

Eh, I wish, I think to myself.

"You understand that you're insulting me by doing this?" I say, hoping that she'll keep it up.

"And you understand that you can't talk to me about money when we've just made love?"

I melt.

She reaches out and touches the hand that's holding the checkbook.

"You don't need to prove anything to me. You don't need to uphold any principles with me either. You know that."

Yeah, right, I think to myself.

"That's not the point," I insist shamelessly. "It's not about what you think. I just want to do my part, that's all."

"You've always done your part, it's not like you're doing it

I HADN'T UNDERSTOOD · 43

better if I take four hundred euros a month from you. The kids
are crazy about you, and you know that I . . . "
Witnesses at a deposition who suddenly realize they've said
the wrong thing catch themselves in exactly the same way.
"You what? Huh? Finish the sentence."
But she doesn't get the chance, because a southern Italian
buffoon on the floor above us is pounding on the elevator door.
"Just a second, for fuck's sake!" I shout.
"Shh," says Nives.
"What is it, are you ashamed?" I say.
She stabs me with her gaze.
"Sorry, sorry," I grovel.
Another series of three loud thumps on the door of the ele-
vator. I look up at the ceiling while I clench fists and teeth,
crushing the checkbook while I'm at it.
"I'm-a come up there and kick your—"
Nives censors me with one hand.
"Come on, just let me go," she says, hastily resolving the sit-
uation.
She runs to the elevator, gets in, closes it. The stairwell swal-
lows her up.
I stand there, in my underwear, on the landing, hypnotized.
Just then, my land line rings. Once. Twice. Three times. I
don't feel like talking to anyone, but since telephones that ring
and ring irritate me, I walk back inside and trace down the
cordless by following the rings. I wind up in the kitchen and
locate it on the tabletop, concealed between the television
remote control and the demitasses of espresso I made when
Nives came by (there's still lipstick on hers, a trace that pro-
vokes an adolescent stirring in my groin).
I pick up the phone. I look at the display.
Identity withheld.
Now what?
I heave a sigh and press talk.

"Hello."

"Counselor Malinconico?"

A woman's voice.

"Who's this?"

"Is this Counselor Malinconico?" she says again, with emphasis, annoyed.

I detest the current wave of telephonic boorishness, which has reversed the roles of caller and callee, with the advent of the cell phone. Nowadays, anyone who calls your cell phone (and therefore also on the landline, because the boundary automatically dissolves) starts the conversation by immediately pronouncing your name, followed by a question mark. Well, fuck you. You called me, why don't you tell me who this is.

"How about you tell me who's calling?"

The woman catches her breath.

"Listen carefully. This is the district attorney's office, and we really have no time to waste. There's a judicial interrogation under way, and Counselor Malinconico is the court-appointed lawyer."

My blood pressure pinwheels.

"Judicial interrogation? Court-appointed?"

I pronounce the words as if they were the surnames of notorious Camorristi.

The district attorney's office-woman withdraws into a contemptuous silence. When she emerges, she lowers her voice almost to the level of complicity, slowly punctuating the words that follow.

"I am talking with the lawyer Malinconico, am I not?"

"Yes," I reply, unmanned. The last criminal case I handled was three or four years ago, and it was just for writing a check without sufficient funds.

"You're on the registry of public defenders. So what'll it be, are you coming? We need a lawyer down here."

Jesus, it's true. In that very instant I remember that I put my name down as a public defender in a moment of overweening professional ambition (they happen, from time to time, these moments of overweening professional ambition: you convince yourself, authentic idiot that you are, that you can afford the luxury of changing sector every once in a while). But I never thought they'd really call me. That'll teach me to rely on the inefficiency of the public institutions.

"Counselor, are you still there?"

"I . . . listen, do I really have to?"

My dismay must have touched a chord of pity, because her voice suddenly softens.

"Well, I'm afraid you do. We don't have time to go through the list looking for others, especially considering that we've found you. I think you'd really better come."

I simultaneously translate the last phrase into "Abandonment of defense, judicial penalties connected herewith."

"Hello?" the talking district attorney's office says, having suddenly lost the connection.

"Huh? Oh yes, sorry."

"So what are you going to do?"

"Okay, I'll be right down."

A moment of silence. I detect hesitation, and even embarrassment, on the other end of the call.

"Counselor."

"What."

"Do you know where to come?"

"Sure I do, the district attorney's office."

Another chilly pause.

"I haven't told you who the assistant district attorney is."

I perspire.

"Ah, right, forgive me."

I imagine her, shaking her head from side to side, on the other end of the line.

"Acampora. Fourth floor, fourth door."

"Thanks. It'll just take me a few minutes to get there."

"Please make it as quick as you can."

I run to my bedroom and get dressed, in a catatonic trance. I'm a fireman who has to rush into a fire without an extinguisher. I'm a student who hasn't studied heading for the blackboard. I leave the apartment, lock the door behind me, call the elevator, push G, and look at myself in the mirror. I see somebody I know, in a jacket and tie, who hasn't got the faintest idea of what he's going to do next.

EXPLOIT

Openly violating a prohibition that by rights he ought to be the first to respect, the assistant district attorney grabs his pack of Rothmans Ultra Lights, extracts one, lodges it firmly between his lips, and stares at us both, as if to say: any objections?

On our side of the desk, me and the guy I've been assigned to defend, a certain Domenico Fantasia, DBA Mimmo 'o Burzone, stare at the floor.

Whereupon the ADA lights his cigarette, fills his lungs, and expels a puff of smoke, creating a little cloud that floats over our heads, just like in a comic strip, with deep thoughts inside it.

A couple of yards away, seated at an old grey metal Olivetti typist's desk (specially made to house typewriter and typist together), the clerk of the court, a skinny guy wearing a pair of counterfeit tinted Ray-Bans and a truly revolting plaid check jacket, is hunched over the transcript form with the unmistakable body language of someone who, if you speak to him, will lose his temper.

We wait.

The ADA takes another drag and leans sharply backward in his office chair with caster wheels, but he overdoes it, shoots backward, and hits the wall behind him. The impact is such that Italian President Giorgio Napolitano, just a yard or so over his head, takes on a slight inclination to the right and the clerk of the court adjusts his bogus Ray-Bans just slightly, even though there is no need.

Mimmo 'o Burzone and I both assume sorrowful faces to express sympathy for the investigating magistrate's embarrassment—a sense of the ridiculous is wheeling over the ADA's desk like a vulture.

At that point the ADA, who shows no signs of possessing a sense of humor, with a flick of the hand that is still holding the pack of Rothmans Ultra Lights, tosses it onto the desktop like a Frisbee, but with a hint of indignation, as if throwing it symbolically in our faces, no different than if it had been our idea for him to shove his chair ingloriously against the wall like an idiot.

The half-empty cigarette pack stutters across the desktop like a flat stone spun at an angle across lake water and skids to a halt at the opposite edge of the desk, teetering at the brink.

Mimmo 'o Burzone immediately lunges to catch the pack before it can fall and there he kneels, curving forward, hands cupped together, his head pointed toward the ADA, as if he were miming the act of supplication.

"Your honor, on the heads of my children," he says, breaking the cringe-inducing silence that ensues, "it breaks my heart to see you having to lose your temper."

The ADA observes this further deterioration of the skit with the reluctant compliance that comes with the sense of being inducted as an involuntary straight man.

I have to say that he has my sympathy, to an extent. We seem to be stuck in a situation that smacks of semantic dementia, in which any and all efforts to shepherd the available information into an even vaguely logical schematic are inexplicably doomed to culminate in shipwreck. As if we were stubbornly repeating the standing high jump, trying to hit a mark and every time coming up a few inches short.

The problem with guys like Domenico Fantasia DBA Mimmo 'o Burzone is that they possess an inborn gift for denying things far beyond the threshold of the reasonable. They lie with a shamelessness that would drive the most methodical of investigators into a blind fury. They downplay their prior convictions, soft-pedaling circumstances that indisputably undercut their alibis, dismissing the testimony of their accomplices, openly denying blood relationships ("My mother? Who says I have a mother?"), dates (accuse them of robbing a bank last Thursday and they might very well tell you that it was last Wednesday). They're moralistic and weepy. They parade their pregnant wives, their children with health problems, the Virgin Mary Herself, the difficulties of making ends meet every month, the bad luck that has dogged their footsteps since childhood, the introduction of the euro, how their fathers beat them and their mothers had to scrub floors to bring them up. It's not that they hoodwink you, because you're as likely to believe their stories as you are to believe in a Gucci bag purchased from a Moroccan immigrant in an underpass. The thing is that they're just so relentless in their insolent recklessness, so confident that they know the way to defraud you, that unless you're very careful you'll stumble into a matter-of-principle trap, obsessed with the idea that now you have to show them once and for all what insincere con artists they really are. They bring you down to their level, in other words. And once you're down there, you don't have a chance. You can't win. No way.

More or less consciously, this young ADA (because along with everything else, he's young, to boot) begins to sense, even though he can't prove it, much less admit it, that Mimmo 'o Burzone is wrapping him up with a Christmas bow. It's an impression that's nettling him like a nasty rumor, a piece of gossip about him that's circulating and that he just happened to overhear, though minus some of the details. It's those missing details that make you want to get straight to the bottom of things.

Which is what citizens like Mimmo 'o Burzone do: they originate rumors about you even when they're talking about something else. And if you let them get away with it, you wind up dangling from their lips.

Which is exactly what's happening right now with our ADA: he's submitting to Mimmo 'o Burzone's process of extortion, instead of slapping him in the face with the criminal charge. In other words, he's making it personal.

This fabulous intuition provokes an unexpected flush of enthusiasm deep inside me. I think I glimpse a way out.

The ADA scoots back to his desk by skating along on the wheels of his office chair, and once there, he folds his arms across his chest and circumnavigates Burzone's face with his eyes.

I shyly hold up my index finger and then immediately retract it, a move that makes me look like nothing so much as a crayfish gasping its last breath on the counter of a fish market. Unsure what to do with it now, I extend my hand toward the arm of my sometime client and grip it ever so slightly, just above the elbow, half in concealment.

Why I should indulge in that particular gesture—the truth be told—I can't even say: it's not as if Mimmo 'o Burzone is confessing or treading perilously close to some pitfall that I would be expected to foresee given my supposed experience (and I've got a pretty strong feeling that actually no one in this room supposes any such thing); all the more so given that I'm completely in the dark about what's really happening in here, to the point that I actually have no idea where to start; but I do it anyway, maybe to convince Burzone that he would be well advised to place himself entirely in my hands (it's a well-known fact that public defenders always hope to be appointed as their client's fiduciary, and to make sure that happens they are willing to promise anything), or maybe just to make myself look useful—apart from the prospect of winning a new client, something that interest me little if at all.

Mimmo 'o Burzone lowers his eyes to stare at the hand that is still hooked onto his arm and then, in slow motion, he raises them again until he's looking straight at me with an expression of deep distaste.

The attorney almost overlooks my interference and starts over.

"Tell me your name again," he says.

"Magistrate, if I may, that line of questioning isn't admissible," I point out. Just to be saying something.

"Admissible! I'll be the judge of what's admissible around here," he replies. The little half-smile that he now rehearses really gives me a pain in the balls.

"You just take care of doing your job"—he glares at me with severity—"instead of making critical appraisals of what's admissible. That's my job."

So now I take a good look at him, freeing myself of the entangling paranoia that's been engulfing me since I set foot in this room, and I perform a mental inventory.

Approximate age, thirty-five (a few years older, a few years younger), the face of the middle class, unmarked, untroubled, the kind of face you can read and commit to memory all at once, a CliffsNotes face; a pair of round gold wire-framed eyeglasses (to think that Grams wore glasses just like that!), hair close-clipped because of the early-onset vertex baldness that he must have inherited from his father (without preamble I decide that his father is a retired school principal, the kind who decided early on that he wanted his son to be a magistrate, and he got his wish, to the enormous self-satisfaction of the anointed one who now goes around living his dream come true), the taut physique of an amateur tennis player (under his jacket he's wearing a long-sleeved Lacoste shirt, WWF green), two days' worth of stubble, a contrivance that's carefully cultivated as a sign of moderate nonconformity. A cool dude. He even smokes women's cigarettes. I have absolutely no intention of allowing this kind of asshole to piss on my head.

"Buddy up on this," I tell him, mentally.

The asshole must sense that something has just shifted, because for the first time since we began, I see a hint of respect in his eyes.

"Your honor, don't misunderstand me," Burzone observes with a submissiveness as slithery as a lizard's belly, "but if you already know what my name is, why would you want me to tell it to you a second time?"

The kind of phrase that a defendant would never dream of uttering, if he had a real live lawyer advising him. I feel a burn of humiliation.

"Listen here, Fantasia, I'm really starting to get fed up with your arguing. In this room, I ask the questions, is that clear?" the asshole inveighs, realizing his misstep just as he finishes his little sermon.

"But you just said it yourself, eh, excuse me very much," Mimmo 'o Burzone points out impeccably, spreading his arms at the self-evidence of the point.

While the cool dude gnashes his teeth, I find myself reflecting on the gesture that Burzone made, and I realize that the symbolic emptying of pockets that are already empty, lending itself to a depiction of both a lack of resources and a complete surrender, is a perfect metaphor for clean hands.

So that's what it means, I tell myself. That money, just like a weapon, spills blood. But the discovery is of no particular use to me, just then.

Meanwhile, the ADA is starting to fly off the handle a second time. He's not going to be made a fool of again, I can see it written on his face.

No question, Burzone is a prickly client to handle. He somehow manages—just how he does it continually eludes me—to defuse every attempt to bring him face to face with the charges. The astonishing thing is that the harder he tries to answer the questions, the more he tends to deflect them, plunging the prosecutor's office into an embarrassing state of suspension. Absurdly enough, I almost expect the asshole at any minute to get to his feet, slap Burzone on the shoulder good-naturedly, and say: "Okay, we've had our fun, you're an undertaker for the Camorra, it's not all that serious, you never actually pulled the trigger, why don't you go home and promise me you won't do it again."

Taking advantage of the cool dude's latest impasse, I regain some semblance of consciousness and discover deep inside me a dialectical determination whose head I can plainly make out, but without even the faintest prospect of a tail.

"Now I'm the one that's had enough, magistrate. I cannot allow you to continue with this death by a thousand cuts. If you want to influence the defendant's answers, that's one thing; but in that case, we should have a written record of the conversation," and at this point, I glare at the clerk of the court, who looks back at me uneasily. The truth is that up till now, it looked as if he were doing a crossword puzzle, so indolently had he been doodling on the preprinted interrogation form. "This is the third, let me repeat, the third time that you have asked the defendant to state his given name. And that, as you know full well, is an unconscionable interference in his freedom to respond."

I let myself sink back into my chair, inhaling deeply in an attempt to fight down the sudden acceleration of my heartbeat that my little improvisation has engendered.

I look up at the ceiling. The plaster is pockmarked with little black marks, as if someone had spent an afternoon scorching it with the flame of a cigarette lighter.

I decorously smooth back my hair. My shirt is starting to adhere to my torso. I'm experiencing a slight dimming of my vision. My salivation is running low. Whatever it is I've just said, I have absolutely no memory of a single word of it.

Mimmo 'o Burzone turns his head in my direction with the cautious slowness of a velociraptor that has just detected prey in the surrounding foliage.

The funny thing is that I feel certain that I'm seeing the same thing as him at this exact moment in time: a defense lawyer who knows exactly what he's doing, spoiling for a fight, and even nicely dressed. A professional who may have looked like something of an underachiever up till now, but that was all part of his clever tactical plan. And it's as if I can see him rapping himself on the knuckles for having underestimated me so quickly. The same expression has suddenly materialized on the face of the cool dude, who is now scrutinizing me with a new appreciation.

And so I give my clothing a quick check, half-expecting to find a shirttail untucked or a fly unzipped.

Not a bit of it. It's all pure respect.

With a renewed surge of vigor, I take the floor again. A little more of this and I'll leap to my feet and start pacing the room.

"Can we finally get to the point? It strikes me that, aside from first and last name, address, and occupation, you have not yet charged Signore—Fantasia, right?—with any criminal act. All right, then, we've all heard his name. Could you tell us, once and for all, exactly what we stand accused of?"

A small tentative smile flutters on Burzone's lips. I used that "we" with utter nonchalance, the phraseology of old-school criminal lawyers. I don't really have a clear role. It's a rhetorical reflex. With a quiver of emotion, I ask myself whether there might really be a lawyer, buried somewhere deep inside of me.

In the meanwhile, the asshole is working on his answer. Because it's obvious that I'm right. He has to bring specific charges before we all go to sleep tonight. What charges? What can he say? "Now then, Signore Domenico Fantasia, I accuse you of being a butcher of human flesh. You receive the bodies of the murder victims in your home, you carve them up in a specially equipped room under your basement stairs—as can be deduced from the long rectangular table with a marble top set in the middle of the room, with unmistakable cut-marks (oh, of course, you'd never be so stupid as to leave the tools of your trade lying around, you know, wire cutters, hacksaws, scalpels; I wonder whether you always use the same tools or change them from one corpse to the next), which you then take care to clean thoroughly with a rubber hose (now that we did find in the room under the stairs, snugly screwed onto the faucet in the wall there), with the additional use of a substantial volume of vinegar, which as we know is an effective way of eliminating even the most stubborn and persistent odors, and channeling the water out of the basement by flushing it out the drain grate located in the right-hand corner of the same room under the stairs; after which you place the hunks of human flesh in a sports bag and then personally take them out into the open countryside and bury them, taking care to scatter the limbs in deep trenches at a considerable distance one from another, so as to make it physically impossible to identify the individual corpses."

Of course he can't say that. He has to move in gradually. Get us to say it. That is, get him to say it. Wear him down. Wait for a contradiction he can pounce on. Convince him that it's in his interest to cough up the names of the instigators to reduce the gravity of the charges. Until shortly before my peroration he was feeling pretty confident. He'd even had the good luck of a defense attorney no one had ever heard of. A stroll in the park, he was assuming.

"Don't you worry about that, Counselor Malinconico"—at least he addresses me by name, a new development that triggers an erection of my spinal cord—"the charges will be brought, and how. It's just that, if you don't object too strenuously, I'd like to do that in my own way, on my own schedule."

"Well, it was my impression that criminal charges must be brought in the manner and according to the time limits established by law," I argue with blinding rapidity.

I can't believe my ears. I feel as if I'm just moving my lips, as if I'm lip-synching my lines.

Nives, if you could only see me now.

"I'd advise you to change your tone of voice, Counselor. Because I might consider it indicative of contempt for the office I represent," the asshole says, losing his temper.

"No, no, no, it's you who are overstepping the bounds of your authority. And be well aware that I intend to use every single word that you say, taken down in the minutes of this interrogation," I add, though I haven't the faintest idea of how I can use them, "to prove that up until this moment you have illegally detained my client and that no charges have been formally brought. I'd also like to take this opportunity to remind you, since we're on the subject, that we have the full legal right not to respond"—and this time I use the lawyerly "we" intentionally and advisedly—"a right that you have taken great care to avoid bringing to the notice of the subject of your investigation, am I right?"

"You have no idea what you're saying," the asshole replies, betraying a hint of discomfort.

"Oh, yes I do," I rebut, shamelessly, "and I'll be even more specific if you continue giving me just cause."

I don't even know what's come over me.

Daddy, is that you?

"We found a hand in your client's backyard. I'm not sure if I make myself clear," the cool dude says, slightly red in the face, turning over his first card.

Oh fuck, I think to myself.

"So what?" I say out loud.

"What do you mean 'so what?'" he says, more disappointed than indignant.

"Well, so what? What you plan to do, charge him with concealing a hand?"

Burzone shrugs, as if to say: "Yeah, right."

The asshole jerks his head back and surveys the scene, like Predator in the jungle raising his visor and activating his victim-identification program, in consecutive order: the window,

Burzone, yours truly, and the clerk of the court. His face assumes a bewildered expression, as if he were thinking he's the only one who doesn't fit in, in here.

"I'm not charging him with concealing a hand, Counselor. I'm charging him with concealing a corpse."

An idea pops into my head.

"Then I'm afraid I'm going to have to differ with you on your very first point. First off, you have no evidence that the corpse, as you insist on calling the hand found in Fantasia's backyard, was actually concealed by Fantasia himself." At this point, Burzone shrugs again, cockier than ever. "And second, before anyone can be charged with concealing a corpse, there has to be a corpse, a whole corpse, not just a hand, and a corpse that belongs to someone, that is, a victim, with a first name and a last name."

I stop to catch my breath. This was such a random shot that I might have actually scored a point. Once, in court, I heard a renowned criminal lawyer, talking to his client, in shackles, say that the important thing is that something *appear* true; it matters much less whether it is or not.

The asshole says nothing, silent and bewildered. Next time, read up on the laws of evidence where concealment of corpses is concerned, why don't you.

I look at him. He's gone limp with frustration.

"Very interesting line of defense, Counselor," he says, wearily. "Too bad that this isn't the forum to present it."

"Oh, it isn't?" I think.

The asshole waves his hand toward himself, but the gesture is for the clerk of the court, who immediately hands over the preprinted deposition form. Then he offers the same form to Burzone.

"Sign here."

Mimmo 'o Burzone stands up and tries to catch my gaze, clearly confused. Then, without waiting for further instructions, he leans over the desk and laboriously inks his name, following the line indicated by the magistrate's index finger.

"What do you mean?" I ask.

"What do you mean: what do I mean?" the asshole fires back.

"What have you decided?" I ask, affirmatively.

"As far as I'm concerned, your client remains in jail," he replies, as if it were the most obvious thing.

Burzone gives me a heartbroken look.

"What is your legal motivation?" I demand, indignantly.

"I can't keep anyone in jail, as you know perfectly well."

"If only I did," I think to myself.

"What I can do is ask," he resumes, "and I'll ask, you can bet on that. Then the preliminary judge will make the decision."

The grand preliminary judge, of course.

"And in any case," the asshole continues, "with the evidence weighing against your client, what did you expect, that we'd just send him home?"

"But I just told you that you don't—"

He cuts me off. I'm thankful for the interruption. I'm pretty sure that at this point my sentence structure was about to go all discombobulated anyway.

"Listen, there'll be an arraignment where you can raise your objections. Write a brief, if you're really determined to bring them up."

An arraignment, huh? Thanks very much for the information.

"You bet I will," I say, feeling cocky again. Then I turn and head for the door.

"Counselor," the clerk of the court calls to me.

I turn around. The asshole and the clerk of the court are both staring at me, mystified.

Now what?

They both go on staring at me as if they were expecting something.

But Burzone tips me off, by gesturing toward the transcript.

Jesus, I have to sign it too, that's right. It's a good thing that Burzone already signed, otherwise I'd have had to ask: "Where do I sign?"

You can picture the humiliation.

I put down my John Hancock, I straighten my jacket, and I nod farewell to the asshole.

Who nods back.

The clerk of the court stands up and opens the door for us.

Mimmo 'o Burzone walks ahead of me. I flash an idiotic smile at the two Carabinieri who have been waiting for us, on sentinel duty outside the door.

At the last minute, the asshole's investigative impulses revive unexpectedly.

"Fantasia."

Burzone turns before I do.

"Yes sir."

"Where on earth did you get that nickname . . . Mimmo 'o Burzone?

Burzone's lips part slightly.

"When I was younger, I was in door-to-door sales."

The asshole rests his chin in the palm of his hand, sketching out a very intelligent little hint of a smile.

"Until next time, your honor," I say, cutting the scene short.

I gently but firmly walk Burzone out of the room with one hand, wheeling after him as I pull the door shut behind me. When the Carabinieri take him, I tell him goodbye.

"Thanks, Counselor," he says, all grateful. "I'll call you."

I'll call you?

For reasons that I refuse to take under consideration just then, that phrase chills the blood in my veins.

W hen your law office is a 200-square-foot room in an apartment you share with others, you have two possibilities.

Either you say:

My law office is a 200-square-foot room in an apartment in a building without a doorman. I don't have a lease, I have a contract of gratuitous bailment (in practical terms, a loan, as if my landlord were an old pal who's just doing me a favor) for tax purposes, and another undated rental agreement, which the owner, a millionaire miser who shuffles around in slippers, holds hostage, just one copy, signed only by me, so that the minute I complain or cause trouble he can date it, sign it, and hurry over to the police station to register it (and I'm certainly not going to waste your time here explaining why the figure reported in the contract is higher than the figure that I pay him on the first of every month, under the table). All my office-mates are in the same legal condition: Espedito Lenza, bookkeeper (but the plaque on the door says "business advisor"); Rudy Fiumara, a wingnut who has no discernable profession and seems to make no rational use of his room, seeing as how we almost never see him (but he has a fundamentalist approach to being neighborly, and he'll have the bar downstairs deliver an espresso in a thermos demitasse even if you don't want it); and the Arethusa cooperative, a cooperative that is made up of a husband-and-wife team—he's one of those guys whose name is Roberto but every time you see him you call him Sergio (you know the ones, the Robertos that you can't help but call Sergio? Or the Giancarlos that you can't get out of your mind that they're really Antonios? You know, those guys)—while she has a refined name, like Iginia or Vitulia or Marosia. They have the most idiotic little Italian spitz, which every time the doorbell rings goes completely bonkers and starts barking, furiously, until Roberto-Sergio and Iginia-Vitulia-Marosia see that they're going to have to pound it silly to make it stop. Since it's a mezzanine apartment, there's a security issue, but instead of installing steel bars, the landlord decided to save a little money and just had holes drilled into the wall on either side of each casement window. So every night, before leaving, you have to remember to slip a steel tube five and a half feet long into the holes to keep burglars from breaking and entering (let me assure you that the sight of a window barred from the interior with an Innocenti steel tube triggers a bout of depression you can't even begin to imagine).

Or else you say:

Now, your professional office suite, these days, certainly isn't what it used to be. The authoritative law office, the office that's located on an upper floor of an impressive palazzo in the city center, with a courtyard and a doorman, a receptionist, a secretary, paralegals, five or six phone lines, a spacious waiting room, original paintings and vintage furniture; the suite of offices designed to crush the will of the client and make it clear from the very first appointment just who it is who holds the whip hand (and especially just how much he can expect to pay in hourly fees), has seen its day. Nowadays, a professional is constantly on the hunt, never in one place; then, every so often, he'll need some downtime. Let's be done with overblown structural rhetoric. Let's be done with the gilded cage that only confines your thoughts and restricts your initiative within the iron bars of ostentation (plainly vulgar and even a little fascistic, if we want to call a spade a spade). Let's be done with underlings and employees who do the dirty work of photocopying and carrying briefcases, let's be done with subordinates, let's be done with the young woman who fields your phone calls and organizes your schedule. Let's be done with the tawdry cliché of the illicit affair with your secretary. Let's be done with ownership of law offices. Let's be done with ownership in general. Don't establish ties, unknot them. Today you're here, tomorrow you're somewhere else. Do you need to meet with a client who's important enough to merit a face-to-face? Tell him to call you on your cell phone and you can have lunch together (or better yet, eat a sandwich at a little table in a bar). Does your cell phone make you feel as if the world is breathing down your neck? Then you just turn it off. You're a freelancer and a professional (just listen to the way those two words chime together), so seize your freedom, do it for real, make use of it. And really, let's level with one another: these days, do you think that the average client is impressed by a handsome law office? The middle class is dead. Professionals are diving into the shark tank. You have to reinvent your career, every morning of every day.

It's great to have alternatives in life.

Anyway, at this point, it just seems right, even if there's no need for it, to swing by the office. How to put this. After a professional performance like the one I just gave, it's the very least I deserve. When you've challenged and baffled a magistrate the way I just did a few minutes ago, and when you're still radiating the afterglow of a new self-consideration, why wouldn't you take the opportunity to head back to your place of business, remove the Innocenti steel tube from its twin housings, swing open the casement windows, take a seat at your Jonas desk, spin a couple of 360s at your Skruvsta swivel office chair, turn on the answering machine, and review your twelve files, eztaking under due consideration the decisions that await you.

taking under due consideration the decisions that await you. To feel up to the task: that's the common man's highest aspiration.

The instant I put my key in the lock, the psychotic toy spitz breaks out into an explosion of yipping and yapping that ought to give him a little canine heart attack by any reasonable standard (the office of the Arethusa cooperative is the first door when you walk in off the landing). But Christ on a crutch, we've been officemates for two and a half years now; everyone knows that dogs memorize the footsteps of the people they know: you know my my footsteps by heart, just as sure as you have four paws, so why the fuck do you bark at me every blessed time? And what's worse, with that deranged fury, as if I'd slaughtered your whole doggy family? Because—and this is the thing that really rankles my nerves—every single time, that fucking dog catches me off guard. You know it's coming, you steel yourself and you're expecting it, but it manages to ambush you anyway, it still gives you an arrhythmia so that you have to stagger in and drink a glass of water. Plus it's mortifying, frankly; it makes you feel awkward to have a little beast barking at you like that, as if it had caught you just as you were on the verge of doing something deeply dishonest. A little self-conscious, a little defensive—that's how it makes you feel, right?

And while we're on the subject, I'd love to say to those twin manger scenes, Roberto what's-his-name and his wife, the doyenne: listen, if you have a psychopathic dog, a dog that barks (and, by the way, doesn't bite) at anyone other than the two of you, leave it at home, pay a dog-sitter, or slip it a Xanax before you leave the house. Why do you insist on inflicting on other people, with all your smarmy friendliness ("Oh, *shiao*, Vin-*shen*-ssso"), the customs of your own household? What right do you have to take your neighbor's approval for granted? Your assault on diversity is ongoing and criminal.

But today I'm in too good a mood to let myself be lured into a fight. To hell with my two subversive officemates and their argumentative nasty little dog: I have a love affair with my office waiting for me, and I'm certainly not going to let them ruin it for me.

With the furious barking in the background, I walk in and close the door behind, huffing and puffing loudly. The quadruped starts clawing the door from inside: he really wants to get out and settle matters mano a mano. Roberto-Sergio smacks him one. The dog yelps, his wife grumbles. I move on. I walk past the office of Espedito Lenza (mine is right next to his). Door half-open. I can hear him talking on the phone.

"You said that already," he's saying.

I open the door, turn on the light (fluorescent, medical-examiner white), I go over to unshackle the window. There's a smell of stale air. But I don't really dislike the smell of stale air, it preserves the days (June certainly doesn't smell as bad as February, for example). I find that olfactory memory is very romantic. And then there are smells that have never repelled me, truth be told. Like the smell of horse shit, for instance. When I was little, every time I went to the train station newsstand to buy *Spider-Man* (at the station newsstand they stocked comic books before the other newsstands got them), there were carriages outside, in the piazza, and . . . oh well, who gives a damn.

I put the Innocenti steel tube away in its hiding place behind the Kvadrant curtain system. I sit down at my Jonas desk, turn on my computer, breathe in the first week of April, vacuum packed in my absence, and I go online, with a yearning for the website of the National Bar Association, just eager to know what my fellow practitioners of the law are talking about these days.

The modem emits a loud raspberry (I have dial-up) and lowers the virtual drawbridge. I type in the URL, I access the website, I pause to admire the home page as if I were somehow partially responsible for its existence, I click to the section "Results of the Elections for Officers of the Bar Association," I navigate at random among the various items on the the pull-down menu, and I read up on the new membership of the board of directors of the bar association of Barcellona Pozzo di Gotto. After that, luxuriating in the vast array of options available to me, I venture into the section devoted to services available to members of the legal profession, loitering for fifteen minutes or so among the submenus of various professional issues. I go so far as to read the first few lines of a random State Council finding concerning auto insurance liability caps and direct indemnification (anyone who happened to be watching me would get the impression that I was deeply interested), but I suddenly break off my reading when a flash of genius almost triggers a surge of cardiac arrhythmia. I quickly navigate back to the home page and eagerly search among the various options for the national online registry of Italian lawyers. I find it and I click. Up pops an electronic dialogue box. I fill in the blank spaces, hit Enter, and there I am, sixth or seventh in a not particularly lengthy list of lawyers with the same last name. I snatch at my name with the mouse and cursor, picking my name out from the competition, and I indulge in a few minutes of leisurely self-contemplation. I savor my name, letter by letter, wiping away any and all senses of ontological insecurity.

Malinconico Vincenzo, member of the bar of, membership card number, lawyer since.

I breathe in, happily.

This must be what success is like, I tell myself. A place for everyone, not just for a few. But a place where everyone looks at you as if you did them a favor by dropping by. As if your very presence brought some inestimable added value. As if after that, in that place, home values increased.

Success—I learn in this exact moment—is something that involves government property.

Once I'm done with my meditation on celebrity, I reach out for the blinking light on my answering machine.

Messages: two.

I push the playback button.

First message: Alfredo.

He's calling from the street (traffic noises in the background).

"Ciao Dad. I tried calling you at home but you weren't there. Your cell phone was turned off."

"I was in the middle of an arraignment," I want to tell him.

Then comes a dripping pause that smacks of: "I was just about to tell you something very personal and very important but now I'm getting the feeling that I'm about to change my mind."

Listen, Alf, could you get a move on?

I wait, already knowing exactly what's coming next.

And in fact:

"Listen, I wanted . . . oh, never mind. It doesn't matter. Ciao."

I look at the far wall, while the tenor of my mood plummets.

Now. There could be a number of explanations for the cold feet of a sixteen-year-old son leaving a message like that on your answering machine. Let me just lay out some alternatives:

a) maybe it wasn't important;

b) it was important but it wasn't urgent;

c) he didn't feel like saying it to an answering machine;

d) he was caught off-guard by a friend who just happened to be walking by;

e) his cell phone battery was dying.

That'll do for now.

If we explore these five options with a modicum of lucidity, we quickly come to the realization that they are nothing other than minor antibodies, pathetic attempts to ignore the obvious.

Option a) is the most threadbare of the five: if something isn't important, you don't even start to explain;

option b) is lawyerly, in the sense that it doesn't fly in the face of the truth, it just disqualifies it: it sidles over to it, but only to chomp it down more thoroughly;

option c) has a certain austere dignity, but it's basically a delaying device at best;

options d) and e) are so blatantly fake that it's not even worth discussing them.

The thing is that reality mumbles. It expresses itself in incomplete sentences. And the translations that circulate are terrible, done by incompetents. Riddled with misreadings, typos, entire lines missing. Without a modicum of professional standards, completely lacking in any sincere effort.

Which is exactly why I'm accustomed to explaining the things that happen to me. I make imperfect translations in an effort to get by until, one fine morning, I meet reality in the street—nonchalant, understated, never vulgar—and I stand there, rooted to the spot, staring as she passes me by and vanishes in the distance without bestowing so much as a glance in my direction. But it's not like I'm completely nonplussed, it's not like I've never met her before.

Same thing right now. Hard as I might try to pretend that I don't get it, this is what I really think: my son wanted to tell me something crucially important, something that's weighing on his mind, something that's causing him pain. He was at such loose ends that he even considered confiding in me (not something he'd normally do), and the one time I might have been able to be of some help to him, he couldn't reach me. So, whatever it was, it's now all my fault.

That's what I think. Forget about a, b, c, and d.

"Counselor," says the turning cassette tape.

The pronunciation of a sewer rat.

I sit up straight on my Skruvsta swivel chair, as if I were a Carabinieri lance-corporal.

Silence.

Street noise.

"Hello," the answering machine speaker insists.

It's hard to believe, but in the third millennium there are still people out there who don't understand how answering machines work.

A few seconds of indecisive breathing, car horns and muffled voices in the distance.

End of messages.

I look at the answering machine display.

Identity withheld.

I don't like the way things are going.

I definitely don't like that voice.

I stand up, I go to the window. I breathe in, I blow out, with a grunt of annoyance.

Right now I'm fighting off overtures from that part of me that wants to convince me to call up Alfredo and drag out of him whatever it was he decided not to tell me (and I can't even imagine how low I'd be willing to sink just to find out what it was), when Espedito Lenza walks in: shirt sleeves rolled up to the elbows, tie loosened, trousers even looser than the tie, crotch of the trousers riding super-low, accordion pleats around his fly, forehead glistening.

All he's missing is a car jack in one hand and a spare tire in the other.

"Vincé' . . . ?" he says.

That's how we say hello where I come from. By uttering the person's Christian name, followed by half a question mark.

As if we wanted to prove to our friend or acquaintance that we still remember what he's called.

I'm glad you knocked on my door, I almost feel like telling him.

"Oh, Espe."

He drops into one of the two Hampus chairs on the other

side of the desk and rubs his forehead, relaxing, as if my office were the ideal spot to unload his cares and worries. He makes no bones about making himself at home.

"I have a fucking problem," he says.

Truth is, I'd sort of guessed that already.

"Actually, it's the other way around," he adds, looking at me sidelong, almost as if there were something inopportune about my presence.

I don't open my mouth, even though the presentation was unequivocal.

The fact is that, however likable I might find Espedito (we have the same fixation with shoes that people shouldn't be wearing, and in fact every time we go downstairs for an espresso, we run an informal competition to see who can spot the most), I'm still fed up with people coming to tell me their problems. It's been happening to me as long as I can remember. As soon as I meet someone, I'm not saying the first time, but at most, the third time that I see them, I wind up having to listen to a minute-by-minute account of the history of their private lives.

Okay, admittedly, I cast certain glances that are like lambent pools of profundity. I consider every word spoken to me as if it meant something, even when I couldn't care less. So other people lose their misgivings, think they can trust me, and start leaking like faucets. It's practically impossible to stop someone when they're determined to confide in you. There are times when you just have to turn and run. One time I abandoned someone in a Feltrinelli book store, telling him that if he'd just wait five minutes in the DVD section I'd be right back.

To be perfectly honest, it's not like this talent I have of getting other people to open up to me ever did me the slightest bit of good. So I finally gave it up, preferring to chase after women with no particular interest in autobiography. Until I actually wound up marrying one whose profession it is to listen to the things that other people confide in her, though she gets paid very nicely for her trouble, unlike me. Even now, despite my VAT registration number, my business cards, and all the accompanying paraphernalia, I can't see why it is that my clients feel entitled to update me in excruciating detail on their personal tragedies, only to be shocked—shocked!—when I ask them to pay me a retainer, for instance.

"I can't do it anymore with my wife," Espedito says, circumstantiating.

"Do tell?" I'm tempted to reply. Instead I give him a skeptical glance, just to undercut the drama. In part because it strikes me as very odd that Espe should have any problems with hoisting the flagpole. If his wife, for it is she whom we are speaking of, had even a vague idea of the number of times—a number that he updates with the dependability of Norton Antivirus and with any woman (only those no longer drawing breath being a priori excluded) that comes within his reach—Espedito had cheated on her, at the very least she would fracture his skull with a ball-peen hammer while he was sleeping.

"No need to make that face. I can't get it up. I can't get it up anymore with Teresa."

I say nothing, then I speak without thinking.

"Do you think it's really over then?"

He lifts his eyes to my face as if I'd just revealed that I was his father or something of the sort. But then I'm just as appalled at myself as he is, I have to admit. I've been surprised at the things coming out of my mouth since this morning.

"Eh?" he asks, rhetorically.

In the face of his complete dismay, I fully grasp how indelicate I've been, and in the full flush of embarrassment I clamp my mouth shut. My response to his dilemma was to reel out the standard phrase for cases in which a friend comes to you to confide that his girlfriend has dumped him. How I came up with it, I really couldn't say.

A reciprocal silence ensues that makes me yearn for station identification or a word from our sponsors.

"Um, no, of course not," Espedito hastens to retract, "it must just be that I'm worn out lately. I've been working too hard, I eat out practically every day, I've been *drinking*"—he says it in italics—"I haven't been getting enough sleep, and then I have to see Valentina at least three times a week . . . "

Valentina, as we were just mentioning, is Espe's girlfriend. Sells perfumes, twenty-nine years old, definitely on the vulgar side. I know her both because she's in and out of the office fairly frequently, and because I've had to help cover up their misdeeds more than once. And on one of those occasions, of this I'm certain, Teresa saw through my evasions, because she called me on my cell phone and asked if I could put her husband on the line, since that asshole had told her that he'd be with me but hadn't bothered to advise me of the fact. Whereupon I had no idea what to say and I simply improvised a sudden and fictional loss of cell phone reception, and just the thought of that embarrassing charade brings a wave of shame, as if I were the one who was screwing the expert in perfumes.

"You see the way it is?" he goes on, making a show of wanting my approval.

I stretch my neck the way you do to show how completely pointless it would be to add any further commentary, since he's just said it all. And with a certain sense of relief I realize that if your goal is to rid yourself of the annoying and persistent buzz of someone who wants to bore you to death with his private life, all you need to do is feed back his version of the facts in the exact same dramaturgical terms in which he first presented them.

"The fact is," Espedito resumes the charge, disabusing me of my naïve hopes, "I function perfectly with Valentina"—and here he illustrates with a hand gesture, like he's shifting an imaginary gear stick into third—"even when I eat badly. Even when I don't get much sleep. Even when I drink a little too much. It's with Teresa that I can't get it up."

I give up.

"Don't fixate about it," I toss out. "These things happen sometimes."

A disheartened expression spreads over his face; he twirls thumb, index, and middle finger of his right hand.

"Three months. I haven't been able to do a thing for the past three months."

I don't know what to tell him. Personally, I've never had to put up "detour" or "out of order" signs up on the approaches to my underground parking garage, as it were, or if so, never any longer than you might expect, say, a head cold to last. I could recommend he take the magic pill, but I'm pretty sure he's already thought of that. For an ideological southern Italian male like him, taking Viagra puts you in the same category as a Mafia stool pigeon.

"It can't go on like this, you understand? I just think about it all the time. And the more I think about it, the more it doesn't work."

He draws a line across his forehead with the tip of his index finger.

"What am I going to do with Teresa? How'm I going to hold on to Teresa? I'm worried, Vincè," he whines.

Look at that, he's even calling me by my first name. Should I be flattered by this mark of extreme familiarity? Should I be touched at the sight of the state he's in? Should I walk over next to him, hesitate for a moment, put my hand on his shoulder, and say in an undertone: "Come on, buck up, you'll see, when you least expect it everything'll straighten out"? Well, I don't have the slightest intention of doing anything of the sort, so there. In fact, I'm actually pretty disgusted at all this pissing and moaning about his lazy dick, so there. I'm going to level with him right now, I'll tell him how he's going to hold on to Teresa.

"Let me explain here and now just why you're worried," I start out, with a rising note of indignation. "Because as long as you give Teresa the full treatment on a regular basis, you can go out and fuck whoever you want with a clear conscience. You've done your duty as a husband to make sure your wife is satisfied, so now you can have a little fun on the side. And sure it's nice enough, from time to time"—and here I'm clearly addressing my own personal demons—"to let yourself be stroked and caressed for an hour and a half by some asshole who knows the way you like to be touched (compare him to that half-faggot you're living with now: where did you find him, in an atelier somewhere?), and then dump him like the miserable loser that he is, and even act all sorry about it. *Oh I'm so sorry, it was nice but you know that the two of us don't really work together* (what do you mean we don't work together, we just fucked like bunnies, didn't we?). It was nice, wasn't it, to keep your full-time job and do a little under-the-table moonlighting in your off hours? Well, the boondoggle is finished. There's been a fucking reform instituted. Your oldest and most trusted friend has just turned his back on you because he's fed up with telling lies, even if it doesn't bother you at all, and so he's thrown a monkey wrench into the works. You're losing your special privileges, that's all. And you can't take it. It's more than you can stand. That's why you're worried."

I stop to catch my breath and figure out what I just said.

Espe stares at me agog. He's probably still reviewing my harangue in his head. Well, okay, it's obvious that I was mostly talking to Nives; but there was plenty of good material there for him, if he has the wit to see it, what the hell.

"Make up your mind who you want to be with, god damn it. Why don't you make a decision for once: do something, instead of helping other people to make decisions about things that are none of your business. Do you realize what an absurd line of work you're in? Eh? Turn this way, idiot: you have someone who knows how to make you happy, who only wants you to stay with her. So stay, by god almighty. What does it cost you to stay?"

Whereupon Espedito gets to his feet, looks down at the floor, and expels a breath of air in a highly self-critical sigh. And as I go on inveighing, relying on his understanding, he turns his back and removes his presence.

I basically walk him to the door.

What If Your Mother Found Out?

I'd never have given a little girl a name like that. Alagia—
please, do me a favor. I remember the first time we
went out together and Nives told me that she had a
daughter, I had to ask her to repeat that off-kilter name, slowly,
before I could even pronounce it. And I can still see her, the
astonishment straight out of Classics 101 that ovalized her lips
when I confessed I'd never heard it before: "But what about
Alagia Fieschi, the niece of Pope Adrian V? Dante even men-
tions her. Why, don't you like it?"

"No, I do. So much," I told her.

So anyway, that's the name of Nives' daughter. She had her
with some goofy loser who took off like a cat with its tail on fire
just a short while after Nives told him he was going to be a
daddy.

"Do you think it might have been the name that scared him
off?" I was sorely tempted to ask her.

Then Nives and I had Alfredo, who couldn't have hoped
for a better big sister, truth be told. And I couldn't have
dreamed of a more adorable daugher.

It's just too bad about the name.

I show up at the airport running ten minutes late, but luckily Alagia has her cell phone turned on, so I call her and tell her
I'm stuck in the line at the parking structure. She tells me she's
hungry so she'll just go ahead and get a Chicken Wrap as an
antipasto while she waits for me to get there.

For the past few months we've had this standing biweekly tryst to eat artery-clogging food, so we meet secretly at the airport, because she has a Burger King fixation, and the only Burger King in Naples happens to be at the airport.

Though if you stop to think about it, there's something deeply maladjusted about driving all the way out to the airport to eat a sandwich, but for your children you'd do This and More. And when you're going through a divorce, the rule is that your ex-wife gets to do the This and you wind up doing the More. In other words, you become open to corruption at levels that someone not going through a divorce couldn't even begin to imagine.

I have to say that even though I'm not a huge fan of the food (if you want to call it that) at Burger King, I do have to admit that the Whopper is a superior hamburger. Can't say if it's the pickles, or maybe it's the onions. But that's the only sandwich that leaves my mouth watering, even while I'm actually biting into it. If you're really feeling ambitious, there's also the Double Whopper, but that's strictly for when you're working through loss and grief.

I generally order a Whopper, onion rings, and soda; for dessert, vanilla ice cream with chocolate syrup. Sometimes I substitute a Chick'n Crisp sandwich, but I almost invariably regret it afterwards.

Alagia on the other hand starts off with the Chicken Wrap (a tortilla with chicken tenders and a curry sauce), then moves on to the San Diego Beef (another wrap, but with beef, lettuce, and various sauces), and then asks me to let her have a bite of my Whopper (which I offer her, however half-heartedly), winding up her meal with vanilla ice cream (but with caramel syrup on hers, instead of chocolate). Between one deeply unhealthy serving and the next, she drinks a medium Sprite.

Every time we leave the airport, we promise we'll never do it again.

I park my car and set off at a run, because Alagia has dance at three, and I want to make it back to the office to review a couple of files.

I hurry into departures, take the escalator up, and emerge into the airport mall. I head straight for the food court, craning my neck in search of Alagia, who's waving a napkin from one of the last tables at the Burger King so I can find her.

It's a bright sunny day and the concourse, overlooking the runways, is drenched in light. Not many people, an agreeable silence, a janitor's trolley blocking the hallway leading to the restrooms.

Come to think of it, it's not a bad idea to come eat lunch here. There is an unbroken succession of planes taking off and landing, and an airplane arriving or departing is always something worth looking at.

And now Alagia stands up from the little fast-food table and walks toward me: tattered low-rider jeans, running shoes with the laces all flapperjawed, so that one of these days she's going to fall flat on her face and remember it for the rest of her life, midriff uncovered. She pops a chicken tender into my mouth, then she plants an affectionate little peck on my left cheek.

"You know that you remind me of Espedito Lenza, with those pants?" I tell her.

She studies the air for a minute, then she gets it.

"Ha, ha," she comments. Still, you can see that she feels like laughing.

"Oh, you know that Espe's not at all bad-looking."

"Ha, ha," she says again. She liked that one.

We grab our trays and walk to the cash register to place our orders. Right up until the last second, I weigh the possibility of being unfaithful to my Whopper, but when the cashier says, "Prego?" I lose my nerve.

We sit down. Alagia polishes off her Chicken Wrap and

starts in on the San Diego Beef, picking out the chunks of beef nestled inside the tortilla with her fingers. I start with the Whopper, so that the onion rings can cool off.

"How's dance?" I ask.

"Great," she answers.

"In fact, you can tell. You're looking much lighter, the way you walk."

"Lighter, you think?"

She takes a sip of Sprite.

"As if you were more on tiptoe."

She looks into the middle distance just over my head, pursuing the concept.

"Mmm," she agrees.

"It's nice when you resemble the things you do," I point out.

"That's true, you're right."

What a nice conversation this is, I think. And I bite into the Whopper again, feeling a wave of sadness at its imminent end.

"There's something I wanted to ask you," I say.

"Mmm," she says, again.

"How's your brother doing?"

She swallows the mouthful and furrows her brow. She's identical to Nives when she furrows her brow.

"What do you mean, how's he doing?"

"In the sense of whether you know something about him that I don't."

"Uh. No, I don't think so," she replies, discounting my observation. "Why?"

She extracts a strip of lettuce and raises it to her mouth.

"He left a message on my answering machine, saying he wanted to tell me something."

"Wanted to tell you what?"

"That I couldn't say. He hung up without telling me."

"Ah, and why would he do that?" she asks, without looking me in the eye.

I set the Whopper down on the tray, in exasperation. Alagia looks at it.

"Are you listening to a word I'm saying?"

"Sure, I can hear you," she answers, scrutinizing her tortilla as if it were a kaleidoscope. It's incredible how my words slide over without engaging her in the slightest when we're at Burger King.

"Anyway, he hasn't seemed quite right for a while now," I go on. "One minute he's cheerful, the next he's all gloomy . . . he doesn't have one of those girlfriends that break up with you and then call you up, by chance?"

A knowing half-smile flickers onto her face.

"No, not at all."

"No?"

She shakes her head no again.

"And how do you happen to know?"

"I just know, that's all."

"You just know, that's all," I repeat.

"Don't worry," she decrees, putting the hollowed-out tortilla back on her tray. That means she's about to ask me for a bite of my Whopper.

"And how do you happen to just know, and that's all?"

She emits a sort of "Pffh" sound through a narrow gap between her lips. A sound that makes me feel like smacking her.

"Have I been annoying you for long?" I ask.

"Come on, Vincenzo."

"Why are you laughing?"

"I'm not laughing."

"Oh, yes you are. You're thinking about something. Otherwise you wouldn't have that stupid little smile on your face."

Her face reddens angrily. She glares straight into my eyes.

Oooh, she's scaring me.

"If I feel like laughing, that might be my own fucking business, agreed?"

A couple of heads look up from the surrounding tables.

I lean forward from the waist.

"You know how they say some girls look prettier when they're angry? Well, in your case, it doesn't apply."

She recoils, drops her arms to her sides, and looks around as if the airport had suddenly become intolerable.

There are times when I think, and I do mean that this is what I think, that we really should give up entirely this idea of talking to one another. Because it doesn't do anyone any good. It's not the question of understanding one another, struggling to agree on given points; that's not the problem. It's that no conversation seems to stay on topic for more than a couple of sentences; the issue is one of pertinence.

Now, for the moment, let's forget about the fact that I'm talking with my daughter, in practical terms. Let's say you ask some friend of yours a question. You notice that he smiles. Since there was no reason to smile, on account of nothing you said was in the least funny, you register the anomaly (which was slightly annoying, by the way) and you let it ride. Then the guy smiles again, and this time you have to go ahead and ask just where that smile of his comes from. And at that point he loses his temper and defends his right to do exactly as he pleases with his own face. As if you had called his right to do so into question. Whereupon you do your best to get the conversation back on track, but he decides he's offended and he barricades himself behind the whole matter of the principle of the thing (which is obviously nothing more than a lateral escape route, because that's all that matters of principle ever really are). So now you lose your temper and you reply sharply, and he gets angry too, and you raise your voice, and he raises his voice, and then maybe just to be offensive you say things that have even less to do with the original topic (which at this point has been completely crushed in the chain reaction of front-end and rear-end conversational crashes), and the only reason you don't actually wind up in a fistfight is because it's not something you usually do, and so you sit there in complete silence for a while glaring at each other in hatred until you start to get a little depressed, and then one of the two of you says something slightly funny (to call it funny is a stretch; it's not the sort of funny that would normally make anyone laugh), and the other one laughs even though he wouldn't normally laugh at it, and then you start over from scratch, without discussing that topic anymore (so it remains unresolved), until the next time that talking together breaks down at that same exact point.

And that's just the way relations are between people, even people who've known each other all their lives, and that's why there's no real difference between talking or not talking, and sincerity is incidental, something that really isn't anywhere near as good or helpful as people seem to think. Talking doesn't solve problems; if anything it papers them over. You can't rely on words, that's all there is to say on the matter. There are times when you find yourself looking at someone who said something to you that you'd set aside, convinced that it had a certain value between the two of you, and you suddenly realize that they don't even remember it, and that's when you decide that it's best to forget about it and you never even think about it again, understood?

"Are you planning to go away?" I ask, already exhausted by the bickering that might ensue or else might already be over, who can say.

I must seem pathetic, because she looks as if she's sorry now.

"Christ, Vincè."

And she requisitions my Whopper.

And I laugh.
And so does she.
And we make peace.
And we never mention the matter again.
I told you.

DESPERATE LAWYERS

P hone call. A number I don't recognize appears on the screen.

"Hello."

"Is this my colleague, Counselor Malinconico?"

I look up at the ceiling with all the tolerance of a chicken farmer. When another lawyer calls me "colleague," I assume he's about to try to chisel a discount of some sort out of me.

"Yes," I admit, resignedly.

"Ciao colleague this is Gaetano Picciafuoco I'm calling for Fantasia okay now the situation is delicate and sure we're talking about a questionable individual and afterward of course you can tell me what you've concluded about this whole thing anyway if you ask me we can get off scot free if we just stick to the facts because okay let's say you found a hand buried in my backyard and it's obvious that the dog is how the hand got there because the license from the dog's collar wound up in the hole too but that doesn't mean it was me, what is this, guilt by association with your dog? Aside from the fact that if it *was* me, first, I wouldn't so stupid as to bury the hand right in my own backyard and second, let's say and I'm not admitting this is what happened, but if it *was* me I would have dug a much deeper hole while the shallowness of the excavation proves beyond any reasonable doubt that we are in the presence of the typical burial style of an animal concealing its prey, which brings us back to square one, which is where are you trying to take this, that I'm legally responsible for whatever my dog does? I don't think so because in that case you'd have to arrest us both don't you think?"

I hold the cordless away from my ear and I stare at it in bafflement. If I was to use a single word to describe my state of mind in the face of this verbal avalanche tumbling over me, I'd say: skeptical. Really, I don't know whether to believe it. And in the meanwhile, as I examine the problem, this guy is still talking.

"In other words a dog is a dog and after all we're talking about a pit bull not a toy poodle that stays wherever you put it, a pit bull is autonomous it's a gladiator it's a criminal it goes wandering around amusing itself, it's not like when a pit bull comes home you ask it if it brought anything with it, what do you think?"

I ought to say something, I imagine; but instead I'm surprised to catch myself in a state of astonishment.

"Wait a minute," I manage to wedge a word in edgewise when lack of oxygen forces him to pause for half a second before resuming the relay race. "Maybe you skipped a section I don't understand. You represent this Fantasia? Fantasia Domenico, a.k.a. Mimmo 'o Burzone?"

"Of course," replies my—let's use the term—colleague.

"Okay, but, hold on, I don't understand where I come in."

"Why, don't you know?"

"Don't I know what?"

"That there are two of us," he says, with an urgency that he can't contain.

I freeze. Even though I knew that Burzone had appointed me as his defense lawyer, I'm fairly troubled by the confirmation that I've just received of that fact. It's not like there's anything unusual about it. Quite the contrary: the substitution and/or addition of lawyers is a common enough practice, especially among inmates. Every day, so many appointments and dismissals stream out of the prison that it looks like a train station. When it comes to counsel for the defense, jailbirds are practically biologically predisposed to experimentation. They hire and fire with a nonchalance that verges on the offensive. They exploit their lawyers, they use them (especially the younger lawyers). At times, they even appoint one but forget to fire the other one (or else they do it intentionally, just to have an extra lawyer on hand, you can never have too many), and what happens then is that when their day in court finally comes, two lawyers show up instead of one, and amid a general sense of embarrassment they stipulate a provisional alliance in the reciprocal hope of eliminating their rival in the fullness of time.

The fact is that down here lawyers have become no different from insurance agents or realtors. There are scads of them, each one hungrier than the last. Just take a short stroll down any street, even on the outskirts of town, and count the plaques lining the street doors of the apartment buildings. A lawyer, these days, in order to get a case, even a court-appointed case, is eager and willing to perform a fanciful array of undignified pirouettes and double gainers. What's driving them isn't even a lust for money or the desire for social prestige—it's not even that anymore. Here it's a matter of maintaining just a bare minimum of logical market presence (that is, pay your expenses and take home a little extra money to live on) or quitting the profession entirely. And the true tragedy is that this general policy of survival now extends horizontally across the entire class of lawyers, shared by the nobodies and the well-connected, the privileged and the miserably poor. In the sense that the cosseted offspring of a successful lawyer is roughly as ravenously eager—if not hungrier—to drum up new cases as people who are, in professional terms, motherless bastards. This is the new culture of competition, spawned in the spirit of gluttonous real estate developers, and it perceives no difference between greed and need, establishing in its majestic equality a false parity between competitors who start out from completely different conditions. The rich and the poor are fighting over the same scraps and bones. There you have it, the demise of the principle of equality.

I've seen things you non-lawyers can't even imagine. I've seen elderly professionals shamelessly brown-nosing magistrates aged twenty-nine. I've seen lawyers, green and youthful, personally bringing trays of espressos to all the body repair shops in a neighborhood in hopes of snagging a car crash lawsuit. I've seen stakeouts at the front door of the city morgue, with ensuing leafleting of business cards at the arrival of the gurney. I've seen Camorra accountants and specialists at inflicting corporal punishment for overdue payments of protection money treated with a lavish regard and obsequiousness that you'd only expect for the highest officials of the state. I've seen colleagues lining up for an audience with the lowliest clerks of the court in the hopes of a court-appointed case, paying a commission in advance based on a fixed percentage of the honorarium. I've seen prison guards boasting of their pull with this lawyer or that to the relatives of inmates in exchange for season soccer tickets. I've seen colleagues barely thirty years old strike deals with notoriously shady clerks of the court to rig a bankruptcy auction, steering the final assignment of the goods allegedly being sold. I've seen their photos in the newspaper a few months later. I've seen car accidents so bogus that you're tempted to step in on the side of the insurance company on a pro bono basis (which is more or less the same as, say, waking up one fine morning with a vocation to become a militant anti-Semite). I've seen lawyers squabbling before the Italian supreme court over a seat on the boards of condominiums. I've seen respected university professors make phone calls to prominent persons of interest in corruption cases offering legal representation, even knowing full well that another lawyer has already been appointed, bragging about their personal friendship with the assistant district attorney assigned to the case and devaluing, between the lines, the professional competence of the colleague in question. I've seen the very same lawyer that the university professor was trying to undermine recount the scandalous professional misbehavior to a group of young colleagues and not twenty minutes later run into the university professor at the front door of the court house and, like on a sappy reality TV show, throw his arms around him as if he were a long-lost brother. I've seen that same lawyer persuade the person of interest that yes, actually, it would be a shrewd move to include the university professor in his defense team, because such a strong lineup of legal counsel would assure an acquittal with a victorious fanfare. I've seen the person of interest sit at the hearing between the court-appointed lawyer and the university professor; frankly he seemed more afraid of his defense team than of the judges. I've heard the professor, in the throes of his summation, stumble over a juridical point of such simplicity that if one of his students had fudged the point during a final exam he would have ordered him out of the lecture hall. I've seen the lawyer shrug and take it, blushing like a guilty confederate, deftly avoiding the astonished gaze of the panel of judges. I've seen the son of the lawyer become a teaching assistant to the university professor who had tried to have his father tossed off the case. I've seen this and much much more, but if I don't stop here, it'll be midnight before I run out of examples.

"Hello," I hear him say at the other end of the line.

My interlocutor sounds irritated, like a smartypants treating you as if you were wasting his valuable time.

"I'm here," I say, enunciating, ready for a fight. And in fact, he immediately becomes all tractable, paper hoodlum that he is.

"I didn't hear you say anything."

"I was thinking."

"Ah."

"Listen, bear with me, colleague," I ask naïvely, "but if

Fantasia already had a lawyer, namely you, why didn't he call you to be present at his judicial interrogation?"

A meditative pause ensues.

"Oh, he called me," he replies, sighing as if I'd put my thumb on a sore spot, "it's just that I had my cell phone turned off that day."

Whereupon it dawns on me that the best thing to do now is to change the subject.

"So tell me something," I say, "what's all this about the dog?"

"Wait, you mean you don't know?"

"Well, you hear me asking."

"Excuse me, but haven't you read the file?"

I look like an asshole.

"No. That is, yes. I mean, I just wanted you to explain a few details."

He replies with telegraphic haughtiness. This time, though, I don't react, considering my misstep.

"The hand. In the backyard. Was put there. By the dog. Fantasia's dog. A pit bull. Ringo."

"Okay. Good. Now we have a name and a breed. Then what?"

"Then nothing, he took it and buried it in the garden. You know how animals do when they're on the hunt, and afterward they conceal their prey? The dog hid it right there, behind the garage. The Carabinieri show up, find the hand, and fasten up the cuffs. In the same hole, they found the dog's tags, with name and address. Ringo must have lost it while he was digging."

"Ah," I marvel, as I organize, then and there, an imaginary projection of the scene, with the pit bull sneaking furtively into Burzone's specially equipped autopsy room in the garage behind his detached villa, it sees the sections of cadaver spread out on the operating table, yelps in excitement, doesn't even stop to think, snatches the hand, and scampers out the door, all unbeknownst to Burzone, who had probably stepped away for some unexpected urgent errand (I don't know, to make a call on his cell phone and the reception under the stairs was no good, or else just to pee, maybe). Then I imagine Burzone coming back, counting up the limbs, and coming up one short. I have to stifle a laugh.

I can just picture him, furious, stepping out into the garden and searching Ringo's doghouse; the pit bull, off to one side, watches him with his ears lowered, fearing an imminent beating; Burzone fails to find the loot in the doghouse, wanders the immediately surrounding area in an unsuccessful search, and so he moves on to Plan B: he seizes the animal by the collar and interrogates it, Talk, you bastard, tell me where you put it; Ringo takes the beating but doesn't spill the beans ("I don't know what you're talking about," his mournful doggy eyes seem to say); Burzone loses his temper and starts flailing clumsily away at the dog; the pit bull takes it like a worn-out boxer but never quite understands what the hell its master wants from him, and it howls brokenhearted out of a general sense of guilt. At that point, I can't help it any longer, and I break out in a nasal burst of laughter.

"Oh," the disinterested colleague calls.

"Eh," I reply, wiping a tear away from the corner of my right eye.

"What are you doing, laughing?"

"A little, yes, truth be told."

"I don't see anything to laugh about. And neither does Fantasia, I'm willing to bet."

Okay, this is when I spit right in this guy's face, I tell myself. And I'd be on the verge of losing my temper, for real, if it weren't for the fact that it all just strikes me as so ridiculous.

"So, what? You want to tell him about it?" I say.

"Oh, now, really," he replies, with the unmistakable sound of his tail tucking between his legs.

We sit in silence for a while.

I think back to the trailer I just watched. I still feel like laughing, but this time I manage to control myself.

"So what do you want to do?" he asks me.

"What do I want to do about what?"

"About Fantasia—what do you mean what?"

Oh, here we are. The poor man finally gets to the point.

"So, you're asking if I'll accept the appointment?"

He says nothing, opting for silence as assent. So I let him dangle uncomfortably for a while, like in the elimination scenes on *Big Brother*, when the contestants slump in their chairs waiting for the presenter in the studio to drop the axe. And in the quagmire of seconds that follow, I realize that the news of Burzone's appointment is making me disgustingly happy. I'm ashamed to admit it, but I still feel gratified by this fiduciary appointment.

"I don't know," I reply, taking my own sweet time. "I'll have to think it over."

"Ah," he says.

"You know, I have so many obligations these days," I add, shivering at the sheer fabrication.

A moment of silence, after which my rival drives home a lunge that I really wasn't expecting.

"I can imagine how much work you have."

I undergo a wave of menopausal heat, culminating in an instantaneous suntan.

Okay, I'm not a particularly well-known name among the denizens of the justice system. I don't represent banks, insurance companies, businessmen, public administrators, Camorristi, or wealthy citizens (in fact, you might reasonably wonder: "So what is it exactly that you do for a living, if I may ask?"). I don't frequent high-society occasions, I don't play tennis with magistrates. I share the rent on a group office. I have no secretary, I have no paralegals or interns. Most of the time that I ought to be devoting to work (which I don't have) I spend inventing occupations that resemble work (like walking up and down the hallways of the courtroom with nothing to do, sticking my head into the hearing rooms to watch other lawyers argue cases, making Xeroxes that I don't need, spending anywhere from a scanty half-hour to an entire hour in the library, pretending to be absorbed in legal research, and other palliatives of the sort). I've got sixteen years of professional activity under my belt, and I file tax returns that are frankly embarrassing. I'm afraid I'm going to be audited one of these days, but even though the numbers on my returns look highly implausible, they are the plain truth. And the Italian tax authorities, it's well known, make a fundamental presumption of falsehood; in fact the burden of proof is reversed in tax cases.

But that doesn't mean you can crack funny. Especially not when you're the one who called me out of fear that I'd snatch the client off your plate, for that matter.

"Well, you know what I say?" I reply, flaring my nostrils. "Now that I've had a chance to think it over, it's a case that intrigues me. I think I'll take it."

The wretch says nothing.

"Well, all right then, listen," he says resignedly after a while. "We should probably meet to plan out our strategy."

I consider the proposal.

"Actually, the first thing I need to do is go see Fantasia."

Pause.

"There's no need for that, you can talk to me."

I stare intensely at the Edward Hopper poster on the facing wall as if it could understand me. I step into it, I have a sudden thirst for a beer. I sit down alongside the other late-night customers there at Phillie's bar, I rest an elbow on the counter. The girl in red doesn't even dignify me with a glance.

Does this guy take me for a complete idiot?

"Excuse me, can I ask you a question?" I ask.

"Of course."

"Is this phone call your idea, or did Fantasia tell you to call me?"

He stalls for time, hamster that he is.

"Are you there, Counselor . . . ?" I ask, enunciating carefully.

"Picciafuoco. Nino Picciafuoco."

Oh, right, James Bond in person.

"Did you hear the question, Counselor Picciafuoco?"

Another guilty pause.

"Yes. No. Well, anyway, don't worry about it."

"Don't worry about what?"

Now he's treading water.

"No, I was just saying there was no need, because anyway I'm very well acquainted with Fantasia's situation, and after all, as you can imagine, I've been his lawyer for years, all I was asking was if you accept, and if so, we can work out terms, it was mainly just to spare you the time and the bother of going all the way out to the prison to talk with Fantasia, that's all."

I let a few seconds go by.

"Well, yes, in fact, I do have a lot of work. But not so much that I can't take the time to meet a client who's asking me to take on his defense."

"Ah," he says.

It sounds like: "Ah, how painful!"

"Anyway, thanks for calling," I cut the conversation short.

"Sure. My pleasure. No. Shall we talk again?"

"If we have something to talk about."

He hesitates. He says nothing.

And then we hang up.

I interlace the fingers of both hands, cradling the back of my head, while I lean against the backrest of my Skruvsta and review the situation. I have no intention of defending that corpsemonger Burzone, but I am enjoying the idea that Picciafuoco thinks I will.

I take a deep breath and smile, but my sense of satisfaction begins to crumble almost immediately. Like a seismic tremor stirring beneath my thoughts, a sneaking suspicion becomes increasingly credible as I manage to get it into focus. Like one of those faint, distant earthquakes that you're not even sure you heard, but your eyes go straight up to the chandelier.

What an idiot you are, I say to myself, are you thinking of turning down the appointment? Who do you think you are, Alfredo De Marsico?

No, it's precisely because I *don't* think that I'm Alfredo De Marsico that I don't want to take the case, I weakly retort.

What a lovely answer, I tell myself. What should I do, just admit you're right, and we can close the debate right now?

I lower my head.

Ah, okay. Let's see, maybe we should try to sum up: first of all, it's not clear why you should do Picciafuoco this favor (did you hear him say, "I can imagine how much work you have"? I felt like slamming the phone down, right in his face), so he can go around telling everyone that you lacked the balls for the job, so you turned it down; second, for years you've been scraping by with fenderbenders, small-claims court, contracts and leases between relatives, leaks and water damage in apartments, insults and quarrels and condominium boards. For once in your life a real case comes along, and what do you do? You turn up your nose?

He's a butcher, I try pointing out. For the Camorra.

So what? I say to myself. What are we turning this into now, a moral question?

Well, yeah, in fact, I venture.

Oh, I see, I say to myself, all of that nonsense you never get tired of spouting about the right to legal counsel and how even the worst murderer has a right to a defense lawyer who will argue his case, if for no other reason than to make it possible to have a trial, because otherwise the alternative is to go back to the Inquisition, and so on—that was all bullshit? Ah? Funny that you should happen to come to that realization now, isn't it?

I'm afraid, I whine.

I know, I say to myself.

I don't want to, I add.

You have to, I say to myself.

I don't know the first thing about criminal law.

Oh yes you do, I say to myself.

Oh no I don't, I insist.

That's not entirely true, I say to myself.

Yes it is, I reply.

But you wrote your thesis about criminal law, I say to myself.

Eighteen years ago, I respond.

About pornography, I say to myself.

I was just interested in the subject, I answer.

Ha, ha, I say to myself.

Eh. Ha, ha, I say back to myself.

You did pretty well for yourself at Burzone's hearing, I tell myself.

Dumb luck.

Are you sure of that?

How the hell do I know?

I find them debilitating, these face-to-face confrontations with myself. Especially when I'm on the losing side of the argument.

The phone again.

Unknown caller. Okay, let's answer and see who it is.

"Counselor Malinconico?"

A woman's voice. Fairly young. I'd say barely thirty. Making a distinct effort to shed her dialect. Vowel formation reminiscent of a suppository. By the time she's said a couple of sentences I ought to be able to guess her hometown.

"Yes, this is he," I confirm.

"*Buon giorno*, Counselor Malinconico, this is Signora Fantasia speaking, am I interrupting something?"

I can't believe my ears: the First Lady herself. I'm on the verge of getting to my feet.

"No, not at all. Please go ahead."

"I need to speak with you urgently, Counselor Malinconico. It's about my husband, Domenicu Fantasia, you represented him just a few days ago."

By this point I'd be willing to stake five hundred euros on Lady Burzone's birthplace. It's a town where not long ago two entire families reciprocally rubbed one another out in broad daylight, over some trival disagreement, as it happens. Like two third cousins (once removed) had a shouting match, followed by a fistfight in the town square over some bitch who dated them both, fully aware of the havoc it would unleash. One of them went home with a fractured septum whining that his cousin had had an easy time of it because he was so much bigger. Whereupon his father said: "Oh, no, this is a problem between you kids, I'm not getting involved." And the cousin with the fractured septum grabs his car keys, goes downstairs, and a few minutes later he's run over his distant cousin in the middle of the town square. At this point, one of the uncles of the guy under the car had been watching it all from his balcony, and now he wades into the melee with a handgun. To make a long story short, it culminates in bloody tragedy. So brutal that, at first, the detectives figured that this must be someone settling scores with someone else who's trying to elbow in on the profits from some local crime ring or bid-rigging (it later emerged that the two parties to the dispute belonged to rival crime clans). That theory was bolstered by the revealing detail of the bedroom slippers on the feet of one of the corpses (this was the uncle who'd watched from the balcony as his nephew was run over on the piazza), a clue that immediately suggested the old technique of an urgent family appointment, a favorite when close relatives are the targets slated for elimination (basically, the victim is hustled outside so fast that he never even has time to put on a pair of decent street shoes; in fact, the corpse is found just a few yards from the front door).

"Ah, well of course, how could I forget," I answer, pretending to emerge from great concentration.

"When could I come see you, Counselor Malinconico?"

I leaf noisily through my half-empty appointment book.

"Well, let's see . . . would Thursday at 5 P.M. work for you?"

"Well, if it's possible, I'd prefer something sooner, Counselor Malinconico."

I don't know why it is, but whenever someone says my name too often, I feel like looking around. As if someone else were about to show up. I don't know if I make myself clear.

"Ah," I say. "Well, let's see. Just a moment . . . Tuesday at 3:30?"

"Well, actually, I could come today, if it's not a problem."

"Today? Today when?" I answer, aghast.

"Right now, Counselor Malinconico."

"But, really, you catch me at a disadvantage, madam. I have an appointment at 5:30 and . . ."

"I'm downstairs, outside your front door, Counselor Malinconico. I could come straight upstairs, if you'd be so kind as to see me right now."

I exhale, outwitted.

"Well, all right, come up right now, what can I say?"

We say goodbye.

Here's another distinguishing feature of the members of the Burzone club: there is no way to get them onto a waiting list. They ignore the concept of yielding the right of way, of waiting for their turn. They are past masters when it comes to break-

ing elementary rules. With their well-controlled obsequiousness, with their insistent good manners, the way they mention
your name in every sentence they utter, in fact they're telling
you: "Look, you might as well do what I'm asking you, because
there is no way I'm leaving until you do." In other words,
they're laying it down in such a manner that you're the one
who suggests making an exception in their case, just to get
them the hell out of your hair. They make you abandon your
principles. Because a principle is theoretical, while nagging
insistence is all too real.

Anyway, to come back to the issue of hearing yourself called
by your name every time, I'm pretty convinced that, in criminal terms, a constant evocation by name is an investiture. The
procurement of a contract. Close parenthesis.

In order to rid myself of the creepy sense of personal com-
promise that comes with having submitted to her demand, I
organize then and there a modicum of set design for the imminent arrival of Her Pushiness: I carefully conceal the Innocenti
steel pipe behind the Kvadrant curtains, I grab a few random
files from the Billy glass bookcase and spread them out illogi-
cally on the Jonas desk, I break open a volume of the civil code
and another hefty tome of criminal procedure (the latter book
with at least half its leaves still uncut, not exactly fresh from the
bindery), and I slap them on the desk facedown, pages open,
one near the phone and the other next to the Dokument letter
tray. The next step is to pull my jacket off the Radar coatrack
and put it on, then I unzip my trousers, retuck my shirt tails,
zip back up, arrange the two Hampus chairs in a symmetrical
array, and finish up with a quick glance at the Bonett mirror,
where I inspect myself, giving myself a searching scrutiny as if
I owed myself a sizable sum of money, in order to impose a
minimum of juridical seriousness on my features. Just then, I
find myself wondering what strange mechanism makes it seem
so natural to people to make an angry face when they want to

appear attractive; but I'm too late to give myself an answer because the sound of the doorbell breaks in, overwhelmed in real time by the yelping of the goddamned toy spitz.

When I step out into the hallway, Virginia-Ignazia or whatever the fuck her name is has already buzzed the downstairs door open, balanced precariously with one hand on the intercom and the other on the handle of her office door, pulling it toward her to keep the little canine kamikaze from bursting out into the open. You can hear the little criminal scratching and yelping away. Obviously, the dog is taking advantage of the fact that Roberto-Sergio is temporarily absent, otherwise by now he'd have already taken a few kicks to the hindquarters for sure.

"Yes, certainly, mezzanine," Iginia-Terenzia or Vitulia-Marcella or whatever her name is says into the intercom.

I walk over to her, doing my best to ignore the canine car alarm.

"Thanks, that was kind of you," I tell her.

"But of course, Vinshenso, if we don't help each other out, who will?"

"We who?" I'm tempted to ask. I can't stand being drafted into categories of humanity that seem destined for failure.

"Well, sure," I say.

"Look at the little scamp, he just won't stop."

She's talking about the four-legged recidivist scratching and snarling on the other side of the door. She's clearly uneasy, and I can hardly blame her. That's why she's constantly offering her services as an unpaid secretary. You can hardly dress her down for her shitty little dog if she's just answered the intercom for you.

"Oh, it's not a problem," I say, as fake as a pirated DVD, "but it's just that, right now, when my client's coming in, if you could . . ."

I don't know, drown him maybe, I think.

"Oh, of course, not to worry," she says, as the doorbell rings.

Before opening the door, I wait for Ophelia-Lavinia to maneuver herself back into her office.

When she turns the doorhandle, angling her right leg into the narrow aperture of the office door, the toy spitz is so excited at the prospect of lunging at the first set of legs he sees that for a moment he actually stops barking. He makes an attempt to feint around the obstacle, rears up on his hind legs, and even snaps his teeth at random patches of empty air once or twice, but his mistress beats him to the punch and slips into her room with a lightning speed that she must have acquired from years of cohabitation: in the blink of an eye, literally the blink of an eye, she's already inside and the door is clicking shut behind her, just like in one of the chase scenes in a *Tom and Jerry* cartoon, when the mouse vanishes around a corner, leaving a cloud of dust to dissolve behind him, like a fart.

I open the door.

"Counselor Malinconico?" the individual who appears on the threshold inquires.

How's that saying go: behind every great man there's a great woman? Let me see if I can describe the subject that appears before me now, though I'm not sure I'm up to the task.

First of all, her age: undefinable. She could as easily be twenty-five as forty-seven, I swear it. You just can't tell. And you can't tell *why* you can't tell either. In the sense that there aren't any noticeable malformations, handicaps, or oddities that might derail the normal process of assessment. That is, if you open the door to a stranger who is suffering from a devastating outbreak of vitiligo, it's understandable that you can't guess how old she is. At least until she says something. Because the disease overwhelms all the other indicators and markers; it demands your full attention.

In this case, on the other hand, we're in the presence of a typical (and I use the term advisedly) instance of a face without signs of the passage of time. One of those sets of facial features that, at a certain point in their personal evolution, come to a screeching halt. They don't know whether to go backward or forward, and in this hovering uncertainty they even wind up losing their sexual attributes to a certain degree (in fact, truth be told, if I hadn't already known that it was a woman coming to pay a call on me, I wouldn't have been a hundred percent certain which little box to checkmark).

The problem, when you're dealing with a genetically equivocal citizen, is that you have to stay constantly on your toes when you talk to them, because if you lower your guard for even a second you're lost. It's a little bit like when you have folks calling into a television talk show from who-knows-where, and the sound isn't synced right. If you hear someone saying one thing while you see their mouth saying something else, the only way to follow the conversation is to look away. But the inconvenient aspect is this: it's no good avoiding the gaze of a person you're talking to, especially if that person is married to a hardened criminal who specializes in butchering mob cadavers.

"Yes, that's me," I reply.

She smiles and nods. Then she comes in.

I almost forgot to describe the rest of her. Height, about five foot three. Round face. Very curly hair, thick and fluffy, with numerous silver streaks, though I couldn't say if they were natural or the aftermath of haphazard salon highlighting. Makeup that stops just short of being overdone, just garish enough to get a mark to pull over. Broad forehead. Incredibly thick eyebrows. Green eyes (not bad, truth be told). The furtive expression of a mouse, vigilant on either side; one of those people who can always locate another exit. Uniform nose, small mouth smeared with lip gloss. A Bahamas smock-shirt.

As for her body shape, completely normal down to the waist; from there on we're looking at the Michelin man, but wearing a pair of black leggings. Running shoes. Cell phone in one hand, car keys and remote in the other.

She dressed special for the occasion, I decide.

She holds out her hand.

"I'm Fantasia."

"So pleased," I reply.

Then I show her the way.

The toy spitz must still be in shock, because it doesn't make a sound.

When we enter the office, Miss Fantasy goes straight to one of the Hampus chairs, takes a seat, turns off her cell phone, and nothing else. A double play that leaves me pleasantly stupefied. Generally, whenever I receive someone in my law office I'm busy justifying myself the whole time, I don't know if I convey the idea. In the sense that I put on a guilty attitude, as if I had to persuade the client not to judge from appearances. To put it in absurd terms, take the client out of this room. Make him or her forget the two hundred square feet and the Ikca furnishings and force him or her to focus exclusively on me, to think that, despite the architectural minimalism, I'll be completely up to the job of winning his or her case. In other words, I can't just sit down at my desk, strike a pose (after all, that's what desks are for), and listen, rationing out my opinion over the course of the session, the way that lawyers with imposing offices can do. Not me—I have to talk nonstop, subtitle every transition, repeat words, nod to the point of damaging my neck, act astonished and understanding, respond at any given point about the entire matter.

Incredibly, for once I can skip the examination entirely, how do you like that. Signora Burzone has made such a spectacular show of disinterest in the formalities, the last thing I would have expected from someone like her. I'm surprised, and I have to admit it.

"Now then," I say with senseless optimism, as I take a seat on my Skruvsta.

"Forgive me if I drop in on you without warning, Counselor Malinconico, but you know, lately I've been so tired, so impatient, I can't get a wink of sleep, you can imagine the state my husband's in, the children are so upset about what happened to us . . . "

I nod, though not the slightest trace of anxiety appears on her face.

"Don't worry, I know what it's like to go through something like this," I say.

"And who could understand us better than you, Counselor," she replies. A phrase that makes me feel as comfortable as if she'd left a kilo of heroin in my office for safekeeping. (I don't know if the metaphor conveys the idea)

"Do you mind?" I ask, pointing to my cigarettes.

"Please, Counselor, go right ahead."

I pick up the pack and, before taking one for myself, I offer it to her.

"Do you smoke?"

She sits, motionless, and saying nothing, for a long time, and then shakes her head no, but with a touch of reproof, as if I'd just committed a gaffe.

I freeze for a couple of seconds, and then I understand.

Je-e-e-e-sus.

I light up, with a new appreciation for my grandmother. As sanctimonious as she was, I never heard her say that only whores put a cigarette in their mouth, truth be told.

"So, as you can understand, it's especially difficult to be all alone at a time like this. I have the apartment to keep up, people gossiping, the kids, their school . . . "

" . . . the dog . . . " I'm tempted to add.

I take another drag and take care not to blow the smoke out in her direction; the last thing I want to do is trigger other progressive ideas.

" . . . and then there's this Carabinieri warrant officer who's constantly buzzing around our house, I look out the door and there he is, he follows me everywhere I go, when I go to do my grocery shopping, suddenly he pops out from nowhere, 'Signora, how's your husband, let me carry your groceries for you, why, what a nice dress you're wearing today . . . '"

She sits there on the extreme edge of the Hampus and talks with half-lidded eyes. A little bit I guess she's putting on airs (who knows, maybe in the circles she moves in she's considered hot stuff), and so she treats me with the slippery detachment of a sophisticated woman who long ago learned to reduce masculine intentions to one kind, and one kind only (if we leave aside the minor detail of what a complete dog she is); and a little bit you can see that she's uncomfortable being all alone in an office with a man (criminals always seem to be disturbingly traditional).

"One of these days, I'm going to accept his advances, too, but I'll have a surprise ending ready for our little evening out."

There it is. Aside from the chilling conclusion (I can already see them in my mind, the seagulls feasting on the warrant officer's dead body, on a deserted beach), at this point I'm really curious to know what the hell this come-on artist of a policeman has to do with Burzone's troubles with the law. What do we care, either of us (and especially one of us)? Not a damn thing, obviously. But still, there I sit, nodding yes-yes with my head, patiently taking part in this dreary remake of the interrogation scene in *Basic Instinct*. It's senseless, I know.

I put my cigarette out when it's only half-smoked. I exhale two streams of smoke from my nostrils.

"In other words, as I was telling you, after the last hearing, my husband trusts only you, Counselor."

"*As you were telling me*, Signora?" I ask, thrown off balance by her filthy logic.

But she doesn't even hear me.

"That's why he wanted you to come as soon as you could, Counselor. He said, Amalia, go see him immediately, I want Counselor Malinconico and no one else."

No, listen, is it possible to carry on a conversation of this kind? And what kind of conversation is this, after all? How can you talk with someone who not only leaps from one non sequitur to the next whenever she feels like it, but sits there, ugly and unblinking, taking it for granted that you're going to follow her lead whatever she decides to say? Really, it's enough to make a person drool idiotically. Enough to make you question the fundamental underlying principles of dialectics. At this point, I feel so deeply choreographic that if, let's just imagine an absurd scenario, I were to go into the adjoining office to shoot the breeze with Espedito and only come back twenty minutes later, I'm not sure that it would make much of a difference to this, shall we say, little chat.

"So he wants me and nobody else but me," I say, as I begin to breathe differently, the way you breathe when you're really starting to get pissed off.

"You see, my husband is a man with lots of habits and routines, Counselor, he takes a bath twice daily, he uses creams, body lotions, lots and lots of personal products, he's obsessed with hygiene, he wouldn't last in prison."

That is indeed a problem, I think to myself.

"So why is it that a certain colleague of mine named Picciafuoco called me up to tell me that he's representing your husband too, Signora?"

I figure I'll give the old system of non sequiturs a shot. You never know when it'll work.

Bingo.

"Don't you worry about him, Counselor. The same way we appointed him we can fire him."

For a second I don't even recognize her anymore. Her eyes have turned blood-chilling and glassy. Her voice has dropped in timbre, vaguely mannish. Her jaw is slack. A manager. This must be her real face.

"Why, aren't you happy with him?"

"Let's just say he could have tried harder."

As if she were talking about some rusty old piece of ballast. A burden of which she would gladly have rid herself long ago, if she'd been able to decide for herself.

"All right. Shall we take a little time now to discuss what happened to your husband?"

"Why, don't you know already, Counselor?"

"I know what I've read in the documentation I was given, but I'd like to hear a little more about it."

"Listen, Counselor, all I can tell you is that the dog buried something in our garden and that's when this whole thing got started."

"Something," I say, in disgust.

She reactivates the partial closure of her eyelids. Whenever they feel threatened, they put on aristocratic airs.

"You know what dogs are like, Counselor."

I scoot my Skruvsta backward, and I slap the sole of my loafer on the floor.

People generally think that lawyers know the truth. That is, that our clients, in the confidential privacy of our law offices, tell us exactly what happened. After which we prepare our line of defense, that is, a rhetorical version of the things that actually happened. Because, as any reasonable person can understand, if you want to make a convincing fake, you need to get your hands on the original.

Nothing could be further from the truth. There is only the slightest relaxation of mistrust between a lawyer and a client. It's all a lurching, pathetic alternation of gossip, ambiguity, enigmas, partial confessions, implausible tall tales, accusations of other people who had nothing to do with it (generally identified as the shadowy mastermind behind everything that happened). No one tells you the truth; you can only guess at it. Drag it out of them and keep it to yourself once you've figured it out. We're accustomed to making our way through the various gradations of our clients' untruths in search of the turds they've stepped in and doing our best to limit the damage. That's what we do. Our job consists of going back to the scene of the crime and doing our best to tangle and confuse the evidence and make the investigator's job that much harder (in a certain sense, a criminal defense always amounts to tampering with a crime scene).

So here I am again, as if I were working off the same old script, asked to perform legal services and given absolutely no trust. As delirious as it might seem when you spell it out, the demands of the particular client sitting across the desk from me today are these: "Don't ask me anything. Don't get me involved in this mess. Treat me as if I were the wife of a solid citizen unfairly accused. Give me a free ride when it comes to the details, the indiscretions, the behind-the-scenes stories, and the whole tawdry mess you're going to have to wade through professionally from here on in. Just tell me yes and send me off, reassured, trusting, and relieved (by the way, don't even ask for a retainer: can't you see I didn't bring my purse?)."

Well, you know what's different this time? My state of mind, all of a sudden, that's what.

"I really do appreciate the faith your husband's shown in me, Signora, but I'm afraid I'm not going to be able to represent him in this case," I say all at once.

"What?" she cries, scandalized. "Why not?"

"I'm very busy for the next few months. I'd be unable to devote the proper amount of time to your husband's case. I'm sorry."

Her face wrinkles up and she tosses her head back and forth.

"Wait just a moment, Counselor, maybe I didn't make myself very clear. If you give me a chance, I'll try to explain."

"No, no, you made yourself perfectly clear, believe me. It's just that I can't take the case, that's all. I simply don't have the time, really."

"But I, I had . . . I came because . . . I thought . . . " she shifts uncomfortably on the Hampus.

Perhaps she'd like me to play a little something while she struggles for words, to accompany her with a string of justifications, my apologies, a nicely crafted circumstantial platitude; but I keep my mouth closed.

She doesn't even bother insisting. She takes the time required to make a careful note of the date and hour of my refusal in the Registry of the Unforgivable and then she gets to her feet.

I imitate her, like a schoolboy, astonished at my own impudent silence.

She dismisses me with a curt nod of the head, lips compressed, the universal demeanor of the Woman Spurned. From that moment she stops looking at me.

I detect an unsettling hint of intimacy.

As she leaves, she walks ahead of me briskly, forcing me into a sort of clumsy chase scene that ends at the door, where I am careful not to extend my hand, because she would certainly refuse to clasp it.

I close the door behind her and think: "Ah, what the hell, fuck her."

Not a sound from the office of Arethusa. They must have left already, I suppose. I poke my head into Espe's room, driven by an urgent need for friendly faces. But he's out too. And so, even though I have no idea of what I'd say if he opened his door, I even knock at Rudy Fiumara's office, but he's not there, of course. So after a while I decide to go back into my little office.

In a daze, I take a seat on one of my Hampus chairs. In the distance, I can hear the steady marching of the troops of remorse: they'll be here before long. And as I do my best to flick away the insistent sensation of inadequacy that's already hemming me in, I say to myself: When am I going to learn not to start something I have no intention of finishing?

FLOATING MAGNETS

A
s I leave the office I bump into a character who's lived on the fourth floor, unless I'm mistaken, for a while now. To be precise, I open the main street door for him and let him go ahead of me. He recoils but then accepts the courteous gesture, eyes lowered, intimidated.

This isn't the first time he's behaved this way, as if there were something left unfinished or unstarted between the two of us. When we run into each other on the street he always displays that slight hesitation of someone who'd like to strike up a conversation but never seems to find the right opportunity.

I don't think that I interest him sexually (in part because I don't usually send unwanted messages to queers); what's more, he has a Polish girlfriend, and I've seen them out and about holding hands together (I've seen them go upstairs together too, more than once). Instead, I think that whatever attraction there is on his part has to do with my previously mentioned predisposition to prompt strangers to confide in me. I say that even though he's not a complete stranger to me: I remember him sitting at a counter in the city offices where I used to go when I was still a student to have the signatures notarized for my applications for the civil service exams that I never wound up taking.

He looks to be fifty, maybe a little older, with the face of a St. Bernard, round and saggy, a mixture of disappointment and *who-the-hell-cares-we're-just-passing-through-this-life*, bags under the eyes, bristly mustache, and a potbelly. One of those civil servants that stick in your memory for the courtesy they always showed you and everyone else waiting in line, who have the gift of a smile when you've encountered any difficulties in filling out a bureaucratic form (and is there a standardized form on earth that any human being wouldn't encounter a problem of some kind filling out?).

In other words, a nice guy, unlike certain bastards you'll run into. In the clerk of the court's office located in the courts building, for instance, on the wall opposite the entry, positioned in a way that you can hardly miss it the minute you walk in, right at eye level, there's a very funny little sign, done on the computer, one of those signs made on a computer that when you see them you can't help but think how funny the guy who made it must have thought he was, and in the middle of it you see the silhouette of a human head, like something out of a handbook of anatomy, over which looms the following instruction: *Make sure brain is engaged before putting mouth in gear* (a dotted line with an arrow describes, in a wavy path, the route from the forehead to the mouth). The kind of thing that if you think about it for a second you can just see it, the Oliviero Toscani of civil servants saying to himself: "Okay, enough is enough," and he sits down at the computer, launches Freehand, redeems his professional category once and for all by pasting over the diagram that masterpiece of a phrase, and then the next day, in the office, he talks to all his coworkers one by one to see if they've noticed the new sign and then they each shake his hand, as if to say that it was about time someone clearly stated the way things really work around here.

Well, I think that it'd be a genuine service to society at large if everyone like that guy were just to jump off a cliff, their bodies never to be found. Let me paint a picture for you: I'm a miserable grunt cooped up in an office that's as grey as the undershirt I change once a week, but I act as if I'm a man of the world, a sophisticate, because this is where you have to come if you want to get your lawsuit docketed or to pick up a copy of a certificate; and if, by any chance, you don't know where in the Code of Civil Procedure you might find information you need (as if everyone studied the Code of Civil Procedure back in high school: try asking most people what a Code of Civil Procedure even is, and tell me what kind of answers you hear), then I feel completely authorized to treat you as a specimen of something whose very survival, in a modern advanced society where even small children know what the Code of Civil Procedure is, constitutes a mystery to me.

This is one of those licenses for bureaucratic frustration that ought to be treated with the same severity as violations of the building code. But the most depressing aspect of the whole episode is that in the entire court house there is not one (1) lawyer who has the balls to address the question of the workplace bullying of the discourteous clerks of the court. These are the reasons that an entire professional category goes to hell in a handbasket, and don't let anyone tell you different.

To come back to the present, that is to the upstairs tenant who is courting me, I let him go ahead of me and I say hello.

Whereupon he replies with *Buona sera*, he flashes me one of those let-me-notarize-that-signature smiles, and he actually gets up the nerve to ask me how everything is going.

"Not bad, not bad," I reply.

After that, he hesitates and, taking advantage of our physical proximity, he manages to find the courage to talk to me. For a few seconds, I'm afraid I'm about to get invited to dinner, but then I discount that theory.

"You know I have a girlfriend, don't you?"

"Excuse me?" I ask.

That's the only way to respond to questions that make no sense, especially when they're posed without a question mark.

"Ludmilla, my girlfriend. We've run into you many times in the street."

"Ah yes, why of course," I say, still unsure what to think about the mental soundness of this character.

"We live together. In this building, on the fourth floor."

"Sure," I confirm, without a shadow of doubt.

"Her name is Ludmilla, but I call her Lulla."

"Ah."

"She's younger than me. A lot younger," he says, with a note of concern.

Well, I wouldn't say that at first glance, truth be told.

"Well, good for you," I reply.

"No, you're wrong there, Counselor. You are a lawyer, aren't you?"

"Yes."

There is a very brief moment of silence, during which the guy looks at me as if there were any number of terribly important things that he needs to make me aware of.

"Do you mind if we use our first names?" he asks out of nowhere.

Well, actually, yes, I do mind, I think then and there. Not that I have anything personal against this guy, quite the contrary. As I said, I actually find him likable; he was (and maybe still is) a courteous civil servant, someone who knew how to treat people and all that. It's just that agreeing to enter into confidential terms with someone who, in all likelihood, has more than one screw loose, is like signing a blank check for pains in the neck and ass. But how can you say no to someone who asks you that question? I've certainly never figured out how to do it.

"No, not at all."

"Well, then," he holds out his hand. "The name is Giustino. Giustino Talento."

"Vincenzo," I reply.

"Vincenzo what?

"Oh, of course. Sorry: Malinconico."

"Sorry to detain you."

"No problem."
And he leaves.

I step out into the street and start walking along the sidewalk, dragging along behind me, like a heavy wheeled suitcase,
that sense of emptiness—no deposit, no return—that oozes
out of my refusal to take on Mimmo 'o Burzone's defense. I puff
in stupid exasperation, I glare miserably at the buildings and
the parked cars, I let myself slip into a series of baseless but savage critiques of life and the inevitable sorrows it produces. I
think of Nives, of how right she was, all things considered, to
dump me. I drench her in a new and unprecedentedly generous golden light, attributing a series of unfamiliar qualities to
her that I only seem able to glimpse now, knowing perfectly
well that this evening, at the very latest tomorrow morning, I'll
retract them all.
        Truth be told, the reason I'm forced to resort to these
lifeboats of complaint is that I'm struggling to ward off the
intolerable feeling that has been washing over me ever since I
turned down the Burzone case. As if I'd acted out the standard
skit of virility—the one, just to be clear, that has you putting up
little or no resistance to the come-ons of a girl that you sort of
like but not really, and you let her venture further and further
out into the open until she reaches the point of no return and
then, just as she's making an outright offer of sex, you find
some despicable excuse and tell you really have to go now.
        And so I sob into my sleeve for three whole sidewalks until
a spectacular showgirl type, eighteen, maybe twenty, blonde,
super-deodorized, with a Nokia bolted to her ear, bare midriff,
and tattered jeans roomy enough to invite a girlfriend to step
into them alongside her, overtakes me, leaving in her wake and
in my ear a grim and categorical: "Well, you just figure out how
to move it back off your schedule: you said we were going and
we're going!" doubtless addressing some Nubian on a two-year

waiting list who's humbly attempting to explain why he won't be able to squire her to wherever it is he promised to take her.

I watch her walk, since I'm in the ideal position to do so. She has a deliberately insolent gait, eloquent of the kind of bitchy insolence that is accustomed to having its way.

Viewed from my vantage point, she's reminiscent of nothing so much as a very expensive motorcycle, so exquisite is the marriage of straight lines and curves at play here. I'd certainly be willing to lay money that the front view is even better. Her skin has a bronzed shade of tan that I don't believe I've ever seen before in my life. She looks . . . orange, this girl.

Taking advantage of the setting provided by the hem of the cobalt blue panties that peep out over the low waistline of her jeans, a slice of right asscheek offers itself to my eyes—through no fault of my own, now the eyes of a dirty old man. As ashamed of myself as I might be, I'm hypnotized by the detail. The most stupefying aspect of the whole matter is this: the body that's swaying before my eyes, rather than pleasing me, rather than appealing to my pornographic imagination, *interests* me. It really does: I feel a yearning to understand, to know more about it. It's as if a sudden spotlight on current events has suddenly illuminated the landscape before me, unasked, informing me: look at what's happened while you were getting old. Get a glimpse of what something beautiful looks like *now, today*, and not the way you remember it. Take a look at how you always overestimated the standard of beauty that applied to your generation. How you always thought that, once your own time went by, *time itself* would have passed by. At the way you've always clutched at your pathetic little culture of the absolute, the beautiful, once and for all. Look at how little you knew. At how you lived with your head turned to look behind you, doing your best to keep things alive that were long dead. Do you think that's why your wife left you for another man?

There we go, I knew that sooner or later I'd come back

around to Nives. Now even looking at a nice ass becomes my cross to bear.

The playmate of the month, while I flagellate myself, goes marching on down the sidewalk, berating the unfortunate on the other end of the line who, to all intents and appearances, can't get a single word in edgewise, until she finally snaps the phone shut right in his face. Then she stops, indignantly, and waits.

I slow to a halt.

The cell phone rings immediately.

Without even bothering to see who's calling, she slips it into the rear pocket of her jeans and resumes her stride.

I follow after her, with no idea of why I'm doing it.

The playmate of this and any month struts briskly along while, like a broken record, the cell phone in her pocket flashes and repeats its intrusive little melody (a horrendous rendition of *Carmen*), proclaiming near and far the current state of banishment of the unfortunate Nubian who is desperately trying to reestablish contact.

Annoyed at the persistent ringtone emanating from the pocket of the inert beauty, the passers-by walking toward us glare at her resentfully; instead of ignoring them, she furiously returns their glares, fully entitled to let her goddamned cell phone ring as loud and as long as she chooses.

It reminds me of a story by Andrea Pazienza in which his comic book protagonist Zanardi is paged repeatedly over a megaphone at a campground. Even though Zanardi's heard the announcement, he doesn't budge from his tent. Whereupon a guy with a prominent nose walking by stops, perplexed, and goes: "?" After a moment's hesitation he peeks into an opening in the tent and says: "Say, aren't you Zanardi?"; and he says: "Yeah"; and he says: "They just called your name a minute ago"; and Zanardi says: "Oh, okay." Then when beak-nose moves off, you see Zanardi lighting a cigarette and humming to himself, "Why can't people mind their own fucking business?"

I'm also reminded of a woman who sat across from me on a Eurostar into Rome who was just lounging in her seat, eyes closed, with an MP3 player turned all the way up so you could hear it perfectly, even though she had earbuds on and . . . well, okay, let's go back to the tremendous babe.

When she just can't stand to listen to all those bleating requests for forgiveness, she denies the call and turns into an entrance of the subway line.

I follow her in.

On the stairs going down, I have the impression she might have shot me a glance.

She walks down to the tracks, without a ticket. My opinion is that a babe of her magnitude just doesn't bother to buy subway tickets on general principle, so that detail doesn't surprise me in the least. I, on the other hand, have been living for many years in the fear that I might from one moment to the next find myself obliged to take some form of public transportation without having time to buy a ticket (or else not being able to find a ticket vendor open, or not having the proper change, or all three things at once), and terrified at the prospect, I always have at least one ticket in my wallet, so I pull it out and punch it. Then I hurry down the steps to the tracks, afraid that the tremendous babe might take advantage of her head start and lose me in the subterranean network beneath the city.

I get to the platform and look around, but it's not difficult to find her; in fact the search is made ridiculously easy by the guilty embarrassment that nearly all the men on the platform share, having immediately zoomed in on this particular specimen and then clustered around her, nonchalantly acting as if nothing in particular were going on.

At that point I join the crowd and act just like the rest of them; in fact, I don't have any clear idea of what I'm doing here. After a short interval I realize (maybe it's the wait, the air of uncomfortable, soul-crushing normality hanging over us) that my irritating rational self-consciousness is starting to row upstream, attempting to undo everything I've done up to now.

Hey, did you get a good look at her? I ask myself.

I sure did, I reply.

Are you positive? I say to myself.

Why don't you just cut it out? I answer.

No, why don't you? I say to myself.

But I'm not doing anything, I reply.

Don't try telling me that, I say to myself.

Anyway, what's going to happen now is she'll get on the train and I'll never see her again, I say brusquely.

Still, the fact remains that you came down here, I say to myself.

It's not the way you think, I reply.

Oh noooo, I say to myself.

Whatever, I act all offended.

You're letting yourself be deceived by appearances, I say to myself.

What do you mean? I ask.

That right there is the beauty of the present day. A Photoshop beauty, I say to myself.

How do you mean, I ask.

Sure, it's a retouched beauty, I argue. Based on the correction of defects and the enhancements of good features.

Um, I answer, rather intrigued.

But just look at it, the beauty of today, I say to myself. They're all the same: idiots with tattoos and gym workouts. There are thousands of them just like her, don't you know that? There isn't an ounce of individuality, of authentic eroticism, of mystery, of genuine difference; they're . . .

Sure sure, of course, I say to myself.

And that's how I conclude the dialectical exchange.

Only now do I realize that I've ventured dangerously close

to the tremendous hottie, and there's a straightforward mechanical reason: in fact, while I was engaged in debate with the opposition, the girl has pulled out a set of earbuds and inserted them in her ears, and she's listening to an old song that I'm beginning to recognize bit by bit. In other words, I'm on the verge of bumping into her just to figure out what song it is.

There it is, I finally caught the whole melody: it's "Alone Again", by Gilbert O'Sullivan.

Incredible. I'm nonplussed, almost moved at the thought that such a young woman might be enjoying a hit single from my own youth (I was just a child at the time). I interpret the odd circumstance as a metaphysical confirmation of the fact that I had tailed her, the purpose of which I had not hitherto suspected. At this point, I have to talk to her.

I brace myself, as the train is pulling down the platform and the people are starting to mass along the yellow safety line.

"It's 'Alone Again', isn't it?" I ask, with a fairly vacant smile. I point to her earbuds, a deeply pathetic gesture, truth be told.

She doesn't glance in my direction even though—I'm positive—she heard me clearly.

"Gilbert O'Sullivan," I try again, pathetically.

She looks at the train snorting to a halt, pulls her cell phone out of her pocket, flips it open, points it right at me, and takes my picture. Then she punches something into the phone and holds the display out just a few inches from my face.

"Now, can you see the number?"

I rock back my head. I can see it perfectly: it's 911.

She looks me straight in the eye.

I look back, nonplussed.

"If I see you on the same subway car as me, I'll hit send. If you even try to get near me again, I'll scream. And if you keep following me, I'll go to to the police station, report you, and give them your picture."

I pinch myself, and at the same time, I think:

"Jesus, listen to the way she enunciates."

A few people are staring.

I stand there, semi-paralyzed, too demoralized to attempt the slightest defense.

The tremendous babe then sidesteps me without a care in the world and boards the train with impressive calm. I hardly need point out that at least five individuals of the male gender offer to let her get on first.

Well, Jesus H. Christ on a crutch, I think to myself.

I head for the stairs and return to the surface, staying close to the walls like a streetwalker. I emerge from that abyss in a state of near-death exhaustion. Is it a coincidence that the worst blows of my life always seem to happen in the subway?

I walk into a café, go to the bar, and order an espresso and a glass of water. I stand there, gazing at the microbes in the air until the coffee is too cold to drink. The barista looks at me without a word, takes the demitasse away, and empties it into the sink. I leave the café and head home, walking down the sidewalks like one of those wanted criminals in an old black-and-white American movie who walk the streets with their head down, hoping to pass unrecognized.

WHAT MALINCONICO WOULD SAY ABOUT
GILBERT O'SULLIVAN, ABOUT HIS SUBMERGED PESSIMISM
AND THE PEDOPHOBIA OF CONTEMPORARY POP MUSIC,
IF ANYONE WERE EVER TO ASK HIM
(A DECDEDLY IMPROBABLE EVENTUALITY)

A lone Again (Naturally)," by the Irish singer-songwriter Gilbert O'Sullivan, was an international hit single at the turn of the seventies. A song that was easy to listen to, with a persuasive charming little melody, one of those songs you feel like listening to over again as soon as the needle comes to the end of the record, even if you couldn't sing along because you didn't know English.

It was so popular in Italy that Fausto Papetti recorded an instrumental version on one of those famous albums with the topless girls on the cover.

My father, who like all the fathers of the seventies specialized in buying only and exclusively shitty music, which he listened to (and forced us to listen to along with him) in the car, obviously had the cassette. I still remember with horror cassette tapes by Fred Bongusto, Stelvio Cipriani, Bruno Martino, and—even though this is more recent—that tremendous pile of shit "A Comme Amour" by Richard Clayderman, infusing with despair the Sunday drives to see the grandparents. Those songs spread through the car, awakening the suspicion in our childish minds that life was actually a fairly grim proposition.

In any case, "Alone Again" was such a pretty song that not even Fausto Papetti was able to drag it down.

Gilbert O'Sullivan, who was actually named Raymond Edward O'Sullivan (he adopted his name as an artist in a tribute to the nineteenth-century librettist and composer duo Gilbert & Sullivan), first debuted in 1971 at the Royal Albert

Hall in London, when virtually no one had heard of him. Other far more famous artists were scheduled to play that evening on the same stage, including The Sweet, Rockpile, and Ashton Gardner.

Well, he went on stage dressed as a sort of latter-day pop version of Buster Keaton, with his cap turned sideways, a pair of shorts, and a puppyish expression. He stole the audience's heart with his genteel, hummable, melodious songs, with a simple well-constructed format, in contrast to the glam rock that reigned uncontested over the music scene of those years.

And it was in fact with "Alone Again" that O'Sullivan won international fame and renown, in 1972.

The distinctive feature of that song is the fact that the words, in sharp contrast to the prettily composed tune, agreeable and easy to listen to, ooze an irremediable sadness and unhappiness. "Alone Again" is the clear-eyed, disarming account of a life marked by loneliness, an essential state that the merry-go-round of life, however many times you might ride it, inevitably brings you back to.

Jilted at the altar on his wedding day, the singer reports events and emotions with shameless sincerity, rejecting the use of metaphor:

In a little while from now,
If I'm not feeling any less sour
I promised myself to treat myself
And visit a nearby tower,
And climbing to the top,
Will throw myself off
In an effort to make it clear to whomever
what it's like when you're shattered
Left standing in the lurch, at a church
Where people're saying,
"My God that's tough, she stood him up!"

No point in us remaining.
May as well go home."
As I did on my own,
Alone again, naturally

The effect that this elementary prose produces in us as we read it is an embarrassing sense of helplessness. If any of our friends were to confide these thoughts in us (and above all, if they told us they had or subscribed to these thoughts), we'd be left speechless. Any attempt to persuade them otherwise, to encourage them to hope, would be be quashed by the commonplace but irrefutable trifecta of subject-verb-object.

For that matter, exactly what would you say to someone who sings lyrics like these to a delightful musical score:

Now looking back over the years,
And whatever else that appears
I remember I cried when my father died
Never wishing to hide the tears
And at sixty-five years old,
My mother, God rest her soul,
Couldn't understand why the only man
She had ever loved had been taken
Leaving her to start with a heart
So badly broken
Despite encouragement from me
No words were ever spoken
And when she passed away
I cried and cried all day
Alone again, naturally

Like many other other artists of his generation, O'Sullivan conceals the pain of life in carefree melody. "Alone Again" is a foot-tapping song. You nod along to the tempo and then shudder in horror at the end of each verse. The music is a booby trap, it's a cunning device that allows him to tell you how life really is. It's so reassuring to listen to, so comfortable to slip on, that the words only reach you later, almost as if you had to make a special effort to listen to them. Like a suitcase with a false bottom that you can lift and look under if you're really interested.

Back then, when there was still some freedom left, even pop music could hatch an occasional conspiracy. The adorable and tuneful young pop artists who wrote ditties to make young girls fall in love and record producers rich were actually just a pack of depressives who had infiltrated the music business with one objective: to infect their fans with a tragic sense of life. They put on a happy face and then calmly proceeded to tell you one chilling story after another when you were alone with them, every time you put them on your record player.

Before vanishing from the scene (artistically speaking, that is, at least here in Italy), Gilbert O'Sullivan reprised the success he'd achieved with "Alone Again" by recording "Clair," another picture-perfect pop song that climbed the international hit parade. The song got stuck in your memory after a first listen. Italian pop singer Johnny Dorelli recorded a very questionable Italian version.

Once again, in "Clair," we find the same dichotomy between lyrics and melody that is such a distinctive feature of the O'Sullivanian compositional style. But "Alone Again" is an undisguised surrender to grief, sorrow, and loneliness, "Clair" is a breath of fresh air in the realm of the greatest and most hopeful of all the emotions that make up the panoply of experience human: love. A love, however, that is openly addressed not to a woman but to a little girl, by the name of Clair.

In this case, the lyrics leave no room for ambiguity:

Clair. The moment I met you, I swear.

I felt as if something, somewhere,
had happened to me, which I couldn't see.
And then, the moment I met you, again.
I knew in my heart that we were friends.
It had to be so, it couldn't be no.
But try as hard as I might do, I don't know why.
You get to me in a way I can't describe.
Words mean so little when you look up and smile.
I don't care what people say, to me you're more than a child.
Oh Clair. Clair . . .

Once again, the composer's sincerity in revealing his feelings takes the form of lyrics that strike us speechless in their sheer elemental simplicity.

Clair, I've told you before "Don't you dare!"
"Get back into bed."
"Can't you see that it's late."
"No, you can't have a drink."
"Oh all right then, but wait just a minute."
While I, in an effort to babysit, catch up on my breath,
what there is left of it.
You can be murder at this hour of the day.
But in the morning the sun will seem a lifetime away.
Oh Clair. Clair . . .

The Italian version of the song (which bears the signature of Daniele Pace, the dean of Italian popular music and a member of the venerable band the Squallor), aside from a few understandable adjustments of the meter, basically adheres to the contents of the original. In fact, Johnny Dorelli sings:

Clair, your mother and I dated once
and you don't know it, but why

are you looking at me that way, with your eyes gazing up,
there's no finer memory for me than that,
and yet since you've come into my life
I don't know whether to think about her or you.
But you have stolen my heart
a thousand times more than that
I'm ashamed to be playing like this
But after all, what do we care what the people say
When you smile at me you're no longer a little girl, Clair.

And there's more:

Clair, now it's too late for you
Let's go to sleep, that's your bed
And I'm not sorry
It's almost dawn by now.
You've stolen my heart and you won't give it back
You can hear my breathing, you've almost taken that away too.
We've had our fun, but tomorrow, in time,
It'll all be over
It's time to get some sleep, Clair.

To read, in the third millennium—and to read *in Italy*, in the third millennium—words of this kind, is something that plunges you deeply and directly into a pool of embarrassment. Something that sends your eyes searching for the gaze of other people. That covers you with a mantle of disquiet, a lurking sense of guilt that you instinctively seek to avoid. It's a safe bet that a song of this kind, broadcast today on a moderately popular radio station or television show, would trigger a population-wide uprising of blistering critiques that, at various levels of hypocrisy, would advocate a collective denunciation of this songwriter's defense of the one crime around which modern society closes ranks and wholeheartedly condemns, in the most absolute terms.

It is obvious that the lyrics, in their impassioned portrayal of childhood, possess all the poetic authenticity required to refute all suspicions and return the accusation to sender.

But it's even more obvious that the simple fact that the song lends itself to potential interpretation as a hymn to the molestation of children would be grounds nowadays for a society-wide disapproval that would sweep it out of the musical marketplace with the irresistible fury of a tsunami, even though it still stands head and shoulders above virtually all of the right-thinking treacle that the contemporary pop music industry foists on its unsuspecting public.

VOLUNTEERS FOR KNOWLEDGE

I'm still asleep when the door buzzer startles me awake. I start to climb up my mattress and my eyes creak open, but of course I can't see a thing because it's dark out and the light is off. I struggle and grope and touch and grab and miss and I keep on until I get oriented, wall, window, Leksvik dresser, Nives getting dressed in front of me, now I remember everything, yes yes, the Slabang alarm clock on the Hemnes night stand, the digital numbers blinking in the dark, the number on the right is missing its central upright but you can still tell what number it is, zero eight colon zero nine, who the hell rings people's doorbells at 8:10 in the morning?

I implore my body to come to my aid and I get to my feet, dragging myself down the hallway like a hunchback. If it's one of those idiotic old geezers who show up before the blood and urine lab opens in the morning and just ring doorbells at random to get in, I swear by the Virgin Mary, I'll give him a stroke this time.

"Who is it?"

"Dad?"

"Alfre'?" I ask. But in the tone of voice of someone who's not sure they have the right name, if you know what I mean. It's schooltime. He should be on his way to school right now.

"Can I come up?" he asks.

I buzz him in.

I give my hair a quick brush with my fingers. I rub my eyes. I yawn.

The first thing I do is open the door to the landing. I leave it on the latch, so when Alf comes up he doesn't have to knock. Then I go into the kitchen and open the wooden shutter, evicting a pigeon who was loitering on the windowsill. I pick up the Bialetti Moka Express, I turn on the TV and switch to the morning news on Canale 5. I don't know why when I turn the TV on in the morning I always turn to the morning news on Canale 5. I hate it with a passion, the morning news on Canale 5. Especially the theme music, that tremendous theme music that seems to have been composed just to remind you of the horrible things that happen out there in the world. In my opinion, the catastrophic theme music of the morning news report on Canale 5 is designed to make you afraid to go outside. That way you can stay home and just watch shows on Canale 5.

So I fill my Bialetti espresso pot, put it on the burner, pull a Stefan out from the kitchen table, turn it facing the television set, and sit down, waiting for Alfredo to come upstairs and the coffee to boil.

I listlessly watch the news roundup, and then I conclude (with a dismissive air that I don't know where I get) that what the hell, nothing happened again today, and finally I hear Alfredo come in, softly close the door behind him, and call me.

"I'm in the kitchen," I call back in a disgusting gummy voice.

I come close to losing it when he walks in to where I'm sitting. A two-tone bruise tattoos half the left side of his face, almost up to his eye. His lower lip is swollen, making him look like an old woman who's had one too many facelifts. He's limping.

I leap to my feet so suddenly that it's a miracle that I don't keel over. The Stefan clatters to the floor behind me, though. My heart shoots off like a billiard ball.

Alfredo waves one hand as if to say, it's nothing, it's nothing; which obviously makes me believe the opposite. I freak out, and even I can't say whether it's out of anger or anxiety.

"What the fucking hell have you done this time?" I ask, without even realizing that I'm shouting.

"Please, Dad," he says, as he pathetically licks his swollen lip, the sight of which sends a wave of pain through me as if I'd just been stabbed.

He pulls out a Stefan and sits down in slow motion.

"Let me get a look at you," I say, leaning over him.

"Everything's okay, I'll be over it in no time."

"*Everything's okay?*" I raise my voice again. "*Everything's okay?* What are you saying, what kind of language are you using, this comes straight out of some American movie!"

They always ask the same idiotic question, in American movies. If somebody hits the edge of a table with their knee, it's not like the other person in the scene asks: "Did you hurt yourself?"; no, they say: "Is everything okay?" as if hitting a table with their knee might shatter much more than just their left kneecap. That's just the way Americans are; apparently they're always convinced something much bigger is going on than meets the eye.

"But just look at what somebody did to you. You need to tell me who it was."

"Dad, stop shouting, please. My head hurts."

"Ah, you see, something hurts. That means everything's not okay!"

He dismisses my stupid retort with a labored sigh, as if to say that this is no time for nitpicking about schematic details. Which, I instantly realize, is true. Suddenly aware of what a shit I am, I impetuously throw my arms around him.

"Sorry, Alfre', I'm sorry."

Suddenly I'm on the verge of bursting into tears.

"Ouch, Dad!" he cries.

I pull back.

"Damn, sorry."

"It's nothing, it's nothing," Alf says, making an effort to

smile. And he reaches up to touch his face, as if I'd knocked it out of alignment or something.

"Do you have some ice?" he asks.

"Yes." I bolt for the fridge.

The Bialetti burbles away. I pull an ice tray out of the freezer, I look for a clean dish towel. Alfredo turns off the burner under the Bialetti. I find the dish towel, I pry the ice out of the tray with my fingers, ice cube by ice cube. Alfredo pours the coffee. I tell him not to worry about it, because I don't want to interrupt what I'm doing for a coffee break, but he keeps on doing what he's doing. I pile the ice cubes in the middle of the dish towel, I make a little ice bag, and I hand it to Alf. With a series of grimaces, he starts to apply the ice bag to the injured part of his face.

I sit down next to him.

"How's your lip?"

He signals "so-so" with one hand.

"Are you bleeding?"

He looks at me.

"In your mouth," I say.

He replies by waving his index finger back and forth like a metronome.

"They didn't knock out a tooth, did they?"

"No, no."

"What about your head? Did you get hit in the head?"

"No, no."

I stand up. At this point, I drink my coffee.

"Who was it this time?"

He shrugs.

"Can't you tell me anything?"

"On the subway. There were three of them. But two of them didn't do anything. In fact, they pulled him off me."

I sigh, dispirited.

"Listen, let me take you to the hospital."

"No, come on, it's not worth the hassle. Then you have to file a police report and everything. It would just be a waste of time, I couldn't even identify them."

I feel hollow. For an instant, just a single fleeting instant, I consider the possibility of exercising *patria potestas* in its most ancient and antiquated form.

Then I resign myself to the facts, and finish my coffee.

It's been a while (oh, let's say six months or so) since Alfredo developed this new fixation with juvenile delinquency. The phenomenon fascinates him, it intrigues him the way a person could be intrigued by heart failure, antipersonnel mines, or white sharks. In the sense that he wants to learn more about it, study it, find out how it functions. So he wanders the city in search of youngsters his age who violate the law, and when he finds them he approaches them, strikes up a conversation and asks them how they spend their days, what they think about, what they hope to achieve, and so on. If he could, I think he'd infiltrate their ranks.

The surprising thing is that, even though he's skinny and small and clearly harmless, he isn't afraid of them in the least. If he crosses paths with four or five hooligans in the street while they molest a young girl, for instance, or just as they're about to snatch a purse, steal a moped, or hold up a married couple, it's a sure thing that he'll change course and follow them until he finds an opportunity to approach them and strike up a conversation with them.

Sometimes it works out for him. And he manages to record documentary material of a certain value. Some time ago, for instance, he let me hear a cassette he'd made (he goes everywhere with his trusty tape recorder in his pocket, like a journalist). He managed to approach the leader of a group of pedestrian-slapppers (the thugs who slap people in the street, but not for money, in fact for no discernable reason at all) and asked him to describe what they did on an average Saturday night.

Aside from the question of how much of what they said was true (because it was blindingly obvious that a lot of it was completely made up), what really made your jaw drop was the complete indifference that rang in their voices, like an accent running through their horrifyingly simple thoughts. Me—this guy—that guy—money—life—death—pussy—balls—freedom—prison. Teenagers who were as hardened as old men.

In this kind of situation, you have to admit it, Alfredo behaves like a complete professional. He listens to the most bloodcurdling details without a hint of surprise. As if he were expecting it, right? Then he asks questions that leave the subjects of his interviews absolutely speechless. Truly brilliant questions, like: "But have you managed to put aside a little bit of money?" or else: "Do you think the girls are having a good time while you rape them?"

In other words, when it goes right, he puts together some documentary audio that you have to respect. Stuff for which the most highly credentialed experts in the sector really ought to go out and buy him cigarettes, as far as I'm concerned.

There are other times, though, when it doesn't go right at all, and that's when they beat him with varying levels of determination, depending on whether they have something to do afterward.

But I have to say that, given how persistent and reckless Alfredo is, he doesn't get beat up that often, truth be told. In six months he's been beaten up three times, including last night, or actually two-and-a-half times, because the time before this one, a police squad car happened to drive by and the thugs cut and ran almost before they got started.

According to Alf, this unusual batting record is due to the fact that when you get up close, nothing is ever as bad as people say it is. Which is a good answer, I know. But I think it's his lack of fear that works as his bodyguard. If you're not afraid of something, then that something learns to avoid you, because it understands that it can only do you so much harm, and with all the harmable people there are around, there's no point in wasting time on someone who's not likely to appreciate it.

So in our family we're trying to come to terms with something that might be described as an anthropological interest— I wonder if you can guess who came up with that terminology. It all started the day that Nives (that's who came up with the terminology) took Alfredo with her to a conference on juvenile deviance, applying the principle that it does kids good every so often to participate in events of this sort, because "even if they don't think they've understood anything, something still sticks in their mind" (which is just a wheelbarrel to transport your balls back home, if you ask me).

In any case, at this conference—after the opening statements from the various prominent officials who express their gratitude, offer their wishes for a productive session, and then are obliged to leave the premises by a variety of prior commitments—a famous sociologist delivered his report, and Alfredo was hypnotized by the sociologist's opinions about the importance of comprehending the malaise of adolescents—that is, comprehending it *for real*, in the etymological sense of the term, by getting your hands dirty and putting yourself on the line as a volunteer for knowledge. He used this exact expression: "volunteers for knowledge." I wasn't there but I'll bet you anything you care to name that those were his exact words because for a good solid month after that fucking conference, Alf made sure he stitched "volunteers for knowledge" practically into every sentence that passed his lips. In that particular period, I'm not exaggerating, talking, for Alf, had become nothing more than a pretext for saying "volunteers for knowledge."

In my opinion, leaving aside the famous sociologist's entire presentation, it was this isolated phrase that tipped him over the edge into complete idiocy. Because, if you really pay attention, people tip over the edge into complete idiocy over the tiniest things, and not because they fall victim of who knows what refined perfidy.

At the same time, even though I have pretty clear opinions on the subject, I also realize that when you're dealing with a son in the throes of complete degeneration into idiocy, you can't exactly start off with such a drastic line of argumentation.

There's one thing I know for sure: that if that day Nives, instead of taking Alf along with her to the double-damned conference on juvenile deviance, if she'd sent him out to play soccer, or even left him all afternoon glued to his super-miserable Playstation, right now he wouldn't be sitting in my kitchen holding a bag of ice to the side of his head.

In any case, as I think is already pretty obvious, Alfredo has already decided, though he's only sixteen, that he wants to be a journalist.

From a certain point of view, I'm glad that he already has such clear plans for his future. From a certain point of view. Because from another point of view—that is, the one from which I'm looking at a bruise that covers half of his face—I'd have to rule out all other points of view.

What are you going to say to a teenager with a fixation of this kind? "Don't go around getting your ass kicked, or I'll kick your ass?"

How do I deal with this problem? Poorly, very poorly. With a sense of guilt that's aggravated by the fact that, because of my marital and family situation, I'm naturally inclined to consider my separation as the source of all our suffering. And the worst part is that it strikes me that I'm the only one who feels any guilt. Because Nives, in contrast, treats the whole matter with a professional detachment that destabilizes me. She acts like a psychologist with our son, in other words.

She says that Alfredo feels an authentic cultural interest, all the more noteworthy because it came to him spontaneously.

She says that if we make an effort to accept this interest of his instead of opposing it, we have some hope that he might become indifferent (to that interest).

She says a few other things, but I can't remember them right now.

"Just think," she explained to me the last time, "Alfredo is doing something strange, unique, and risky, something none of his friends would do. That makes it irreplaceable for him. You and I have nothing as exciting to offer him as an alternative."

She says—I just remembered—that, despite the risks to which it exposes him, *this need our son feels to use his body to understand the world makes him a body endowed with an experimental intelligence* (those are Nives's italics).

Which, all things considered, might even be true. It's just that whenever Nives issues these fine diagnoses, first of all, it twists my balls into a knot because it always seems that she's just issuing them for herself and not for anyone else, I don't know if I convey the idea; and second, if you ask me, when you're talking about your own children, anybody who can lay such a clear-cut, impeccable line of reasoning is nothing but an idiot. You can't be clear-cut and impeccable with your children. Because it's a well known fact that children were created precisely to contradict any and all principles. And if you use your own son as an underpinning for a principle, it really does mean that you haven't understood a single god-damned thing.

I've always turned up my nose—truth be told—at the idea of principles as a basis for action, even leaving aside my role as a parent. I remember perfectly well the moment that it first happened. I must have been ten years old or so. One evening my father's brother, a self-centered individual with a completely unjustified but extremely elevated opinion of himself—and no one in the family seems to know where he got such an opinion—told my mother that he didn't want his son (my cousin) eating pre-packaged ice cream treats. At that point I broke in to ask him why. And he replied: "On principle." Just like that, flatly. Whereupon I asked just what principle that might be. And he said again: "On principle." As if he'd said: "God exists." Exactly, precisely the same. Whereupon I told him that maybe he hadn't understood the question. And he told me that I had absolutely no right to dare to insinuate that he was the kind of person who misunderstood questions.

If at the age of ten I had understood the meaning of the verb "to insinuate," I would probably have replied to him that no, I had by no means insinuated that he had failed to understand the question, I had stated it, clearly, outright.

That very evening I decided that a principle, inasmuch as it is a conceptual motive upon which a doctrine or a science or even simply a reasoning is based (definition taken from the 1979 Devoto-Oli dictionary, Euroclub, Milan, pg. 884), was simply a cheap rhetorical contrivance employed by people who have no other arguments to employ. In fact, I still think so, if for no other reason than that the idea of a principle was so appealing to my idiot uncle.

So that's the way it is, as far as Alf is concerned.

"I'm guessing you don't want to go to school today, right?" I ask Alfredo.

He pulls the ice pack off his face, he licks his swollen lip.

A stab of pain right here, in the arm, like a myocardial infarction under way, when your son licks his swollen lip.

"I don't feel up to it, Dad."

I can already see them, his classmates, sort of pitying him and sort of mocking him. Truth be told, I would have gone to school if I were in his shoes, because in cases like this the girls take turns comforting you and you get rides from people who wouldn't normally even take you under consideration.

Just look at the things that go through my head.

"You know you don't have to talk me into it. I wouldn't think for a second of sending you to school."

He smiles, reassured.

"Why didn't you go home?"

Meaning Nives's home, which used to be my home too, until just a short while ago.

Yes, I know, it's a bastard question, it's sort of like asking: "Who do you love more, Mommy or Daddy?" But if I don't take advantage of these situations, just bear with me.

"I just didn't," he says.

Head up, shoulders straight, like a gentleman.

But I'm disgustingly pleased at the idea that he chose to come to my house.

"Listen, let me ask you something, but I want you to tell me the truth. Are you sure you haven't banged your head or anything like that? Don't give me the runaround, because if you have we need to get you a CT scan."

"No, no, it was just a couple of punches, not even straight on, they just grazed me, I swear."

"Okay. Listen, I have to go into the courthouse, I've got a case. You stay here and wait for me. Let me give Totonno a call though and ask him to drop by and take a look at you, okay?"

Totonno, that is Antonio Rossi, is our public health general practitioner. He's a lifelong friend of mine. One of those people who, when you're on the verge of a breakdown, you don't even have to tell him what's wrong and he's already fixing you up.

"Okay."

I touch his forehead. It's cool.

So I go and get ready for work. Alf gets comfortable on the Klippan sofa and turns the other TV on, with the sound down very low. He puts his feet on a stool that I keep there for the purpose. He wedges a cushion behind his head and hugs another to his belly (classic pose of self-consolation). I call Totonno, who assures me he'll swing by before lunch. Before I leave I ask Alf if he needs anything. He doesn't need anything. So I tell him that I'm leaving and later that day we'll have lunch together. Whereupon he asks me if I can call Nives to let her know that he won't be coming home but will be staying at my house. I say okay and head downstairs.

On the street, the thought of Alfredo, safe and sound, waiting for me at home, serves as a kind of morphine. All things considered, it's not bad to be able to keep the people you love in a cage, if you understand what I'm trying to say here.

You Could Feel It in the Air
(That I Was Going to Become Famous)

I stop outside the main entrance of the courthouse to call Alagia, since inside my cell phone doesn't hit on all four cylinders.

"Vincè. What's up."

I snort through my nose in irritation. You work yourself blind to teach your kids manners, then one day they invent caller ID and in just a few weeks they wipe out the efforts of a lifetime.

"Good morning to you, eh. Where are you, at the university?"

You can hear noises in the background that sounds vaguely like a party.

"Eh."

"Listen, I need to talk to you, is there some way I can see you today?"

"When, today?"

"No, at midnight the day after tomorrow. I told you I need to talk to you—bear with me."

"Is it really that urgent?"

"Sweet Jesus, Ala', what do I have to do to have a conversation with you in person, file a request in triplicate?"

These are the small things that remind you of your status as a separated father. They say that happiness consists of small things. That goes double for unhappiness.

"But what's happened, something with Mamma?"

Not yet, I think to myself.

"I dunno. Alfredo."

There's a brief pause. I can clearly hear the voices of a group of kids talking, not far from Alagia. First one says: "Whatshisname, you know, the professor who looks like a flea market version of Umberto Eco, has invited the students in his course to a reading of his book of poetry at the Feltrinelli book store." Another one says: "Are you going?"; and the first one replies: "Of course, I'm going to have take a final exam with that miserable hobo"; "Ah, okay," cuts in a girl's voice, then she adds: "Ask him to sign the book, with a dedication, that way he'll remember your name."

"Okay, listen," says Alagia, "I have three classes today, I'll be here all day long. Why don't you catch up with me at the cafeteria and we can eat lunch together?"

At the cafeteria? I'd already planned on a nice lunch with Alfredo. I wanted to buy country bread, prosciutto, Vannulo mozzarella nuggets, all that stuff he loves.

"At the cafeteria? At the cafeteria. Okay. Fine. I'll come meet you at the cafeteria. I can do that. All right. I'll see you there. At the cafeteria."

A reflective pause.

"Oh, Vincè."

"Eh," I reply.

"Are you okay?"

"Am I okay? Of course I am, why?"

"What do I know, it's just that you said like five times: 'At the cafeteria, yes, at the cafeteria.'"

"No, it's just that I was thinking about how to . . . oh, Christ, but what a pain in the ass you are, Ala'."

She laughs, idiot that she is.

"Okay, I'll expect you about two o'clock," she says, clearly making a tremendous effort to finish the sentence.

"Eh. And you just go on laughing," I say. But I'm laughing too, truth be told.

"At . . . o'clock . . . pffst . . . "

"Hold the phone closer," I say. But the only result is that she laughs again.

So we go on like that, until one of the two of us, and by now I can't even remember whether it was her or me, finally hangs up first.

I immediately call home to tell Alfredo that I won't be back for lunch. I ask him what he's doing, how he feels, how his bruise, his lip, his leg are coming along. I fire a volley of questions at him.

He snickers and replies: "Like Wolverine." Which is the name of one of the X-Men, the one with the bone-claw sabers that project from his knuckles, who also has the power to heal his own wounds (Alf was only referring to the power of self-healing his wounds). In practical terms, if he's shot with a bazooka, or stabbed with a red-hot spear, or if he bangs his head against the wall at 225 mph, you can see the injury retracting all by itself, like an octopus retreating into its underwater cavern. One minute it's there, the next minute it's gone. It's called "healing factor," I think.

So with my tail between my legs I start explaining to Alfredo that I'd forgotten about a prior engagement, and he interrupts me to say that I don't need to worry about it, I certainly hadn't known that he'd show up this morning.

I tell him that for lunch he can make himself one of the Healthy Choices that are in the fridge, and he says okay, I'll be healthy if I have the choice, and I don't know what to say for a second, and then I laugh politely and say, okay, see you later, and he says okay.

And at last I go to work.

Today in the courthouse there's pure bedlam. A number of different divisions are in session at the same time, so there are hearings under way everywhere, with plaintiffs, defendants, prosecuting magistrates, defense attorneys, witnesses, expert witnesses, defendants' relatives, and all the rest, producing that typical temporary surge of overcrowding that plunges the Hall of Justice into an evocative frenzy of self-importance—an automatic effect of concentrating large numbers of human beings in any given place.

When you happen to walk into a building crowded with people, after a while you just naturally start to walk as if you were in line waiting to audition for a part. That's perfectly understandable, because it's very rare for someone to feel relaxed in a crowd. You can tell me you don't give a damn about what other people think of you until you're blue in the face, but I know better: you care. Bodies know when they're being observed. That's just one of their basic traits. And when a body senses that it's being observed, it generally tends to become exceptionally clumsy. That's why when you walk into someplace that's crowded, even a place where there are normally lots of people, like a courthouse for instance, or a lecture hall in a university, for instance, everybody seems to be remarkably clumsy. That diffuse sense of clumsiness washes over you, and before you know it, you feel clumsy yourself. As if you were about to do something glaringly idiotic any second now.

In that case, you have two options: either you become insignificant and you try to blend into the herd—and when that happens a friend you've known since you went to elementary school together might look you in the face and fail to recognize you—or else you study the behavior of the others around you, you pick the ones who strike you as the most successful, and you imitate them.

Most people try to blend into the background. Those who don't are mostly lawyers. And lawyers, in their efforts to stand out from the crowd, necessarily wind up striking fairly oafish poses.

If you watch them closely—lawyers in a crowded courthouse—you have a hard time believing that they're deadly serious about their behavior. They shuttle from one hallway to another, from one courtroom to the next, or more likely from the courtrooms to the bar, weaving in and out, dribbling around people in a way that seems intentional, as if they're trying to show them they're taking up vital space. They make a display of their well-established sense of direction and skill at maneuvering through the hallways and hearing rooms to make it clear that they (the lawyers) are at home in the building, while the others (consumers of the service dispensed by the justice system) are merely guests.

When they run into other lawyers they jovially call out to them, using their professional title and surname in jest, and exchanging absolutely meaningless phrases at the top of their lungs, for one reason and one reason only: to make themselves heard. What on earth are they thinking, that afterwards the people they run into comment in an undertone to their colleagues: "Oh, did you notice, that lawyer we just ran into, how nicely he yells?"

Sure, I know, not all lawyers are like that, thanks for the information. But I'm talking about the lawyers who *are* like that, obviously.

I take the main hallway and slide into the flow of traffic. After a short distance I glimpse an overweight lawyer who strikes me as familiar, and at the exact same moment he glances at me as if he just had the same impression. And so we each look at the other the few extra seconds that now oblige us to the minimum professional courtesy: the requisite exchange of greetings.

But now it dawns on me that the other lawyer is Picciafuoco, my horrendous colleague. I might have seen him three or four times in my entire, shall we say, *career*, and yet I recognize him.

"Picciafuoco, right?" I call, pointing to him from within hailing distance.

144 · DIEGO DE SILVA

"Yes," he says.

But already from the tone of voice in which he said it, it's obvious that he has no desire whatsoever to stop and talk.

As if I'm dying to.

I extend my hand and remind him of my name. He nods, as if to say there was no need to remind him.

"The place is packed today, eh?" I point out.

"Yes, yes it is," he replies.

By which point our conversational resources are completely exhausted.

I can't stand people who give monosyllabic answers and then refuse to volunteer another single stinking word, you know the kind, and after a while there's a pool of shitty embarrassing silence stagnating between the two of you, and you just feel like telling them: "Aw, go fuck yourself."

People like that, I hate them, for real.

Which by the way, I am deeply tempted to remind him, this shameless individual who's suddenly acting all terse and telegraphic, when he called me on the phone yesterday he had quite a different attitude, unless I'm much mistaken.

In the end, to extract myself from that miserable plight, I decide to bring up our former shared interest—that is, Mimmo 'o Burzone—in part so I can give him the news that I turned down the appointment, which I imagine ought to make him happy.

"Oh, say, colleague," I lead off, as if it had just popped into my mind, "I meant to tell you that Fantasia's wife dropped by my office, just a little while after you called me."

"Ah," he says.

An "ah" that sounded a lot like "And who the fuck cares?" A reaction that honestly baffles me.

"And so," I resume, "it turns out that I had to turn down the appointment. Too much going on, I really can't keep up with it all. I was sorry, though, I have to tell you."

He takes in the news and begins to nod, looking around repeatedly with a certain arrogance, as if—I don't know—as if the people around him owed him money or whatever.

"So then you have to wonder who they're going to get now," he says, after a short pause.

"Who they're going to get?" I ask. But I already understand.

At that point my shameless colleague snorts in generic resentment, slaps me philosophically on the shoulder, and vanishes into the crowd.

I stand there, staring distractedly into the middle distance, if there is any such a thing as the middle distance in a hallway packed with people.

They retracted his fiduciary appointment.

Obviously.

But why?

They must have someone else, of course. Burzone's not going to deprive himself of all legal representation at a time like this.

Do you remember what the wife said to me? "Don't you worry about him"—referring to Picciafuoco—"the same way we appointed him we can fire him."

Sure, but she meant that they could fire him so they could hire me.

But I turned them down, and now what?

Exactly.

And now nothing.

Now they must have hired somebody new.

Eh.

Necessarily.

With all the criminal lawyers looking for work.

Then why do I have this horrible cloying sensation?

Who knows.

The civil court division is on the top floor. And since the

vast majority of lawyers are civil lawyers, there are white-sale lines for the elevators. So I brace myself psychologically for taking the stairs, and I take the stairs.

I'm holding up pretty well when, on the last flight of stairs, I glimpse the unmistakable calves of Alessandra Persiano, who is leaning against the railing and waiting for me, with a semiserious scolding expression on her face. All around her is a gymkhana of wolves and dirty old men jostling to be the first to say hello to her.

Well aware that she is the uncontested star of the hall of justice, AP dismisses the pathetic suitors, liquidating each of them with a glance and a smirk (just then, she reminds me of the scene with Totò tossing the suitcases that Mario Castellani hands him out the window of the sleeping compartment on the train).

I look at her again and I stiffen, in part because it's normal to stiffen in the presence of Alessandra Persiano, and in part because I'm suddenly swept by a sense of guilt that I can't place right then and there, baffled as to the reason, though the fact that A.P. is waiting for me is makes it clear that she has something she wants to scold me about.

Standing there, I catch myself thinking that if through the intervention of a merciful god I should one day happen to get A.P. into bed, after a bout of lovemaking as grueling as it would be unforgettable, I would reach out for the pack of cigarettes on the side table and, suddenly inspired, say to her: "You know, that morning, when I saw you waiting for me on the stairs, no matter how packed the courthouse might have been, suddenly the place was empty: there was no one there but you and me."

And then I'd light the cigarette.

I file the pitiful scene away and laboriously climb the last few steps separating me from her.

Jesus, she really is one hell of a woman, Alessandra Persiano. Like any true work of art, she has one unmistakable trait: every time you see her it's like the first time.

I walk toward her, crossing unharmed through the magnetic field of all my fellow lawyers who are dying inside as they watch me in disbelief, wondering what I could possibly have that they don't (I'm asking myself the same thing, as it happens). In this particular moment, I am without a doubt the most roundly despised lawyer in the hall of justice (or at least on this flight of stairs in the courthouse). I wonder if she realizes that she is making me famous.

"Ciao, Ale," I say. My tone of voice is just pathetic.

She stares at me in a way that forces my guardian angel to intervene, taking up a position just behind my shoulder and whispering in my ear: "If you fail to fuck this one, I'm never speaking to you again as long as you live."

"Come here," she says.

I go there. That is to say, one step below the one she's standing on. Guys, where on earth does she buy her perfume?

She lifts her left hand to chest level, braces the fingernail of her index finger behind the pad of her thumb, forming a horizontal "Okay" (she has magnificent hands), takes careful aim (sort of like when you pick your nose and then flick the snot) and mischievously smacks her nail against the knot of my tie. An incredibly sexy gesture, truth be told.

"That wasn't very nice of you," she says.

I look at her, clueless. I think my forehead might be a little sweaty.

"Listen," I say to her, catching my breath, "I have no idea what you're talking about, but whatever it is, I'm ready to get down on my hands and knees to beg your forgiveness."

She holds her breath for a second, reemerges, and laughs right in my face.

I swear to her that I wasn't kidding.

She looks me straight in the eye, to judge my degree of sincerity, I have to guess.

"You really don't know?"

"I swear I don't."

She sighs. She decides to trust me.

"Okay, then do I really have to explain to you that it's not very nice of you not to call me, after I gave you my cell phone number?"

You remember the jaw of the Tyrannosaurus rex after King Kong rips it half off with one hand? Well, that's the way my jaw is dangling right now.

"Ah. The cell phone . . . sure. Of course." Brief pause to collect my thoughts. "No, listen, do you seriously think that I forgot? Do you think that I'm so stupid that I don't want to call you?"

"You're probably that stupid," whispers my guardian angel, from just over my shoulder.

"Well, but you didn't call," she says.

Only then do I realize that the episode of Alessandra's cell phone, the opportunity that she'd implicitly offered me when she gave me her number, the sheer wanton waste that is staring me in the face. In other words, I hadn't forgotten it at all. It's just that I'd set it aside for later. Like when you put a check in your wallet instead of cashing it. Have you ever walked around for days with a check in your wallet instead of going to the bank and cashing it or depositing it? I mean, you practically have the money in your pocket, you could get your hands on it, but you don't. You just wait a little longer.

When you leave a check in your wallet, or when you decide to forego calling Alessandra Persiano, you're putting on airs. You're behaving like those wealthy landowners who have a villa in Sardinia and never bother to go.

The problem, to come back to the issue at hand, is that with A.P. I had been putting on worldly airs while at the same time pretending I didn't know that there was a statue of limitations ticking on my opportunity. Because when God Almighty bestows a blessing of this sort upon you, he always assigns a peremptory time limit, and when it expires, he rightly runs down his list of names and calls up the next candidate. Because our forefathers were expressing an age-old wisdom when they said: "Get moving, because if you don't take her to bed, someone else will."

"I was going to," I answer. "I swear."

She lowers her head, still vaguely dissatisfied. How can you blame her, after all?

"Is it too late?" I ask, shamelessly.

Just then Maria Laura Francavilla, a fellow civil lawyer, catches up with us, hurrying down the steps. She nods hello to me (and I nod hello back), and lays a hand on A.P.'s shoulder.

"Sorry, Ale, but the witnesses are waiting, are you ready to come?"

"I'll catch up with you, you go ahead," she replies.

Maria Laura turns on her heel and climbs the stairs alone, evidently annoyed.

"I don't know if it's too late," says Alessandra, returning to the topic of us. "Why don't you try and find out?"

Excellent answer.

She turns to go.

I grab her arm.

She turns around.

What just happened to her? All of a sudden she looks so unhappy, as if I'd hurt her somehow, without realizing it. Instinctively, I loosen my grip.

She won't look me in the face. As if she's on the verge of tears.

"Listen," I tell her, "I'm not having an easy time of it right now."

I realize that I'm spouting bullshit, so I try to make up for it.

"No, I'm not having that hard of a time, it's just that I don't want to see you leave like that."

She looks up. I'm certain, absolutely dead certain, that I could kiss her right now, if I tried.

"Listen, Vincenzo, it strikes me that we're taking things a little too far. We're in the courthouse, you do realize that? Omigod, listen to what I'm saying . . . "

Oh how I love the second act of any courtship. Who is the playwright who came up with such a perfect script? At times like these, we don't have anything to do with what happens, really. We're just actors. The script is all written, we mouth line after line, better than if we'd memorized them.

"Listen, let's get together tonight, you feel like it? My place, your place, anywhere you name," I suggest. Just like that. Without preliminaries.

"What?" she asks, somewhere between scandalized and amused.

"Please. If I think that I have to call you, you'll see, I won't be able to do it. I can't even tell you why. I have a million things pending that I can't seem to get done, but I don't want to risk the run of . . . Oh shit."

I freeze.

Alessandra is about to laugh but she stops herself.

It had been a while since I last got tangled up. And to think that the first time it happened she had been there. The same morning she gave me her cell phone number, in fact.

I can't say another word, maybe because I'm afraid it'll happen again, or else because I don't have anything more to say.

So Ale covers her nose, holds her breath again, and then bursts out into a laugh that's pure tenderness.

I imitate her.

And it lasts for a while.

And in that way we both manage to get rid of our awkwardness.

EGG

My professional obligations today have occupied roughly 1 m. 40 s., the time necessary to walk halfway down the hallway to the civil division to the courtroom, where I find tacked to the door a nice white A4-format sheet of paper on which is written that the hearing has been officially postponed because the judge is indisposed. In other words, it's barely 10:15, and I no longer have a fucking thing to do. Which presents me with the problem of how to kill time until noon/1 P.M., so that I can return home at a presentable time of day to a son who is understandably convinced that his father is a lawyer, a profession that makes it highly unlikely he'd have leisure time any given morning. And so I call a brief meeting with myself, at the end of which we agree to drop by my law office, which is certainly not close by.

The minute I leave the courthouse, I see the chairman of the bar association, just outside the main exit, being held captive by a couple of time-wasters in jacket and tie who are telling him an anecdote that they seem to consider highly amusing. Every now and then, the more histrionic of the two smacks the chairman on the forearm to accompany the latest punchline of the story. The chairman smiles with each smack, but I can see all the way from here that he's wishing the guy misery and pain.

I look at him as if to say: "Life is hard when you're chairman." He tells me to go fuck myself with a gesture that we both recognize, after which he acts as if he just remembered something very fresh and recent and he launches a lascivious wink in my direction. I get the reference immediately and I put on my *Ihavenoideawhatyou'retalkingabout* face. He falls it for it the way he would if I told him that pigs have wings, and to show me that he doesn't believe me he tilts his head to one side and arches his eyebrows. Aghast at the speed with which the tip seems to have reached him, I take the bait and, without even realizing what I'm doing, I walk over to him, obedient little sheep, as if I have to justify myself. He, old slut that he is, reads my approach as a surrender (he's been playing this game all his life, and I fall for it every time), and so he laughs disgustingly right in my face. When I get to normal conversational distance I praise through clenched teeth the quality of his mother's amatory performance, ignoring the two idlers, who take a step back at the sight of our evident intimacy. He mutters something incomprehensible that I, by virtue of my uneasy conscience, manage in some absurd way to decipher; like an idiot I ask him who told him, and he replies in triumphant glee that the courthouse stairwells are monitored by video surveillance cameras. I'm on the verge of laughing but with a last-minute visceral lunge I manage to convert my laughter into a pompous pose of indignation that comes off as entirely unconvincing. "You turn my stomach," I say, addressing him in the categorical second-person plural, and I turn on my heels, pursued by his gales of understandably self-satisfied laughter.

Remember, in terms of ethical turpitude, we lawyers have a very specific reputation on the market, but above and beyond every other shortcoming, even the most despicable kinds of self-interest, what we are is gossips. We're worse than shampooists, worse than concierges, worse than journalists, worse than body-builders, worse than university professors, worse than elementary school janitors, worse than barbers, worse than politicians, worse than neighborhood poets, worse than lifeguards. Name any other category or profession you can think of: we're worse.

While I'm walking along, Nives calls me on my cell phone. At first I'm afraid she's going to ask me about Alfredo, with the vague suspicion that she might have found out something via some vestigial umbilical impulse; then I remember that she has always been completely insensitive, umbilically speaking, so I ask her impassively how she's doing.

"How do you think," she says, and nothing more, a response that catapults me into a hopeful sea of melancholy that I should have long ago learned to ward off, considering my long experience with my ex-wife's sentimental flip-flops.

"What is it?" I ask, instead, in an objectively despicable tone of voice.

"I don't know, Vincenzo, I just can't seem to find a center of gravity to this situation, really, I can't . . . "

A center of gravity? Really, could you ever have imagined a phrase of that kind? Would you ever come up with a center of gravity, I mean a spontaneous center of gravity, in your life? Well, she would. And the stupefying thing is that she actually *sincerely* means it. When she says that she can't seem to find a center of gravity, she *actually* feels the lack of a center of gravity. She's so dazzled by herself, by her unconscious adoption of the Stanislavsky Method (whereby actors live for months in the role of the characters they are supposed to play), that she's actually accustomed to thinking in terms of centers of gravity, bedsheets that come clean after a last laundry cycle, significant relationships, emotional frictions, internal broom closets, the parking garages of the soul (that last one I made up myself), and all the rest of that ridiculous bullshit. It's the grammar of acting according to Stanislavsky, and then Lee Strasberg, Elia Kazan, the Actors Studio, and all the rest of that stuff that's put her into a trance, even if she doesn't know it.

Truth be told, to put it in terms of the most perfect clarity, from time to time, at irregular intervals, but intervals nonetheless, Nives needs to have sex with me. Why that should be I've long since stopped wondering, it's enough for me to know that I fuck better than the architect, evidently (of all the sources of male satisfaction that you can imagine, there are none greater than this one). When she makes these apparently purposeless phone calls to me, that's where she's heading, even if she doesn't know it.

I could just say to her: "Okay, understood: when?"; and we'd spare ourselves a vast quantity of centers of gravity and other metaphors of that kind. But instead we always have to rehearse the same little vignette over and over again, so that she can feel justified in cheating on the poor cuckold yet again.

But today it's not going to work out for her, because all of a sudden—just think!—I don't feel like it. I still don't know exactly what's happening to me, but you can bet your hat that this sudden mood swing must have something to do with Alessandra Persiano. So I blurt out a junk store allegory that I must have heard years and years ago on *Dancin' Days* or *Água Viva*, or some other Brazilian telenovela. And I throw a monkey wrench into her plan.

"They're just clouds passing over, Nives."

Her feelings are hurt, I can tell by the prolonged silence that follows.

"Maybe you're right. I'm sorry," she replies resentfully.

Whereupon I say, "Sorry for what," and she says, "Oh nothing," I say "Did I say something wrong," she tells me, "Absolutely not a thing," and after another exchange of hypocritical tropes we put an end to this meaningless phone call.

I quicken my step, expecting the angel of argumentativeness to appear at my side at any moment, clapping his hands and crying "Nice work—nice work" (subtitle: "Now she'll never go to bed with you again; proud of yourself?"), but instead, nothing happens. I can hardly believe the silence-as-approval. I walk along guilt-free, and after a while I reach my office, with a bounding step, light as air.

As I'm approaching the street door I cross paths once again with Giustino Talento, the demented tenant who summarized his problems with his live-in Polish girlfriend, Lalla or Lilla or whatever her name was.

Terrified at the prospect of a second run-through of our last, let us say, conversation, I briefly consider the possibility of taking shelter behind a car, but then I discard that hypothesis, square my shoulders, and continue on toward my encounter with the inevitable.

"Hey there," I say.

"Vincenzo, how are you?" he asks me, beaming.

We're already old friends, apparently.

"Oh, not bad. And your . . . girlfriend?" I ask, just to have something to say.

I must have put my foot in it, because all of a sudden he turns very serious on me. His eyes are lost in the middle distance.

"Last night she cooked dinner and set the table just for me. 'Aren't you going to eat?' I asked her. And she told me that from that night forth we were never to eat together again."

I'm at a loss for anything to say. But he's not done confiding in me.

"'But why?' I asked her. And she told me that she's always had problems eating in front of other people, because it embarrasses her, and she doesn't want to do it anymore. And she took her plate into the other room, just like that. And that was it."

"Well," I toss out, "it doesn't seem like anything aimed at you personally. Sure, it's not much fun, I realize, but we all have our fixations."

"Sure," he replies, clearly ready for my objection, "but I didn't know anything about this particular fixation until last night. I'm just presented with this immutable state of affairs, from one day to the next. From now on, I have to get used to the idea that I can no longer sit at the dinner table with my girl-friend, do you understand that?"

I nod, making it clear that I'm on his side, as I think: he certainly has a point, poor guy. It's just that I don't give a crap about his girlfriend's unprecedented unilateral diktats.

"I'm about to make an important decision," he says, staring me in the eye in a way that intimidates me.

"What . . . kind of decision?" I ask, humoring him.

"I need to talk to you about it," he declares.

"To me?"

"Tell me a good time to drop by your office."

"Ah, well, right here and now I couldn't say," I pull my wallet out of the inside jacket pocket, "call me and we'll decide on a time."

I try to hand him my business card, but he doesn't even deign to glance at it.

"I could do tomorrow afternoon at five o'clock," he says.

I think it over for a moment.

"Maybe I didn't make myself clear," I observe.

"See you tomorrow, then."

He nods, walks around me, and heads off.

I stand there in the middle of the sidewalk, business card in hand, dazed. From a billboard across the street, a jerk in a double-breasted suit points his finger straight at me, addressing me with the informal "tu" and advising me to turn to him with trust and confidence if I ever need a loan.

Given the hour, the Arethusa cooperative hasn't opened, so to speak, for business yet, which means I'm spared the psychopathic toy spitz's ritual bark-fest.

As I'm heading for my room, Espedito calls my name. I hadn't even noticed he was in.

"Vincè?"

I go back and look in at the door.

"Ciao Espe, how you doing?"

He's sitting at his desk but I practically can't see him, there's so much smoke in the room. He looks like Mysterio, Spider-Man's arch-enemy with the lightbulb head, emerging from billowing clouds of smoke like a rock star.

He swivels the thumb and index finger of his right hand.

"Not great."

I express my regret that the problem doesn't seem to be going away.

"Why don't you open your window a crack?" I ask.

"Why don't you go open your own window in your own room?" he replies.

"Are you still angry about the other day?"

"What? No, what are you saying?"

"I did sort of lecture you."

"But you were talking about your own problems."

"Yeah, but I was supposed to be talking about yours."

"Oh, will you cut it out?" he cuts in abruptly. "Here, this is for you," he says. And reaching across his desk he picks up a padded envelope, a handsome baby-shit yellow-brown. It's about the size of a magazine and it's nice and fat; but it looks like it's light, from the way he's waving it.

"What is it?" I ask, baffled, as I head over to the desk.

"Search me. The courier dropped it off half an hour ago. I even signed for it."

He waves the receipt in the air.

"For me?" I ask.

He pushes the flimsy sheet of paper closer to my eyes.

My mouth turns into a pair of inverted parentheses. I take the package.

"You probably just ordered something you can't remember," Espe observes.

I turn the package over in my hands, I read my own name in the space for the recipient (it's funny how sometimes reading your own name makes you feel like a stranger to yourself). The return address is a well-known electric appliance chain.

"No. I don't think I did. In fact, no. I never buy anything by mail order."

"Well, open it up," Espe resolves. He hands me his letter opener.

While I'm cutting the packing tape, I come to a halt.

"What if it's a mail bomb?" I say.

"What are you, an idiot?" says Espe.

Still, you can see that he took the possibility seriously for a second or two.

I slowly rip open the envelope and proceed to extract the contents. Espedito watches my every move in a silence you could slice like butter.

I suddenly stop.

"Oh, Espe."

"Eh?"

"We look like a couple of fools."

"Eh, I know. You going to open it already?"

I give a sharp jerk to the two edges of the envelope and rip it open, liberating the sealed package contained within.

"But it's a cell phone," says Espedito.

"Yeah, it is," I concur.

"Lemme see."

And he snatches the box from my hands with the confidence of a past master in appraising cell phones.

"Look at that, they didn't even shrink-wrap it."

He turns the package over a couple of times and then hands it back to me in disgust.

"It's a piece of shit. It doesn't even take pictures. They might as well have sent you an old TACS phone."

I stand there, the box under my arm, looking at Espe, undecided whether to tell him to go fuck himself then and there or wait until later.

"Wait a minute," I say. "I didn't buy any cell phone."

He stops to focus.

"It must be one of those things where you build up points, and after you recharge your card a certain number of times they give you a new phone. That happened to my brother-in-law last year."

"Whatever," I say. And I head for the door.

"Is it really that pathetic?" I ask, just before I turn the corner.

I go into my—I use the term reluctantly—office, I remove the steel pipe from the casement window, pull open the shutters, sit down at my Jonas desk, and contemplate the gift pack.

I wonder why—I subscribe to the observation that Espe made a short while ago—the package isn't shrink-wrapped?

An answer to that question starts to take form after I open the box, and I find that the cell phone is already assembled. The charger cord is rolled up ineptly. The instruction manual is roughly shoved into the space between the plastic shell and the cardboard box.

I pull out the cell phone, remove the battery, and look at the two slices of this technological sandwich. There's already a SIM card inserted.

Just what's going on here?

I reassemble the phone, push the power button. As I do, I have the unpleasant sensation that I'm doing exactly what somebody expected me to do.

The screen comes to life, depicting a digital duck waving at me with one hand.

I go on thinking about nothing in particular and after a short while I drift into a reverie, with the cell phone spread out on the palm of my hand like a pet hamster.

How much time has passed: five, maybe six seconds? When

I hear the phone vibrating, I feel as if I'm in the middle of an old silent movie.

I suddenly regain possession of my cerebral functions; I furrow my brow and stare at the screen.

A message.

MISSED CALLS: 11.

What the—? Eleven missed calls. Eleven calls to whom?

Whereupon I think back to Espedito's theory of building up points and I decide to call my cell phone provider and ask for an explanation.

After a little more than fifteen minutes of irritating homogenized wait music, a young woman answers and—before listening to my version of the facts—informs me that her name is Silvia. I tell her what happened and she puts me on hold. Another seven minutes go by, during which the background song ends and starts over at least sixteen times. Silvia finally gets back to me, apologizes for making me wait so long, and tells me no, the company hasn't sent me anything, much less a cell phone with a working SIM card. I ask her if she's sure. She thinks it over for a couple of seconds and then asks me if I'm sure that I received the cell phone in question from them. I answer yes in order to avoid having to admit that the return address that appears on the envelope is in fact that of a well-known chain of electronics retail stores, because at that point Silvia could easily tell me that I should be talking to the well-known chain of electronics retail stores, not to her. Except that at that point I could respond that I assumed that they probably subcontracted this kind of service out to other companies, but I don't feel like arguing and so I retrench to the impossible-to-verify falsehood. Wherepon Silvia makes a further effort of goodwill and tells me that if I give her the serial number of the cell phone she could try to do some further investigation, but at that very moment my eye happens to light on the Dekad wall clock and I realize that it's really gotten late, so I start to clear out of the office with the speed of Road Runner, and as I'm positioning the metal security pipe across the window I suddenly realize that I might just have hung up on her without saying goodbye.

I go back to the Jonas to get the cordless, just in case Silvia happens by some miracle to still be on the line, and at that very moment, the cell phone rings.

Uncertain what to do now, I look at it, lying flat on my Jonas in the throes of ring-tone epilepsy, and after a while I finally answer, accompanied by a sensation of unreality.

"Hello?"

"Aah, at last, there you are, Counselor."

"Who is this?"

"*Buon giorno*, how are you doing? We just wanted to know if you liked our gift."

An adult voice, male, confidential with a sinister edge.

I look at the screen, still covered with a plastic film. Caller unknown. A light sheen of perspiration cools my forehead.

"Who is this?"

"So did you like it, yes or no?"

"I said: *Who is this?*"

"I get it, you didn't like it."

"Look, you might have called the wrong number."

"Why are you losing your temper, Counselor?"

I hadn't lost my temper, by any means, until he asked that question. As the unknown voice on the other end of the line knew full well.

"Listen, I've had enough of this buffoonery. I don't know who you are and I'm not interested in knowing. And your lovely little gift, you can go pick it up at police headquarters, because that's where I'm taking it right now, understood?"

The other takes a long, leisurely pause, demonstrating to me that my tirade made him go *Wa-a-a-ah*.

"So when it's all said and done, do I have to get on my knees and beg you?" he asks, conveying a sense of determination that annihilates me.

"*Beg?*" I ask, disconcerted.

Another pause. The tone that follows is pure accommodation.

"It's not nice to say no to a lady. Are you going to say no to me too, Counselor?"

I reconstruct events at the speed of a videotape being rewound. I'm assailed by a mixture of fear and disgust. I leap to my feet, recoiling. The Skruvsta falls over, slamming against the Effektiv, which, however, remains immobile. I immediately turn off the cell phone and extract the battery. I let the two dismantled parts of the phone drop onto the Jonas and I start pacing back and forth in the room, waiting for a reaction that never comes.

"Ah, so that's it, eh? Is that how it is?" I grumble, furious and confused.

Espedito appears in the doorway.

"Did you drop something, Vincè?"

"Eh?" I say. "What?"

Espedito walks in and looks at the overturned Skruvsta on the floor. I look at it with him.

"Yeah. In fact, the chair," I say.

He stares at me in concern.

"Do you feel okay?"

"I don't know. I just got a strange phone call."

"What phone call?"

I'm looking him right in the eyes, but I don't hear the question.

"Do you still have the envelope?" I ask.

"The one the cell phone came in? Yes, it must be in my trash can."

"Give it to me. And get me the receipt from the courier, too."

I gesture for him to go ahead of me toward his office.

"What on earth is happening, Vincè? Who was that on the phone?"

WHAT?

At police headquarters, they took what seemed to be ten minutes or so to take down my complaint against parties unknown. The cell phone and the box wound up in a metal locker with a number tag on it, the envelope and the receipt from the courier in a file folder, along with a printout of the complaint.

Then we said goodbye.

That's how I dealt with the problem.

The wait in line for a parking spot at the university is brutal. Among other things, everything is cement as far as the eye can see, the sun is pounding the pavement like a streetwalker, and my car isn't air conditioned.

While I'm waiting in line I find myself noticing, with a certain degree of horror, the luxury that surrounds me. Kids who are barely twenty, dressed in indeterminate style, generically wealthy, get out of cars whose cost, at a rapid glance, would probably suffice to cover the household needs of an average family for two years straight, even with a grandparent to take care of.

Okay, I'm not trying to moralize here. In that moment I feel like a penniless loser, I admit it. But that's not the point. And the point isn't that the aggressive ostentation of wealth (the plenary remission of this age-old form of oafishness) annoys me. The fact is—I'm going to go ahead and say this even though I can't really explain it—that I don't believe in this wealth. It looks so unstable, so provisional to me. Extraneous. Wealth that has no real residence, just a pied-à-terre. Money that's bound to be confiscated by an investigating magistrate, sooner or later, I don't know if you get the picture. Like one of those shops with five plate-glass windows that suddenly appear from one week to the next in the heart of downtown, and as you walk by it you say: "It won't last." Just like that, instinctively. You don't even think it over, you don't drill down into the concept. You don't need any evidence, to put it the way Pasolini might have. You just know that the money behind that shop is no investment, it's money with other uses that just needs someplace to stay for a little while. Money that serves as a cautionary tale, I guess you could say.

At last a parking spot frees up. The student who's getting in his car—imitation handsome, bumpkin-Bieber hairdo, charcoal gray suit meant to make him look like a young executive but the effect is that he looks like he ought to be showing model homes—sneers at my automobile as he pulls out.

With a sense of relief, I park and set off down the access road leading to the central pavilion. On the other side of that, according to Alagia's directions, I ought to run right into the main dining hall.

My God, this university is a blight to behold. Now I remember why I never came to class when I was enrolled here. It looks like a low-security American prison for people sentenced for financial wrongdoings. The only nice thing about the place are the dogs lying around everywhere on the lawns and flowerbeds. When you walk past them, you have to envy them their openly fatalistic view of life.

I walk into the central pavilion, cutting through a café that I seem to remember was here when I was going to school. (A vague sense of déjà vu creeps through me.) Gathered in this bar is a fair sampling of college-age youth. There's a line at the cash register. More kids are talking on their cell phones than to each other. With an abrupt surge of anxiety, probably caused by the thing with the cell phone earlier, I head up the first staircase I come to and find myself on the second floor where I hunt around impatiently for the exit as if I were feeling the onset of an attack of claustrophobia, a pathology I don't happen to suffer. I get outside and suck a deep lungful of air. I lift one hand to my forehead to shade my eyes against this blinding cement wall of sunlight.

That must be the student cafeteria across the street. If not, I don't know how to explain the throng of dogs dotting the surrounding flowerbeds and lawns. I cross the street, still shading my eyes with one hand.

Alagia is walking up and down outside the front entrance pretending to send text messages on her cell phone. I do the same thing: when I'm in the street waiting for someone, I scroll through my contacts at great length (in fact, I think that one of the reasons for the popularity of cell phones is that they give you a way to keep your hands occupied when you don't know what else to do with them).

Hot as it is out, she's stripped down to her T-shirt. Her sweater (or whatever it is) is tied around her right thigh, like an emergency tourniquet to stop hemorrhaging. She's tied up her hair in a ponytail that has pride of place on top of her head like the topknot of a Kendo master.

It's not because she's my daughter (well, Nives's daughter, but mine, too), but she really is cute. She has that tenderness that springs from the aesthetic contradiction between candid spontaneity and contrived pose, meaning, for example, that if you aren't aggressive by nature there's no point trying to put on an aggressive act, because your true nature just becomes all the more transparent.

She walks toward me and then—*smack smack*—a kiss on each cheek.

"You're late," she says.

"There was a line at the parking structure," I explain.

"Mm," she comments.

And she takes a quick look at the Swatch Folkloral Chic that I gave her a few months ago.

"Come on, I have class in half an hour."

As we walk in, she sort of waves hello to a big café-au-lait-colored dog sitting philosophically a few yards away from the main entrance. The dog looks up and sweeps the sidewalk with his tail.

"Friend of yours?" I ask.

We share a table with a pair of coeds. It's normal, in cafeterias, to share a table with strangers. Which is actually a problem for me. Alagia notices I'm not comfortable as she pops the cap off her little bottle of mineral water.

"What's the matter?" she asks.

"Nothing," I reply.

She doesn't believe me. But it's not like she devotes a lot of effort to doubting me.

The fact is—and I can't tell her about it now—many years ago I had a traumatic experience that involved a shared table. I went out for dinner with a girlfriend and because we hadn't called ahead to make reservations and there was going to be a long wait, the waiter told us that if we wanted, there were two seats open at a table for four. Turns out that sitting all alone at that table was a retired school principal who was eating a mixed greens salad. So we said hello to her, just to be polite.

Hands down, one of the most deeply unpleasant evenings of my life. You couldn't get a fucking word in edgewise while she banged on, telling you how wrong you were. One diatribe after another, for the entire duration of the meal. And it's not as if once she was done with her salad she toddled out of that shitty restaurant to collapse in a corner somewhere; oh no, she stuck it out, right up to and through the grappa, correcting every damn word that came out of our mouths. What. The. Fuck. You wanted to set her on fire, really. It's like I'm still always looking around, afraid I'll run into her, every time I go out to eat.

But anyway, I have to admit that the experience only brought us closer, me and that girlfriend.

"So, what's happening?" Alagia asks me as she spears a chunk of roast potato, and as I'm asking myself why I didn't think to get roast potatoes.

"Your brother showed up at my front door this morning. Someone had just beaten him up."

I take a sidelong peek at the plates of the two young women sitting next to us to get some idea of how much longer they're likely to be sitting there.

"Yeah, I heard," she says, frowning.

"Ah, you heard," I say in surprise.

"He called me," she adds.

Whereupon I wonder why I even drove over here. I feel like someone trying to tell a joke to someone who's already heard it. But I didn't want to see her just so I could give her that news.

"How is he?" she asks. And she lays her fork across her knife in her plate, as if she'd lost her appetite.

"A couple of punches that just grazed him, is what he says," I reply.

She glares at me with one of her looks of resentment.

"Is what he says? Sweet Jesus, Vincè. He came to your house. You saw him, didn't you?"

Which pisses me off. It's not that I mind being told when I'm off track, especially when I deserve it. It's just that when Alagia starts nitpicking over phrasing and words, she turns into an updated model of her mother. And sooner or later I'm going to stand up to her, since I don't seem to be able to do it with her mother.

"Well, he called you, didn't he? And you fell into line with his version too, if I'm not mistaken. Unless I'm mistaken, you didn't hurry over to see him so you could form your own personal opinion, did you?"

She looks at me in astonishment. She doesn't even try to come up with a response.

The coeds sitting near us sense the tension and fall silent all at once. Which is just one more way of butting in.

Alagia picks up her utensils again and starts operating on her cutlet with slow, gloomy gestures. I no longer feel like eating. I'm inhibited by the presence of these two women sitting next to us, I feel guilty about what I said, I'm happy that at least I said it though, seen up close this tomato-and-mozzarella salad becomes repellent, and suddenly all creation strikes me as intolerable.

"You're right, sorry," says Alagia, after a while.

I melt. The cyclonic mood-storm that was raging inside me until just a few seconds ago is suddenly over. A fundamental awareness colonizes my mind: I'm a piece of shit.

I try to reach out for her hand, and then a wave of shame sweeps over me.

"No, I'm sorry, darling. I hate myself when I'm rude with you."

She feels like crying, I can tell from the way her lower lip is trembling ever so slightly. She used to do the same thing when she was small.

"Never mind," she says.

And she cuts off a wedge of cutlet.

We sit there, bobbing in a melancholy silence.

"Could I have one of your potatoes?" I ask, after a while.

She looks up from her plate.

"A potato?"

"Um, hm."

She lowers her eyes to her plate again and then looks up sharply, slyly.

"All the same with you if I throw it in your face?"

So we start talking like a father and daughter again. We go back to old topics, we say things that we've already said a thousand times before, just readjusting the arrangement slightly, without getting anywhere or learning anything we didn't already know, comparing our respective senses of impotence in order to decide whether we should continue to honor the pact of resignation that all of us in our, so to speak, family, have underwritten, or whether it might not be a good idea to actually try to do something about the way things are.

At a certain point, Alagia interrupts me. Or maybe I should say, she approaches the topic from another angle.

"Can I ask you something?"

"Of course you can."

"Why did you come to see me? Why don't you talk to Mamma about it?"

Eh, good question, I think.

"Eh, good question," I say.

What follows is a scene from a silent movie. For that matter, what should I do, lay out an essay on the subject of intimidation? Should I tell her about the sense of inferiority that comes over me when I'm with her mother? Explain to her that I listen to her raptly even when I disagree with her? And what am I supposed to explain to her, if I don't know anything myself? I know the effect, I'm baffled about the cause. Leaving aside the fact that even if I understood the cause, the effect would remain the same.

Alagia acts like one of those tender-hearted teachers who assume they're not going to get an answer and so they ask another question.

"Listen," she veers over into a philo-conspiratorial tone of voice, "there's something I need to tell you."

I plump up properly in my chair. At last the unwanted neighbors get to their feet and hit the road.

"Alfredo," she says.

"What."

"He asked me to tell you this, when I had an opportunity."

"To tell me what."

"At first I told him I wouldn't; then I said to myself: 'Oh, why not.'"

My blood pressure shoots northward of 160/99. One more preamble and I'm going to start doing some self-cutting.

Alagia issues an affectless statement, as if she were reading the weather report.

"He likes boys."

I feel an involuntary twitching of my lip muscles. Something intrinsically moronic sets out to conquer my face. What's happening to my mouth? I feel as if I must look like the Mona Lisa. I even have my hands crossed in my lap.

"*What?*"

Alagia looks at me skeptically.

"*What* does he like?"

She throws her head back and ranges the room quickly with her eyes, as if I were an over-insistent would-be boyfriend who won't take no for an answer, an insurance salesman, a Jehovah's Witness, or some other form of persistent annoyance.

"Listen up, Vincenzo," she tells me, leaning forward with a comforting, paternalistic demeanor, "this kind of curiosity is normal at that age. It's not like you know what you like or don't like. You just experiment, don't you see?"

I'm a piece of real estate right now. I'm not going anywhere. They could rent me out.

Where am I? How did I get here?

I'm not where I think I am.

That isn't Alagia talking to me.

It isn't May.

It isn't true.

"Oh, Vincè."

"Eh?"

"Are you all right?"

"All right. Yes."

"Look at you, you're white as a corpse. Take it easy, hey, nothing terrible's happened."

My eyesight is all blurry.

"Jesus, you're having an attack of some kind. I have to say I didn't expect this. Or actually, maybe I did."

She's fiddling with the balls of bread gum from the dinner roll that she's gutted while we were talking.

"Are you sure?" I ask, just to have something to say.

"*Vincenzo.*"

"Do you think he'll get over it?"

Jesus, I can't believe I said what I just said.

"It's not a disease, you know."

Standard answer for blinkered morons. Like me.

"Well, what I meant is do you think it's something permanent?"

Holy Mary, why can't I stop myself?

"I told you that I don't think so. When I was his age, I had a thing for a while with a girlfriend of mine, and then I fell in love with Francesco and that was the end of that. And anyway, even if it did turn out to be something permanent, I hardly think it's something we should turn into a tragedy."

"Who did you have thing with when you were his age?"

"Oh, enough is enough, Vincè," she squirms in her chair. "I can't believe this is you."

I touch my hair, overwhelmed at the thought that with all the people sitting in this cafeteria, I should be the one who feels worst.

"But listen, there's something else I'm worried about," Alagia says, changing the subject with chilling nonchalance.

"Ah, something else," I say, under partial anaesthesia.

"This thing he does where he goes around getting beaten up," she says, as if pursuing a line of thought that she'd already been pondering in her head.

"Well?" I ask, fully expecting her response.

"I hope it's not something he enjoys."

I hear synchronized bells, I see blinking colored lights, and I recognize the sound of a score counter running way faster than normal. My internal alarm has gone off, a manifestation of my terror. When I was a kid, that was part of the experience of playing pinball. Once you reached a certain score, the machine would go into a trance for a few seconds, putting on a celebratory show for you with its entire spectacular arsenal before spitting out another ball.

"I'm not following you," I lie.

She doesn't look at me, still lost in her wandering thoughts. The ensuing silence triggers an irresistible need to defuse the tension.

"No, no, of course not," I resume, as insincere as a flight attendant reassuring the passengers as the airplane plunges to earth. "You know how deeply he cares about this stuff. He has a cultural interest in these things, a normal cultural interest. Even your mother says that . . . "

Oh God, the horror.

Alagia looks up at me, still half distracted, and fails to focus.

I need to sleep. I want my bed. Sheets and blankets. A dark room.

"You're right, Vincenzo," Alagia comes to, all confident and upbeat. "What are we worried about? After all, what's happened? Nothing's happened."

I take a breath.

"Yeah, in fact, that's what I say."

"That's right, come on. Let's behave like adults."

"Right, let's behave."

Exactly forty minutes later, I charge into Nives's office like an avenging fury. The minute her secretary Marianna sees me coming she knows this is no time to intervene. She doesn't even make an effort to intercept me, the way secretaries do in movies when someone busts into the boss's private office, and the secretary comes running up right behind the intruder just as they open the door and calls out: "I'm so sorry, Mr. Thus-and-Such, I told him he couldn't go in but he refused to take no for an answer."

But what does happen behind me is that a guy who was sitting in the waiting room jumps up and yells: "Hey, where the hell is he going?" to which Marianna replies: "He's the doctor's husband," and he says: "Ah."

I throw open the door and interrupt the session so vehemently that Nives and her patient—a woman I know, by the way—practically jump into one another's arms in their startlement.

The time that it takes for Nives's expression to swerve from surprise to indignation is the exact same amount of time it takes for a child to progress from the astonishing realization of the boo-boo to the explosion of tears.

Nives's patient hides her face in her hands, as if I'd caught her necking with my wife or something like that. In effect, I would never have guessed that an oafish social-climber like Felicia Parisi was in analysis. She's the kind of person who, when they do condescend to speak to you, seem to be saying nothing but: "Problems, me? Oh, good Lord, the very idea."

"How dare you?" Nives raises her voice, red in the face. She's so angry that her lips are trembling.

At that point I realize what a complete fuck-up I've just committed, but I stay cool. Fuck-ups don't legally entail proactive restitution. Which is why in a process of criminal escalation, like when somebody goes out to commit a robbery and then commits murder, e.g., the murder is preceded by other actions that are of lesser criminal importance. A murder committed by a hooligan is always a dirty, vulgar, wasteful murder, awkward and bloody, committed with a violence that squanders and spoils. That's why, in contrast, a murder committed by a professional is described as "clean" or "perfect." Professionals don't leave a mess.

In other words, in view of the aspects of criminal law that I've just explained, I stand in the door and begin clapping my hands.

"Well, well, my compliments, eh; nice job," I say.

She registers my incomprehensible sarcasm with a mixture of curiosity and indignation that, among other things, makes her particularly attractive. She throws the notebook that she was holding until just a second ago onto the floor and strides toward me, all ligaments, as if she were walking in a suit of armor.

"What the fuck are you talking about? What are you saying? What right do you have to interrupt one of my sessions? You could be arrested for this, did you know that?"

Eh, you could have the police confiscate all my Ikea furniture, I say to her in my mind.

"Of all the masterpieces you've put your signature to in your career, this beats them all, no question," I say.

Nives's nostrils flare, practically emitting smoke.

"Get out of here immediately," she commands.

"Nives, what's happening here is very serious, I hope you realize that," Felicia Parisi puts in her two cents.

"Who asked you anything, mind your own fucking business if you can manage it," I say to her, slapping the back of my hand in her general direction.

She turns red as an Apache.

Nives looks at her and immediately afterward turns to look at me, as if she can't believe what she just heard.

"WHY HOW DARE Y—"

I level my index finger straight at her.

"Do you want to know why I'm here? Eh?! You want to know?"

She clenches her jaw, frustrated by my interruption, but she's dying of curiosity. Felicia Parisi too has retracted her neck like a bulldog. I don't have the slightest idea of what I'm about to say.

"Listen closely. Probably up till now I haven't been as good a father as I ought to have been, but from today forward, everything's going to change, understood? The mother's exclusive on this story has expired. I want to have a say in raising my kids, I want to stop you once and for all from doing exactly as you please and prefer, knowing full well that Idiot Boy here isn't going to contradict a thing you say. Have I conveyed the idea? So brace yourself: a new era is about to begin!"

I fall silent and just breathe, waiting for my heartbeat to stop racing. In the meanwhile, I do my best to remember what the hell I just said.

Now Nives is looking at me uneasily.

"Vincenzo, do you feel all right?"

I let fly.

"Oh, go fuck yourself. Now I have to hear it from you? Since this morning all I've heard from anyone is that same fucking question! Enough!"

At that point Her Highness Lady Felicia grabs her purse and her cell phone and prepares to leave the office in disgust.

"Goodbye, Nives," she says, walking past her and taking up a point on the wall-to-wall carpeting exactly midway between the two of us.

"Hold on, Felicia," Nives says. "This is just an unexpected disruption. Don't leave, we can still finish the session."

"No, it's lasted long enough for me," Felicia says, tartly.

God, how I feel like slapping her in the face.

"Then this is our last session," Nives declares unexpectedly, as sharp and spare as a scalpel.

"What?" the turd cries.

"You heard me," my ex-wife snaps decisively.

Hey, I can't believe my ears.

"You're telling me not to come back? Did I undertand you correctly, Nives?" Felicia demands in outrage.

Exactly, I reply mentally. In fact, she just told you to go get fucked by a choir of gospel singers. Didn't you hear her? Because that's precisely what she just said.

"If you can't handle this kind of situation, Felicia," Nives points out dryly, "it means that you're refusing to do your part in this therapy. In which case there is no reason for us to go on meeting."

You can't even imagine the look on that turd's face now. She just stands there, like a TV antenna, incapable of deciding what to do next. Boys, that is some woman I married.

"Your husband is a boorish oaf," says the turd. And glares at me.

I plaster a Walter Matthau smile across my lips.

"I'm not the one who asked him to break into our session," Nives replies. "I'm not responsible for what he does. I don't even know what he's talking about."

Nives's logic proceeds like a seeing-eye dog. It accompanies the turd's thoughts, preventing them from walking into the sides of buildings, signaling contradictions and incongruities.

"I want you to do something," the poor thing finally croaks.

"I just told him to leave. And I just asked you to stay. So what are you going to do? Are you going to stay?"

At that point something truly incredible happens: Felicia Parisi—Felicia Parisi!—tucks her head back down into her shoulders and goes back to her place, like an embarrassed little schoolgirl.

Nives levels her eyes straight into mine, with a look of reproof that is completely devoid of vindictive anger. She leans over the carpeting, picks up her notebook, walks over to Felicia, puts a hand on her shoulder, and then comes back to me.

Behind me, at a safe distance, is Marianna, slack-jawed. I see her out of the corner of my eye.

"Now please leave," Nives tells me, brooking no contradiction. "Whatever this is about, we can discuss it later."

I nod, turn on my heel, and finally leave the office, as she gently closes the door behind me.

I return home with a feeling of serenity that I don't know where it even comes from, but it's there. Get this: I find a parking place not far from the front door of my apartment building, which is, how to put this, something verging on the miraculous, as these things go. Once I've parked my car, in fact, I stop for a second and just look back to admire it, as if I'd achieved something. I don't know if you ever catch yourself doing things of the sort.

Sometimes I think that when you straighten your back, and you start knocking on doors and demanding things, instead of submitting to everything by exerting the basic bare minimum level of resistance (which, let's face it, is the way that I live), the world takes notice. Just develop a little bit of respect for yourself and life makes things easier for you. Which is why all of a sudden you find a parking place right outside your own front door, or a woman gives you a lingering glance, or someone offers you a job. Like when you get into a relationship, and all of a sudden four or five different women suddenly call you up on the same day (including a couple of your exes that you haven't seen in years), and you wonder: "Hey, but where the fuck were you all until the day before yesterday?"

Here's the way it is: reality makes inquiries about individuals. When life offers you these special bonus discounts, it's basically opening a line of credit. It's telling you: okay, here you go, but don't be a loser, don't turn around and squander it all so that you're penniless again tomorrow morning. You didn't find this on the sidewalk: I gave it to you, to you and nobody else. So give me some evidence that I wasn't wrong about you. Keep up the good work: change.

The problem, at least as far as I'm concerned, is that I can't seem to get anyone to change their mind about me for more than a day or so—maybe a day and a half.

So I stick with the bonus discounts.

As I stick my house key into my front door lock, all the thinking, rethinking, and sense of guilt that I've been wallowing in up till now about Alfredo lose a significant percentage of their burdensome weight. That's the way it always is with me, where problems are concerned. From a distance, they always prompt a bunch of complicated considerations. Then, once we're face to face, we always find a way of coming to terms.

Just now, fr'instance, the kind of awkwardness I feel at the idea of seeing Alf for the first time after getting the news is the same as when you have to explain to your children the process that leads to birth. Maybe it's that too many things have already happened today, who can say? One thing I can rely on is that by now, that chucklehead of a sister of his has certainly already told him the expression that appeared on my face in the cafeteria.

I walk in, toss my keys onto the hardwood Monga bench that was actually originally a piece of bathroom furniture but who really cares, and I call out Alfredo's name, followed by an entirely rhetorical question mark.

No answer.

"Hey, let's not try to be funny, no one's in the mood," I say, a little louder.

More silence.

"Alfre'? Come on, don't be an idiot."

I stick my head into the, shall we say, living room.

He's not there.

Into the bedroom.

Not there either.

Into the bathroom.

Nothing.

I hurry into the kitchen (which is the last room in the apartment).

On the kitchen table, in plain view, there's a sheet of paper.

THANKS ALL THE SAME DAD.

I THOUGHT IT OVER AND I REALIZED THERE WAS NO REASON NOT TO GO TO SCHOOL AFTER ALL.

I'LL GET THERE IN TIME FOR SECOND PERIOD, SO WHATEVER. AND IF THEY ASK ME WHAT HAPPENED, I'LL JUST TELL THEM THE TRUTH.

I'M GLAD YOU WERE ON MY SIDE.

IAG

ALF

XXX

I pull out a Stefan and take a seat, reading the note over and over again from the beginning until the words on the paper have become incomprehensible scribble.

I put down the piece of paper and stare into the middle distance.

I'm rich, I think to myself.

That's what goes through my head.

Then I sniff.

Aw, go to hell.

Those are the words that come to mind when you unexpectedly feel a wave of happiness, without warning.

Outlet

There's nothing gradual about the way things happen. When things happen, they just happen. And it's not like you can walk them along, guide them with one hand to keep them from veering out of control and sweeping you away with them as they crash into the void. There's no way to slow things down when they happen. You can't control them, you can't manage them. Even understanding them is beyond our reach. In fact, the most common recurring phrase in this connection is the following: "I don't know what's happening to me." Certain phrases don't exactly come about by chance. If something happens to you, there's nothing you can do about it, and that's that. It's not true that life changes little by little. Either it changes or else it remains the same. After your life changes, you might say: "Yeah, but before that, this and that and the other thing happened," and you talk yourself into believing that the change was in the air somehow. But deep down you know why, or really, deep down you *don't* know why your life has changed. You just don't know the reasons why things happen. It's like when you come down with a psychosomatic disease: the natural countermove is to look around for a triggering event. You thoughtfully review the recent events in your life that were bound up with choices or sacrifices (which are actually pretty much synonymous), and you decide to put the blame on one prime suspect. You open an investigation into suspect number one, and you bombard it with damning evidence until you've pinned it down as the instigator behind your psychosomatic disease. But the truth is that no one knows what events produce psychosomatic diseases. Because the array of events that can trigger a psychosomatic disease (which, by the way, no one really can define or understand) is so vast that one is as suspicious or likely as another.

But you don't even really have to go into the realm of psychosomatic diseases to prove how unreliable explanations that attribute specific causes can be. Take a head cold. You apply the same inquisitorial procedure. You get a cold and you think to yourself: "It must have been that one time I left the house dressed too lightly." Which is obviously only one of an array of potential explanations, since it's a well-known fact that you can catch a cold in any of several million ways. The fact is, though, that once you've spent the night sleeping with your mouth wide open and at half past midnight you realize that you've already gone through a family-size box of Kleenex, you have to find some way of rationalizing such an enormous pain in the ass. So you put the blame on that one time you should have dressed more warmly. And with the passage of time you become absolutely convinced of it. Even if it would be sufficient to remember the thousands of times you left the house dressed much more lightly than that one time (times when it was even colder, what's more) to completely demolish the prosecution's case. All of this long and intricate explanation leads up to the fact that I can't tell you how it is that I wound up in Alessandra Persiano's bed, but, unless I happen to be in the throes of a prolonged hallucination, the naked woman sleeping alongside me right now is none other than her.

As soon as we walked into her apartment, that is, here, I threw myself at her with a vehement impatience that my subsequent performance couldn't possibly hope to live up to. So before it was all said and done, or really before any of the saying and doing even began, just forty seconds after I entered the home of

Alessandra Persiano, I also entered Alessandra Persiano herself, but I remained inside her such a short time that, after the
first and last thuds, she called my name beseechingly, as if wondering where I'd vanished to. Whereupon I thought to myself:
"Now I look like an asshole," but I didn't say it out loud,
because really there was no need. And then she, who at that
moment was on top of me and was objectively somewhat ridiculous, all rumpled and disheveled on account of me, said to me,
"Why don't we just start over from square one, but taking it easy
this time, since there isn't anyone actually in hot pursuit of us?"
In response to which I asked, in perfectly good faith, whether
by "from square one" she meant going right back to where we
started from, that is to say, on the landing outside her apartment, or even better, in the elevator, and she burst out laughing right in my face (Alessandra Persiano always bursts out
laughing right in my face), and that helped to break the tension
so that no more than five minutes later we started fucking but
for real this time and we didn't stop for a good solid four
hours, filling our heads with good talk in the intervals, along
with everything else.

So anyway, at this point I have to say that I feel pretty discombobulated and even a little dopey after everything that's
happened, truth be told.

In the meanwhile, the first state of mind that I register is
that of a generic gratitude toward existence at large. Which is
a condition of beatitude verging on the Franciscan, if we
accept that St. Francis ever felt a sensation like this one. And
I'm not just talking about the Zen tranquility that is so typical
of the post-coital state, when you feel all invigorated and it's as
if your body were sending a message from deep within that it
was about time you paid a little attention to it for a change. I'm
referring to the sudden intrusion of hope. The ability to grasp
the meaning of every single act that allows you to earn a living.
To think of the future as something that you can't wait to start.

And to be sure, it wasn't written in the stars that a piece of woman like Alessandra Persiano should come along and bestow this incredible favor on me of all people.

Reasoning about it coolly, I think that this New Malinconico Miracle is due to the fact that I reacted fairly passively to her first approaches.

There's a short story by Proust that deals with this very same subject. It's called "The Indifferent Man." It's about a marquise who falls head over heels in love with a man who treats her with complete indifference. Put in those terms, it seems about as obvious as a hot-water faucet, but you try making a hot-water faucet sometime. Anyway, this marquise, even though she is one of the most beautiful women in Paris, and, being a wealthy widow, is constantly pursued by a vast throng of suitors, winds up falling incurably under the spell of this guy who systematically ignores her. It's not that her beloved is all that much better than the various nobleman panting after her with declarations of love (and the marquise knows this perfectly well); it's precisely the unaffected way in which he becomes hard to track down, rejects her invitations, and dismisses her repeated advances that makes her so unhappy. And even at the end of the short story, when she agrees to marry another man, it's obvious that the indifferent man is the one she couldn't get out of her mind.

In other words, without even realizing it, I must have behaved like Proust's indifferent man. With the niggling difference that, unlike Proust's indifferent man, when Alessandra Persiano came charging back at me, I didn't even make her ask twice, truth be told.

The fact is that I belong to a generation of men who are pathologically skeptical when it comes to the idea that a tremendous babe might actually be coming on to them. I'm an outlet-store man. And outlet-store men, since they are invariably last season's model, have a troubled relationship with the latest things. They feel like they're past their sell-by dates, second choice. If anyone ever wants us, it's only because we're on sale, with deep discounts. So it's obvious that we would never dare to think that a woman like Alessandra Persiano, who is a Prada woman, might ever consider dropping in here to do a little shopping.

The other state of mind that I am registering just now, and with a sense of relief that I'm not even going to bother trying to describe, is the complete absence of any guilty feeelings that the thought of Nives triggers in me. I don't give a damn: it's a beautiful sensation. Whatever else people might say, a man who doesn't give a damn is a free man.

I'm so rapt in my conjectures that I don't even notice that Alessandra Persiano has turned in my direction, and is contemplating me with post-sexual curiosity—the kind that amounts to taking a closer look at the person you just had sex with, to get a better idea of whether or not you just made a mistake.

"Oh," I say, "I thought you were asleep."

She smiles, and then she sketches out the oval of my face with her enchanting right index finger.

I breathe in her vaguely fruit-scented aroma (beautiful women always give off a scent of fruit) and I scrutinize her, overjoyed at my complete inability to find one single defect.

"What were you thinking about?"

I give her a partial answer.

"About Francis."

"Francis?"

"The one from Assisi, you know the one I mean?"

She opens her eyes wide, momentarily taking into consideration the possibility that I'm just joking, then dismisses that thought, and thrusts her head against my chest, sputtering out a crescendo of laughter that is only amplified by my thoracic cavity.

"I just don't know. I mean, you're amazing." She remerges, half dazed by the absurd sensation that she's evidently experiencing.

"Why?" I ask, seraphically.

She shakes her head. I get a mouthful of hair. I blow it away.

"The things you say never seem to fit in with the place. Or the time."

"Naturally, I'm nothing but an outlet store" is what I feel like saying. But then I'd have to explain it all, and I don't feel like it.

"Ilikeit*Ilikeit*Ilikeit!" she says over and over, electrified like a little girl, and runs her hands over me.

"But you women," I ask as I do my best to pin her down, "why is it that you're always attracted by defects? I mean, a guy wears himself out trying to seem promising, reliable, convinced of the things he says; a guy studies, works hard, gets ahead, goes to the gym, does his best to dress fashionably, in other words, ruins his life, and then when you finally decide to take him to bed, what's the secret that you confide in him? 'I don't really like handsome men'; 'Your belly makes me feel safe'; 'You're so adorable when you misspeak' . . . Jesus Christ, what a pain in the ass. Couldn't you at least tell us in advance?"

She looks up at the sky, or really, at the ceiling, and shakes her head.

"God what an idiot you are, Vincè. It's exactly because you try so hard to conceal them, your defects, as you call them, that we like you. A truly inept man is pathetic. But a man who's trying to act self-confident, and then you realize that he's inept, it just does something to you, you understand?"

I think it over.

"In other words, you're trying to say that you women are still fascinated by 'what's underneath the surface' and 'Now you see it/now you don't.'"

She points her hand straight at my face, having formed all

four fingers into a flat plane, the universal gesture meaning, "Take this for example," however, when used at this distance from the subject, means in many parts of the world: "Now listen to this guy."

"As if you men are equally as captivated by the same things? When you look at a woman, you're not imagining anything else, are you?"

"Touché," I reply.

She kisses me.

"You're just the way I imagined," she says.

"You're much better," I rectify.

"I imagined you at your best," she shoots back.

"I can do better than that," I insist.

"Maybe the best thing is for you to shut up," she says. And she seals my mouth with her own.

We're squirming and caressing each other again when a cell phone—my cell phone—rings. I curse myself for not turning it off and I pretend I can ignore it, busily pursuing the activity now under way, but after a little while Alessandra Persiano, with impeccable feminine pragmatism, taps me twice on the shoulder.

"Come on, answer the phone so we can forget about it," she recommends.

I snort in annoyance and roll over onto the other side of the bed, reaching out toward the nightstand. Alessandra Persiano fixes her hair, stands up, and walks to the window, walking indifferently past her clothing folded neatly on the chair, a detail that cheers me up as it clarifies her future intentions.

"Hello."

I speak slowly and in a low voice, just to eliminate any doubts my caller might have as to whether this call comes at an unwelcome moment.

"Good afternoon, Counselor, so when can we have a meeting?"

I sit bolt upright in bed.

"Who is this?"

Of course, I immediately recognized the voice.

"What are you saying, have you already forgotten about me?"

He says it in an indulgent tone of voice that gets on my nerves.

I start to sweat.

"Who is this? How dare you call me again? Who gave you my phone number?"

"Counselor, if you don't mind my asking, why do you have to make it so complicated?"

I turn to look at Alessandra Persiano, who is looking back at me with a worried expression, standing naked and beautiful in front of the window curtains.

One time something happened to me that resembles this situation very closely. A case of intrusiveness that verged on extortion. I was selling a family apartment through a real estate agency. One day a guy calls me up from a rival agency and says why don't you fire the agency you're with now and let me sell that apartment for you. I ask him why I would do anything of the sort. He replies that he has some people who are interested in buying my apartment. I tell him that I don't give a damn if he does. So he asks me if I'm trying to be funny. Whereupon I tell him that our conversation has gone on long enough and that it'd be better for him if he never tried to call me again. He apologizes and hangs up. I think back on this phone call for at least a couple of days, so shocked am I at the existence of such people (you ask yourself: "Does God exist?"; whereas "Do people like that exist?" is what you ought to be asking yourself). Incredible to say, a few days later the same guy calls me back and asks when he can come and show the apartment. Come and show what? I say, with a horrible morbid curiosity that drives me to find out more. What do you mean, to show what: to show the apartment. Just like that, as if the last time we talked I'd hired him as my realtor. I tell him that I have no intention of letting him show my apartment and he replies, in a tone of voice that almost seems friendly, that he needs to sell the apartment so that he can get his percentage. Whereupon I start shouting and I threaten to report him to the police for attempted extortion. And at that point he vanishes, never to be heard from again.

The resemblance between these two episodes triggers a dizzying implosion of fury. I hurl my cell phone at the floor. The battery detaches and winds up who knows where.

Alessandra Persiano comes over to me, uneasily.

"What's happening, Vincenzo? Who was that?"

"I don't know."

"You sure? You're so angry."

I stand up.

"What the fuck do they want from me? Now you tell me," I say to myself, walking aimlessly back and forth. The funny thing—so to speak—is that I'm naked, too. Which is not something I'd normally do.

Alessandra Persiano remains on the bed, sitting in silence.

"Sorry Ale, forgive me," I say after a while.

"What's going on?" she asks.

So I sit down next to her and explain. I start with the judicial hearing of Burzone, pausing to savor the finest moments of my performance as a public defender. Then I tell her about Picciafuoco's phone call, the invasion of my office by the First Lady, the cell phone, the threatening phone call, and the report to the police.

"So what it means is that they want to hire you," she says after I'm done summarizing the salient points.

"That's the way it looks."

"It must mean you're good."

I strike a pose.

"Oh, please."

"And you turned them down."

"Exactly."

She taps her lips with the index and middle fingers of her right hand, tosses her hair back, gets to her knees on the bed.

"You know what I think? The fact that you turned them down is exactly what convinced them that you're the right man for the job."

"It strikes me as a somewhat optimistic opinion," I say, wondering at the same time what's become of my underpants.

"Look, I can think of hundreds of lawyers who would falsify documents to be in your position. Whoever it is has powerful people behind him, don't you doubt it."

I'm on the verge of responding, but Alessandra Persiano's gaze blurs as she pursues another thought, so I skip it.

"But there's something that strikes me as strange," she says.

"What."

"I mean strange. Odd, I guess."

"What does."

"The interrogation."

"The interrogation?"

"Yeah. The judicial interrogation in the assistant district attorney's office."

"Strange how? I don't get what you mean."

"Usually the ADA doesn't conduct a judicial interrogation in cases like this. That is, he ought to, in theory, but in practice he skips it. The Carabinieri just send him a transcript of their interrogation, he checks to make sure that the arrest was done in compliance with the law, and then he immediately asks the preliminary judge to confirm the detention."

Really? I think.

"Yeah, I know," I say.

She goes on thinking, staring into empty space.

"As if he were interested in talking to him, this Burzone."

"You think?"

"Well, I don't know. I could be wrong."

She drops her suspicion.

"Why would someone send me a cell phone?" I ask, changing the subject. "What's it mean?"

"I don't know. But with people like that you can't always go looking for a meaning. It's not like it's the Mafia, communicating metaphorically. If you ask me, that's exactly what they want, for you to wonder what it means. They want you to feel confused, frightened. They're trying to hem you in, you see."

"Yeah, I thought the same thing, though maybe not in such analytical terms," I reply, feeling depressed.

She strokes my hair.

"Oh, stop worrying, it's not like anybody's threatened to kill you. They just want you defend the guy. And since you told them you wouldn't do it, they're asking you again, in the only buffoonish way they know how, that's all."

"Yeah, I know, but still . . . "

She moves closer to me.

"It's complicated, the work we do, you know that, Vincè. I understand the way you feel about it. That's why I got out of criminal law. People don't understand these contradictions."

I say nothing.

"Anyway, don't make a big deal about it. If you don't want to take the case, they can't force you to. They'll get tired of asking, and they'll look for someone else."

I nod, but I'm not convinced.

"There's just one thing," she asks me suddenly. "Why don't you want to defend this guy?"

"Because I wouldn't know where to begin" is the answer that I can't give her.

"I don't want to get mixed up with these people."

She glances at me, skeptically.

"So, wait a minute, how did you wind up representing him at the interrogation? Were you standing in for someone?"

"No, I was appointed by the court," I answer without thinking.

"Now come on, Vincè," she says, clearly not satisfied. "You don't just get appointed as a public defender. *You have to sign up for it.* You signed up, didn't you?"

There's an accusatory note in her voice now.

"In fact," I admit.

"And when you signed up to work as a public defender, who exactly did you think you would be representing? The crème de la crème?"

Hm. Well, you'd better answer her.

"You have a point. I don't even know why I did it. I thought it was something that interested me, maybe."

She turns all understanding again.

"But then, when it came to it, you lost interest."

"Right."

She strokes my forearm.

"I was afraid that you'd do the same thing with me."

"My self-esteem is not exactly flourishing," I say.

She takes me by the chin and turns me in her direction.

"That's why I like you."

We kiss.

"I don't want to take this case," I whine a second later.

"So don't take it."

"Oh, you make it sound so easy."

"If you ask me, you shouldn't have let the wife come up to your office."

"I told her I wouldn't take the case."

"Yeah, but afterward."

"So are they going to make me pay for the insult?"

"No, on the contrary, the minute you turned them down you confirmed that you're a good lawyer, I told you that. And in fact, they went ahead and fired Picciafuoco."

"I don't get it. It's not like I'm a famous lawyer."

"And it's not like they're asking you to represent Don Vito Corleone. Mimmo 'o Burzone, as he calls himself, is a complete nobody."

"Oh, thanks so much."

"It was just a way of telling you that they're not trying to put you through some test. You did nice work for them and they want to try you out, you understand," she becomes more and more convinced as she talks, "so they start you out defending an underling, a foot soldier. Burzone is just like a fence for stolen cars, his little basement workshop is like a chop shop. They bring him the loot and he breaks it down. He's probably never even seen his employers. Look, this could be a big opportunity for you, if you're interested in getting into criminal law."

"Are you recommending I take the case?"

She fans herself with her hands.

"Oooh, Vincè. You know what time it is?"

"Why do you ask?"

She glances over at the radio-alarm clock on the bedside table.

"I have an appointment in my law office in less than an hour. And if you consider that it takes me at least half an hour to shower and get ready, you tell me how much time we have."

"Ah," I say, finally catching her drift.

HERE COMES THE CAVALRY

Everyone knows—though nobody seems to know the reason why—that as soon as it starts raining, sidewalks become crowded. Hordes of pedestrians with furrowed brows suddenly pour out into the streets, with the obvious objective of getting home. People are suddenly there—who knows where they were just a few seconds ago—as if they had hurried outdoors just to hurry back indoors. So you see these columns of streetwalker-men that form along the walls of the apartment buildings, taking turns standing under the balconies.

I too, having just left Alessandra Persiano's apartment building in an enviable psychic and physical condition, join the line. It's sort of like queueing up for a vaccination—that's how slow the line is progressing. The more impatient line-standers lift up on the tips of their toes to try to identify the obstacle. One elderly gentleman right behind me says that he's going to be late paying a bill, and then starts laughing to himself. Somebody else emits a series of unrepeatable vocalizations. I have that delightful sense of warmth in my veins of having just made love, and I take it all very tolerantly. It's not raining all that hard.

The line starts moving again, and a short distance later I discover that the cause of the pedestrian traffic jam consists of a piece-of-shit thug sending text messages on his cell phone, stretched out practically full-length on a motor scooter that he thoughtfully parked on the sidewalk, directly under a sheltering balcony.

What would you estimate the width of a city sidewalk on a secondary street to be? Five feet, to be generous? Place in the middle of that sidewalk an overweight motor scooter of the latest generation (the ones with seats that look like club chairs and all of the various accessories that go along with them), and you can easily guess how little room is left over. Of course, there's not a policeman around, even if you called one in. And if there was one, you can just imagine how that would go.

I take a look at the perpetrator of this scandalous occupation of public property. He is tall, unmistakably reckless, with the physical arrogance of someone who chooses to appear dangerous and most likely is. His mouth is half-open, and even though half his face is concealed by a pair of sunglasses absolutely outsized in relation to the oval of the underlying face, he wears an idiotic expression, the kind of expression people put on just to annoy anyone looking at them. He's wearing a fishnet T-shirt and a pair of multi-lacerated jeans whose crotch, even in that languid position, sags practically to his knees. He has the bulked-up arms of a body-builder and tattoos that are even more despicable than, to use a debatable term, the *clothing* that he's wearing. His cell phone probably cost, at a glance, 400 euros or so.

But the most depressing aspect of this act of open contempt for pedestrians is the fact that nobody says a thing. People snort in annoyance, and they might even curse through clenched teeth, but they navigate around this abusive squatter and move on, leaving the affront to public utility behind them. The consequence of this forced detour is that the aspiring Camorrista has pissed on the territory, marking it as his own.

All this is an official communiqué, a memorandum, sent periodically to remind that you are living under a state of siege.

I can't take any more marketing campaigns hatched by disorganized crime, by dogs off their leashes who engage in criminal narcissism and gratuitous murder as a form of self-promotion and propaganda (because that's what they are, the purse snatch-ings that end in violence, the robberies that are preceded by murders, the pedestrians beaten bloody for no discernible profit, the faces slapped by motor scooters passing at speed, or even just the simple exhibitions of rudeness and annoyance like this one: they're commercials. Display ads. Press releases).

The point is that you can refuse to accept certain provoca-tions. It's just that you pay for that kind of refusal with your self-respect. And here's the problem with paying in self-respect: it seems like you're not spending much, but then you find your-self throttled by the interest.

And so, what's new, you say, Well, this time, I'm not paying. I'm not going to play along with this ring around the motor scooter. Fuck 'em. And I don't even give it a lot of thought: when it's my turn, instead of going around him, I stop.

After a few seconds the hooligan registers the fact that I'm motionless. He looks up from his cell phone and focuses on me from behind his super-boorish black sunglasses.

"Something you need?" he asks.

I think of Alf, of what must go through his mind at times like these, of his complete lack of fear, and I screw up my courage.

"Yeah, the sidewalk," I answer him, expecting at the very least a head-butt in the face in response.

Instead he snaps his cell phone shut, removes his sun-glasses, puts them on the handlebars of his scooter, tilts his head to one side, bugs out his eyes, opens his lips, sticks out half an inch of tongue, and starts drooling intentionally, getting his T-shirt all wet. The most disgusting thing I've ever seen in my life. Why doesn't he just drop dead?

"You really are a piece of shit, you know that?" I say, unable to control my words.

The thug's eyes realign and focus on me with all the cun-ning of a reptile. A grimacing sneer is stamped on his lips. He immediately suspends his pantomime of an epileptic fit, he wipes his mouth clean with the back of his wrist, and he prepares for the massacre.

I can't hear or see a thing. All around me, everything is silent and motionless. I squint my eyes to see as little as possible, sort of like when you're about to have a car crash and your instincts automatically censor the horror that's about to arrive.

How much time goes by, an instant or two? It feels like ten thousand instants. But the strange thing is that none of what I'm expecting happens. Because the arm of a third party intervenes between us, and a fist flashes down like a cleaver onto the hooligan's shoulder, knocking him back into a seated position with an impact so powerful that the motor scooter almost drops off its kickstand.

"*Aaah*," moans the unfortunate thug, and he touches his shoulder with genuine compassion.

At that point, I start to focus again.

Where did this savior, maybe 5'3" tall, short and stout, thick tar-black hair, square jaw, marginal forehead, disproportionately short legs, K-Way jacket, and running pants, come from? And how on earth, with the body type that he has, does he manage to hit as hard as he does? From the way the miserable hooligan's arm is dangling, I'd have to guess he fractured his shoulder.

I step forward impulsively, in a completely reckless manner, to take part in some way in the events that I've caused; but as I'm on the verge of stepping into the combat zone my defender halts me with a wave of his left hand, as if to say: "Don't worry, I've got this."

The stunning detail is that in order to show me this act of courtesy, he actually turns in my direction, completely ignoring his adversary, who in fact immediately takes advantage of the opportunity to land a straight punch with his good arm, striking him on the right cheek with a sound that comes out, roughly, *chock*.

Whereupon we all three go to our corners and take a pause.

I expect at this point that my volunteer gorilla is going to fall to his knees and then pass out, leaving me to the tender mercies of the thug, who will take advantage of the opportunity to take his revenge on me, giving me change back from my dollar, as we used to say when we were kids. Instead, the gorilla looks down at the ground, adjusts his jaw with one hand, and then turns toward his unfortunate assailant.

Then everything happens in a sequence straight out of Italy's Most Horrible Home Videos. The dwarf—and I now notice what remarkably long arms he has—grabs the hooligan by the hair at the back of his head. The thug doesn't even try to put up resistance, as if he were curious about the treatment he's about to receive. The little powerhouse jerks the thug's head toward him with one sharp pull, preparing himself for the toss.

The sound of his nasal septum stamping violently down on the scooter's handlebars comes just a second later.

Ooomammamia, says a fishwife, grabbing my jacket and hiding behind me.

An unnatural silence descends over the street.

The thug emerges from his encounter with the handlebars looking like a Futurist version of himself. Disfigured and with one arm dangling, he starts his motor scooter and putts off, sobbing.

Whereupon, like a videotape when you take it off pause, reality begins to flow normally again. Traffic begins flowing, people get moving, the knot of rubberneckers begins their post-game commentary. You can already hear the voice of the impromptu editorialist, pleased at the thoroughness of the beating.

I'm standing there, semi-traumatized.

The cave-dweller turns and looks at me.

"That's all taken care of," he says.

I nod, automatically, since it strikes me as in poor taste to express my gratitude.

"Are you hurt at all?" the beast asks me.

"Me?" I reply. It sounds like a joke to me.

"Yeah, you."

"No, not at all."

He moves toward me and wraps his left arm around my waist, inviting me to come with him.

"Come on, let's get something to drink, you're pale as a sheet."

I comply. The audience parts to make way for us. We walk past a first bar, and then a second, whereupon I start to wonder if I understood his invitation. We cross one street, then another, and then my unexpected bodyguard ushers me into the place that he evidently prefers.

"This is very kind of you," I say, accepting his offer to let me go in first.

He sketches out a courteous bow with his head.

"The least I could do."

The least I could do? I think to myself.

At that very moment, I recognize the voice.

The bar we've just walked into is called the Love Café, and it stinks like a heap of carrion, wafting odors of late-night casino, narcotics dealership, and marshaling yard for prostitutes. It has, I don't know, four picture windows overlooking the street, each of which is surmounted by a sign touting the varied attractions of the place: "Pastry Shop," "Gastro-Pub," "Coffee & Wine Bar," "Snacks & Foods," "Smith & Wesson" (just kidding), and other modern-day novelties. I've walked by it more than once, but I never dreamed it was like this inside. That is, I don't know if you're familiar with this impression, but it's an unmistakable impression: there are places that, even if you see that they've spent lots of money fixing them up, and used top-notch materials and hired professional designers, still the minute you walk in you catch a whiff of organized crime. Like you'd be willing to bet a large sum of money that if you started banging away at any given wall with a pickaxe, before long a human leg would flop out.

I swear there are times when I have to if wonder if there is a specific curriculum for a degree in the architecture of the Camorra. If not, then I don't know how to explain this recurrent style in the buildings occupied by the Camorristi. In fact, I almost have the impression I could identify it from the materials, the architectural style in question. Most of all, it's the marble that transmits this horrendous sensation. And also the Venetian-style fauxing of the walls.

Among other things, if you ask me, the Camorra has a distinct preference for fuchsia. I wonder if it's the wives, or even more likely, the daughters of the Camorristi who impose this touch of class on the family places of business. Now, I don't want anyone to take me for a racist when it comes to fuchsia. But, when I walk into a restaurant or café or bar and I see a fuchsia wall with Venetian-style fauxing, I can't wait to get out of there, truth be told.

Among other things, these bars all seem to have names that drip with such a pornographic sentimentalism that you can spot the chip on the owners' shoulder from two hundred feet away: Love Café (in fact), the Inamorata Bar, Guys & Dolls, Walking on Air, Love a Little . . . (with the ellipsis), Let's Got Lost, The Last Kiss (okay, I invented most of these, but it was just to convey the style of the latter-day Camoralist).

So anyway, this is where I am right now.

The interior room we're ensconced in now is enormous, with mood lighting, and is practically empty, aside from a leather jacket draped over the back of a chair at the far end of the room, not far from certain horrible draperies that conceal the entrance, I imagine, to the restrooms.

Fuchsia continues to dominate in all directions, depressing

me, and on the facing wall—overlooking our little café table
with its floral ceramic surface and its wrought-iron base—is a
gigantic liquid-crystal television screen transmitting images of
a twenty-year-old woman in a workout costume, telling the television camera how unhappy and miserable she was until she
discovered Ab Swing. Just talking about the days when she still
wore size 18 pants makes her voice break (the show is dubbed,
by the way).

While waiting for the cavern-dweller, who has gone to the
counter to place his order in the meanwhile, I listen to her talk,
and as I notice that the television shopping channel is somehow (I can't say exactly why) perfectly in tune with the surrounding environment, I suddenly feel a frantic need to run
away, and I look in all directions for an emergency exit, which
a place like this must certainly have.

The troglodyte makes his return, this time in the company
of a young waitress with an irritated look on her face, probably
Polish by nationality. He pulls out a chair and takes a seat at
the café table.

"What'll you have, Counselor?" he asks, with the tone of a
part-owner of the bar.

"I'll take an espresso and a glass of mineral water."

"Mineral water how?" asks the waitress.

I don't bother to answer, because I find her tone to be
rather irritating.

And she snorts in annoyance.

"Bubbly or still?" the cavern-dweller prompts helpfully.

"It makes no difference to me," I say. And I glare at the
rude waitress, who misses it, turns on her heels, and heads
back to the front room.

"Aren't you having anything?" I ask my host.

"She already knows," he replies, tilting his head toward the
oafish waitress.

We sit in silence for a while, pretending to watch the televi-

sion shopping channel, which continues with a series of testi-
monials by miraculously fit young women who give all credit
to the Ab Swing crunch. By the time the second woman breaks
into an emotional lament, I can't take it anymore and I come
to the point.

"Listen, can I ask you something?"

"Of course you can."

"Were you following me?"

No answer.

"You were following me," I state.

He looks at me, doing his best to refrain from making a
comment that he'd prefer to spare me. A demonstration of delicacy that I would never have expected from a plantigrade of
his kind, truth be told.

"It's a good thing I was following you, Counselor. Otherwise
they'd be trying to put you back together right now."

For a split second I see myself, stretched out on a filthy gurney in an emergency room, half-conscious, while a couple of
rough male nurses slap me in an attempt to bring me around,
shouting into my face, demanding that I tell them my name.

"That may be," I admit, sensing the advent of a light facial
sunburn, "but I don't remember asking for a police escort."

The cavern-dweller raises both hands. It's a gesture that
makes me think of the tossing of the bone in the opening
sequence of *2001: A Space Odyssey*.

"Not a problem," he says.

And I translate: "This one's on the house."

"I have to say I enjoyed it," he adds.

"In what sense?" I ask.

"In the sense that you weren't afraid of that runt."

"No, in fact I wasn't," I confirm, with a lavish dose of vanity.

The bad-mannered waitress returns with our beverages; she
sets her tray down on the café table, offering an involuntary
glance down her shirt front to the cavern-dweller (who I

notice, to my astonishment, is no lecher), turns on her heel, and leaves.

I lift my left hand in the direction of her receding back, as if to say: "What, are you just going to leave the tray here?" but I immediately realize that I'm the only one who's noticed the oafishness of the service, because the cavern-dweller happily picks up his drink (one of those eighties-style cappuccino drinks), toasts me with a hoist in my direction, and takes a generous gulp, frothing his mustache with a coating of cream and some undefinable granulated substance.

"Do you think she attended hospitality school?" I ask, indicating the yokel-ette with a jerk of my head.

He turns to look in the direction I indicated, and stops to think about my observation. He thinks for a good long while. In any case, when he answers, he doesn't smile.

"Don't think that, she's always like that when new people come in."

"I imagine that's why the place is empty."

The guy keeps his cool. I can't tell if he's just not interested in the things I say, or if he doesn't understand them.

"Anyway, I haven't introduced myself, sorry," he says suddenly, remembering, "Tricarico. Amodio."

I wonder which is the first name and which is the last.

He puts down his drink and holds out his hand.

I shake his hand.

"I guess there's no need for me to tell you mine, right?"

He smiles. That one he understood.

I take a sip of water, pour some sugar into my espresso, stir it with the demitasse spoon.

"So what's that you're drinking?" I ask.

He replies, enthusiastically.

"This? It's a Bailès on the rocks. It's made with vodka, cream, nutmeg, cinnamon, ice, and of course, Bailès. But why are you laughing?"

I almost choke on my espresso.

Invent something, and don't waste any time doing it.

"Oh, it's nothing, I was just thinking about how the waitress left without taking the tray with her," I improvise, as I contract my lip muscles in a spasm and do my best not to choke.

He lowers his gaze to take in the tray and he sits there, contemplating it, wondering what's funny about the tray. Then he evidently gets tired of that, and shrugs.

I exhale a deep inner sigh, relieved to have dodged that bullet.

We go back to watching the Ab Swing show, and after a while I decide it's time to get up and get out of this local edition of "Candid Camera."

"Listen, I want to thank you, really very much. It was so kind of you to beat that guy up for me; I enjoyed the coffee too, but now I have to go."

I start to get to my feet.

"So, you're really not interested," whatshisname, Tricarico, catches me off guard.

I stand there, bowed over the café table, or actually over the tray, as if I'd just thrown my back out. I utter the next sentence in a tone of self-justification that I don't know where it comes from.

"No, look, don't take it personally, but I just can't do it."

He looks into the middle distance and shakes his head.

"That's too bad. That's really just too bad."

"And why is it too bad, if I may ask?" I say, even more of an idiot than before.

"It could have been a nice opportunity for you."

"How do you mean?"

He gazes at me compassionately.

"It's not like you've got much work."

I flush red.

"And what do you know about how much work I have?"

He waves his left hand, as if to brush away an annoying fly.

"No, that's okay, let's forget about it, if you're not interested there's no point talking about it."

I get stubborn.

"No, no, let's not forget about a damned thing. *What. Do. You. Know. About. How. Much. Work. I. Have?*"

Which is of course a completely moronic question. As if it were difficult to gather information about a lawyer. As if no one knows which lawyers are successful and which are just scraping by. As if you needed to hire a private detective to find out who's doing fuck-all. There's lots of us, that's how I comfort myself when I feel bad about my lack of work. We are the new invisible poor. The ones who'll never admit it openly. We're devastated by our professional sense of dignity, in the name of which we're ruining our lives. Give it a try yourself sometime, if you have nothing better to do: you will never find a lawyer or any other freelance professional, however desperately they're actually struggling in the market saturation of contemporary society, willing to tell you: "I make less than a waitress; if it wasn't for my family I'd shut down my law office tomorrow morning, but instead I walk around in a jacket and tie and pretend nothing's wrong." No two ways about it. No one'll spit out the truth. We're a majority locked in a conspiracy of silence. We have no union, we have no demands for better conditions. We're not dangerous. We live in a tepid bath of awkwardness and guilt complex. And all we do is grow in number.

"Well?" I ask, since the guy seems to be taking his time.

"Do you think that we don't know who we're talking to, Counselor?"

I take the point and recoil.

"Fine," I reply indignantly, "maybe I don't have a lot of work, as you say, but that doesn't mean I drop my pants the minute the first Camorrista who happens along decides that he wants me to work for him."

I lean back in my chair, resigned to the reaction that I imagine is going to follow this little volley of mine. But instead the cave-dweller looks at me as if I'd just passed some test with flying colors.

"That's exactly why we want you, Counselor."

Alessandra Persiano, I think, you're a genius.

"Meaning?" I ask, obscenely gratified at the idea that I've just enhanced this thug's opinion of me.

"That you're somebody who, when the time comes, really shows that you've got a pair of balls on you. You're a first-class lawyer, but nobody knows it. You just need an opportunity, that's all."

I couldn't agree more.

"What of it?" I say, continuing my lofty, indifferent act.

"Why should you miss this opportunity? Here you can make money, get into a river of work that just never stops; are you any lousier than the others, excuse me very much? Why shouldn't you profit from it yourself?"

I agree by saying nothing.

"And what would I have to do?"

A rhetorical question.

"Practice your profession. Be a lawyer."

Impeccable answer.

"I don't care much for your manners," I say primly, rapping knuckles at random.

"I do what they tell me, Counselor," he says, disarmingly.

"Why the cell phone?" I ask, now disgustingly accommodating.

"I don't know why."

"Ah, that you don't know! But you do know exactly how much work I have, don't you? What's going on here, you're intermittently knowledgeable?"

"There are lots of things I don't know, Counselor, believe you me. I do what they tell me, as I told you."

I don't know why, but I believe him.

"Now listen to me," he resumes, "this is the last time we're going to bother you. After this, we won't ask you again. We're looking for new lawyers, fresh, untested, so we don't have to put up with the same old ones."

"Why is that?"

"Because they charge too much, and they never lift a finger."

Whereupon I imagine a plenary working session of Mafia capos, maybe sitting around an oval conference table, making a collective decision. "Sure," they say, "let's get some young blood into the organization, we should recruit young lawyers." So they send out Tricarico to do some scouting.

"If you accept, we'd treat you with the utmost respect and courtesy. We've always been professionals with our lawyers, just ask around. Give it a try, what would it cost you? If we get along, it's a win-win."

"But what if we don't get along? What if, let's say, you're not happy with my work?"

He stretched both arms out wide.

"I don't see what you're getting at, Counselor. What are you afraid of? If we're not happy with your work, we'll just hire someone else. We're not idiots, we're not going to try to hold on to someone who loses cases, excuse me very much."

I sit there saying nothing, rendered speechless by his impeccable argumentation, to the point that I wonder how I could have failed to see things in such a clear and uncomplicated light before this. But what truly overwhelms me, because it qualitatively alters my state of mind, is the fact that a tough little hitter verging on dwarfism, who pronounces Bailey's "Bailès" and works as a PR advance man for the Camorra, is actually putting his trust in me. I hate to admit, but I get a thrill out of it. Jesus, am I really that desperate? Does it take so little to win me over?

"So, what's it going to be?" Tricarico sums up.

I wonder to myself why it is that decisions always have to be made on the spot. The answer's simple: because that's how decisions are made. People who take more time to make a decision are just putting it off, and when the time comes, they'll still have to decide on the spot.

"I have to think it over," I say after a short while, well aware that I'm on the verge of accepting.

"We can't wait any longer, Counselor, the hearing is tomorrow."

"What do you mean, tomorrow?"

"Eh. Look: they arrested Mimmo on Monday; you attended the judicial interrogation the next day, that is, within twenty-four hours; the ADA asked the preliminary judge to validate the grounds for detention within the following forty-eight hours, and in the next forty-eight hours after that, the preliminary judge scheduled the hearing, which will be tomorrow morning. What with one forty-eight-hour deadline and another forty-eight-hour deadline, you get to the maximum time frame of ninety-six hours, right? You get the same numbers, don't you?"

There you are. The first embarrassing oversight.

"Ah, certainly, of course I do. You know, after all this time, I'd completely forgotten, seeing as how I'd turned down the case the first time."

Pause.

Tricarico smiles with satisfaction.

I hadn't even meant to put that clause into the pluperfect tense. "The first time."

I swear.

FOUNDATIONS

I spend the evening poring over a handbook on the code of criminal procedure, like one of those students who think they can pick up, maybe not the entire curriculum, but at least the fundamentals, the night before finals.

Clearly, the idea that you can pick up the fundamentals at the last minute, as if they were lying there waiting for anybody who happens along, ready for a one-night-stand, reveals a vulgar and opportunistic concept of fundamentality.

Only somebody who believes they are a genius—which is to say, only an idiot—can hope to perform that order of mental acrobatics. Because you don't know in advance just what the fundamentals are. And most importantly, you don't know exactly where to find them. They shift around, is what the fundamentals do: it's why they're so tricky. It's my very frequent experience, for instance, that I set out to look for something fundamental where I left it last time, and it's just not there anymore.

And to make a long story short, long live sincerity, I spent the evening, and well into the night, hunting down those fundamentals of criminal procedure that I ought to know before the hearing to determine whether or not Mimmo 'o Burzone's detention would be confirmed. At this point, I don't even know when the hearing is supposed to begin, since we've already been sitting here waiting for an hour and ten minutes (Burzone, escorted by prison guards, hasn't been waiting anywhere near as long) and nobody seems to be calling us.

To be fair and to be truthful, I should point out that my search for fundamentality was rendered considerably easier by the fact that I could restrict that search to the field of activity in which we are about to engage, that is, the confirmation of detention. So, even in the bookstore, literally then and there, I went straight to the letter C in the index of the handbook that I then purchased, but the entry for "confirmation of detention" was conspicuous by its absence.

Whereupon I experienced an onset of panic (theories that are confirmed in practice almost always result in an onset of panic), because there I was, in the actual presence of a case of the self-concealment of a fundamental that refuses to be found where you would logically think to look for it. You read: "co-conspirator," and directly below it, "contempt of court." Between them, nothing. Where the fuck has confirmation of detention gone, you start to ask heatedly; is this or is this not a list in alphabetical order, after all? Obviously, at this moment, you are simply encountering the cold hard reality of your own profound ignorance. Later, when you do find it, the confirmation of detention (because, after extensive rummaging through the index, you do find it), you feel like telling yourself: "Ah, why certainly, of course." The truth is that you're a donkey and you know it perfectly well, because your initial instinct guided you to look for it in the wrong place, the place that all the donkeys who take the easy way inevitably wind up, not to put too fine a point on it.

And anyway, when I finally did find it—the confirmation of detention, that is—(it was a short inset under the longer block of entries in a chapter devoted to precautionary measures of the judicial police), I concluded with a considerable sense of relief that a few hours of hard concentration ought to get me through this after all. If you want to know the whole story, I even had the vague impression that details and notions were starting to come back to me.

In fact, after a couple of hours of full immersion, my criminal law joints were starting to creak a little less. At a certain point, I even realized that the fingers of my left hand were holding the placket of my shirt front, just beneath the collar—the ancestral posture of the Roman jurisprudent, a pose that Italian criminal lawyers assume when they grip the lapel of their judicial robes, their hand roughly over their heart: a detail that when you notice it, you're not sure whether it inspires a note of anthropological appreciation or a Bronx cheer.

Around 9:40 P.M., I had developed a preliminary working reconstruction of the procedural state of affairs, noting the following points:

1) we were still in a phase of preliminary judicial investigation;

2) the preliminary judicial investigation was under the supervision of the assistant district attorney, to whom the judicial police reported directly;

3) the judicial police, who had probably been keeping an eye on Burzone for some time already, or else perhaps were operating on a tip, must have caught him red-handed in the unearthing of a hand in the backyard, arrested him, and taken him before the assistant district attorney within the initial twenty-four-hour period required by law;

4) the ADA had questioned Burzone (represented by me as court-appointed counsel because it had been impossible to track down Picciafuoco), and had then requested within forty-eight hours from Burzone's arrest a confirmation of detention from the preliminary judge and now, that is to say, in the forty-eight-hour period following the ADA's request, the preliminary judge would have to issue a finding concerning the confirmation of detention—every step of this process falling within the span of ninety-six hours as prescribed by Article 13 of the Italian Constitution, a point that had been

cogently and brilliantly underscored by Tricarico during our meeting in the Love Café;

5) the hearing for the confirmation of detention would take place in the deliberation room, that is, in an office, without an audience, with the preliminary judge and the required presence of the defendant's legal representation, which is to say, me, at least at this point. The ADA could just stay home as far as the procedure was concerned, simply forwarding his requests in written form. If he wanted, Burzone could skip the hearing as well. In the case that Burzone was present (and I hoped he would be, since I had accepted his case), the preliminary judge would question him, then he or she would listen to my points in all cases (that's exactly what the code of criminal procedure says: "in all cases," as if it was reluctant to leave that up to the discretion of the judges), and then proceed to issue a finding, either confirming the detention or declaring the arrest illegitimate and setting Burzone free (this second hypothesis was one that I felt I could safely rule out).

That takes care of the procedural aspects.

As for the matters of fact, I wondered on the other hand exactly what Burzone was being charged with. All right, they'd found a human hand in his backyard. So what? Exactly what crime was Mr. Cool ADA planning to try to pin on him? Murder? Concealment and/or elimination of a corpse? Article 416-*bis*, seeing that Burzone was working for the Camorra? And even if they chose to pursue the theory of Article 416-*bis*, is it enough to catch somebody with a human hand buried in their backyard to charge them with association with the Mafia? Or were there other elements of evidence pending against Burzone that were far more incriminating but about which I knew nothing? It was all pretty muddy.

According to Article 388 of the code of criminal procedure (which I now knew), when an ADA interrogates an arrestee, he must inform the suspect of the crime under investigation, the reasons for his arrest, the evidence or testimony against him, and even the sources of that evidence or testimony, unless so informing him might undermine the investigation. But now, thinking back, I could no longer say whether the ADA had done those things or not during the judicial interrogation. I was too focused on finding a way to get out of that office as quickly as possible. The one thing I know he did, Mr. Cool, was to ask Burzone over and over what his name was. In fact, when I objected that he was hammering at Burzone with this continual repetition of first and last name instead of telling him what he was accused of, I think that instinctively I was referencing Art. 388. Maybe I even remembered it, who can say? There are so many different ways of remembering things.

Anyway, I'd had nothing in my hands, no paper, no photocopy, no document, that stated the crime of which Burzone was being charged. At the end of the interrogation, this I remember clearly, I had signed the transcript (in fact the clerk of the court had called me back to sign it, since I was walking out of the office blithely forgetting that detail), but I hadn't stayed long; in fact, I hadn't even bothered to read what was written on it. So I had to study up on the concealment of corpses, the elimination of corpses, murder, and, as long as I was at it, Article 416 *bis*, which can always come in handy. I had only crude approximations to work from, in other words.

One thing struck me as certain: Burzone must have found the hand that the dog had made off with only after getting rid of the cadaver, because if he had interrupted his butchering to go out into the backyard in search of the hand and then been arrested, the police would have found the *corpus delicti*, or maybe I should say the dead-body *delicti*, or better still, all-that-remained-of-the-dead-body *delicti*, in his little, let us say, basement autopsy workshop, and in that case he would have been well and truly fucked.

This evidence of far-sighted planning proved two things:

one, Burzone was no fool, and two, the prosecution had nothing other than the hand that was found in the backyard.

I was feeling a rush of reassurance at this second conjecture when, at exactly 10:12 P.M., I received a text message from Alessandra Persiano: THIS IS STARTING WELL, it said. Whereupon I immediately tried to call her, but her cell phone was turned off. It serves me right, I said to myself, what an oafish pig I am.

I walked back and forth in my bedroom for a while, talking to myself and continually losing the thread. Then I went back to studying, and after rereading the hearing for the confirmation of detention for the eleventh time I said, Enough is enough, Vincè, you've learned the hearing for the confirmation of detention, you've even repeated the hearing for the confirmation of detention aloud from memory, you're going to dream about the hearing for the confirmation of detention tonight, don't you think you've done enough? I was heading for the kitchen with the general idea of poking around in the fridge when my cell phone rang, so I ran back into the bedroom, all excited at the thought that Alessandra Persiano had seen my phone calls and was calling me back; I was so impatient that I didn't even look at the display and when I said hello, who did I hear at the other end of the line? Not Alessandra Persiano but Nives, who said, "Ciao, I didn't think I'd find you home at this time of night."

"Where did you think I'd be?" I replied. Baffled and more than a little confused, I have to admit.

"I don't know," she said, all sugary. "I don't have any idea of what you do with your evenings since we stopped living together, Vincenzo."

At that point I got my bowels all in a twist. What the fuck, I thought to myself, where is all this sweetness coming from? My emotions crossed their arms and put down their tools, as if to turn to me and say: "Uh, what are we supposed to do now, boss?"

Listen here, Nives, I should have told her at this juncture, I should tell you that *probably*, and I ask you to note that I qualified that with a *probably*, I'm at the very beginning—I really don't even want to say this, you know—the beginning of a relationship with another woman, and guess what? I like her, in fact I like her a lot, we made love for the first time this afternoon, in fact, and how was it you ask? Great, in fact, better than great, if you really want to know. What? you can't think of anything to say now? And after I left her apartment a PR executive for the Camorra with arms longer than his legs beat some hooligan bloody on my behalf, after which he invited me to come have a drink with him in an absolutely ghastly bar where he tried to convince me to represent one of their employees who specializes in the butchering and disposal of dead bodies (before that, he had also given me a cell phone as a gift, a cell phone that I took to the police, but we can skip over that part of the story). I'm not even going to try to explain it all to you, but in the end I took the case, it would just be too long and complicated to explain, anyway I agreed, and I've just spent the last two hours studying up on hearings for confirmation of detention and in the midst of all this confusion, as you can easily imagine, I forgot to call up the woman I was telling you about, and by this point she is well and truly pissed off at me, and in fact she's turned off her cell phone, and who can blame her, so to top off the day that I just described to you, what do you do? You call me? You act all jealous? You ask me how I spend my evenings? You hint (oh, it's the second time that you've tried this, what do you think, that I don't notice?) that you want me, do you think this is the time for that? After I told you off in the middle of a therapy session, among other things? Why do you have to make my life more complicated, when I'm already plenty confused without any help from you, thanks very much? Why is it that you never take these initiatives when they would do some good? Where are you when I'm banging my head against the wall in despair and I feel as lonely as a coyote so that I practically start howling at the moon? And when these waves of disquiet come over you, instead of destabilizing ex-husbands, why don't you just wrap your arms around your monumentally insipid architect and go out to dinner with him in one of those minimalist restaurants that serve curled ribbons of tuna in an orange mousse or fagottini with hazelnut butter in an amarone wine sauce or whatever? Maybe you should go plan a weekend in Cortina or Cortona, why don't you take your pick, and just let me try to forget what's happening with this other woman?

But what I said was, "No, I don't go out nights."

She waited a little while before asking the next question, nasty thing that she is.

"Are you alone?"

Now you're going just a bit too far, I thought to myself.

"No, I'm not alone," I replied.

But I don't know why I said it. Maybe because there was a kernel of truth in it, all things considered.

Then she plunged into a glacial silence and then she started stammering and saying excuse me, I didn't mean to, I didn't know that, I couldn't have imagined, I never should have, and things like that.

And she almost hung up on me in her haste to get off the line.

I looked down at the cell phone in my hand, as if to say: "How about that." And I took a few short strolls around the perimeter of the bedroom, just to stretch my legs.

I called back Alessandra Persiano but her cell phone was still turned off. So I tried her landline, dialing *67# before the phone number so that my own number would be concealed. I didn't feel like making her abstinence official after I'd tried her in vain on her cell phone, what the fuck, but either she wasn't home or if she was, she didn't want to answer, so I said, Fine, she wants to make me pay, and I went into the kitchen and made myself a Harmonious Cream of Zucchini and Squash. Then I went to bed, but I left my cell phone turned on, in fact I had it within easy reach on the nightstand, truth be told.

After a couple of hours of partial sleep, I saw my cell phone was blinking. It was Nives again, a text message. I WANT TO TALK TO YOU, it said, YOU OKAY FOR LUNCH AT TWO O'CLOCK AT IL SERGENTE?

SI, I wrote back, without even putting the proper accent on the 'i'—*sì*—and at that point I turned off my cell phone because it really was time to call it a day.

So now here I am, sitting in the vestibule of the prison office reserved for judges, waiting for the hearing to begin. Tricarico came to pick me up with his Vespa, even though I had told him not to bother.

"Good Lord, Counselor, it's the least I can do," he had argued on the phone. "What are you supposed to do, take a bus to the prison?"

"What do you mean, take a bus?" I said, skipping the second half of the response, which goes: "Look, you bumpkin, I do own a car, you know. Okay, it's a 1999 Ford Fiesta, but I just installed new floor mats."

And it's not like he drives a Rolls Royce, after all.

But I was in no condition to explain all that to him, worried as I was about the hearing, Alessandra Persiano's protracted eclipse, and Nives's phone call; so I told him, "Fine, okay, don't worry about it, swing by and have done with it."

Then, when we pulled up in front of the prison, a colleague of mine whom I know and who was just leaving the building, stopped to watch me dismount from the Vespa as if to say, What are you doing on a Vespa driven by that guy? Whereupon it occurred to me that it was a pretty good question, so I adjusted my blazer and turned to thank Tricarico for the ride,

making it unmistakably clear in that manner that it was time
for him to clear out and get gone and stay gone. For good.

"At your service," he replied, completely missing the point.

I started toward the front gate, but since I didn't hear the
sound of the Vespa taking off, I turned around and glimpsed
the erect figure, shall we say, of Tricarico, contemplating the
street with the passivity of a taxi driver waiting for his fare.

I sketched out an interlocutory "No" with my head, as if to
say: "Why on earth aren't you leaving?" Since he didn't react
in any way, I went back and asked him, clearly, why he hadn't
left yet.

"Then how would you get back home?" he said.

"That's not your concern," I replied.

"Then what am I doing here waiting?"

"Exactly," I said.

And I turned on my heel, just to emphasize the point.

In the yellowish-grey waiting room where I'm sitting right
now there are two other lawyers that I've never seen before.
They're talking about soccer, exchanging insipid observations
and the kind of wisecracks that sophisticated professionals
turn out all day, so jaded that they no longer pay any attention
to their surroundings, because they've seen it all. In their opinion, anyone who lays eyes on them will remain captivated and
intimidated by their false cynicism.

Except that false cynicism has to have the right sort of context to be properly appreciated. And in this place, there's
nobody—except for me, Burzone, and the guards, and you can
imagine how little they care—who can appreciate the false cynicism of these two.

I mean, if you go in to have a sonogram and the sonogram
technician is talking about taxes with the nurse while he rubs
the probe back and forth over your belly, then you're in the presence of a successful example of false cynicism, because while on

the one hand it might strike you as disrespectful for a doctor to talk about taxes while he's composing a Futurist portrait of your digestive tract on the computer screen, just try to imagine the state of paranoia that would assail you if he did the sonogram in silence, concentrating exclusively on the blobs and squiggles chasing each other around on the monitor and maybe even stopping now and then to think about them.

False cynicism is the conceit of a professional who wants to show the world that he's elsewhere while those who rely upon his professional services are in a state of enforced immobility. Now it's obvious that there is no one in this waiting room who relies upon the professional services of these two bags of hot air and who would therefore have any reason to hang around and drink in their unwelcome false cynicism.

And the unbelievable thing is that these two sad sacks don't even realize that they're staging a show without an audience. They're putting on a whole song and dance for themselves, as we like to say down here. And yet they keep it up. They laugh, they slap each other on the back, they discuss and debate, they egg each other on. How they manage, I couldn't say. The guards huff and puff in annoyance and fan themselves, among other things. Why do these guys think the guards are huffing and puffing and fanning themselves, because it's hot? After all, we're in the cooler, everyone in here's on ice, ha ha.

Burzone's sitting in a chair, arms folded across his chest, legs crossed, looking as if he doesn't want to confide in anyone. When the guards (two of them, with potbellies and paintbrush mustaches: whenever you see two prison guards, they almost always seem to have potbellies and paintbrush mustaches) brought him in here, he looked at me as if to say: "So you're here, eh?"; and then not even *Buon giorno*.

I pulled out the standard form for appointing a defense lawyer, I walked over to him, and I practically slapped him in the face with it, telling him to fill it out and sign it.

"I got no pen," he said.

"Me either," I replied.

And I went back and sat down in the horrendous steel-and-green-plastic chair I'm sitting in right now.

Whereupon—I would have bet twenty euros that he was going to do it—one of the two false-cynical lawyers immediately hustled over to Burzone, slithering like an iguana, and offered him his fountain pen (which is more or less like someone in the street witnessing a furious spat between you and your girlfriend and the minute you walk off trying to pick her up).

Then Burzone showed the iguana how a real lady behaves: he turned away from him with disgust, obviously totally indifferent to the tacit proposal, shot me a glance of renewed esteem, asked one of the guards to lend him a pen, filled out the form to appoint me as his lawyer, signed it, and gave it to the guard to take it to me.

The iguana went back to talking about soccer, but the complete humiliation he had just endured remained embossed on his face.

At last the door of the office opened and a male secretary appeared, with farsighted glasses, a comb-over, a preprinted form in one hand, and the general demeanor of someone whose work is miles beneath him.

I instinctively get to my feet, and am immediately filled with embarrassment at the action—Burzone is still seated, as stolid and phlegmatic as a viscount.

"Oh," I feel like telling him, "you're the one who might be staying in prison or might be going home; really, I'd recommend that you cross yourself because the odds are good in my opinion that you'll be eating in the prison dining hall again tonight, I don't know if you follow me; so why the fuck are you acting all imperturbable?"

The thing that has always annoyed me most about the arrogance of Camorristi, personally, is the nonchalance with which they put it on or take it off, depending on the circumstances.

Look at how self-sufficient he acts now. But the odds are good that before long he'll stage a pitiful show of begging for his freedom, and that he'll confide to the preliminary judge that for the past two days he's been doing nothing but thinking longingly of his family, speaking to the Madonna of Pompeii, and drinking nothing but water.

Because then, when they're down on their knees and imploring, Camorristi trot out fetishes and metaphors that even the hyper-Catholic militants of Communion and Liberation would feel the need to edit at least somewhat: his first-born son's first communion, his toddler boy's little pony, the drawing that his grade-school daughter did, with him coming home and the family waiting for him at the window (with an attempt at exhibiting said drawing by the defendant, halted in the nick of time by the presiding judge just as the defendant was extracting it from the breast pocket of his jacket), the wife who had an operation for her tumor though it looks like it might not be in remission after all, the pilgrimage that the whole family took to Lourdes, the medallion of Jesus Christ, kissed and rekissed after answering each question, the little villa in the subdivision purchased only after much scrimping and saving and sacrifice (the closed-circuit video cameras on poles sticking out of the walls at the corners of the villa, providing video security surveillance 24/7/365, I'm deeply tempted to add, just to see the expression on their faces). But then, when they're done begging, the look of sheer arrogance reemerges.

The false cynics take two steps back and call out in chorus, "*Buon giorno*, Carpinelli," to the secretary.

The secretary, who is obviously called Carpinelli, responds automatically but then gives them a look as if to say he must have met them somewhere before, but he can hardly be expected to remember, with all the lawyers he meets every day, leaving aside the famous ones, so there's really no point in the two of them greeting him by name as if they were famous themselves. Which they're not.

"Fantasia," he then announces in a loud voice.

The false cynics withdraw into a corner. The guard with the less-prominent pot belly of the two gives Burzone a shove on the shoulder, urging his ass up out of the chair. As I lightly touch the knot of my tie, I feel as if my heartbeat just accelerated slightly, and in fact it just has, but I almost get it muddled with the vibration of the cell phone that's bouncing around in the breast pocket of my jacket. I thought I'd turned it off.

I pull out the cell phone, look at the display in its frenzied announcement of an incoming call, and then I freeze to the spot.

Alessandra Persiano.

I'm so nonplussed by the obvious fact that she chose the worst possible moment to call me that I read and reread her name, as if I couldn't quite manage to remember who she is.

The guards lead Burzone into the office. I glimpse the preliminary judge sitting at his desk; no, make that: I see the preliminary judge sitting at her desk, since she's a woman, reading through the file.

The secretary stares at me in disbelief, completely scandalized at the idea that I might choose to answer my phone at this exact moment.

So I scandalize him.

"Hello."

My tone of voice is absolutely ambiguous.

Alessandra Persiano takes a good long pause before answering.

"What do you mean 'Hello,' don't you have my number in your cell phone directory anymore?"

I have a hot flash.

"Ale, I'm sorry, I can't talk right now," I say, lowering my voice, while Carpinelli, or whatever his name is, continues to stare daggers of disapproval at me that jar my nerves.

Another pause, grimmer than the first.

"No, *I'm* sorry. Forget it."

"No, what do you mean forget it?" I say, in horror. "Wai—"

But I'm talking to myself. She's already hung up.

I examine the unfamiliar object that's sitting in the palm of my hand. It's made up of two components: a tiny alphanumeric keyboard and a backlit screen at the center of which the name of an Italian company that I think I must have heard somewhere enjoys pride of place; surrounding it are an array of graphic squiggles that resemble, from left, a megaphone, a walkie-talkie, a magnifying glass, and a notebook. Beneath them, today's date and the time. I wonder just what purpose this curious device might serve.

Fucking pigshit.

Possible interpretations of Alessandra Persiano's sudden termination of the phone call:

a) she guessed that I was in a sticky professional situation and just hung up in order to avoid distracting me, intrinsically discreet person that she is;

b) she got the impression that I was acting aloof, since she hadn't answered any of my repeated phone calls (which is exactly what was happening), and she immediately expressed her opinion on the subject;

c) she thought that I was with another woman (because when a woman goes to bed with you she is automatically liable to assume that every other woman who meets you wants to do the same, even though you try to tell her that you only wish that were the case);

d) none of those options occurred to her, but the simple fact that I told her I couldn't talk offended her deeply and now she never wants to see me again.

I hardly need to tell you which interpretation strikes me as the most plausible just now.

In the meanwhile, Burzone has taken a seat across the desk from the preliminary judge, the guards have come back outside, and Carapelli or Carpinelli, whatever the fuck his name is, is still standing there, looking me up and down as if I were adjusting my fly or who knows what.

"Excuse me, but are you here for Fantasia?" he finally resolves to ask.

"Um-hmm," I say, distraught over the situation. I'm still holding my cell phone in my hand.

Then he says the wrongest thing he could ever have thought of saying.

"If you'd like to step in. And it might be best if you turn off your cell phone."

I put my cell phone back in my pocket. I take one step toward him, and I stop just *this* far away from his face.

"What did you just say?" I demand point-blank, with blood buzzing in my ears.

Piece of shit that he is, he turns pale.

"Only . . . that . . . maybe you could turn off your . . . phone," he stammers.

You know, I've had it up to here with the rules of etiquette invented by frustrated bureaucrats. I must have developed an allergy of some kind.

"Get the fuck out of my way," I demand through clenched teeth. I wave him aside with a scornful gesture, then I walk into the office.

The preliminary judge senses a squall brewing, looks up from her file, and focuses first on me, then on her secretary, who's standing right behind me, still dazed from the way I body-checked him.

Burzone, too, turns around to look with some alarm.

"*Buon giorno,*" I say.

"What seems to be the problem, Counselor . . . ?" asks the preliminary judge, suspiciously.

"Malinconico," I fill in the blank, satisfied that she recognized me as a lawyer; then, without measuring my words in the slightest, I come to the point.

"The problem is that this idiot"—and I point out the idiot in question by tipping my head in his direction—"had the gall to tell me to turn off my cell phone."

The secretary turns red, but he keeps his mouth shut. Burzone gives me a glance of mixed respect and concern over how things might turn out for him at this point. I just stand there, in the middle of the room, proud as punch and completely unrepentant.

The preliminary judge removes her reading glasses and looks up at me. She has a long, vaguely masculine face, pronounced cheekbones, a slightly off-center nose. She so strongly resembles Anjelica Huston that I have to make an effort not to tell her so.

"What?" She pretends not to understand. I'd bet thirty euros that she actually liked my entrance.

"I said 'idiot,' your honor."

"Moderate your language, Counselor."

If that was a smile that looked like it was trying to get onto her lips, she was very good at concealing it.

"I beg your pardon, judge. I'm mortified at appearing before you for the first time in such a, shall we say, informal manner."

She thinks that over.

"We don't allow cell phones to remain on during a hearing, Counselor."

"You are perfectly right about that, your honor. But in point of fact, the hearing had not yet begun. My cell phone rang outside, before I ever set foot in your office."

She looks at me. She looks at the idiot. She inhales. She exhales. All through her nose.

"Take a seat, Counselor. Let's get started."

I take a seat, beaming. Burzone too looks like the cat that ate the canary. The idiot sits at the right corner of the desk, bowed over the transcription form. Without bothering to glance at him, as if she were talking to a spinning tape recorder, Anjelica Huston begins dictating the elements of the hearing, and he takes down every word.

The ADA, as I expected, hasn't bothered to show up. For that matter, when the presence of one of the parties isn't required, why on earth go to the trouble of attending? He must have sent his written conclusions on confirmation of detention and, no doubt, a request for continued detention in prison. Nothing seems more likely than that this hearing will be over in ten minutes, or even less, with Anjelica Huston accepting the request of Mr. Cool by issuing a lovely decree of cautionary detention, Burzone going back to doing pushups on his cot, and me without a clue of what to do next.

I begin to resign myself. And I weep inwardly, thinking that I've spent my whole life waiting to see how things turn out.

The preliminary judge acknowledges the presence at the hearing of Burzone, she acquires (that's the way they say it) to the official case file my appointment as Burzone's fiduciary representative, and then she proceeds to interrogate Burzone, stating his first and last name, place of residence, marital status, certificates of study (completed junior high school), profession ("Currently unemployed"), real property ("None"), prior criminal convictions ("None": an entry that sounds even less likely than the preceding one): all information that she garners from the record of his arrest and which she dictates to the idiot in a totally flat voice, with the exception of his monicker (or, shall we say, his pseudonym). That she asks Burzone himself to confirm with measured (and just slightly bitchy) irony.

Burzone looks at me, I nod my head yes, and he confirms. I expect La Huston is going to want to have some fun by asking him the origin of his nickname; instead, to my relief, she skips over that detail.

"Well, now," she says, having gotten through the introductory ceremonies of the hearing, "we have here a case of disposal and concealment of a corpse."

Okay, I think to myself. That much I know.

"Would you care to tell me, Signore Fantasia, just what happened and how you come to be here?" she asks, crossing her forearms on the desk. It's a pose that I must have seen in at least four hundred movies. Okay, I know I'm repeating myself, but it really is incredible how we fail to realize how completely clichéd the poses that we continually strike really are. We ought to pay closer attention to it, I believe. For instance, now that I think about it, I seated myself in a very uncomfortable way, with my back rigid and my legs crossed without the slightest suppleness or relaxation, making an enormous effort to keep my shins aligned, and in fact my calves hurt now. In general, when I sit down, it's not anything like that.

Burzone shoots me another ocular request for authorization to answer the question. I nod yes again.

"Your Honor, what can I tell you? It was my daughter who wanted to get the dog, and she was going to drive me crazy if I didn't make her happy. What do I know about where the creature gets to and what it brings back home?"

"So you're saying that you have a dog that likes to collect souvenirs, Signor Fantasia?" La Huston observes.

"Sooveh-whats?" asks Burzone; he even leans over toward the secretary and tried to peek at the minutes, like a little boy trying to copy off the student at the next desk over. In these situations, you have to admit, his timing is impeccable. The preliminary judge, in fact, has an uptick of embarrassment, or really, a paralysis of embarrassment, and is rendered speechless.

"Listen, Your Honor," he resumes, taking advantage of the interval, "I told the assistant district attorney the same thing: I saw a little pile of dirt in the yard, I went out to take a look, I did some digging, and the next thing I know I'm in trouble. I don't know anything about the object that was in the hole, I swear it on the head of my baby daughter."

"The object," Anjelica Huston repeats, as if the generic nature of the expression had offended her intelligence; then she looks at me to make me feel guilty about representing him. It's a form of investigative racism that I've quickly become accustomed to, luckily for me.

"Your honor, excuse me," Burzone shoots back, "but are you saying that if someone comes to your house and finds a handgun, then that means it's yours?"

"Why, if they find a handgun in my house, who should I accuse, my next-door neighbor?" the judge retorts.

"Exactly," says Burzone, then falls silent; as if the preliminary judge had just confirmed his theory, instead of demolishing it.

Here the preliminary judge stumbles, doubting her own logic. She looks into the middle distance, probably doing her best to remember what she just said. Burzone sits there, with a face oozing good faith, as if the matter was all taken care of now.

Madonna, what a clever son of a bitch.

"I'd have to agree with your observation, judge," I break in, in a frantic attempt to hijack the interrogation from the ridiculous morass it's sinking into, "but, if you'll allow me the point, it is precisely when we come to the concept of *home* that the detention that I'd imagine the ADA has certainly asked you to uphold is most clearly baseless and false."

"Oh, really?" she tells me with her expression.

I go on, since by now I've got a running start.

"The *hand*, because what we are talking about is a hand, you're quite right on that point," I take a moment to lick her ass, because if you want to cover your own you've got to lick someone else's, "was found in Fantasia's backyard. And what is a backyard if it is not a virtual extension of an enclosed space, a sacred domicile, an unwalled piece of property?"

I take a breath. It strikes me that Anjelica's nose has gotten sharper. I continue.

"Inasmuch as it reproduces a greenery whose general lack is felt keenly in our modern world, a backyard is a bridge between the open air and the enclosed interior. It lies vulnerable to the intrusion of any and all passersby. It negates the concept of the home, even though it is at the service of the home. The master of the house is the master only when he is inside the house: the backyard strips him of that role. It is an architectural alternative to the claustrophobia of private ownership. It gratifies a desire for exposure. It's mine, and yet I allow the rain to muddy it, the wind to dishevel it, the stranger to enter it. And that is exactly why we cannot reasonably state that the limb in question was *in my client's home.*"

Here I break off. I have the feeling that Burzone, even though he hasn't understood a word, is dying to slap me on the back. Anjelica Huston listened to me the whole time with an expression hovering somewhere between "How about that?" and "Okay, okay, we get your point" and "What the fuck does this have to do with anything?"

I'm pretty satisfied with my own performance. A couple of lines I'd planned out at the drawing table, truth be told, but the rest was improvised. It's times like this when I think I can understand jazz.

"So you're of the opinion that the ADA has requested a confirmation of detention," the preliminary judge comments. "I wonder how on earth you found out such a thing. In any case, your definitions of *premises* and *property* are quite evocative. You really ought to be a writer, you know that?"

Burzone and I exchange a glance.

"I have a novel in my desk drawer, but the publishing houses keep sending me rejection letters," I reply.

La Schnozzola makes a superhuman effort to keep from bursting into laughter. Look at her, she's turned all red. That'll teach her to crack funny with lawyers she doesn't even know. Burzone also acts as if he's stifling a laugh, but I'm pretty sure he didn't even get the joke.

"Anyway, I'd like to know what you think of my observations about the backyard," I continue.

Hey, being a criminal lawyer is starting to look like fun.

"I'll tell you in my decree, Counselor, don't worry about that."

"It was out of interest, not worry."

"Well, then. Now, Signor Fantasia, you have stated that you know nothing about this object, as you call it, that was found in your backyard, and you believe that it might have been the dog that picked it up who knows where and then buried it, again, in your backyard."

"Eh."

"Would you mind answering 'yes' or 'no'?"

"Yes," I say.

"I need to hear him give the answer, Counselor," the preliminary judge sets me back on my heels. But from the way she scolds me I can tell she likes me.

"I apologize," I say. She nods, but with the simulated scolding that women use when they seem to be trying to convey to you that you have an account to settle, a reckoning to be made, I don't know if I convey the idea. I wonder why it is that for the past little while it seems as if women are aware that I exist.

"Yes," says Burzone, "that is, no, it's not that I believe it: I'm completely certain that it was the dog, and in fact, you found the dog's collar in the hole along with it, didn't you?"

"True," admits La Schnozzola, very seriously.

Whereupon I have a strange presentiment. Strange in the sense of positive.

"Your dog visits some eccentric places, Signor Fantasia," Anjelica resumes.

Burzone is about to say something, but I intimate silence with a wave of the hand.

"Why won't you let him speak, Counselor?"

"I didn't hear a question, judge."

She slumps back in her swivel chair.

"Okay," she says, giving me that point.

She puts on her glasses and lowers her head over the file. She turns to the idiot and resumes dictating rapidly.

"There's no point in my informing you of the ADA's recommendations, since the counsel for the defense has informed us that he is already privy to that information; I would imagine that counsel, in view as well of the lack of a criminal record on the defendant's part, would like to request that he be freed or, subordinately, be given house arrest. Would you concur, Counselor Malinconico?"

She looks up from the file and gazes at me.

"Quite right," I confirm, concealing my utter surprise, since I had forgotten or never known that at some point in the course of the hearing I might be expected to put forth a request or a demand myself. If not, what in hell was I even doing here, for that matter? Aside from explicating my theory of the backyard as an illusory negation of private property, of course.

The preliminary judge nods in her secretary's direction, and the secretary takes down her words fairly promptly.

"Okay," she concludes, "you can have a seat in the other room. It'll take us a moment to prepare the decree."

Burzone and I stand up in unison. I sketch out a sort of bow, he doesn't. At Anjelica Huston's behest, the idiot stands up to see us to the door. As he opens the door, he scrupulously avoids meeting my gaze. The guards greet me. One of them asks Burzone how it went. Burzone tilts his head in my direction (I notice it out of the corner of my eye, feigning complete ignorance as I do), and he traces a virtual comma down his cheek with his thumbnail, an age-old Italian signal that it's all good: I experience a warm glow, as I discover to my horror just how eagerly I aspire to win the esteem of this piece of flotsam washed up from the sea of organized crime.

In the waiting room, in the meanwhile, another prisoner has arrived, dressed in a tracksuit, loafers, bald dome, and facial features that would make anyone conclude then and there that Cesare Lombroso understood everything there was to know. The two false-cynical lawyers, who to all appearances constitute his defense team, cluster around him like squeegee men at a stoplight, one on this side, one on the other, talking at top speed, finishing each other's sentences, showing off transcripts and documents that the prisoner glances at with annoyance. A stomach-turning display.

"Who's that?" I ask one of the guards under my breath. I nod toward the prisoner.

"A piece of shit from hell," the cop replies to my question.

Oh really? And I was just assuming that once again the system had dragged in the wrong man.

"Okay, but what did he do?" I specify.

He lifts his pudgy hand and sketches out a couple of spirals in the air.

"Ah," I say, as if I'd understood.

Burzone comes over to me.

"How do things look now, Counselor?"

I shrug my shoulders.

"What can I tell you? Let's just wait and see."

"What if they send me back inside?"

"Not a forgone conclusion," I reply, in the tone of a scholastic hypothesis.

"Maybe if I told her something that she wanted to know, Her Honor would send me home."

I stiffen, hoping that Burzone isn't about to provide the answer I'm afraid of in response to the question I'm about to ask him.

"In what sense, if I may ask?"

"I was at least hoping for house arrest."

Which actually means: if it hadn't been for you, I might be about to get out of here.

In other words, not only have I defended this filthy creature, but I have to listen to him tell me that maybe things would have worked out better if I'd just stayed home.

I'm starting to wonder if I'm cut out for criminal law. Something about Camorristi seems to make me touchy.

"Are you guilty, Fantasia?" I snap, staring him in the eyes.

"Ah?" he says, startled.

"Do you dismember dead bodies and then bury them in the mountains, scattering the limbs to keep anyone from identifying the corpse?" I spell out in a crescendo.

"Counselor, what are you saying," says Burzone, with a very guilty little smile playing across his lips.

"You don't know anything about the hand they found in your backyard, do you?"

"No. Yes. That is, what do you mean? Of course I don't know anything," he gasps.

"Then what else could you have told the judge? You told her the truth, didn't you?"

Silence. He doesn't even answer that one.

"So, if you told the truth, then we have nothing to worry about. You have nothing on your conscience and I have nothing on mine, because I have represented a client who told the truth."

Full stop. Burzone is wrung dry. He has nothing left to say.

Well, he asked for it.

The preliminary judge's door swings open again. We see the idiot stick his head out with the usual sheet of paper in hand. We all stop talking. He just stands there, without a fucking word. We look one another in the eye. What is this, a guessing game?

"Fantasia," he finally decides.

We go back in.

"Have a seat," the preliminary judge invites us.

I take a seat. Burzone sort of sits down and sort of doesn't. The preliminary judge inhales a lungful before she begins expelling words.

"All right, Signore Fantasia, you're a free man."

"What did you say?" I ask.

"What'd you say?" asks Burzone.

The preliminary judge looks at me with something bordering on tenderness.

"We're releasing him, Counselor. He can go home."

I don't know if I'm capable of controlling the joy that's colonizing my face. I turn to look at Burzone. He's so overwhelmed by the news that he has practically no reaction. He's just standing there, his hands in midair, as if someone had hit pause on a remote control.

"There is insufficient evidence to order any measures of detention in your case," Anjelica Huston explains. "The one judicial order we will issue is for periodic scheduled visits to a parole officer."

At that point, Burzone starts giving off blazes of light. "Periodic scheduled visits" was, evidently, the password. He clasps his hands together, crosses his fingers, puts them to his lips, and kisses his crossed fingers a dozen times or more. Then, in a completely unexpected twist, he leans over me and gives me a hug. I try to extract myself, but he just grabs me tighter and goes on panting and drooling into my ear, muttering words that I can't understand. I'm not only immobilized, I'm baffled and embarrassed by this sudden piece of theatrics. Instinctively I work around the bulky thorax of Burzone as he continues to wrap his arms around me and sob with happiness to get a look at Anjelica Huston across the desk. She covers her mouth with one hand and laughs. I throw open my arms, signaling my surrender, in order to convey to Burzone that now it's really time for him to release me. And he finally lets me go. He's soaked the collar of my shirt and half my tie, I'm revolted to discover. I try to sort myself out with both hands, combing and straightening, while he dries his tears and does his best to recover, after which he thanks the preliminary judge and hurtles out of the room.

PRESSING

I emerge from the prison, catatonic, with my briefcase in one hand and a copy of the decree—which I don't even want to read—in the other.

"It was a pleasure to meet you, Counselor. I hope to see you again soon," said Anjelica Huston, ushering me out with an expression of professional esteem that veered dangerously close to the realm of the ambiguous. I glossed over it, because I have to say that I always find come-ons in the course of my duties just a bit awkward.

To be perfectly honest, I'm not a hundred percent sure that I'm happy with how it all went. Okay: Burzone was released from prison despite all expectations to the contrary, I come off looking masterful, the preliminary judge flirted with me throughout the hearing, and yet something doesn't add up.

It's like when you buy a house, and the minute you walk out of the settlement office you're suddenly assailed by an inexplicable and paranoid suspicion that you've been the victim of some form of fraud. And you ask yourself why on earth the seller and the closing agent exchanged that glance at a certain point during the document signing. So you slow from a brisk walk to a crawl, and in your mind you see the local television news, opening the evening broadcast with a report on a multi-million-euro ring of false real estate transactions. At that point, unless you manage to calm down, you're on the verge of retracing your steps, ringing the buzzer, going upstairs, and knocking on the office door: the secretary is surprised when she opens the door and sees you (her surprise only adds to your suspicion), you apologize and ask whether by any chance it was in their office that you left the cell phone that you can't find anywhere, she says that she'll be glad to go take a look for you and would you mind taking a seat in the waiting room, and there you sit, scrutinizing every detail of the place to make up your mind whether it's really a settlement office after all; you stick your head out and look up and down the hallway, well it certainly does look like a typical Italian settlement office, antique furniture and paintings, rows of law books in the bookcases lining the walls, hardwood floors, Persian carpets; then you wonder why the secretary is taking so long; ah, maybe she rushed into the fraudulent settlement agent's office to warn him, and he—having already doffed jacket and tie to return to the natural shirtsleeve state of the con artist (it's amazing how quickly con artists resume their natural appearance, as soon as they're done with a con job)—quickly puts on his jacket and knots his tie so that he can receive you with the most nonchalant of expressions, in case you happen to demand to see him; oh, there she is now, "No, I'm sorry, there's no cell phone in the conference room, you must have left it somewhere else"; and you say, "Oh, that's all right"; "I'm very sorry," she says, and accompanies to the front door; you hesitate, then you wonder if you might ask the settlement agent just one last question, and the secretary tells you that he's in the middle of a long phone call right now (how can she know that he's on the phone if she just went into the conference room to look for your cell phone?), but if you like she'd be glad to take note of the question and then let you know the answer, and at that point you decide to put an end to this Stations of the Cross that you've voluntarily chosen to undertake, "Oh, it's not important, don't worry about it," you say, and so you head back downstairs; on the way down you shake your head and even laugh about it, you decide that you really ought to have your head examined

I HADN'T UNDERSTOOD · 237

for the unlimited credence that you give your overheated imagination; but the next morning you call the settlement agent, the secretary puts you through, and you ask him when you can have a copy of the title to the property, whereupon he says, "The title? We only did the closing yesterday, and you already want a registered title? Listen, don't worry," dismissing your request with unconcealed annoyance, "as soon as the title's ready I'll have my secretary give you a call, all right?" and you finally put that worry to rest, but not so much.

I walk out the front gate, and in the little roundabout in front of the prison building, not far from the intercom, is a small knot of women with their children standing there, in a tight cluster, waiting for I can't imagine what. You often see them outside the front gates of prisons, these mothers staging the symbolic dismemberment of their families by implementing this form of open-air detention. It's unclear whether they want to go in but are not allowed, or if they've already gone in and, after emerging, they've just done some socializing with other women who share their unenviable fate, or if they've brought their children on this pilgrimage to the hermitage of their fathers, or whether they're organizing a sit-in, or if this is already in fact a sit-in. They're free to go, but they stay there. They're not demanding anything, but they're waiting. There they stand, proving that they don't count for anything, but still they won't go away.

What I wonder whenever I find myself in the presence of a spontaneous representation of a common social problem is whether or not those who have staged it—usually people who have little if any experience with the notion of metaphor—know what they're doing. In my opinion, they don't know, so they *do* it.

The air is filthy and muggy, I'm hot, it's hot, I'm bracing myself psychologically for the hike I'll have to take to get to the

238 · DIEGO DE SILVA

bus stop when, as I happen to glance around, I spot Tricarico's Vespa, with Tricarico sitting on it, exactly where I left him, like a stalker who can't bring himself to accept reality. His insistence is starting to irritate me, even if I have to admit that a ride would be more than welcome right now. This must be what the first stage of corruption feels like, I say to myself, and I walk toward him just to reiterate the concept. He seems a little intimidated as I walk toward him.

"Why are you still here?"

He bows his head.

"Unless I'm mistaken, I told you not to wait for me," I add, since he doesn't answer me.

"What do you think, that I'm having fun, Counselor?"

"I don't give a damn whether you're having fun or you're bored to tears. I just want to stop finding you underfoot all the time."

"Listen, what harm am I doing you, excuse me very much?"

"I'll be glad to tell you exactly what harm you're doing me, I really don't like the fact that . . . "

And that's when I suddenly say nothing, because I don't know what to say anymore. You know, it's a horrible thing to be asked to explain something that strikes you as self-evident. You just can't find the words, you can't get them up. Among other things, to be perfectly straightforward, I can't tell if the question is reasonable (in fact, what harm *is* he really doing, after all?) or just so stupidly mulish that the mere effort of searching for an answer makes me feel as if I'd just stepped into a pile of shit. So I try to get out of it by spreading my arms and then letting them drop to my sides, playing the part of someone too deeply disgusted by the level of the conversation to go on any further; then I turn on my heels and leave, hoping at least that that works.

Of course it doesn't work, because as I reach the street and turn onto the sidewalk, I hear the Vespa starting up. I go on walking, minding my own business, concentrating—no, distracting myself—to the extent possible in order to ignore the annoyance in motion behind my back. Out of the corner of my eye, I can register the constant distance of the slow-motion chase. The unit of measurement is provided by the puttering engine.

From a repair shop across the street, a mechanic with nothing to do watches us. From the way he's watching us (and I'm not even going to bother describing how he's watching us), it's unmistakable that we must strike him as a couple of queers. Especially Tricarico, I imagine, since he's following me.

Now what am I supposed to do? Turn around and make a scene? Run? Continue walking at a steady pace as if nothing had happened? Accept the ride? None of the four options would rescue me from the mechanic's bias.

Well, Jesus H. Christ on a crutch.

On the verge of complete exasperation, I come to a halt. With great precision, Tricarico stops as well. There we stand, looking at one another, motionless, in a pathetic pantomime of the crucial scene in *Duel*. The empty-handed mechanic actually lights a cigarette at this point.

After a while my nerves give out, and I wave Tricarico over. He walks hopefully toward me.

"Are you going to fucking stop buzzing around me or not," I blurt in a fury. "I mean what do you imagine that guy thinks is going on between us?"

Tricarico turns to look at the repair shop, glances at the mechanic, who promptly looks away, turns back to me and lip-syncs "Huh?" as he lobs the problem back into my court.

I'm speechless.

"Do you mind if I ask how the hearing went?" he asks.

"It went great: your colleague's getting out of jail," I blurt out, in the hope—based on nothing in particular—that this piece of good news might get him out of my hair, once and for all.

"Seriously?" he says, in shock.

I enjoy the scene in silence.

"Counselor, do you realize what this means?!" cries Tricarico in excitement, letting off electric discharges of contentment like a blinking turn indicator.

He kills the engine, pulls the Vespa up onto its kickstand, and starts to get off and throw his arms around my neck, but I freeze him to the spot with such a murderous glare that he instantaneously desists.

I look at the mechanic, who's enjoying himself as he smokes his shitty cigarette. I wish an angina pectoris upon him, and I tell myself that the next time I have business in the prison, like fuck I'll go by this place. I'd rather wear a burqa, in fact.

"So now you see that we were right?" Tricarico comments enthusiastically. "But how on earth did you pull it off?"

"Search me. Wait a minute, what do you mean how on earth did I pull it off?"

"No, sorry, I just meant to say that you did a great job."

"Well, thanks so much. Now would you very much mind getting out of here?"

"I can't do that."

"What do you mean you can't do that?"

He shrugs.

I get the message. I inhale, and then I exhale loudly.

"Ah, I get it, now you're my handler, is that it? You drive me around, you act as my secretary, chauffeur, and when needed, bodyguard, so you can keep an eye on everything I do and report back to whomever it may concern, right?"

"Only for the first few days, Counselor."

"What am I, on probation?"

He laughs. This is the first time since I've met him that he's gotten a joke.

"Anyway, I'm taking the bus."

"I'll follow you anyway."

"Oh, really."

"Eh. I have no choice."

I head off. This time he gives me a considerable head start before starting up his Vespa.

As I approach the bus stop, I decide to regain control of my personal life so I turn my cell phone back on, with all the enthusiasm of a Sunday afternoon in mid-November. I half-heartedly select Alessandra Persiano's number in my phonebook, almost completely convinced that our, shall I say, affair has already vanished under the surface and sunk to the bottom of the sea, even though I really wouldn't be able to say why, if someone were ever to ask me.

If she doesn't answer, it's disagreement by silence.

It rings once. Twice. A third time. A fourth time.

"Hello."

My heart suddenly stops beating, I swear. I'll die if it doesn't start up again.

"Ale. Vincenzo," I gasp. I don't have the slightest idea of how I managed to manufacture the sound.

"I know that," she says.

The reception is impeccable. I manage to capture every nuance of her tone of voice. I could describe it (I don't know, maybe I'd say that it's somewhere between disappointed tenderness and renunciation, for instance), if I hadn't been trying so hard to stay on my feet, right here and now.

"Eh. Can . . . can you hear me?"

What a pathetic question.

"Like an iPod, Vincè."

What really puts me through the floor right now (because it's incredible, but at the same time, inevitable), is that I have so many things I'd like to tell her, but now, I mean right this instant, it strikes me that there's not a single thing, not even one, of all the things that I could tell her, that is sufficiently interesting to be worth telling; I don't know if these self-critical panning shots with a resulting laconic silence—at the very moment when the most useful thing would be to start talking—ever happen to other people, but I sure do hope so.

"Where . . . where are you?" I ask, venturing further into the realm of the inappropriate.

An extended pause follows, which sounds more or less like: "Why, what a great question you just asked, oh, I'm just so eager to answer it," after which Alessandra Persiano replies, in a tone of semi-resignation:

"You want to know where I am. So I'll tell you. I'm outside the judicial offices. I just got done. I just served two restraining orders and a preliminary injunction. Now I'm in the main lobby of the courthouse, in fact; can you hear how it echoes in here? Now that I think about it, there's a shoe store not far from here: I might just take this opportunity to drop by because I really need a pair of closed-toe slippers."

I let a few seconds go by, then I ask:

"With or without the fluffy trim?"

"What?" she says, but she heard me.

"The slippers. The kind with the fluffy trim, or do you mean espadrilles?" I specify.

Whereupon I distinctly hear a snort and a hint of laughter. I feel as if I can see her, Alessandra Persiano, looking around, disconcerted and a little annoyed with herself because she can't manage to tamp down this hemorrhaging surge of cheerfulness.

"You always manage to catch me off guard, and there's nothing I can do about it," she admits, overwhelmed and amused.

The return of hope is like the jolt of a strong drink, straight to the head.

"If you only knew how you catch me off-guard," I add.

She says nothing. God, how I want to fuck her. Now. Here and now.

"Ale?" I call her name.

"Hmm," she goes.

"I called you a lot yesterday. Over and over."

"And I waited all day for you to call me."

" . . . you jerk," is the unmistakable kicker to the line, perfectly present in the subtext.

Tricarico, sensing the delicacy of the conversation, keeps a considerable distance. This isn't the first time he's shown that he has the gift of discretion, which, I have to say, confuses me more than a little.

"Can I explain what happened?"

"Let's hear it."

"Right now?"

"Why not, is someone bugging your phone?"

"Ale, I want to be with you."

"That's your explanation?"

"So you never want to see me again?"

"What the fuck does that have to do with anything right now?"

"Beats me. But I need you to answer the question."

She keeps me hanging for a few seconds. My God, those are the longest seconds.

"Do you think I'm the kind of woman who loses her memory the morning after, eh, Vincè? Is that what you think of me?"

No, it's that I think that I'm the kind of man who makes women lose their memory the morning after, is what I feel like telling her. But it would be pitiful, so I skip it.

"Ale, please, don't take every word that comes out of my mouth and turn it against me, I can't even think anymore. I don't know if I really believe the things I'm saying, or if I'm just trying to make sure I don't say anything wrong. And when that happens, I wind up not talking, and I come off like the kind of guy who doesn't have anything to say. But in fact I have a lot of things I want to tell you, if only you knew. I just have to find a way to get started, that's all."

There follows an extended silence of data being computed. When Alessandra Persiano finally answers, she's practically surrendered.

"You're incredible, Vincenzo, really. When I talk to you, I feel as if I'm constantly jumping from place to place. I don't recognize my surroundings anymore."

I can't figure out if these are compliments or warning signs of an eviction. While I think I remain silent, just for a change. On the wall across the street, I marvel as I read a spray-painted message:

I DNT LV GETTING LOST IN WORDS . . . BUT I LV GETTING LOST IN YOUR BLUE EYES . . . ONLY 4 U . . . BY MARCE

Jesus.

"Anyway, you're right," Alessandra Persiano says a minute later.

"About what."

"That I nitpick the things you say."

"You do?"

"Sure. It's just that . . . I don't know. I get nervous."

"Why?"

The timing leading up to the line that follows is, how to put this, just perfect.

"Because it's your fault, you idiot."

When a woman calls you an idiot, it generally means she's falling in love. And I feel like such a complete idiot right now that I start walking down the middle of the road without any concern for the cars that have to steer around me, without even honking, because of what an idiot I must look like, I'd have to guess.

What Malinconico Would Say About the Most Common of All Autoimmune Diseases, If Anyone Ever Asked Him About It (*Quite Likely*)

L ove, if I may give my views on the subject, is a disease that affects a person's sense of dignity and self-respect. It operates by highs and lows. It buys and sells. You can recognize it immediately. It has symptoms—how to put this?—symptoms that are unmistakable.

First of all, it makes you feel like a chosen person. It sends you out to observe other people and pity them. Deep down, it approves the idea that we really aren't all equal.

It's not true that when you're in love the whole world looks beautiful to you. It's just that you look down on the whole world from a point of extreme elevation. You look at people going by and you think: "Poor miserable dopes, look at the way they run around, living their drab lives. You see how they hustle and bustle, work, get stuck in traffic jams, wait in line at the cash register?"

In other words, when you're in love you turn into a god-damned cynic. Worse: a new-money oaf, who discovers that the minute he has some personal wealth he values the things he used to look down upon when he couldn't afford them; so he goes around trying to palm himself off as a sensitive soul, with a yearning for the beautiful and the spiritual.

But there's no point in you saying how you love sunsets, because if you didn't like them before then you really don't like them now. Likewise, it's pointless for you to inhale great lungfuls of fresh air, saying how much you love the scent and flavor, because you know you've never given a damn about breathing deep like the veterinarian in the television commercial for Amaro Montenegro, otherwise you wouldn't have started smoking. Just like it's pointless for you to go into bookstores and ponder the blurbs on the back covers and inside flaps of the books, because you know perfectly well that you can't wait to get out of there. And it's useless for you to stop and talk to everyone you meet, even people you don't know, and patiently listen to every word they say to you, implicitly repeating that tired old sermon about how everyone deep down has something interesting to say as long as you know how to listen, because really, other people are of no interest to you whatsoever. And there is no point in you talking and talking, because anyway you don't really believe the things you're saying. Just as it's useless for you to start playing an instrument again, because when you stopped fifteen years ago there must have been a reason.

This sort of mental defectiveness, which ushers together both a resurgence of cynicism and metaphysical yearnings, not only undermines laboriously constructed reputations and damages decades-old friendships; it can also have serious repercussions on political elections, so that parties need to be worried about the vote of people in love.

And then there's cosmic depression, which threatens the very process of evolution.

Let's say you're at the station waiting for a train. You're in love and you're in a relationship (but she's at home, or at work). It's not like you're leaving on some extended trip; you're going to be back the next day. You're reading the newspaper, everything's normal. All around you are other people waiting for a train. It's not raining, it's not hot out, it's not cold. In a situation like this, here's what can happen: the public address system, for instance, might announce a ten-minute delay, or else a middle-aged woman might ask you if this is the platform for the train to Bologna, and you, for no good reason, just like that, I mean from one minute to the next, feel yourself sliding into a completely meaningless state of disappointment, a sadness based on nothing, and your entire immune system turns in its resignation en masse, and the world suddenly becomes the worst possible place to live, so that you have the impression that you can sense all the injustices that blight this planet gathered into a single unpleasant bundle, and everything starts to go a sort of drab blue-grey, and now you want your momma, and your shoulders start to slump, you turn into a living triangle, and then your hand of its own accord seeks out your inside jacket pocket in a desperate quest for an antidote, and now you've found it, you dial the number and then you give the death blow to whatever remaining pathetic shreds of your dignity are trailing along at your heels like a big-eyed seal pup imploring you not to do it but, there, you've done it, the phone rings once, twice, a third time: "Ciao," you say to her; and she answers: "Oh," as if to say: "Why'd you call?"; and you say: "It's me"; and she says: "I know" (understandably—what else is she supposed to say to you?); so then you say nothing and you even act slightly offended; she vaguely perceives it but she can't really be certain (because if she were certain she'd tell you to go to wherever it is that you ought to be told to go in that case), and at that point she asks you, in no uncertain terms, what's wrong, and you say: "Oh, nothing," but you say it in the key of D minor, understood, with that nostalgic harmonic shift in your voice, the ambiguous, guilt-inducing intonation that in your devious intentions ought to be sufficient to make her melt at the other end of the line and respond: "Ah, now I understand, darling, you just want me to tell you that I love you, and of course I do, I'm so happy that you called me, call me again whenever you want, I hope you do"; but instead she justifiably says: "Ah," which amounts to: "Well then, why did you call me in the first place, if you don't have anything to say to me?"

Whereupon the phrase brings you back to your senses with the immediacy of a bucket of cold water, you straighten your back, the train station becomes a train station again, and you feel as ashamed as if you'd been caught molesting fifteen-year-olds when you fully realize the depth of the level to which you just sank, because you know perfectly well that your dignity should be safeguarded from these deplorable sideshows that, among other things, have nothing at all to do with love, since what they amount to is premeditated bouts of whining, indecent petty episodes of extortion, demands to be picked up and carried like a baby and even taken to the park to feed the ducks.

Another masterpiece of love is that it invents a series of coincidences and cause-and-effect relationships. It constructs improbable geometries linking events that have nothing to do with one another, making a mockery of hindsight and prompting lines like this: "I mean, do you realize that if that morning my car battery hadn't died, I would have driven to X, instead of accepting the invation of Y, when he asked me to come join him at Z, which is where I met you for the first time, and everything that's happened since then?"

Which might, after all, even be true, in the sense that no one can deny that something took place in a certain order of events, if that's the way it actually happened.

It's just that car batteries run down, and in fact they run down every day, it's not as if they run down in some kind of special way when you're about to start a relationship with someone. The fact that you start dating someone on a certain day doesn't authorize you to create a cause-and-effect linkage between a dead battery and your new relationship, because (leaving aside the fact that the battery would have run down anyway) your dead battery might also have been the cause of a variety of other events far more worthy of consideration than the one you're so proud of right now.

Without taking into consideration the fact that, as far as your new relationship is concerned, the dead battery has no more and no less significance than the other events that conspired to ensure that you'd enter that relationship (the fact that you accepted the invitation, for instance: you could just as easily have decided to stay home, and then so long, new girlfriend), and so, with all the other factors that come into play, it's not clear why the dead battery should be at the root of it all, unless you're trying to prove that chronology is the guiding criterion in new relationships.

Which, by the way, if you always thought in terms of dead batteries, and not just when you're trying to prove that your love affair was written by destiny in the stars—a destiny that on that particular day was plotting on your behalf—and instead you considered that all the billions of circumstances that make up your life each has a significant relationship with each and every other circumstance, at the very least your brain would creak and collapse as it struggled to uncover all the various significant relationships among things.

And in any case, without even bothering to delve deeper into all these considerations: it's not like it's such an amazing story you're telling. It's not like your girlfriend was sitting perched on the very edge of your building's roof and you just happened to look out the window right below her (oh, it's even better if it wasn't even your apartment), and you happened to notice a pair of feet dangling just overhead, so you engaged her in a lengthy conversation about whether it's worth the trouble to go on living, and you talked her down from the roof, and since then you've never spent a moment apart. If that was how things had gone then sure, you'd have grounds for talking about occult forces at play, because really there's no comparison between a dead battery and an averted suicide attempt.

But that's not what happened at all. All that happened was you met a girl you liked, she liked you, and now you're a couple.

This yearning for a starring role in hindsight, which drives people to rewrite virtual scripts long after the play is over, is in fact a defect in one's self-respect, a clear side effect of love, because it's obvious that if a person had a shred of dignity and any awareness of the things that he says, he wouldn't talk that way about a dead battery.

And then there's the last, worst symptom, where your dignity is so completely pummeled and crushed that you might as well get it out of your head that there's any chance of recovery, and that's when you find yourself depending on the other person's mood.

This phenomenon has to do with the phase in which the relationship is lurching and staggering (you've already stopped inhaling lungfuls of fresh air, lingering in bookstores, etc.) and she's not even all that certain that she wants you around anymore; in fact, she's more there than here, more over it than into it, so there are times when she's affectionate and other times when she treats you like shit.

The truth is (and you know it perfectly well) that you no longer really interest her, in fact, if you want to be completely honest, you're even starting to get on her nerves just a little, but it's just that every so often she feels guilty and so, in the grip of passing waves of pity for you, she turns all sweet and loving, and you, dangling shamefully from her little finger, start wagging your tail like a fox terrier and kidding yourself the minute you sense a hint of reconsideration.

There's no need to say at this point that your love affair is dead and buried with a cross planted on the grave because, in the end, you know that if a woman wants you she'll come looking for you, and when she stops coming around it's because she doesn't want you anymore, and really there's not much more to say on the subject.

You on the other hand go on dragging yourself through this

sort of emotional methadone in the hopes that things might work out, but there's no cure for this particular kind of malfunction, there's no fixing things and, whatever people might say, it's never happened, never, that anybody succeeded in straightening out this kind of situation, just try asking around.

Depending on someone's mood, this thing where if she's nice to you then you can make it through to the end of the day in one piece but if she treats you with indifference then you're just a shell of a man and you can't get a thing done and your work piles up along with debts of various kinds, it's just a completely shitty situation, ignominious, something you should get out of once and for all; it leaves a stain on your heart.

And the most pathetic thing is that at this point whatever love there was is now dead and gone (what are you going to love when your dignity is in tatters?), but you go on talking about love. You've become the emotional equivalent of an Elvis fan, a misfit who's incapable of living in the present, and in the way you dress, the way you talk, the way you listen to music, in the books you read and the things you write, and even in the way you go to bed with someone, you're looking for something that no longer exists—that's it, that's all.

SHOCK THE DOG

The situation in which I find myself is completely anomalous. It violates all the boilerplate rules of chase scenes.

Being followed is one of those typically cinematic sensations, the kind of thing that when it actually happens to you, you immediately feel as if you're at the center of attention, as if you're being followed not only by the person who's following you but also by an audience who's eager to know who's following you and why.

In these cases, in fact, the first thing you do when you're out walking is to slow down, take a deep breath, and square your shoulders, as if somehow you felt incredibly interesting all of a sudden. The second thing you do is look around to get the best possible vantage point of the street you're on, and pay careful attention to the things surrounding you (parked cars, moving cars, an indeterminate point on the sidewalk across the street, pedestrians walking ahead of you, pedestrians coming toward you—and in fact as they pass by, they give you looks as if to say *What the hell are you looking at?*—shop signs, and so on), with a view to coming up with some way of gaining leverage and turning the tables on the person following you, just like in the movies, in fact, when the person being followed suddenly disappears from the field of view of the follower, who immediately comes to a sudden halt in the middle of the sidewalk, disoriented (you know, so that anyone who happens by would swear that what this guy is doing is following somebody), and then kind of fumbles his way forward for a while until the guy he's following, in magnificent athletic condition, appears from around a corner, grabs him by the scruff of the neck, hurls him up against the nearest wall, and beats him silly until he confesses who sent him.

That's as far as tailing somebody on foot. When it comes to car chases the boilerplate is slightly different (for instance, in the car being chased there's almost always a woman in the passenger seat next to the driver, upbraiding him for having flirted shamelessly for the whole evening with another woman; just then, he shoots an eloquent glance up at the rearview mirror, returns his gaze firmly to the road ahead of him, doesn't even bother to answer the woman, whereupon she flies into a rage but she doesn't even have time to start dressing him down before he shifts gears, jams his foot down on the accelerator, and takes off like a rocket, and after the woman comes this close to doing a face-plant into the windshield, he says: "Better fasten your seatbelt"), even though, at the end of the chase scene, it's always the car following them that goes hurtling off the road.

Obviously in your case this is all just a farce, because if you really did think that a criminal was following you in order to rob you or settle some account that you know nothing about, at the very least you'd start running like a sewer rat or you'd scream for help in the general direction of the first policeman, traffic cop, or mailman (anyone wearing a uniform, in other words) you happen to see; I very much doubt that you'd waste time acting like the poor man's James Bond, a part, furthermore, that no one has assigned you.

The fact is that reality, in these cases, gives you a distorted idea of things from the very beginning, and you are only too eager to jump right in because, obviously, everybody needs a dose of self-importance now and again. They're false dangers, situations with an induced, facilitated risk. It's kind of like the inhabitants of Rome, if you've ever noticed, who always seem to be on the verge of trading punches but then they never actually come to blows, like on a train when people are lined up down the corridor of a passenger car, and the guy up ahead takes forever to get seated, so one guy says: "You wanna get a move on?"; and the other guy answers him: "Yeah, sure, if you just give me a second here"; and the first guy says: "Well, as long you don't take the whole damned afternoon"; to which the other guy says: "Excuse me, do you have a problem here?"; and the first guy: "Maybe my problem is you, what do you say?"; and the other guy: "Ah, you think so? Well, that being so, I'm not sure I'm going to help you with your problem"; and the first guy: "No, I'm pretty sure you're gonna take care of it, like it or not"; and the two of them are perfectly capable of going on like this for a solid fifteen minutes without ever actually trading punches unless the people behind them in line don't start a shouting cascade of objections, so they have to shut down their debating session. You just picture the same kind of exchange in Naples, and try calculating how many (or how few) seconds would pass before the first fist crunches into the nasal septum of the other debater.

In reality, the chase scene that actually does take place usually involves an acquaintance who spots you on the street from an average distance, not too close and not too far, and calls your name but you don't hear him, whereupon he raises his voice by an octave, but you go on walking, minding your own business, and at that point your acquaintance has already kind of overdone it with the decibels, embarrassing himself with the other pedestrians who look at him with a certain distaste, so he decides to take it to the limit, and he comes after you, only by now you've gained a considerable headstart on him, and so the chase is on.

My current situation, as I was saying, doesn't even comply with this elementary plot structure. I'm riding in a city bus, comfortably seated among family members of convicts, construction workers, and little old men (and why do you always see little old men riding the bus? It's not like they have to go to work), and despite the miserable clattering of sheet metal produced by the rattletrap bus, I can't help but obsess on the puttering noise of the Vespa following close behind us, faithfully slowing down for every bus stop. The driver has even noticed it, I saw him glancing into the rearview mirror a couple of times as if he's about to stop the bus and get out.

I try to ignore what's going on but I can't seem to do it, the engine of the Vespa is drilling through my brain, I even go so far as to suspect that Tricarico might have intentionally doctored the muffler (it certainly wasn't making this much noise this morning). He's just trying to wear me down, there's no mistaking the pattern. They're tremendous, the guys who set out to wear you down. They're more or less like hyenas—the way that hyenas tag along behind wounded animals so that they can devour them at their leisure once loss of blood and exhaustion has laid them by the heels.

This thought makes me so furiously indignant that suddenly I can't stand to just ride along quietly without saying a word so I decide to get off the bus and dress Tricarico down, but good. Only, at the next stop, when I hop down from the bus and see him pulling up (beaming at the sight of me again so soon), the whole scene of the clobbering of the hooligan on the sidewalk unreels before my eyes, and my aggressivity shrinks so radically that I unexpectedly find myself saying:

"Let's do this. You can give me a ride to my office, but I don't want to hear a word out of you, understood? Not one word."

He nods his head yes with some display of confusion.

"Did you hear me talking, Counselor?"

"You starting again? I said *not one word*, do you understand Italian, yes or no?"

He raises both hands.

I climb onto the scooter.

And we go.

When I do this sort of thing, that is, peel out in high gear for a vicious argument and then desist, converting my impulse for a brawl into a simmering and inoffensive broth of resentment, I find myself hemmed into that very particular variety of unproductive conflict, exquisitely aesthetic in nature, in which you do your best to make it clear to the other person that you can't stand them, and yet there you remain. Which is, after all, a typically matrimonial situation: instead of telling your spouse to go fuck himself, you sulk. Practically speaking, you deep-freeze the conflict. You put it in the freezer, in the lowest compartments, and you make use of the daily chill drawer until one fine day you decide that a trial separation is the one and only way to defrost it. People break up to defrost their conflicts much more frequently than you'd be likely to guess. Because at a certain point you've got to get over the cold wars. You have to make something happen, at last. Which is why, when people break up, even people who aren't stupid, they discover that they're so stupidly determined not to let their spouse come out the winner, and they do everything they can to engage in a form of obstructionism. Separation and divorce, once you start down that road, produces chain reactions that are virtually unstoppable. It turns into a matter of principle. A way of saying, too late, the words that you wish you'd said that one time when you couldn't think of anything to say. It doesn't do you a bit of good, but it's one of those things you decide you just have to do, even if you don't exactly understand the reason why.

"Separation," by the way, is a word that has an inexplicable driving force, a sort of linguistic front-wheel drive: the minute you utter the word you've started separating, even if it doesn't seem that way. It brings misfortune, in a certain sense. It pulls down decisions on your head without even giving you the time to make them. It conditions your behavior, undermines existing relationships, launches itself into the future with immediate effect. It's a sort of virus. That's why you have to be so careful about saying the word. If you ask me, most people who have broken up up only did so because one day they uttered the word.

In short, on the Vespa I act all offended the whole way to the office, even when we pull up in front of the street door and I finally get off the scooter.

"Well, thanks very much," I say. "Take care."

Tricarico grimaces and raises a finger.

"Can I say something?"

"What are we, at school?" I comment.

He snickers.

"Can I come up for a minute?"

"Eh?"

"To your office. Just for a minute."

"What now?" I say, indignantly. "Do you want to take a look at my office?"

"No, what do I care about your office, Counselor?"

He seems to mean what he's saying.

"Don't you dream of it," I decree.

"Please," he says, and puts on a miserable expression.

If he's acting, he's very good.

"What's got into you?" I ask.

"I have to go to the bathroom."

I'm flabbergasted, bowled over, flummoxed.

"Oh, my God. And you need to come to my office? There's a bar across the street, don't you see it?"

"I don't use bar bathrooms."

"Why not?"

"They're disgusting. And I have a problem with closing the door."

258 · DIEGO DE SILVA

I stand there, arms akimbo, and tilt my head to one side.

"For real?"

He looks at the pavement.

"You mean, you're afraid you'll be locked in?" I ask, realizing as I speak that I've lowered my voice.

He doesn't answer, but he's answered.

I run my hand through my hair, accompanying the blazing recollection of a trauma I experienced many years ago. Something like twenty-seven, twenty-eight years ago, at a party at a classmate's house, I was locked in the bathroom. Actually, I didn't even really need to go to the bathroom, in the sense that I didn't have to pee, but I went into the bathroom anyway because when you're at a party where there's a girl that you like, every so often you have to disappear for 15-20 minutes at a time; that way after you've been gone for a while she'll start asking other people where you are and even come looking for you, if she can't figure out why you've suddenly vanished. In general, in these cases, you go out onto the balcony to smoke one cigarette after another, running the risk of contracting bronchial asthma while waiting for her to turn up and instead she promptly fails to turn up (while your friends, who have figured out your little subterfuge, emerge from indoors, asking questions like: "What's up, too hot inside?"; or else, in an even more diplomatic show of delicacy: "You want me to go get her?"); but the problem at the home of this classmate of mine was that there weren't any balconies and so, not knowing where else to implement my strategy of disappearing from circulation, I went into the bathroom, and after a while, when I was ready to return to the party, I turned the handle but the door wouldn't open. I tried everything I could think of to get that fucking key to turn but nothing worked, it was as if someone had cemented it in place with liquid steel.

After I'd been locked in there for fifteen minutes or so, Stefano Cavallo showed up. I told him in a whisper that he had to help me get out of there, and discreetly, if there was any way he could pull it off. And do you know what that traitor, that son of Cain did in response to my request? He started shouting: "Oh, everyone, come running, Malinconico's locked himself in the bathroom!" And a minute later the entire party had rushed en masse from the living room to the door of my little prison, with my classmates eagerly debating the best way to get me out of there, and me having to pretend I thought it was fun and funny, taking part in the discussion and laughing at their shitty jokes on the other side of the locked door. I swear, I can still remember every minute of it, the look of pity on the face of the girl I liked, when I finally managed to get out of there.

All this just to say that since that night I've never locked a bathroom door in my life, not even at home; so now I can't help but feel an irresistible impulse of solidarity toward Tricarico, after his confession.

And anyway, I found Stefano Cavallo's diary later and I pissed in it.

"Okay, whatever, come on up," I concede. "Just a minute, though, and then off you go."

"Okay."

As we head upstairs, I realize the degree to which the discovery that even a Camorra hitter suffers from fears of this kind has already improved my relationship with him. Take a look at me: suddenly I'm even walking differently. I've stopped worrying about him coming after me; I'm no longer pacing myself in accordance with his gait, but I even accelerate.

Reinvigorated by this development, once we get to the front door of the shared office, I culpably fail to warn him that the instant I insert the key in the lock the canine burglar alarm is going to go off. And so, when I unlock the door and the damned toy spitz explodes in furious full-throated yelping, Tricarico leaps straight into the air with fright and puts one hand on his heart.

Whereupon I burst into laughter and open the door.

"What the fu—" Tricarico grunts, but afterwards he starts laughing, too. All things considered, he's a funny guy, truth be told.

"It's the dog that belongs to this cooperative here," I explain, gesturing toward the door of the Arethusa while I close the front door behind us. "It always does that."

"Well, you could have warned me, couldn't you?" he objects, justifiably, with one hand still on his chest, and even a little red in the face.

"Oh, well, you know," I lie, "by now I don't even think of it anymore."

Maybe because it's detected the presence of a stranger, the toy spitz is yapping even more furiously than usual. It's howling itself hoarse, hurling itself against the door, head-butting the door so powerfully that it's a wonder that it doesn't sustain a canine lapdog skull fracture. At this point, I'm sure that the dog is alone in the office, otherwise Roberto-Sergio or Clelia-Ginevra, in there, would already have forced it to pipe down. It's incredible how angry a little dog like that can make a person.

I haven't even finished composing the concept in my mind when, as if through some kind of telepathic conjuncture, I turn toward Tricarico with the chilling certainty that he's thinking exactly the same thing.

"Wait, didn't you need to go the bathroom?" I ask, subconsciously hoping to prevent him from doing something that I don't even want to imagine.

"Would you excuse me for just a moment?" he says. A request that, to judge from the expression on his face, translates roughly as a firm injunction not to even think of trying to stop him. And so, with the presence of mind of a guinea pig, I step aside.

He knocks at the door.

No answer. Aside from the toy spitz, obviously.

He looks at me.

Don't do it, I think.

He does it.

I silently pray that they've locked the door.

The door doesn't open.

I heave a sigh of relief.

Tricarico turns his head and looks at me, arching his eyebrows in a compassionate expression.

Don't do it, I think again.

He lowers the handle and delivers a sharp, decisive shove forward, as if he were shifting into first gear. And the little tongue of the door-lock reveals its precarious fragility. The great thing is that it doesn't even break.

Tricarico looks back at me and smiles, with a diabolical glimmer that back-lights his right eye.

For a single fleeting instant the toy spitz is silent.

"Oh, be careful!" I cry when he opens the door and the little beast hurtles straight at him with a snarl, latching on to the right sleeve of his jacket.

Without losing even a smidgen of composure, Tricarico lifts the dog level with his face, and with the other hand he grabs it by the scruff of its doggy neck. The toy spitz clenches its jaws, scrambles its legs furiously, snarls and foams at the mouth, its eyes rolling frantically, its crescent-shaped tail whipping back and forth through the air. Seen from up close, in an oblong version, the dog is obscenely rickety and stunted, pathetic in its senseless blinding rage. It's not biting anything but the sleeve of a jacket, the little moron, but it has no intention of releasing its grip. Without even realizing it, I barricade myself behind my bodyguard; in fact, he turns as if to ask me to give him a little room.

I comply.

Tricarico takes a step forward and enters the office of the Arethusa cooperative.

I follow him with bated breath: in fact, this is the first time that I've had the experience of entering this office. Before today, the office of the Arethusa cooperative was Bluebeard's Room for all of us in here. I can already picture Espe's incredulous face when I tell him about it.

While the toy spitz dangles from the enemy's forearm, savaging the fabric of the sleeve, we look around. Tricarico seems rather interested in the poster of the Robert Doisneau photograph, "Kiss by the Hôtel de Ville," which I personally find super-trite. I stop instead to gaze in rapt admiration at a magnificent Klappsta easy chair, a sober Le Corbusier imitation, which I've been thinking about getting for years.

Once we're done with our respective appreciations, Tricarico tears the dog's jaws away from the sleeve of his jacket with a sharp yank, and the rest of the dog comes away with the jaws. At this point the toy spitz flips out; it probably doesn't even realize that it's no longer chomping down on anything. Its jaws continue to snap at empty air as it alternates each bite with a pathetic snarl; all the while, Tricarico holds it suspended in midair, waiting for it to come to the realization of the way things now stand.

In fact, after a short interval, it dawns on the dog that its situation has changed. For the first time, it looks straight at its new adversary. At that point, it finally falls silent. A slightly pathetic interlude, truth be told.

Continuing to dangle the diminutive quadruped, Tricarico turns his head and glances at me, as if to say: "You see?" I shrug my shoulders to deny the existence of any prior bet or understanding between the two of us, whereupon he, with the impassiveness of someone setting out to demonstrate a theorem, lifts his right arm, opens his right hand flat, braces the toy spitz, and then delivers a straight-armed slap in the face with such intense violence that the poor little dog, recoiling against the palm of the other hand that's gripping it relentlessly by the scruff of the neck, reminds me of nothing so much as a crash-test dummy when its shoulder harness jerks it back against the seat back the instant after the car hits the wall.

The sound of the impact (flat, vaguely metallic) is just as chilling as the yip of pain that accompanies it. After which the office of the Arethusa collective is plunged into a horrible silence.

Tricarico kneels down and gently places the dog back on the floor. The toy spitz, now catatonic, sits there tucked back on its hind legs, between the Rebus rattan wastebasket and the sawhorse legs of the Galant desk, without making a single solitary sound.

Tricarico stands up, turns toward me (I'm more or less as shocked as the dog), puts one hand on my shoulder and permits himself two little pats, as if he were telling me: "There, there, it's all over." Then he turns his gaze to the Robert Doisneau poster, which he must really like a lot.

I open my mouth, wondering if all this really happened. In the space of just a couple of minutes, and without any particular effort, my unorthodox bodyguard and handler has solved a problem that has been the bane of my existence for the past two years every time I returned to my office.

The truth is that, just beneath the surface of my repulsion for the crudeness of the method, I feel an intriguing sense of admiration for this elementary ability to triumph over situations. I'm ashamed to say it, but I like his openly anti-cultural attitude. Even if it disgusts me.

The secret of the Camorra's success, I think as I'm standing there, must be the way that they eliminate the whole idea of problem-solving. In their cognitive system, probably, there's no human situation that can't be solved in a brusque and direct manner. Life is objective, it responds to elementary input: why make things complicated? You want something? Take it. Does someone you know have more money than you? Make him give you some. Do you yearn for a woman who won't give you the time of day? Rape her. Whatever the topic, they approach it in terms of elimination and appropriation. Nothing remains uncertain. There are no pending questions. That's why Camorristi have such a natural and practical relationship with death; they kill and are killed continuously. It's because, as far as they're concerned, there's absolutely nothing tragic about death.

Whereas I'm constantly overwhelmed by imponderables. I have a horror of death. I perceive life as something that continually opposes an obstinate and dignified resistance to my every desire. I have, so to speak, a mortgage-holder's attitude to life. Life gives me a series of deadlines, life obliges me to make a number of periodic payments, if that conveys the idea. It's not something I take for granted, the idea that I'm here and that life is here too, that we're both in the same place. Life isn't free, you know. I have always nurtured this idea of life as a mortgage that extracts a portion of what I make every month, while at the same time preventing me from turning into a complete savage, in a certain sense.

In other words, unlike Tricarico, I've never had the nerve to break into the office of the Arethusa collective and deliver a nice straight-armed smack right to the snout of that shitty little toy spitz that's been giving me heart attacks every time I come to work, though I can't tell you how much pleasure it would have given me to do so.

Which is to say, I can't seem to bring myself to simply take what I want. It strikes me as ridiculous to think that things are simply there, and that it's your fault if you fail to take them. I have never believed in the idea that all you have to do is reach out and grab. And the fact that someone else manages to do it still doesn't make me believe that it's true, and that's all.

"The bathroom?"

Tricarico's voice breaks into my thoughts like a doorbell.

"Eh?" I ask.

"The bathroom," he repeats.

"Oh, right," I say, "all the way down the hall, on the right."

He heads down the hall.

I call after him.

"Oh, wait a sec."

He turns around.

"What is it?"

"The door," I say.

He turns his gaze in the direction of the lock he just forced a few minutes ago.

"What about it?" he answers, or really, he asks.

"Will they be able to tell?" I ask. It strikes me as incredible that we're in the same room as the now-silent toy spitz.

"No o-o, absolutely not," he rules out categorically. And he waves me out of the room, as if to say: "Come on, I'll show you."

So I catch up with him, placing myself in his competent hands. As I do, I glance over again at the dog, staring into the void from its position on the floor, and I actually feel a twinge in my heart, truth be told.

Tricarico lets me go first (he's practically obsequious, as far as that goes), he pulls the door shut behind him with a sharp yank (at first the lock opposes some resistance, but then it yields to persuasion), and he gives the handle a couple of strong shakes, twisting it up and down, up and down, until you hear something sliding into place. At that point he steps to one side and, assuming the pose of an apprentice elevator operator, he points to the door handle with both hands, inviting me to give it the acid test myself.

I accept the offer.

I push down on the door handle.

I lean into the door and try to open it.

I wonder what profession Tricarico's mamma does or did.

That door is *closed*. It's what you'd call a perfectly clean job, and I contemplate it with candor of a boy scout.

Tricarico flashes me a smile that says "mission accomplished" and heads off down the hall toward the bathroom.

I stand there for another couple of minutes, reviewing the various scenes of the imminent detective mystery, where Attilia-Germana does her best to snap the toy spitz found in the locked room out of its inexplicable state of shock and Roberto-Sergio inspects the door and window of the office in search of any signs of breaking and entering.

I emerge from the spell and I walk over to my, shall we say, office. I pull the Innocenti steel tube away from the window and I turn on my computer. After a while, the sound of a flushing toilet heralds Tricarico's return. I sit down on my Skruvsta, I open the file on a car accident lawsuit that was taken care of last fall, I furrow my brow, and, in other words, I strike a pose. Tricarico walks in and starts getting acquainted with my office without betraying even the slightest appreciation for the overarching Ikea-ism of the place. I am once again obliged to recognize that he possesses a discretion that continually astonishes me, in someone like him.

"Listen," I say to him as he's standing there, absorbed in *Nighthawks* with his back to me (he clearly has a thing about posters, I guess), "I wanted . . . well, it wasn't a pretty sight, but still, thanks, that's all."

"For what?" he says, without even turning around.

"I meant the dog."

"Ah. Don't mention it, it was nothing," he replies, continuing to admire my reproduction of Hopper's famous coffee shop.

Since the silence that follows an expression of gratitude always embarrasses me, I return to the subject, just for the sake of something to say.

"It was a misery to have to deal with that toy spitz yelping every time and . . . hey, are you listening to me?"

At the very instant in which he turns to answer me, it's as if his face has suddenly become more pointed. Evidently what I said must have aroused his interest, and now he wants to explore it in greater depth.

"So it isn't true that you never even noticed it anymore," he points out.

"What do you mean?" I stall for time.

"When we came in, that's what you said."

"Well, what is this, a lie detector test? Aside from the fact that you never even asked permission," I counterattack, reddening.

"Permission?" he asks, bewildered.

"Permission, permission. You did it all on your own. You just up and went in there. What if I hadn't wanted you to do it? What if they'd come back and found you in their office? Eh? What would I have said to them?"

"Counselor, what do you mean, first you thank me and then you scold me?"

Whereupon I don't know what to say, since it's obvious that he has a point. It's pure good luck that someone knocks at the door just then.

"Now who the fuck is that," I grumble in relief. And I start to get up from the Skruvsta.

"Don't bother," he says, "I'll go."

"What do you mean you'll go, wai—"

But I'm not fast enough to stop him before he's out of the room and down the hall. I'd like to yell after him that he's not my secretary, but instead I sit there, half curved over the Jonas, astonished at how intrusive he is.

Reality hits pause until I hear him open the door and say *Buon giorno.* When whoever it is returns the greeting and asks if I'm there, and from the voice I recognize the demented tenant who recently confided in me about his disquieting problems with his Polish live-in girlfriend, I'm reminded of a television commercial that ends with the phrase: "Help me," with Christian De Sica flopping over helplessly onto the steering wheel of the car.

In fact, I sit back down.

Tricarico comes back, letting the tenant go ahead of him, the tenant whose name I absolutely can't remember just now, actually.

"Ciao, Vincenzo," says the guy, walking in so briskly that then and there I have to wonder if by some chance I might have given him an appointment.

"Oh, ciao," I reply in some confusion.

Before I can even inquire as to the reason for this visit, he takes a seat on one of the Hampus chairs without asking.

"Oh please, come in, make yourself comfortable," I feel like saying to him.

I look him up and down: he's wearing a worn-out polo shirt, once dark blue, that looks as if it hasn't been changed in the past two days at least, and a pair of horrible pleated jeans for fifty-year-olds, so drab that they trend worrisomely toward beige. I've never seen him looking so bedraggled. And since I believe that the state of a person's clothing more or less reflects their psychological state, I'm starting to get apprehensive about the potential development of this unscheduled entertainment.

He leans forward and starts scrutinizing me, as if he were trying to predict my next move. Whereupon I look at the surface of my desk, sensing the sudden lack of a chessboard.

Behind him, in the door, Tricarico eyes me closely, awaiting further instructions. I transmit no signals, but I find his presence pretty comforting just now.

We all remain silent and motionless for two long minutes until the tenant whose name I continue not to remember finally says:

"Sorry if I didn't come by the day before yesterday, for our appointment. I still needed to think it over."

What the fuck are you talking about? I think.

Tricarico puts his hands in his pocket and stands there listening.

"I'm losing control of my nerves, Vincenzo. I'm thinking things that I shouldn't think. I don't where this is all leading."

"Where what's leading?" I ask.

He closes his eyes and then opens them again. The thought that just went through his mind must have made him wince.

"She wants me to move out. To move out of my own home, you understand?"

Tricarico pulls one hand out of his pocket and traces a couple of circles in midair. I slap him down with a ferocious glare. He desists.

"I'm sorry to have to get you involved in this," he resumes, "but you're the only person I trust."

There we go. Let's say that up to now, it was all within the bounds of the acceptable. But I don't like that last phrase, whatever it meant, even a little bit.

"Listen, can you tell me what you're talking about?" I try saying. But it's like trying to start a conversation with an answering machine.

Giustino Talento. His name suddenly appears in my memory like a lightning bolt.

"I can't blame you if you don't find it in your heart to forgive me, I just want you to know that, Vincenzo," he goes on, talking to himself, "But I have to share this thing somehow. You understand me, don't you?"

"No."

He looks at me, glassy-eyed, and clamps his mouth shut. At that point I realize that the objective of his off-kilter mind is to use me as nothing more than a recipient to whom he can serve his demented subpoena. For this kind of wingnut, what matters is not that you interact with his lunatic plans; it's enough that you listen to those plans, that you become a party to them. Knowledge becomes consent. Obviously, a deranged form of extortion. In the sense that he starts out from an absurd pretext, but still one that is articulated in accordance with a comprehensible logic. And in fact, you can even sort of understand it. That's what's so disturbing about wingnuts, what makes them so truly invasive and unpleasant: the suspicion that, if you stop and listen to them, they might actually wind up convincing you. As if their way of thinking could somehow infect yours. It's because when they bend reality to their wishes, they bend you with it. Which is how they destabilize.

"Listen to me," I tell him, "I don't know what you have in mind and I don't want to know. And just to be perfectly clear, I didn't understand a single word of whatever you just said."

He lowers his head, but his lips are twisted with the victorious smirk of a properly served subpoena.

Without even realizing it, I give Tricarico a glance, and he intervenes like a radio-controlled bouncer.

"Oh," he says, putting a hand on his shoulder, "it's time for you to go."

Giustino turns around, looks up, focuses on him.

Goodbye victorious smirk of a properly served subpoena.

"Did you hear me?" Tricarico explores the concept in greater depth. As if to say that, otherwise, what comes next is physical ejection from this office and probably from the apartment building itself.

Giustino looks at me, but I don't say anything. He gets up.

He turns on his heel and leaves, freeing up some space.

One time, at the zoo, I saw a gorilla curve his shoulders in that exact same way, turning his back on a crowd of rude little boys clustering around the front of his cage, jeering. Identical.

As for me, I feel like a complete piece of shit, if you really want to know.

FLIRTING WITH YOUR EX

S ome sort of avoidance mechanism must have made me completely forget about my appointment with Nives, because when my ex-wife calls me at 2:15 to ask: "Vincenzo, are you having problems?" I instinctively start to ask: "Problems of what kind?" but I manage to hold it in, remembering that we had agreed to meet for lunch at Il Sergente. I tell her that in fact I did have a problem so I'm running late but I'll be there soon—ten minutes at the most, I improvise, even though from where I am when she calls me—that is, in an Expert electronics store browsing color television sets—it'll take at least twenty minutes, if not longer.

That's me all over. A true master of the improvisational jazz of complications. Give me a situation that's already compromised, and watch me launch into my virtuoso solo. The funny thing is that I work hard at complicating my life, in an almost invariably unsuccessful attempt to simplify it. The thing is, when I don't know what to do, I fudge. Not in a fraudulent way. I'm just always trying to cut corners, catch up. Because alongside the survival instinct, there's also the instinct to cut corners, which is why, for instance when you're late for an appointment and you want them to wait for you, you declare ten when the actual time required is twenty minutes. Thus, you force the person waiting for you to give you a discount on the time you're already running late, as if you had restarted the clock on that appointment from the moment when you stretched the truth. Because otherwise the other person could reasonably tell you: "Go fuck yourself," or maybe even say nothing and just leave, while you're still on your way.

Of course, it would be great if that's how things went. But that's not how they go at all. There's always a basic, concrete reason why people wait for you. And that basic, concrete reason, whatever people may say, is far more compelling than the lovely internal flights of rhetoric you indulge in about how intolerable it is for people to show up late. It's not really all that simple to say: "I'm leaving now," and then actually stand up and leave. If there's a woman you want to see, let's say, just to pick a random example, and even if she makes you wait and that's something that normally gets you upset, there's nothing more likely than that you'll wait for her anyway, well past your normal limits of what's tolerable. And even though at first glance it might seem like a typical case of male submission to female with the expectation of a fairly radical short-term reversal of positions, what is really happening in that situation, what you're really doing, is you're plea-bargaining with life. Because life (and it becomes especially clear to you when you're waiting for something or someone who is running late) is made up primarily of plea bargains. It's made up of transactions in which—and this is the revelation that blows you away—you discover that you're capable of a degree of downward-trending comprehension that you normally can't understand when you see it in other people. And there are things that become clear to you, for instance the fact that leaving now would be tantamount to telling the nasty thing you're waiting for that, as far as you're concerned, she can go get fucked (by some other guy? Just the thought of that possibility is enough to catapult you into bottomless despair).

And anyway, to come back to the topic at hand, this time it's Nives who has to stoop to a little plea-bargaining.

"That's all right, it doesn't matter," she says to me, but she says it as if something were happening that mattered, "but get here quickly if you can, okay?"

I remain speechless for a couple of seconds with my cell phone in my hand, and then I roughly triple my walking speed.

When I get to Il Sergente, I can scarcely believe my eyes. Sitting at the table with Nives is the architect. I see him through the plate glass window, before entering the restaurant. What the fuck does this mean, I wonder. Then, without thinking twice, I walk in.

The restaurant is a large open space with a wood-burning oven in plain view, crowded with tables jammed one up against the other. The place is packed. The diners are all talking at once at an intolerable volume, which only confuses me even more. The waiters, red-faced and frenzied, hurry to and fro, their arms loaded with dishes. None of the staff seems to notice me. Perched on a high stool behind the cash register, a matron with dyed blonde hair and outsized seventies smoke-grey sunglasses is talking on the phone at the same time that she rings up a customer (a lack of respect that I find galling, just as much as if she were doing it to me, I have to say). Hanging on the wall behind her, a Last Supper featuring Totò, Peppino, Sophia Loren, Massimo Troisi, and Pino Daniele enjoys pride of place, a classic of local pop art that always prompts an indescribable surge of sadness in me. I stand there looking toward the table of the newlyweds until Nives catches sight of me, stands up, and waves me over, while the miserable cuckold blatantly avoids meeting my gaze.

"You, sir, are an idiot," I mouth mentally; next I glare at my ex-wife, just long enough to let her know that I'm going to make her pay for this one; then I turn on my heel and walk out.

Compared to the deafening din in the restaurant, ordinary street noise seems like silence. Even the air is nice out here. I look at a one way/no entry sign as if I found it rather interesting. A couple about to enter the restaurant asks me if there's much of a wait. I tell them I have no idea and stroll off down the sidewalk at a snail's pace, counting down from ten. Before I even reach six, Nives runs out of the restaurant and calls my name. I turn and give her another murderous glare. For a second I see in her eyes that she's afraid I might smack her.

"Why the fuck did you ask me to come, eh? How dare you pull this kind of move on me?"

Guys, let me tell you, there's nothing as satisfying as acting offended when you are unmistakably in the right.

"Ah, how dare I? You gallop into my office, burst into the middle of a session of therapy, put on your little cabaret act, and now you decide that you can preach to me?"

"So that's what you wanted? To get even? Nice job, you did it, congratulations. Now you can go back to your table. *Buon appetito.*"

I turn to go. She grabs me by the arm.

"Wait. He's leaving right away," she says. She spoke in a low voice, I notice.

"I don't give a goddamn if he's leaving right away," I snap back at her, flying into a rage. "I wouldn't have come in the first place if I'd known you were bringing him with you."

"I didn't bring him," she goes on explaining with perfect calm. "He showed up while I was waiting for you. I didn't tell him I was having lunch with you."

"So, what, is he following you?"

"He told me that he was walking by and he saw me from the street."

"And you believe him?"

"What does that matter, since I lied to him in the first place? Anyway, he and I have just finished having a fight. I told him to leave. He said he was leaving."

"Then how come he's still inside?"

"He waited for you to get here. He wanted you to see him. I think he's trying to show you that he's not giving you a free hand, he's not going to get out of your way."

I think that over for a second.

"Why, what a lovely analysis, Nives. And what do you expect me to do, fight a duel with that pathetic loser?"

"He's afraid of you, Vincenzo."

"Oh, he is? I can't tell you how sorry I am, really. Wait a minute, what do you mean he's afraid of me?"

"He says there's a distance between him and me, that I'm growing further away from him. That it's ending between us, and that I don't even realize it."

And that's how you tell me? I feel like saying to her. Let's go inside and I'll order a bottle of champagne, right?

Instead, I riposte with a textbook comeback:

"Listen, Nives, those are problems between the two of you. You don't have any right to involve me in your architect's mood swings."

"I'm not the one that's involving you, he's the one who's taking his time. I told him to leave, but I can't expect to snap my fingers and have him obey my every command. What do you want me to do, throw him out of the restaurant? After all, he does have a point. He just found out that I lied to him."

"Ooh, for God's sake, Nives, what do you want from me? You want me to say that he's right, now?"

"Quite the opposite. I wanted to stay and have lunch with you, and I still do. It's up to you. If you come in, he'll leave: practically speaking, the two of us can send him away together. But if you leave, then he'll probably stay."

"But you could leave."

"And what difference would that make for you, if you're leaving anyway?"

"Eh. No difference."

"Exactly."

Well, Jesus H. Christ on a crutch.

You really ought to see the sequence of expressions that are projected onto the face of that idiot when we get to the table. The gamut, from astonishment to knowingness, from incredulity to pure scandal. It's like a film trailer. The problem, I think then and there, is that often people don't have very clear emotions, let alone clear ideas.

Nives sits down. I don't, since it's a table for two and the idiot seems incapable of making up his mind to clear out and free up a place. But he's already starting to get on my nerves, so unless he decides to get moving, chairs and other things are going to start flying in here.

"All right then, can you leave us now, please?" she says to him.

"Is that what you want?"

What a ridiculous question. I have to say, when someone asks that stupid a question, do they really think they're going to change the other person's mind?

"I need to talk to Vincenzo. Alone. Do I have to tell you again?"

"I wouldn't have had any objections, if you'd told me about it in advance," he protests.

"We've already talked it over, and I told you that I was sorry. I could have rescheduled my meeting with Vincenzo and seen him some other time, whenever I liked. But I don't want to lie to you again. Right now I want to stay here with him, and I want you to know it."

The asshole registers the impact, picks up his napkin, crushes it into a ball, lets it drop next to his plate, and stands up. Such a cornball piece of histrionics that you won't even find it in a made-for-television movie these days.

"All right," he says, "the two of you win."

Wow, what a retort.

I tense my muscles in preparation for a last-minute assault even though, judging from the debate that I've just witnessed, the likelihood is decidedly theoretical. In fact, the architect meticulously ignores me (which only makes me sketchier, as if

I had "Cut along dotted line" written on me), takes the long way around the table in order to avoid passing in front of me, walks out the door, and vanishes. Nives follows him with her gaze, vaguely sorrowful.

I sit down.

For a little while we say nothing.

The sound of voices all around is overwhelming.

"I'm not that hungry," I say.

"You're telling me," she says.

"You want to get out of here?" I say.

"And go where?" she says.

"Search me," I say.

"Your place?" she says.

"What?" I say.

"Just kidding," she says.

"Ah," I say.

"But why?" I think.

Just then a sweaty waiter materializes next to us, with his Bic already poised over his order pad.

"All right then, what can I get you two," he says, as if he couldn't wait to come take care of us. And he wipes the sweat off his brow with the back of his right hand.

We quickly read the menu, then the young waiter takes our orders with all the focus of a journalist (Nives orders a fruit salad, I order a steak salad, and a carafe of house wine for the table), apologizes for the haste and confusion, and hurries off.

I pick up a breadstick.

"What were you trying to tell me the other day?" Nives asks after looking at me for a while, in that way of hers that I know all too well.

"The other day?"

"When you walked into the session. Why did you attack me that way? What did I do?"

I snap the breadstick in half, and with it, I break something else. There really aren't that many times in your life when your ideas are crystal clear. And I'm not talking about carefully deliberated decisions, with a judicious balancing of pros and cons, those ridiculous processes whereby you look for a sage middle ground that makes the rest of your life miserable. What I'm talking about is the kind of logic-free awareness that makes you say, from one minute to the next, with no conceivable reason: "I'm not doing that." Full stop. Why not? Because. What do you mean "Because"? Just because. Sometimes you get these moments of intense awareness at the altar. I just had one, even if we're not at the altar. Suddenly I have no desire whatsoever to talk with Nives about Alfredo, about how upset I am, about me, about the blame I put on her and on myself for the way in which I left her the leadership in the education and rearing of our children, for all the bullshit with which she furnished their lives, and so on and so forth. I don't want to tell her a damned thing, what do you think about that? Let her come up with her own explanation of my attack, as she calls it. It'll be my 9/11, let's say, oh, what an intelligent metaphor I just engendered.

"I don't want to tell you," I tell her.

"What?" she says in astonishment.

I look at her. I'm proud of myself.

"You're joking."

"Not at all."

She ventures a tremulous smile.

"Are you going to exercise your right not to answer that question?"

"Yes. You could put it like that."

She torments little balls of bread crumb. But I remain unmoved.

"Do you want to make me feel guilty?"

"Cut it out, Nives. I'm sick and tired of you explaining to me what I'm doing."

She thinks that over for a while.

"When did you turn into such a bastard?"

"Well, I like that one better than I like the one about making you feel guilty."

God, I don't know how long it's been since I felt so good. Nives is completely baffled. She's struggling, she doesn't know what to say or where to look; her hands are fumbling clumsily, her whole body seems to fit her a little too tight. Twenty years of psychology defeated by a simple no. The funny thing is, I swear, I can see it in her face that she is feeling authentic admiration.

"You said you wanted to have more of a role. That the mother's exclusive had expired. That you wanted to have a say."

"Yeah."

"What did I ever exclude you from? And how did I do it?"

"Are you starting again?" I could say to her. But I don't even bother. I chew my food, and I even enjoy it a little, truth be told.

"Why won't you tell me what you're talking about?" she says in despair after a while.

"Because I don't want to."

She grinds her teeth, she chokes back tears, she stares into the middle distance and administers a sort of emergency autotherapy that consists of inhaling, exhaling, and passing in review a series of rapid thoughts that seem to flow past her eyes in a virtual braille that only she can read.

The exercise must have been successful, because she appears more luminous when she speaks to me again.

"Okay, it's all abundantly clear. You want to use me as a punching bag in your aggressivity training. Maybe I'm a masochist, but you know what? Be my guest."

Oh, at last, a bit of metaphorical anal sex, I think.

"You're too kind," I say.

She looks at me and, from one second to the next—I intercept the exact interval of time when it happens—her eyes take on a different light, cunning and crafty.

"What's come over you?" I say.

She leans forward until she's practically wiping the plate with her breasts, she grabs the two edges of her side of the table, whereupon I assume she's about to tip the whole thing over onto me, but instead she contracts her belly muscles, lifts her right leg, extends it, uses it to wedge my legs apart under the table, and jams the tip of her shoe straight against my junk.

"Don't try to be funny or I'll crush them for you."

I panic, I throw myself backward; recoiling brusquely against the back of my chair, I look around in terror, and I cup her foot in my hands. It's an unquestionably grotesque maneuver, as well as deeply embarrassing. In fact, people turn to look.

"Have you gone crazy?" I say. Still, I feel like laughing.

"You think you have the exclusive on aggressivity?" she says, pressing hard.

I grab her foot just above the ankle, I try to push it away, but all I achieve is another pathetic recoil, which leaves things exactly the way they were, and only attracts more attention.

"Would you get that fucking foot off of my balls? Because everyone is looking at us."

"There was a time when you appreciated initiatives of this kind."

"That was before you left me, you imbecile. And anyway, you used to take off your shoes."

"You've never called me an imbecile before."

"That's not all I'll call you if you don't get your foot out of there."

The waiter arrives with our plates. But not even this persuades her to release her grip. If anything, she presses harder.

"Fruit salad?" the young man asks.

"That's for me," Nives replies without taking her eyes off me, or her foot, more importantly.

He serves her.

"Steak salad?" he continues, turning to address me.

Try to guess, I'd think of saying to him, if I wasn't otherwise occupied in the head-to-head combat going on downstairs. They always ask questions like that in restaurants.

He sets my plate down in front of me, and only then does he notice the rigidity of our postures. My face is fire-engine red, and my back is as tense as if I were trying to convince a suppository to find the straight and narrow path. Nives is sitting with her chin resting on the knuckles of her right hand and a mischievous idiotic leer on her face, as if to say: "What were we saying?"

Seen from outside, her attitude, unlike mine, might be all right, all things considered; but that something shady is going on underneath this tablecloth even a child would understand. The waiter, in fact, with the discretion of a narcotic-sniffing dog, actually starts to bend down and take a peek; whereupon I tell him to bring me more wine before my steak salad gets cold, and that gets rid of him.

"Listen, I'd like to have something to eat," I tell Nives once we're, so to speak, alone again.

The witch laughs at me. And she finally removes the weight.

I regain my composure.

We start eating in that typical tense aftermath of a prank that's gone too far, with half your mouth still cramped into a smile that won't go away. After a while, I notice that Nives is staring at me.

I cross my legs. Then I look up from my plate.

Do-o-on't look at me like that, I think.

"I wasn't kidding before," she says.

"I beg your pardon?"

"Why don't we go to your place, right now?"

"*Nives.*"

"Sorry."

Don't mention it, I think.

But the outing resumes a few seconds later.

"I don't know what's come over me," she says. "I've never felt like making love with you as much as in the past few days."

She spoke quietly, but I still look around instinctively. One thing is certain: you're not going to catch me back at Il Sergente any time soon.

"It's been since that day you broke into my therapy session, and I haven't been able to think about anything else," she confesses, at once astonished and liberated.

I look at her, amazed at the unmistakable fact that she's undressing me and fucking me with her eyes. I don't think anything of the kind has ever happened to me before. All right, she's my ex-wife, but still.

"My . . . um . . . meat is getting cold," I say.

The waiter comes back with the wine. This time he doesn't ask who it's for. I intercept it before it touches the table and take a generous slurp. The waiter moves off somewhat uneasily.

"Why are you so embarrassed?" Nives asks.

"Maybe it's because you've never been so explicit before."

"I thought I'd get a more enthusiastic reception."

"But you didn't."

She edges backward with her shoulders, as if my answer were a slap in the face. When she speaks again, she seems to be on the verge of resignation.

"Are you with someone else?"

Alessandra Persiano's nude body, waiting for me in front of the window of her bedroom while I argue on the phone with Tricarico, appears before my eyes like a hologram.

"Well, another woman, to be specific. But it's none of your business."

"Is that so? And you think you can decide it's none of my business?"

"Listen to me, Nives. You have to get it out of your head that you can do with me whatever you want. I'm not your second car, understood? And I'm a little sick and tired of being your stud bull upon request."

"I didn't like that one."

"Well, I don't like you all that much anymore, if you want to know the truth," I shoot back, completely unintimidated.

"Ah, now I see."

"And stop acting all offended, Nives. You know I'm right. You don't want to make decisions, and that's the truth. You're always very knowledgable when it comes to other people, this thing goes here and that thing goes there, but when it comes to yourself, you like to keep a foot in two different shoes. Well, it's time to be done with the time-shares. Do you want something? Choose what you want, and act accordingly."

I lean back in my chair, exhausted by my summation, and I look at my steak salad sadly. I'm hungry, but to start eating after a diatribe of this kind is aesthetically inconceivable, truth be told.

Nives looks at me as if she had suddenly been given a new perspective on everything.

"So you're saying that if I decided to get back together with you . . . "

I turn pale.

"I have to . . . answer my phone," I say.

"But it's not ringing."

"Yes it is, actually, it's that thing, the, you know, the . . . vibration," I stammer, struggling for words. I raise my hand to the outside breast pocket of my jacket, and without the slightest idea of what I'm doing, I leap to my feet, as if I had a sudden onset of angina. There is a sudden plunge in the general volume in the room. Everyone turns to look at us.

"What on earth are you doing, Vincenzo?" Nives asks in astonishment.

"Let me just go outside for a minute so I can answer, excuse me," I say, completely incapable of putting a halt to this crescendo of ridiculousness; then, behaving in a truly indefensible fashion, I pretend to pull my cell phone out of my pocket as I make my way through the tables and I reach the exit, abandoning Nives to a state of embarrassment from which I can't even imagine how she'll emerge.

My head is actually spinning once I get out into the street. Even though there's no reason to go on play-acting, I pull out my cell phone, I place it against my ear, and I answer an imaginary caller (for the occasion, I don an intolerant demeanor). I take a first step, then a second step.

Then I accelerate.

Then I slow down.

Then I accelerate again.

Then I cross the street.

And finally I leave.

A Kind of Closet for Skeletons

J ust look at your refrigerator," she says.
   When she's wearing it, my I LOVE NY T-shirt makes a completely different impression. That's partly because it's all
she's wearing.

"What's wrong with my refrigerator?" I ask, standing in the
Grigioperla boxer shorts that Alagia gave me for my fortieth
birthday, two years ago.

She pulls open the refrigerator door and explains, as if I
didn't know what she's talking about.

"It's depressing. You've got . . . " And she gives me a run-
down of my food supplies, one item at a time: "A bottle of
Greco di Tufo with a paper napkin rolled up and jammed into
the neck in place of a cork, another bottle of Borsci San
Marzano liqueur, a lopped-off length of Galbanino soft cheese,
a stick of butter, a package of prosciutto dating back at least to
last Wednesday, a package of hot dogs, a squished-down tube
of ketchup, a jar of mayonnaise, a jar of pickles without a top
and with a few lilypads of mould floating on the surface, two
individually wrapped cheese slices, and an open can of tuna
with a coffee saucer on top of it."

"Don't forget my collection of frozen meals on the lower
levels," I point out.

She doesn't laugh.

I grab her by the hand and pull her to me. She wraps both
arms around me with a worrisome degree of intensity.

"Oh," I say, "what's up?"

"Nothing."

I don't believe for a second that it's nothing, but the kiss she gives me immediately after that distracts me from exploring the matter in any greater depth. So we go back into my bedroom and we make love again. And it's more wonderful every time.

Then I tell her everything. About Tricarico, about the offer that in the end I accepted, about the confirmation of detention hearing and its unbelievable outcome. I leave out nothing, not even the garishly appalling experience in the Love Café.

She listens to me, and she asks plenty of questions, too. She seems happy for me, even if she's slightly puzzled about the preliminary judge's decision to release Burzone. While we're on the subject, I ask if she too has noticed the striking resemblance to Anjelica Huston.

"It's true," she says.

Then we do it again.

When she leaves I stay in bed, wait half an hour, and then text her.

I PUT A SET OF HOUSE KEYS IN YOUR PURSE, I write.

Well, I gave it a shot.

I head into the kitchen, pull out a frozen package of breaded flounder filets, slice a pat of butter into a frying pan, and turn on the TV as the butter starts to melt.

I leave my cell phone in the bedroom.

On a local television station, real estate listings scroll by on the screen, just words, no pictures. In the background, I recognize the melody of "Scimmia," or "Monkey," an old song by Eugenio Finardi about heroin. Flabbergasted by the absolute lack of any connection between real estate listings and heroin addiction, I continue to listen as I cook the filets. Like a buried flashback my mind is filled with a sort of video clip of this song that was broadcast on Odeon at least thirty years ago. It shows a strikingly young Finardi wandering through an amusement park, his mind evidently elsewhere, because it was just a few days after he shot up for the first time. He could already feel the quicksand of smack shifting under his feet, and he watched the families with little kids having fun, while the song goes: *But I kept thinking about it / couldn't get it out of my mind / and as time went by / it was becoming the most important thing of all.* I don't even know if that's how the video really was or if my memory thawed it out for me like that, speaking of breaded flounder filets.

Whereupon it occurs to me that if an Italian pop singer tried to pull something like this on TV nowadays, they'd kick him out of there faster than Mastelloni when he cursed on live TV.

Anyway, Odeon was a wonderful RAI TV program: the closing theme music was a masterful rendition of "Honky Tonk Train Blues" by Keith Emerson.

The song comes to an end. I switch channels to La7, I eat my flounder filets, I head back to the bedroom and glance nonchalantly at the cell phone blinking on the night stand. But up till now I've been so good that I decide to persist in my delaying tactics. I go into the bathroom and brush my teeth, and then I come out.

I sit down on my bed and I sigh as I pick up my cell phone.

I PREFER TO KNOCK, she wrote.

Oh, well.

I get up, walk to the window, cross my arms, and just stand there for awhile looking at the slats of the venetian blinds. Then I turn off the light, get into bed, close my eyes, and sing "Scimmia" over and over in my head as if I were counting sheep, hoping that I can fall asleep before being lynched by a mob of sad thoughts.

Ares Tavolazzi was on bass.

S cimmia" was the last song on the flip side of *Diesel*,
Eugenio Finardi's third album. *Diesel* came out in 1977,
which is to say, a period when the communist movement
in Italy not only existed but had real meaning, with a variety of
forms and gradations, so that there were those who occupied
schools and universities, putting up with vastly dull, inter-
minable assemblies where hundreds and hundreds of cigarettes and the occasional joint were smoked, there were others
who had already started a solo career based on adroit and
strategic political ass-kissing, others still who were on drugs
and didn't understand a thing, and of course those who just
one year later would go on to kidnap and kill the chairman of
the Christian Democratic party.

So while the political landscape was fairly lively and diver-
sified, the musical state of affairs (since music was a sort of
mystical membership card for the younger generations of the
left) was pretty much immobile. In the sense that in those
years, what we mostly listened to were the *cantautori*, or singer-
songwriters, largely self-taught musicians, not all that gifted or
experienced, who adapted disproportionately long lyrics, intel-
ligible only here and there, now and again, to melodies that
anyone could reproduce with a month or two of basic guitar
lessons.

The incredible thing is that, aside from selling truckload
after truckload of records (some of them with just one song on
only one side of the disk), the Italian *cantautori* could count on

a vast audience of mannered depressives who not only learned every verse by heart with the dedication of a Taliban gang, but even sang them themselves, competing to be the first to memorize the most challenging ones. The distinctive feature of these artists, in any case, was not their political engagement, which was implicit (and in fact, whenever an interviewer would ask a notoriously politicized singer-songwriter: "Now, do you consider yourself to be a politically engaged *cantautore?*" he would always give an answer along the lines of: "What can I tell you, I just write the things I feel; I write so that I can express myself and my sensations. Whether that's political involvement, I really couldn't say"), as much as the unmistakable predominance of lyrics over melody, so that the music wound up constituting a sort of extra bonus tacked onto a minor literary work with world-changing ambitions.

In other words, the Italian singer-songwriter of the second half of the seventies was a non-card-carrying political militant who had zipped his literary and/or poetic aspirations into the popular digital file of a slightly overgrown pop song (with a few admirable exceptions, of course, that over the years proved just how exceptional they were, proving the rule once and for all).

Nobody really liked the *cantautori* all that much, truth be told (more than anything else, they were an act that people tended to put on), and in fact when disco music burst onto the scene (which, okay, was crappy as could be, but at least it involved some possibility of fun), the new younger generations didn't think twice about defenestrating the *cantautori* in exchange for some enjoyment and perhaps a little sex.

Finardi, despite his discography, was press-ganged into the ranks of the *cantautori* of his generation (in part because he was politically engaged), but, unlike his fellow singer-songwriters, he was a rocker hiding in plain sight. He wrote his songs and sang them, but he was yearning for a rock band, a band that he reconstituted with every record he made, recruiting cutting-edge musicians. Unlike his contemporaries, who played sitting in a chair onstage, delivering long-winded speeches before playing each song, and accompanied at most by a back-up guitarist and maybe a bongo player, Finardi appeared onstage with a full complement of rock musicians (electric guitars, bass guitar, drum set, keyboards), and he danced, broad-jumped, and grimaced: he overdid it, but at least he played the rock-and-roll game. He tried to impose the model of the rock band in a marketplace dominated by acoustic guitars and bongo drums. In fact, he was the first one to identify the musicians who played on his albums by name and musical instrument. Maybe that was his real idea of rebellious music. In any case, he paid for it. "Scimmia," from this point of view, is the song in which Finardi best exemplifies his rocker notion of how to tell the story of a life in songs. It starts on such a caustic and peremptory note that it could just as easily have ended right there, having already fully served its purpose right at its inception:

The first time I shot up
was one night
at a friend's house
just to see what it was like.

A verse like that, for an era in which every act of juvenile transaction had to be analyzed, politicized, and explored in depth, has the probative value of a full confession. Because it has the courage to tell the truth. Because it denies the act of shooting up its supposed higher meaning and motivation. It takes it back down to its own level: the desire to try something new. Which is the real reason people do things.

That was what rock music did, back when it existed (not today, when it serves as a soundtrack for fashion designers' runway presentations): it addressed reality by its first name. It bodychecked reality, put reality into words and music, without extenuating circumstances. And if it created poetry, that was incidental, something it happened to find on the floor. When it lost this function of telling the truth, revealing hard facts, rock music died.

Now Finardi is over fifty, and he's playing the blues.

SUDDEN REVELATION OF AN OXYMORON

I'm up at 6:15 in the morning so I can get over to the claims center of the Generali insurance company as early as possible, in hopes of finally closing the file on the case of Pallucca, Maria Vittoria, a client of mine who suffered a nasal septum fracture when she walked straight into the automatic front door of a clothing store. The automatic-door mechanism, all things considered, must not have been working very well. And even though at first the owners of the clothing store rushed to the woman's assistance, saying, "We are so sorry, nothing like this has ever happened before, we're insured, don't worry about a thing," when in fact I went into the insurance office confident that I'd be able to take care of the matter with a minimum of effort, I discovered that the people from the store, the day after she broke her nose, had written a letter to the company stating that on thus and such a date a certain Pallucca, Maria Vittoria claimed to have injured her face by striking it against the automatic doors of the premises of their place of business, period: that is, a revoltingly ambiguous statement that, while it may not have completely reneged on the promises made the day before, certainly seemed well on the way to doing so. Among other things, with all the claims adjusters who work at the Generali claims center, I had to be assigned a particularly oafish claims adjuster, the kind of adjuster who seems to resent the existence of the world at large, so that when I pointed out to him that the store owners had repeated over and over to my client that they would immediately write to the insurance company to settle her claim, he told me that that's not the way it looked to him, in fact from what he could see my client's claim was completely unproven, and he saw no evidence that his policy-holders were in any way at fault, which may even have been the case, but the way he said it was so arrogant and disdainful that I really had to force myself to count to ten to keep myself from hauling off and punching him right on the kisser.

So the case was left dangling in the breeze; in the meanwhile, Pallucca, Maria Vittoria had gone in for her medico-legal physical and now I was back for another meeting to see whether the insurance company would at least meet us halfway, splitting the liability fifty-fifty so that we could just settle the case amicably without having to take it to court. I'm never very happy about going to court, in part because, as my old friend Angelo Puzo likes to say, every out-of-court settlement is a victory.

So to make a long story short I pull up outside the main street door of the Generali insurance company just a few minutes after 7:30, and I think to myself, look at that, for once I'm the first one here, but when I step into the lobby I can't find the sign-up sheet anywhere. The sign-up sheet is a miserable piece of paper ripped out of a notebook fastened to the front door with a strip of scotch tape, and lawyers write their names on it to make a reservation before the office opens for the day's business, and the claims adjusters take the lawyers in order by running down the list of names on the sign-up sheet—which is what wasn't there.

I step back into the street to look for the concierge, since the doorman's booth is empty, and I immediately spot him in front of a café across the street talking to some loser. I wave my arms to attract his attention, and when he finally sees me I pretend to write on an imaginary sheet of paper. He holds up his index finger and goes on talking with the loser, leaving me to wait like a child, and I start to get annoyed, because waiting for

294 · DIEGO DE SILVA

the concierge who's chatting with someone outside the café across the street instead of sitting in his booth doing crossword puzzles and occasionally making himself useful is just one more of the many things to which I've developed an allergy.

After a while he condescends to cross the street, and without so much as an apology or a good morning, he just strides briskly into his little booth and, whistling an unrecognizable little tune, pulls open the drawer in the counter, pulls out the sign-up sheet, and sticks it up in plain view on the wall across from the mailboxes, using a single strip of scotch tape that he made materialize from who knows where.

Pen in hand, I step forward to sign up, but when I finally come to this crucial moment, I see that there are already three names marked on the sheet. Whereupon I close my eyes and then open them again, accompanying the sudden wave of heat.

Now, if yesterday Alessandra Persiano hadn't told me that she preferred knocking on my door, if I hadn't sung "Scimmia" in my head last night until three in the morning (especially the last verse: *And if you hang tough six weeks you'll see / you won't think about it again / practically ever*), if only this knuckle-dragging lummox of a doorman hadn't made me use the sidewalk as a waiting room, then probably right now I'd have pretended not to notice that he's certainly taking a tip on the side from some despicable fellow-lawyer so that the lawyer in question can sleep in, not bother to come in early to sign in, butt to the head of the line, and, practically speaking, screw his fellow lawyers.

But this morning I don't really feel like letting it slide, because it's just not possible that every time you leave your house to try to earn your daily pittance you have to be a good boy and swallow another teaspoon of shit. I just can't take these small-scale atrocities anymore, this shake-down of your personal dignity that's implicit in every single phase of every single transaction. Freelance professional is an oxymoron. And it's not even knowing that that's how things work that I can't take anymore. What I can't take any longer is pretending I don't care.

So I decide to rebel. I rip the sheet of paper off the wall and thrust it into the doorman's face, waving it just inches from the guy's ugly mug.

"What the hell is this about?"

He recoils, astounded by my sheer impetus.

"What's what about, Counselor?"

Ah, so you've suddenly decided I have a law degree, I think to myself. *How's that work?*

"Right here, what you wrote on the sheet of paper, you see it? Where are these three names, when did they sign up?" I continue, blindsiding him, with documentation in hand.

"Oh, bef . . . earlier," the little shit stammers.

"Oh, really? Earlier when? In the middle of the night? Did they sleep at your house? Are they hiding in the elevator? Huh? You want to know what we're going to do now?"

The concierge takes a step back, perhaps fearful for his personal safety. A well-dressed matron who just happened to be coming downstairs stops halfway down the last flight of steps. I brandish the pen, I slap the sheet of paper against the wall, and with three slashing lines of ink, I cancel the three names.

"Let's just take these three names off the list. And let's put my name at the top of the list, seeing as how I was the first one here this morning, understood?"

And I put down my name in block letters.

The corrupt doorman doesn't say a word.

"See you later," I conclude.

I turn on my heel and leave.

The middle-aged woman stands motionless on the stairs.

I feel better now. I'm walking briskly, as if I had some idea of where I'm going. Maybe it's just an impression, but it strikes me that the pedestrians I pass notice me. If you ask me, if you really want my opinion on the subject, when someone changes their stride, people notice it. Even if they had no idea of the way you walked before. Because the times you actually display some balls, even if you tuck them away again immediately, you still look ballsy for a while afterward. It's a sort of aesthetic afterglow of manliness, a draining charge that keeps emitting sparks of energy that hit the people walking past. Like periods of intense sexual activity, which produce undefinable diffuse aesthetic enhancements, so that people who have sex look different than when they don't have sex. Not to say that when someone has sex they change all that much (because by and large people generally tend to look the same), but still there are a series of microtransformations instantly perceptible in a fleeting manner, somewhat reminiscent of apparitions. A series of apparition-transformations, that's right. As if somebody who has sex emanates, as it were, waves of low-frequency sexual gratification that make the air around him just a little more electric. As if there were an intermittent subtitling, in a certain sense.

Anyway, ripping the doorman a new one has certainly done me good. I feel as if it's got my blood flowing or something. I'm even feeling a little peckish. I think I might just get myself a pastry.

It's good to rip someone a new one every so often. Maybe that's why bosses are always ripping their employees a new one. It's not because they're so damned worried about continually reiterating the corporate regulations governing productivity. No, workplace bullying must just be good for your personal well-being.

Since I have absolutely no idea of what to do with myself until 9:30, which is when the claims center opens, I decide on a purposeless courthouse incursion. But by the time I get there, my residual charge of virility has drained away entirely. In the semideserted hallway of the Labor Division, a clerk who's listlessly pushing a metal trolley loaded with judicial files gives me a quizzical glance that clearly underscores how unmistakably gratuitous my presence must seem. Because it's obvious that you can't show up in a courthouse, and especially not first thing in the morning, without some good reason. Self-evidence, in a courthouse, is an invaluable trait. You can't go into a courthouse wihout an evident prupose. And in fact, people who go into a courthouse without some good reason are noticed immediately. Especially if they're lawyers.

I don't even try to count them anymore, these episodes in which I flee from a sense of inadequacy. And not only in courthouses, truth be told. In fact I believe that places, just in general, tend to make people feel inadequate. People don't pay enough attention to how places tend to discriminate; places impose behaviors, they divide and pigeonhole people; and those people hardly realize, or maybe they just pretend not to notice. It's not true that you can go wherever you want. I mean, a person can pass by, move through a place, but unless that person has something specific to do there, then they have to leave. You can't just hang out in places. Try walking into a bar, say because you have an appointment to meet a friend who hasn't shown up yet, and you'll see how quickly it becomes intolerable just to be there, unless you order something.

So I head for the exit, and just then who do I see arriving, coming straight toward me from the opposite direction? None other than Anjelica Huston, the preliminary judge with the schnozzola who ordered Burzone released for me, walking side by side with the cool dude ADA who held Burzone's first judicial interrogation.

Of course, there's nothing odd about the fact that two magistrates who've worked on the same case in different roles should walk into the courthouse together. Maybe they're just old friends, or maybe they're having an affair, or maybe they can't stand one another and they're just pretending. That's their business. But the question is: why on earth would the two of them so obviously avoid meeting my gaze?

At a loss for an answer, I head back toward the insurance company, where the claims center should be opening for business soon.

The three pieces of shit whose names I canceled from the sign-up sheet have written their names on the list again, which strikes me as a notable act of arrogance on their part, because it's obvious that if someone strikes your name off a list, it must mean something. You can't go around falsifying lists. It would mean the demise of the guiding principle of standing in line, one of the very few principles, if not the only one, that people allow to govern their lives. Even though it's a principle based on getting there first, which doesn't amount to much as far as underlying foundations of principles go, truth be told. Still, standing in line is an incarnation of an egalitarian principle that states: all human beings are equal in the face of the right to get someplace before other people get there. Which is a pretty loopy principle, if you stop to think about it.

Anyway, my name is still at the top of the list, so I sit in the waiting room of the claims center, enjoying the warm glow of pole position to the clear discomfort of my fellow lawyers, who are already starting to look impatient, considering the number of people already crowding into this dimly lit cubbyhole at just 9:05 in the morning.

Unless you've spent time in the waiting room of an insurance company claims center, you can't really have much of an idea of how depressing it is to witness the most common occupations that come with a degree in jurisprudence. The kind of thing that makes you wonder whether it was really worthwhile to spend all those years studying just you so could find yourself speculating on a car crash. Because when it's all said and done, that's what you're doing. You're bartering a court case (that you try to avoid pursuing) for a check for damages that includes a certain sum for your legal representation. Practically speaking, you're skimming something off the top. And lawyers (who work in the field of traffic accidents and insurance cases) can be grouped along a continuum from the relatively honest to the outright criminal, according to how much they skim off the top.

Finally, after we've been there for a while, the claims adjusters make their entrance. One after another, they walk to their drab little offices like so many aging showgirls heading for their dressing rooms. They love their morning stroll down the cat-walk. This is the one moment when—you can see it on their faces—they find genuine satisfaction in the line of work they've chosen. You can see their point, for that matter. If you started out thinking you'd do who knows what for a living, and now you find yourself haggling over a body shop estimate, try-ing to limit the reimbursement of damages from a car crash to the lowest accepted minimum, what could be more gratifying than a waiting room filled with mendicants with law degrees, all willing and ready to kiss your ass in exchange for favorable treatment?

My adjuster, true prima donna that he is, is the last to arrive, and this morning he looks to be even nastier than usual. As he walks through the waiting room, he looks at everyone, not just me, with such scorn and contempt that, taken a little further, he would have just spit in our faces. In fact, we exchanged a lot of long, searching glances in here, among us lawyers, after he came through.

While I'm lingering over the procession of claims adjusters, with the poorly concealed objective of keeping my mind off the memory of Alessandra Persiano's message (which has already tied lead weights to my love of life, despite the fact that I'm doing my best to behave as if that weren't exactly the way things are), I glimpse, right there, at the entrance to the claims center waiting room, in an unexpected and to my mind absolutely unforgivable manner, like a slap in the face, a broken promise—and to make matters even worse, with a horrible friendly smile on his face—Tricarico.

I have to look at him a couple of times before I can be sure it's him. He's coming straight toward me, amid the embarrassed glances of a few fellow lawyers who evidently dabble in criminal law. The guy sitting next to me stands up immediately to give him his seat. And he sits down without so much as a thank you, the nonchalant recipient of an act that is expected if not required.

"*Buon giorno*, Counselor."

So now we're publicly friends.

Well, Jesus H. Christ on a crutch.

"What are you doing here?" I ask, making an effort not to shout.

"What you mean what am I doing here? For the first few days, don't you remember?"

I could tell him that I've changed my mind about the intrusiveness clause, that I don't want him around me anymore, much less sitting next to me, but suddenly I'm seized with a sense of curiosity about something else.

"How did you know I was here?"

"I saw the name on the sheet of paper downstairs."

I jam my tongue hard against the walls of my mouth while I craft my answer. Then I run it back for him in a replay.

"So you just happened to be passing by the street door downstairs, you liked the place so much that you just walked in, you saw a sheet of paper stuck up on the wall with scotch tape, you read it, and since my name was on it too, you just said to yourself: 'You know what, I think I'll go upstairs.'"

He laughs. But awkwardly.

"Eh, let's say that's how it was."

I must have caught him off guard, because he jerks his head back when I start shouting.

"Just who do you think you're talking to? Eh? Do you think

you can just put your feet on anyone's face you feel like, you *Camorristi*?"

I must have raised my voice a lot louder than I realized, to judge from the ensuing silence. And at that exact moment, my claims adjuster sticks his head out to call the first lawyer on the sign-up sheet, that is, me.

"Counselor, there're certain words that you might be better off not saying," says Tricarico, doing an admirable job of maintaining a deadpan. You might not think of *Camorristi* as restrained and understated, but in a certain sense that's how they are. Well, I've already gotten started, so I might as well take it all the way.

"Or you'll do what? Wait for me outside? Shoot me right here, in front of everyone? Come on, why don't you tell me, I'm curious to know!"

There's not even a fly buzzing in there after that. It's like being in a library. My fellow lawyers, aside from the ones staring open-mouthed, are looking at the floor. A couple of them are scrolling through the directories of their cell phones. The claims adjuster stands at the door, mouth half-open.

Tricarico takes it like the consummate gambler that he is: he stands up and, without a word or a sign of annoyance, he leaves the room.

My embarrassment is so profound that I can hardly feel my face anymore. I smooth back my hair, I fan myself for a moment, and then, while everyone looks at me in silence, I stand up and walk toward the claims adjuster.

"I believe it's my turn," I say, tilting my head to indicate the file he's holding in one hand.

He emerges stammering from his trance. First he looks me in the face, then he drops his gaze to the file, and then he looks back up into my face.

"Oh, of course! Pa . . . Pa . . . "

"Pallucca, Maria Vittoria," I finish his sentence for him.

"Right. Of course. Absolutely."

Absolutely? I think.

The office visit that follows verges on the distasteful. Even though there's an element of satisfaction, witnessing the metamorphosis of a renowned misanthrope into a worm on a hook is an experience you'd just as soon do without, if you have even a shred of respect for the general notion of personal dignity. Long story short, ten minutes later I walk out with the check in my pocket. I practically never had to say a word, because the claims adjuster seemed eager to take care of everything himself, and so I settled the case, for nearly twice as much money as I would have been willing to accept.

I head downstairs in a state of partial depression, turning that odd and unexpected winning lottery ticket over and over in my hand. Is that all? I say to myself. Is being seen with a criminal all it takes to improve the manners of the notoriously rude? Does it take so little to settle a case with spectacular results? Is the Camorra right after all?

I pull out my cell phone and immediately call Pallucca, Maria Vittoria to tell her the happy outcome of her case, with the feeling that this money, dirty in its way, is burning a hole in my pocket. She practically screams with happiness when I tell her the amount of the check and, after I let her shower blessings on me for a while, tell her that I'd appreciate it if she could drop by soon to pick it up.

She says, "I could drop by this morning."

I reply, "This morning?"

She suggests we could go to the bank together, where she could cash the check and pay me then and there.

I look at my watch and think it over. In fact, I don't have to be anywhere, aside from my clandestine Whopper with Alagia at one o'clock. Though I have to factor in the time to get to the airport, of course.

Since I don't seem to be coming up with a response, at a certain point she asks me, with unmistakable shame in her voice, whether my fee is still what we agreed on.

I reply, "Of course it is."

She tells me that I'm a gentleman.

I think to myself: Sure I am.

Se we make a date to meet at eleven o'clock at the Feltrinelli bookstore, which is very close to the bank where she'll be cashing the check.

I walk out the front door of the insurance company, deflated.

I wish Alessandra Persiano would call me right now. Stupid as it is, I touch the cell phone in the breast pocket of my blazer to see if it's vibrating.

Of course it's not vibrating.

On the sidewalk across the street, Tricarico is waiting for me, tail between his legs. I cross the street unenthusiastically and walk over to him. He looks at me, embarrassed, probably expecting another dressing down.

"Nice job," I tell him. "You just settled an insurance case."

"Just did what?" he asks.

"Nothing, I know what I mean."

He purses his lips as if to say, Huh?

"Counselor," he says, after a little while.

"E-e-eh."

"I wanted to apologize."

"Oh, please, do me a favor."

"No, you were right. I made a mistake when I came upstairs. I put you, how do they say it, in an awkward situation. It's just that I don't see myself, when I do things."

"Excuse me, what do you mean?"

"That is, I only understand things after I've done them."

"Ah. Okay. But could you just leave me alone now, do you mind?"

"Why? What is it, are you sad about something?"
"Oh, please."
"Still, there's something I want to tell you."
"Now what."
"There's a person who wants to talk to you."
"And just who would that be?"
"She's waiting for us in that car, over there."
And he tilts his head to indicate a Mini Cooper double-parked with the emergency blinkers on a short way up the street. There's a woman behind the wheel.
"I asked you who that is," I repeat.
"The CPA."
"The CPA?" I ask, as if the professional title didn't fit in somehow.
"Oh, what do you want from me? That's all I know."
"And what does the CPA want to talk to me about?"
"What do CPAs usually talk about, Counselor?"
"Taxes?"
"Which is to say?"
"Money."
"Bingo."
Maybe I shouldn't get into that car. Maybe I'm just making one idiotic mistake after another. But then and there I have so little self-esteem that I can't imagine that anything I do could have any significant consequences.
So I accept.

According to Tricarico's categorical instructions, I get into the car through the right rear door. He waits for me to get seated, then he shuts the door, walks around, and gets in the car and sits down next to me. And to think I'd meant to tell him to sit in front, since the seat is available.
"*Buon giorno* Counselor Malinconico, it's a pleasure to meet you," the so-called CPA says without turning around.

She has a nicely trimmed pageboy haircut and a youthful, slightly mannered voice, and a nice, non-vulgar scent of perfume wafts off her. Even from back here, she seems to be dressed quite tastefully.

"The pleasure is all mine, Dr. . . . ?"

Tricarico wags his finger admonishingly at me, out of sight.

"First of all, I'd like to thank you for having agreed to represent Fantasia, Counselor," she says, ignoring my question and continuing to talk without turning around.

I crane my neck in an attempt to see her in the rearview mirror. She reaches up quickly and grabs it, positioning it so it faces downward.

I look at Tricarico as if to say "What the—?" He pretends not to understand.

"You're quite welcome," I reply, not knowing what else to say.

"We're very pleased with you. You've mounted a truly brilliant defense. We certainly didn't expect him to be released so quickly," she declares, with a cadence straight out of Human Resources Management.

"Oh, is that so?" I say, with the beginning of a flush of annoyance.

Tricarico must have sensed my irritation, because he shoots me a stern sidelong glance. She also heard the gall beneath the flip remark (something tells me), but she smooths it over.

"The decision to take a risk on new names has proven to be a wise one," the talking pageboy haircut continues. "You see, we feel certain that there are excellent lawyers like you around, and that all they need is an opportunity. It's just a matter of giving them a chance."

Well, listen to that, I think.

"The famous lawyers are just so many brand names by now. They don't study, they don't keep up with the latest developments. They are just managers of themselves, they live on public relations and political contacts, and they have galley slaves to do all their work for them. Young and not-so-young lawyers and paralegals who run their law offices for a monthly salary . . . well, we're interested in emancipating these worthy professionals from a state of dependency. We want to invest in them. Invest in all of you, who work in the shadows, far from the recognition that you deserve."

I take a deep breath, doing my best to control myself. All right, I agreed to step into this car. I was curious to see what would happen. But I can't take it.

"So what are you, some kind of labor union?" I say, in a chilly, cutting voice.

Tricarico trains his gaze on me suddenly. In all the time we've spent together, he's never looked at me that way before. The Camorra PR executive lets the seconds drip past before answering me.

"You're a funny man, Counselor. But there's nothing to laugh about here."

"I couldn't agree more," I say. "But now I've really got to go."

I reach out to open the car door.

Tricarico grabs my wrist.

"Get your hands off me," I order.

He ignores me, but his grip doesn't tighten either.

"Just a moment, Counselor," says the whore.

Tricarico releases me.

"What else do you want?"

"We're very impressed with the fact that you haven't asked for the payment of your honorarium."

"I assumed that Fantasia would pay me."

She reaches out her hand, opens the glove compartment, pulls out a rectangular envelope and, still without turning around, hands it to me.

"This is for you."

I've always needed money, all my life. Maybe because I've never had money. So why is it that this morning, of all mornings, just when I don't want any, everybody's trying to give me money?

"What's the meaning of this?"

"Take it, Counselor."

"I don't even know how much it is."

"It's more than enough."

"I think I should be the judge of that, if you don't have any objections."

"You're right. I may not have made myself clear. I just meant to say that I consider it to be a reasonable sum."

"I need to make out an invoice."

"You can invoice Signore Fantasia."

I don't answer. But I don't make up my mind either.

"My arm is getting tired, Counselor," the Corporate Camorrista says.

I inhale. And as I exhale I realize how deeply offensive it would be to them if I refused to accept the money.

So I take the envelope and I open the car door.

"Counselor," the union representative calls out to me.

"What."

"We'd be deeply honored if you'd be willing to work for us again."

"I'll think about it," I say.

The dirty city air has a wonderful taste when I finally get out of that piece-of-shit car.

I, for what it's worth, don't even know what the Camorra is anymore. Not that I have any special knowledge on the subject, because I know more or less as much as everybody else. And what people know about the Camorra is essentially the popularized version of what is written in the verdicts handed down by trial judges, which are after all the primary sources for any study of the phenomenon. Because it's clear that in order for something to be studied, it must be written down, at least to some extent. Of course, direct experience is also a form of knowledge (generally—though not necessarily—the most reliable form); but those who study things refer to written documentation, because, for the purposes of study, that is to say, the critical understanding of a subject, a written account is always preferable to an oral account. On the other hand, when we're talking about the need to convey a cumulative personal experience, that is to say, writing it down (since writing is the natural extension of experience), we immediately sense the need for other bodies of writing as a point of reference. And where is someone who writes about the Camorra going to find these other other bodies of writing as a point of reference? They're going to turn to the verdicts handed down by judges in Camorra trials. Because, let's face it, the Camorristi don't write. Or perhaps we should say: they pick up a pen and paper when they're turning their back on that life, in order to provide, in a certain sense, the written proof of a change of heart (what Camorrista still in the business would put his dealings in writing?). And it's obvious that a personal account, even a written personal account, by someone who has had a change of heart lacks the degree of reliability found in a legal verdict, which is the product of an extended, painstaking, complex effort, adhering to certain criteria of objectivity and, most important, a text that has been written by people who have no need of a change of heart in order to start writing.

There are plenty of stories in circulation about the Camorra. But what makes these stories so durable, and what takes them out of the realm (in an absolutely inexplicable way) of gossip and hearsay is that you believe them when you hear them. By which I mean that these stories immediately convey that distinctly Camorristic sense of déjà vu, so that as soon as you hear the beginning of the story, you've already figured out what it's all about.

This impression of having already experienced the thing is a trait that is peculiar to the Camorra, a faint but lasting aftertaste, like the faint hint of vanilla in a Brunello di Montalcino or the nuance of blackberry in a full-bodied Amarone della Valpolicella, details that immediately make you nod in recognition. As if the Camorra spoke to a special dedicated sector of the brain, which is capable of filling in sentences automatically. The sentence structure of the Camorra is invariably missing a piece: they give you subject and object, or else predicate and complement, or subject and predicate, leaving you to supply the rest of the sentence.

I suspect that this grammatical privilege is a product of the fact that the Camorra, if you were born in the lands that it controls, is one of those things you learn from an early age; but if you try asking around about exactly what the Camorra is, no one will tell you. It's like the mystery that surrounds the question of how babies are born, a mystery that they try to unveil only when you've reached a certain age, as late as possible, when you're old enough to understand, but by then you've already figured it out for yourself. The surrounding community basically teaches you about the Camorra by hinting at it and doing its best to scare you. It reports the news by censoring it. It gets you used to looking away, pretending not to understand; and then, when you grow up, it blames you when you fail to report something to the police.

Anyway, what I'm trying to say is that it's my impression that in recent years the Camorra has changed a great deal, in the collective imagination even of people who experience it as nothing more than another form of atmospheric pollution. In the sense that it's no longer only one single thing, and especially in the sense that it's something that never stays put, in one place. It has kind of shredded, spread out, muddled itself into an indistinct criminal genre where there's room for professionals and dilettantes, militants and wildcat operators and loose cannons, without any certainty of a distinction between legitimate operators and fly-by-night gypsies, the careful and the out-of-control, originals and cheap imitations.

Let's take one of the best-known aspects of the way that the Camorra exercises its power: its control of the territory. Until just a few years ago, it was unthinkable that anyone might be shot and killed, or stabbed and killed, over a cell phone, or for a small amount of money you just withdrew ten minutes ago from an ATM. The rigorous application of an occult system of rules, forbidding the commission of any criminal act outside of those prescribed or specifically authorized by the Camorra, was a fundamental and indispensable condition of exercising its power.

But these days, there's a nondescript grab bag of criminals roaming the streets, generically Camorristic, deepy irresponsible, casually practicing a level of violence that's absolutely disproportionate in terms of its criminal objectives. So you can be shot in a two-bit robbery, or because you talked back when ragged and bullied by a small-time thug, high and on the streets looking for a fight, or else just because you committed the error of looking at somebody in a way that nobody even noticed but him.

Whereupon you're forced to ask yourself: where is the Camorra? Why doesn't it do something? Has it transferred its criminal interests elsewhere? Doesn't it care about its territory anymore? Where is it doing business now?

If the Camorra can't be defeated, then at least it ought to liberate the citizenry from the barbarity of disorganized crime. It shouldn't abandon its victims. The Camorra should get back in the trenches, fight the good fight, make it safe to walk the streets again.

We want a sustainable Camorra.

Turn-Downs

I take advantage of the ample fifteen minutes that I'm running early on my appointment with Pallucca, Maria Vittoria to hole up in the bathroom of the Feltrinelli bookstore so I can examine the contents of the envelope I was just given by the intern in Encouragement of Unknown Lawyers for the induction of new blood into the Registry of Criminal Lawyers on the Camorra Payroll.

Given the restroom-claustrophobia syndrome that keeps me from locking bathroom doors, I walk into the toilet and adopt the so-called technique of the artist's compass: legs spread wide, left foot jammed against the base of the door (though I take care not to lean against that door, given the suspicious fingerprints that besmear it), tip of the right foot against the opposite wall. I then proceed to open the envelope.

I pull out the wad of bills, which are intimidating in the way they rustle with freshness and give off a distinct sense of confidence in the future (it's undeniable that tomorrow strikes you as sunnier when you have a wad of cash in your pocket), I fold it over like a sandwich (actually, I should say, like a triple cheeseburger, given the sheer bulk—and I can't say whether I find that bulk more exciting or worrisome) and I proceed to count it.

In this case, I make use of a money-counting technique I learned from an ex-girlfriend who worked as a bank teller; actually I called her up recently, in a period of absolute sex famine, beating around the bush for a good twenty minutes and winding up with a friendly turn-down, one of those turn-downs that's cushioned by the fact that the two of you have a shared sexual history, but that doesn't mean it's not still a turn-down. In fact, even now when I think back on it, I'm left with a burning pain in my ass, truth be told. Because there is something intrinsically unacceptable about turn-downs from ex-girlfriends. They start with an unexpected and completely decontextualized phone call from you: in practical terms, you pop out of the distant past; she immediately understands what you're driving at; you give it the long wind-up to the pitch but that just makes it worse; she matches you in tone and spirit, but it's obvious that she's just waiting for you to get to the point, and when finally, after a long and cringe-inducing series of circumnavigations, she makes it clear that it's completely out of the question, you change the subject with the lightning reflexes of a motorist swerving into the oncoming lane a split second before impact, to the soundtrack of an absolutely gratuitous giggle that she validates by laughing along with you, even though nothing funny was said. Then you say goodbye and hang up, and you walk up and down in your apartment for a while.

But the turn-down in question is especially upsetting because the ex-girlfriend we're talking about—who dismisses me as if as long as we've known each other I'd done nothing but proposition her—is just pretending that she can't remember which side the scale was tipping toward, back then.

When she told me on the phone that "it didn't strike her that there was any basis for us getting together again in that context" (which in and of itself strikes me as a piece-of-shit phrase), I could have reminded her, oh I don't know, of when she used to say things to me like: "Do you realize that in the time I've known you I've seen you more with your pants off than on?"; and I would tell her that she had every right to be proud of the fact (in fact, after telling me that I was an oaf and a pig for saying it, she had to admit that she was in fact proud of the fact); or else (my personal favorite): "You and I don't talk enough!" when, immediately after walking into her apartment, I started taking my pants off, in fact; or else, reemerging after a blow job in my car: "No, listen, this is absurd. There's a boy who's been courting me for three months, a real sweetheart, believe me, gentle, polite, caring, a perfect father for my children. And it's not like he just loves me: he worships the ground I walk on. He takes me anywhere I want to go, and money is no object. When he takes me home he waits to make sure I get in the front door, and he even wants me to wave to him from the window before he'll drive away. And he hasn't laid a finger on me, you see what I'm saying? Nothing, not even a kiss on the cheek, and look at what I'm doing right now"; and I say: "Exactly: don't stop."

Anyway, I count the money, I put it back in the envelope, I slip the envelope into the inside breast pocket of my jacket, I step out of my solitary confinement cell, I walk over to the sink, I rinse my hands without soap; the electric hand dryer doesn't work, so I shake my hands freely, scattering drops everywhere; I look at myself in the mirror as I wait for my hands to dry themselves, but since someone has just walked in and I suddenly realize that I have no apparent reason justifying my continued presence in there, I walk out with both arms outstretched and dangling, and find myself in the children's book section looking like a zombie. A little boy holding his grandfather's hand looks up at me. I go to the home video section and contemplate with lively interest a "Teletubbies" DVD while I think to myself: *Good God Almighty, I have 15,000 euros in the inside breast pocket of my jacket.*

I head over to the bookstore café, I sit down at one of the high stools by the counter, and I order an espresso. The barista takes one look at me and asks if I feel all right. I say, "Yeah, sure."

I sip my espresso as I analyze the facts at hand. Okay, I'm not exactly an expert when it comes to legal fee structures (which for that matter is a field that belongs by feudal right to famous lawyers: if small-time lawyers talk to their clients about fees, they lose them as clients). I have no idea what the normal cost of the kind of defense I just provided would be, nor have I really given the matter a great deal of thought before now, accustomed as I am to taking whatever people pay me without objection. The one thing I'm sure of is that in the course of my entire, shall we say, career, I've never earned anything like this much money at a single time (and let's not even try to imagine how much time it would take me to earn this much money). But the question that suddenly begins to torment me is this: What if this money isn't just limited to the Burzone case? What if this money is also a down payment on future cases? The problem with these people is the language. Since they speak only through actions—accomplished or attempted—you've got to try to decipher them each time. It's not like a person can just take the money he's due and then forget about it; he's also got to worry about whether by taking this money he might not discover that he now has an uncomfortable fiduciary responsibility as a Camorra lawyer. Obviously, that's the kind of thought that contaminates whatever money you earn (which in my opinion is something that Camorristi know: it's why they pay you).

I finish my cup of espresso and walk off stiff-legged, like someone who's just stepped in dog shit, but I have to go back because the barista practically yelled after me that I've forgotten to pay.

I head upstairs, I loiter around in the nonfiction section in a catatonic state, I leaf through a book called *The Antibiological Man* that I don't give a damn about, and then I head for the exit.

Across from the wall where the new titles are on display I

run into Pallucca, Maria Vittoria as she contemplates the latest best-sellers with a look of bafflement, and, come to think of it, now I seem to remember that we had an appointment.

"Counselor," she says, overjoyed to see me.

"Ah, hi there," I reply.

"I got here a little late, sorry."

"What?" I ask.

"Are you okay?" she asks.

"Of course I am," I reply.

Why is everyone asking me that question?

"Well, shall we go?" she says.

"Where?" I ask.

"What do you mean, *where*, Counselor?" she asks with a note of concern in her voice. "To the bank, right?"

I touch my brow.

"Oh, of course. But I can't come with you."

"Why not?" the woman asks, perplexed.

I pull the check out of my wallet and hand it to her. Her face lights up when she sees the figure.

"I have an appointment," I say.

"Then what are we going to do? I can't pay you unless I cash the check."

"That's all right, you can drop by my law office this afternoon."

"This afternoon?" she says again, incredulous that I'm willing to let her go, since the check (which includes my fee) is made out to her, and so there would be nothing to keep her from cashing it and then claiming that she had paid me.

"Why, are you busy this afternoon?"

God, it's heartbreaking to see how she clutches that piece of paper to her heart.

"No, no, I'm not busy."

"Well, all right then. Would six o'clock be convenient for you?"

"Six . . . o'clock. Okay."

"Don't hold that check so everyone can see it," I say.

"Oh, right," she says, looking at her hands, uneasily. And she stuffs the check into her purse.

"Then I'll expect you."

"All right, Counselor."

She shakes my hand, uncertainly.

Then we walk out into the street and part ways.

I head off for my date with Alagia, but before I've gone more than a few yards, as I expected, my critical angel starts off on his diatribe.

Ah, excellent work, I have to say, my compliments. You know, don't you, that you're never going to see her again?

She's an honest person, I reply.

Oh, really? And how do you know that?

She would never do anything like that to me, I reply.

Who is she, your sister?

I just decided to trust her, I reply.

So what you're trying to tell me is that she's coming to your law office this afternoon to bring you the money?

Sure, I reply.

Truly noble on your part, I say to myself, but don't come crying to me later.

Fine, now would you mind leaving me in peace for a while? I reply.

And before I can ask myself another question, I pull out my cell phone and consider an array of alternative text messages to send Alessandra Persiano: her absence is starting to take on the general appearance of an abandonment that is threatening to devastate me.

Here is the range of options that presents itself to me, after a while:

318 · DIEGO DE SILVA

A) WHERE DID I GO WRONG?
B) OKAY, YOU PREFER TO KNOCK, BUT THEN WHY DON'T YOU KNOCK?
C) WHATEVER THE PROBLEM MAY BE, LET'S TALK ABOUT IT
D) IF IT'S OVER, AT LEAST DO ME THE FAVOR OF LETTING ME KNOW

So I write:

HOW ABOUT GETTING SOME CHINESE FOOD TONIGHT?
KISSES, VINC

Hitting SEND demands an enormous effort, I'm so disgusted with myself.

Then I dial Alf's number.

He only answers after it rings repeatedly, and in a whisper.

"Dad, I've told you three hundred times not to call me at school."

"I know, but there's something I need to say to you."

"All right, okay, just hold on while I step over here."

"What are you doing?"

"Phys ed. Would you mind telling me why you're calling me?"

"Listen, is there something you want?"

"What?"

"Something you want. Tell me something you want, anything at all. I'll buy it for you."

Pause. He must be in the hallway at school, because the voices of his classmates have that unmistakable echo.

"Dad, what are you talking about?"

"What's the matter, you don't know what to say?"

"What happened, did you win some money?"

Thanks for the vote of confidence, I think to myself.

"Is there something you'd wish for or not?"

He takes a moment to think.

"For you and Mom to get back together?"

"Ha, ha, funny guy."

"What do I know, Dad. Just let me get off the phone."

"You don't know what you want?"

A short silence follows.

"No. Really, there's nothing I want."

"That can't be."

"Yes it can."

"Alfre'," I say, after a pause, "I've never given you a real gift."

"That's not true. Why are talking such bullshit, Dad?"

"Trivial stuff aside, I mean. You've never really asked me for anything."

"Maybe that's because I had everything I needed."

"Because your mother took care of it."

"And who gives a damn about that, Dad? Do you really think that I bothered to wonder which of the two of you had paid for it when I got something?"

I hadn't actually considered that, I say to myself.

That'll Teach You to Set Another Place at the Table

Y
ou caught him off guard," Alagia says, referring to my phone call with Alfredo. Today the airport is half-empty, and our line at the Burger King actually seems like a lot of people.

"I didn't ask him a particularly hard question," I point out, as I look up at the backlit transparent display photograph of the Whopper as if it were women's lingerie.

"No, actually that's a pretty challenging question," Alagia says.

The guy ahead of us in line, a gentleman in his early sixties, fit for his age, with a distinguished appearance and a dark suit, orders a large Coke and a Double Bacon Cheeseburger XXL—the advertising slogan for which is: "When you could eat a wild animal."

"So if I asked you the same question, you wouldn't know what to say?" I ask her.

Alagia thinks it over while the Burger King cashier serves the unsuspectable *paninaro*, whose Double Bacon Cheeseburger XXL is so massive that it's leaning to one side like the Tower of Pisa. I'd be embarrassed to eat that monster in public, truth be told. I have to admit that I'm starting to like the guy.

"You know what?" Alagia resumes. "When you suddenly come into a lot of money, you're going to be worried about squandering it, so you wind up buying something that you don't really like. And that only makes things worse. If you ask me, the best thing to do is just put a thousand euros in your pocket and go out and spend it freely on crap of all kinds. At least you'll have fun."

My personal hero picks up his tray and walks off.

It's our turn.

"So you're saying you want a thousand euros?" I ask.

"Why don't you start by paying for our burgers."

We go over to a table and sit down.

"Your mother didn't say anything to you, did she?" I ask her, after gulping down my first onion ring.

"No, why, what should she have told me?" she says, and chomps into her San Diego Beef, spilling a fair amount of filling onto her tray liner.

"Let's just say I screwed up big time."

Alagia grabs a chiclet of meat and stuffs it back into the tortilla; she rapidly surveys the biggest lettuce leaves scattered across her tray and browses on a couple of them.

"Like how big time?"

"Super-rude."

"As in?"

"We were having lunch together and I walked out."

"I don't follow you."

I pop open my San Benedetto and take a swig from the bottle.

"Look, let's take you and me right now, okay? Now imagine that I stand up, pretend I have to answer a cell phone call, even though the phone doesn't even ring, then I walk out and leave you sitting here."

Alagia puts her San Diego Beef back in its basket (I've never seen her do anything like that before) and stares at me.

"Did you really do that?"

"Mm-hm," I reply, my mouth full and a hint of satisfaction in my voice.

"You're a complete idiot, Vincè, you know that?"

I brush my hands together to get the crumbs off.

"Oh, thank you for the in-depth analysis."

"What did you want, for me to say nice job?"

"No, not nice job. But why'd you do it, maybe."

"There is no reason to do anything that idiotic. At least not what you just described."

"In fact, I don't even know what made me think of telling you about it, if you want to know."

I doubt that she even heard me, to judge from the intensity with which she's suddenly started brooding.

"Wait, does Emilio have anything to do with this, by chance?" she asks, after a while.

Emilio would be the name of the architect.

"Why do you ask?"

"Because for the past few days, Mamma's been treating him like shit."

"Oh really?" I ask, straightening my back.

"When we're at dinner she practically refuses to look him in the eye, and she's really rude to him whenever he tries to talk to her . . . frankly, I don't know how he can put up with it."

"Imagine," I say, repulsively delighted. And I take two consecutive and super-carnivorous bites of my Crispy Chicken Deluxe.

"So does he have anything to do with it or doesn't he?"

"Who, the architect?"

"He wouldn't have happened to be there, too, the time that you walked out on her?"

"Eh. That is, yes, up till a certain point. In the sense that he'd already left by the time that I left too."

"Look, can you just tell me what you did?"

"Me? Nothing."

We both turn almost simultaneously toward the plate glass windows to watch a plane coming in for a landing. I take another bite of my CCDL.

Alagia rips open a packet of ketchup and drizzles it over her French fries.

"To get back to the question of money," I say, "should I give it back, in your opinion?"

On the way to the airport, I had told her everything.

"Or else you know what I could do," I resume, before she can answer me, "seeing that neither you nor Alfredo want anything, I could set up a nice insurance policy in both your names, what do you say?"

"That it's not a huge amount of money, so why don't you take it and use it to live without worries for a while."

"I'm not sure that I really want to do that."

She raises her eyes skyward before answering me in a slightly exasperated tone of voice, that is if you can combine slightness and exasperation.

"Vincenzo, you're forty-two years old, you realize that, don't you?"

"And what does have to do with anything?"

"What it has to do with is that you can't dither endlessly every time you have to make a decision. The last time we went to the movies together we walked in after the film had already started, because right up until the very last second you didn't know if you wanted to see this movie or that one."

"You're wrong, I couldn't have any doubts about *Spider-Man 2*."

Not even a smile. She must really be determined to complete her presentation of the concept. She can be a little ponderous at times, this girl.

"Or take the question of the money. It's not a huge amount: you did a job, they paid you, so keep it."

"Maybe you don't realize the kind of people we're talking about."

"Then give them back their money, if you think that's the best thing to do. But do it. Stop dithering, because in the meanwhile the movie's starting, if you get what I'm saying."

"Hey, how do you know all these things about me? Have you been taking lessons from your mother?"

"You want to know what I think? That you're drumming up all these problems about things because you just don't want to do them."

I stare intently into the middle distance, beyond her talking head, horrified at what I see.

"Well, here's something you might want to know."

"What might I want to know?"

"That your mother's architect is coming this way, heading straight for our table."

Alagia turns around, and when she sees him she actually starts to get to her feet, she's so surprised. But there's no need, because he's already standing by the table. He's wearing a peach-color Lacoste shirt, super queer, and he even has a suntan, to make things worse. If you ask me, he's exactly like her father, even if I've never met her father.

"Emilio, what are you doing here?" Alagia asks.

"Forgive me, Alagia. And forgive me, Vincenzo. I'm sorry to barge in, but I need to talk to you."

By which he means the undersigned.

"Did we have an appointment, by any chance? I can't seem to remember that we did," I observe.

"No, we didn't. I was driving on the beltway, I saw you, and I followed you."

"Well, isn't that a coincidence. The other time you told Nives that you just happened to be walking by the restaurant and you saw her inside waiting for me. Do you have a GPS device that indicates the location of my next lunch appointment?"

Alagia smiles, even though she finds the situation embarrassing.

The cuckolded goat ignores the provocation and puts on a slow half-lidded blink of the kind that says: "That's not the point."

Like hell that's not the point, I think.

"That's exactly what I'd like to talk about with you, if you give me an opportunity, Vincenzo," he says, with a reasonableness that smells fishy to me.

Alagia gazes apathetically at our favorite dishes, which also now strike me as somehow tainted by the intrusion.

"Don't take this the wrong way," I say, "but I just don't feel like ruining my lunch with Alagia so I can sit here and listen to you."

"Vincenzo's right, Emilio," Alagia breaks in. "You really could have tried to find a better opportunity to talk to him. Plus, this hamburger lunch of ours is a little secret between me and Vincenzo, not even Mamma knows about it. All the more reason that I wish you weren't in on the secret."

The turd emits a pained sigh through his nostrils. Then he turns to me, in a sort of exasperated request for compassion.

"You see the way things are, Vincenzo? This is your family, not mine," and he nods toward Alagia with a tip of the head, as if she were a surprise witness or something. "You feel as if you're in the minority, you think they're holding you at arm's length, but it's not true. Alagia comes to have secret hamburger lunches with you, Alfredo has never confided a thing in me, Nives is constantly reaching out to you (and the two of you probably go to bed together—I don't know and I don't want to know), but I'm part of their lives too, and I love them just like I love Nives, and you need to give me a little room, because I can't win anything for myself if you keep competing with me, you understand that, don't you?"

For a moment, Alagia and I exchange a glance dripping with an oozing blend of pity and respect—and in fact he immediately takes advantage of our weakness to sit down at the table next to ours and join our little party, uninvited—then I suddenly say to myself, "Oh, wait a second, what the fuck is this guy saying? What does he know about coming home late at night to an apartment furnished entirely in Ikea, closing the front door, hearing the noise of the refrigerator and nothing else, and then rushing to turn on the TV as if it were an emergency inhaler? And the public television programming on RAI Educational at three in the morning, what does he know about that? And the frozen meals?"

"Listen here," I say, increasingly impassioned, "if there's one thing I find distasteful it's this insistence on a dignified approach with just a sprinkling of humiliation. This idea of treating marital problems as if they were corporate mergers, asking your rival to make a contribution, you hand over this block of shares and in exchange I'll promise to do X. But we're not talking about transactions here: this is a vicious goddamned jungle, you understand? It's win or lose, and it's not like you can smooth everything out with a nice balanced discussion. When Nives dumped me and set up housekeeping with you I didn't come around butting into any of your lunches, as I recall. If this is still my family, as you said just a few minutes ago, that just means that you weren't successful in your takeover. So what do you want from me now? You want me to lend you a hand? Well, it's admirable on your part to pretend to get down on one knee and beg like this, but my answer is no."

Alagia nods, enthusiastically, I think.

The miserable cuckold's self-serving façade of dignity collapses in a pitiful heap. And he's left there, revealed as the frantic loser that he is.

"Then I'm going to put it to you in somewhat different terms," he declares, assuming a ridiculous tone of voice, as if signaling that he's about to issue a threat.

For some reason that's unclear to me, I look Alagia in the eye instead of him, then and there.

"Oh, really? And how exactly are you going to put it to me?"

Whereupon he points his index finger straight at me and says:

"You stay away from . . . your wife."

I'm baffled for a second or two; then I look over at Alagia, and she bursts into laughter.

"Hey, that's priceless. Do you realize what you just said?"

The miserable wretch realizes he's shot himself in the foot, and he turns red as a beet despite the suntan.

"Don't let's get lost in wordplay," he says, clearly struggling. "If being civil doesn't work, I can stop being Mr. Nice Guy."

"Now that's enough, Emilio. Cut it out immediately," Alagia says.

"Why don't you just go fuck yourself?" I tell the turd.

And then I couldn't say who started it, but in the blink of eye we find ourselves rolling on the floor of the airport food court, thrashing and wrestling but without a hint of technical skill, while Alagia hops back and forth around us, shouting, "Stop it, stop it" and nobody tries to separate us and a woman says, "The police, there's a police station on the ground floor, call the police," and finally at a certain point I manage to get one arm free and at last I'm about to haul off and really punch the shitbird good and proper but I don't get a chance because at the very last second someone pulls him off me, I have just enough time to get a full-screen close-up of his astonished expression, understandably incredulous as he feels himself being lifted straight up into the air like a big old hambone and then hurled with unspeakable violence against the counter of the Burger King, taking one of the cash registers, a pile of trays, and the promotional cardboard totem pole of the Double Whopper with him as he goes, whereupon I haul myself to my feet to find just who bowled this unconventional strike and I say to myself, no, this can't be, Tricarico again?

The Value of Lost Things

Oh how pleasant it is to spend half your afternoon at the airport police station with a cop nitpicking everything you say and completely disbelieving your version of what happened. Alagia explained to him over and over that everything that happened was the fault of that cuckolded goat, but the cop ignored her, he couldn't believe his good luck at finally being able to sink his fingers into something that in his mind vaguely resembled an investigation. The police must get bored silly at airports.

"And to think you're a lawyer, you ought to be ashamed of yourself," he said to me when I showed him my bar association membership card instead of my identity card or my driver's license, in the hopes that my professional standing might help me to clear up what had happened.

"Ashamed of what?" I answered.

"Getting in a fight like that, in public, over a woman—and in front of your daughter, just to make things worse. Aren't you ashamed of yourself?"

"Leaving aside the fact that the only one who's itching to fight over a woman is my ex-wife's live-in boyfriend, do you realize that I took an elbow to the ribs because I was trying to protect him?"

Because in fact I actually had tried to save the architect from Tricarico, and all things considered, I had been successful. As soon I realized that he was the one wading into the brawl to protect me, I jumped on his back to try to keep him from slaughtering the faggot. Tricarico, unaware that it was me pummeling him on the back, had crushed his elbow into my ribcage, making me fall to my knees, coughing and dragging myself across the floor in a desperate quest for oxygen. Once he realized the seriousness of his error, he renounced his intention of executing the architect and came to my rescue, just as the police hurried onto the scene, having been summoned there by Alagia. The police, at the sight of Tricarico intent on slapping me gently in the face to bring me around, just assumed he was a good Samaritan and therefore detained only me and the still semi-conscious architect (who had already taken a couple of kicks to the face in the meanwhile), deeming the two of us to have been the sole protagonists of the brawl. Whereupon Tricarico took advantage of their misunderstanding to heel-toe it out of the airport without any of the onlookers—especially not Alagia, who knew nothing about his role in the fight, since she had immediately hurried off to summon Naples Airport's Finest—daring to point him out to the police as a participant in the melee.

"So there you were," the policeman was summing up, with a very disobliging tone of voice, truth be told, "having a fight with your wife's live-in lover; suddenly out of nowhere appears this other guy who starts beating up your wife's live-in lover, and you hurl youself on him to protect your wife's live-in lover."

"Yes, that's right," I answered without shame.

"And why on earth would you have done anything that stupid?"

Come to think of it, why on earth would I have done anything that stupid?

"What do I know? You don't really stop to think, in that kind of a situation," I told him.

"What are you saying, do you find yourself in that kind of a situation on a regular basis?"

"Oh, sweet Jesus. Listen, there are at least twenty people who saw what happened. Why don't you go back upstairs and ask them, if you don't want to believe what I'm telling you?"

"I'll go, I'll go, don't you worry about that. For the moment, why don't you just answer my questions."

He uttered that last phrase with a visible shiver of emotion. Whereupon I decided that he must be one of those cops who take their final police academy exam with the dream of one day being able to say things like "For the moment, why don't you just answer my questions."

"And just who is this guy who wades into the fight and starts beating up your wife's live-in lover?"

"How would I know?"

At that point, he finally deigned to get Alagia's point of view.

"Signorina, would you happen to know anything about it?"

"Of course she doesn't know," I intervened on her behalf. "She had just run downstairs to get you when the other guy showed up."

He turned to look at me, brimming over with bumptious arrogance.

"The question was directed at her, if you don't mind."

You could tell that he couldn't wait to say that either.

"It's like he said," Alagia confirmed.

"Isn't that a nice coincidence," the cop mused with a crafty leer. "You rush off at the exact moment when the mysterious brawler shows up, Signorina . . . ?"

"Cervi."

"Cervi, and after that?"

If anything, that should be "and before that," I thought to myself.

"Alagia."

The cop craned his head forward and cupped his ear with one hand.

"Ala . . . ?"

"A. La. Gia," she broke it down for him, in annoyance.

"What an odd name, I've never heard of it."

"There you go."

"Wait a second. Did you say Cervi?"

Whereupon Alagia and I exchanged an objectively ambiguous glance, which we meant as "Okay, now how're we going to explain it all to this guy?"

And of course he took it in a completely different way.

"You told me that this was your daughter," he immediately challenged me, as if things had turned mighty damned serious all of a sudden.

"Not my biological daughter," I replied.

Alagia stood there saying nothing but disapproving of my choice of adjectives with her eyes. I could have put it differently, I had to admit.

He looked at her. Then he turned back to me.

"Are you two trying to pull some kind of prank?"

"You're kidding me," I said.

"Who is this girl, and how old is she?" the cop demanded, raising his voice.

"Hey, wait a minute, are you trying to insinuate . . . "

"What are you saying, how dare you?" Alagia shouted in turn.

Luckily that's when the architect showed up, fresh from the nearby public health clinic, and cleared up everything, thanking me publicly for having come to his rescue.

"What have I been telling you for the past half hour?" I railed at that moron, who stood therefore dolefully, looking at his shattered dreams lying scattered across the floor.

Then we signed a complaint against unknown parties and left the office, pursued by the cop's preachy advice, as he exhorted us to set a better example for our children next time.

We both decided to forego a visit to the hospital.

The pathetic cuckold's face was all swollen, and he asked Alagia not to say anything to Nives; he wanted to tell her that he'd been attacked in the street.

She said that she wasn't sure she felt like doing him that favor, after the deeply uncomfortable situation he'd put her in.

And at last we left the airport.

Alagia accompanied me back to my office (where I was supposed to have an appointment with Pallucca, Maria Vittoria to receive payment of my fee), and when she said goodbye she added that now at least we had a good reason to give up eating Whoppers, since it was unlikely that we'd ever be going back to the airport.

And there on the spot, when I realized that we'd never go back for one of our secret junk-food meals together, I felt myself plummeting backward, dragged down by such a powerful wave of sadness that I told Alagia that I had to go because my client must already be upstairs waiting for me, and I practically turned and ran without looking back and not even a kiss on the cheek.

PEOPLE IN LOVE HEAR VOICES

I turn the key in the lock, open the door, and walk into the group office, amazed that I've succeeded at that undertaking. By now, I'm so used to the yipping and yelping of the bellicose toy spitz that I have to focus my mind to summon up the explanation of the unnatural silence that unexpectedly drenches the place. The door of the Arethusa collective is actually open for once, a detail that confers a vaguely funereal atmosphere to the place.

I stick my head in.

The only person in the room is Roberto-Sergio, sitting at his computer, with a screenful of email.

Uh oh, I think.

"Ciao," I say, avoiding any use of his name, since I'm not sure exactly what his name is.

"Oh, ciao Vincenzo," he says, turning to look at me.

"Your wife?" I ask, so as not to ask: "The toy spitz?"

"At home," he answers gloomily. "We have a problem."

"A . . . problem?" I ask, with the exact tone of voice of the guilty party in an episode of "Columbo," when Peter Falk informs them that the guy they just killed is dead.

"The dog, Vincenzo," he says, with such a face.

"What? Is it dead?" I ask, in a crescendo of anxiety.

My interest must strike him as heartfelt, because his voice gets a little husky.

"No. We really don't know what's wrong with it. It's as if from one minute to the next the dog had lost its will to live. It seems . . . depressed."

"What do you mean depressed? Do dogs get depressed?"

"We've taken it to the veterinarian, but he says there's nothing wrong. But the dog has practically stopped eating, it mopes around, it won't leave the apartment, if we try to put the leash on it, it backs away. In fact, Virginia's at home with it right now. It's just so heartbreaking."

"I'm so sorry to hear it," I tell him. I even mean it, when I put a hand on his shoulder.

"Thanks, Vincenzo. Let's just hope the dog gets over it."

I leave the room.

"Should I close your door?"

"No, thanks."

I step out, and at the far end of the hallway I see Espedito lip-syncing some show tune, sketching invisible spirals in midair with both arms, and swiveling his hips like a Hawaiian hula dancer.

I hurry down the hall and shove him into my office.

"Vincè, God Almighty has bestowed a miracle upon us," he says.

"Shh!"

I close the door, turn on the light, and go over to remove the steel tube from the window. I swing open the shutters, take off my jacket, drape it over the back of the Skruvsta, sit down at the Jonas, and drift into a trance, as I hadn't made up my mind whether to feel guilty or not.

"Can you believe it? The toy spitz is depressed, what a beautiful stoke of luck," Espe exults, intoxicated with joy, and starts shaking his ass again in celebration.

"You know that I'm almost sorry about it?" I say, even though I do feel like laughing, truth be told.

"Nah, don't let them chip at your emotions," he replies, dismissing my comment with a semicircular gesture of the left forearm that makes me think of a windshield wiper on a car. Then he hikes up the waist of his trousers, as if to get the fit of the crotch just right. "That little fucking ball-buster has done nothing but make us look like assholes. Last week I had to rush to get a glass of water for one of my clients, it threw such a scare into him. I don't know about you, but I have to go see some of my clients in their offices, because they won't come here anymore on account of that turd of a dog, believe you me."

"Seriously?"

"What do you think, I'm kidding?"

I'm doing my best to think whether anything of the sort has ever happened to me (and just the difficulty I'm experiencing trying to come up with a memory of a client in this office before the visit from Lady Burzone is humiliating) when my landline rings. I look at the number on the screen, recognize it instantly, and my heart leaps into my mouth. I can hear the thump-thump so loud that it sounds as if I have a couple of houseguests fucking in my chest cavity.

Before now, I discover, I hadn't realized how tremendously important it had become to me to hear her voice again, and to grasp this ordinary event as concrete evidence of her existence. It is a typical trait of love that it makes the people you love cease to exist, so that when you love someone you're continually obliged to prove that, no, they actually do exist. Because a person who falls in love isn't all that certain that what's happening to them is real. People in love are suspicious of reality, they always keep their eyes wide open: that's why they get so little sleep. When they get the phone call they've been waiting for for hours, they're practically talking with phantoms and specters. If it happens to you, the way it does to me right now, that you start breathing normally again when you hear the voice of a ghost, then you have something to worry about.

I put my hand on the receiver, let it ring one more time, and then I look over at Espe. He holds up both thumbs as if to say, "Way to go, dude," and he oils out of the room with all the discretion of a consummate playboy.

I take a deep breath and, at last, I answer.

"Hey," I say cheerfully, in a pathetic attempt to exorcize the feeling of apprehension that has been haunting me ever since I received her last text message.

"Ciao, Vincenzo," says Alessandra Persiano.

Which already strikes me as horrifying, as greetings go.

"So, how's everything?" I insist, sticking to my cringe-inducing cheerfulness, like someone with a terminal illness but a good sense of humor.

"So-so," she says.

"Well, how about Chinese food?" I ask, desperately skirting the issue.

"I'm not all that hungry."

"Ale," I say, after a brief pause.

"What?"

"Is what I think is happening happening?"

She doesn't answer right away. A pause that's already an answer.

"I couldn't tell you, Vincenzo."

The Edward Hopper poster blurs. The humiliation has turned me nearsighted.

"I'm sorry," she says, after a while, since I don't say anything.

"Did I overdo it? Was I trying to go too fast? Could you tell me what I did wrong?"

"Don't do that, Vincenzo. What you did is what you did, don't you think?"

"What do you mean by that?"

"Would you be willing to repudiate the things you did, Vincenzo?"

"Would you just stop calling me Vincenzo?" I snap at her, before I realize what I've said. In fact, I immediately regret it.

"Why, isn't that your name?"

"It's just that repeated over and over, like a term of address or a post-graduate degree, it's so damned impersonal, it makes me feel like some horrible stranger."

"You're right, I'm sorry," she says, after thinking it over.
One point to me. Which doesn't make me feel any better.
"Would you explain the thing about repudiation?" I ask.
"What thing? I don't remember."
"If I was willing to repudiate the things I did."
"Ah, right."
"Well, affirmative, if you're still interested in the answer.
You name it, I'll repudiate it, if it would help."
Silence. I can hear that she's a little closer to laughing.
"That's a side of you I'm not sure about, Vinc . . . sorry."
"What do you mean?"
"You don't know why you do things."
Which is completely true, even if I don't see anything strange
about it.
Since I don't have the courage to say that, though, and I still
feel obliged to defend myself somehow, but since at the same
time I lack any original ideas at the moment, I rummage around
in the most recent information at hand.
"No, it's just that I don't see myself, when I do things."
"What?"
"That is, I only understand things after I've done them."
"So you just do them, whatever, without meaning anything
by it."
Embarrassment sweeps over me like heatstroke. I wonder
why I so frequently trap myself in such ridiculous situations.
It's hard enough to be consistent with yourself; trying to be
consistent with someone else's opinions, especially when the
only reason you said what you said is that it was the first thing
that came to mind, is a deeply unrewarding task.
"Why, is there a firm commitment with every single thing
you do?"
Jesus, I can't believe that I'm having an argument because
of Tricarico.
"I'm talking about the two of us, Vincenzo."

338 · DIEGO DE SILVA

"So am I, talking about the two of us."

"Then why do I have the impression that we're saying different things?"

"What do I know, Ale? It all seems much simpler to me than you're making it out to be."

"So it's just me complicating things."

I let a moment of silence go by, then I veer suddenly in a new direction.

"It's unbelievably wonderful making love with you," I say.

"What?" she says. But her voice sounds different.

"If you were here right now, I wouldn't let you say a single word, you know that?"

"Vin . . . cenzo."

This time, she said it in a completely different way.

"You're at the other end of the line, but I can smell your scent as if you were here. You can't even imagine how badly I want you."

She says nothing, but I can feel how close she is right now.

"You see how you are? You're always accelerating."

"Please, Ale, don't walk away from me. If you leave now, you'll never come back, I know it," I say, one step short of a supplication.

She sighs.

"Just give me a little time, Vincenzo. It's all happened so quickly. I need to think it over. And I can't understand a thing if you're all over me."

"I just wish I was," I say.

She sighs again.

"I don't know if I made myself clear," I add, since she hasn't picked up the reference.

"Oh, I got it, I got it."

"Are you smiling, at least?"

"Of course I am."

"I already miss you."

"I'll call you soon, Vincenzo."

"Ale, wai—"

She's already hung up.

I sit there, with the receiver of the cordless pressed to my ear, listening to the busy signal that repeats frantically like the *beep-beep-beep* of an EKG in an operating room when they're losing the patient.

Lucikly, Espe's head pokes in through the half-closed door.

"Come in," I say.

"You done?" he asks, nodding at the phone.

"Yeah, I'm pretty sure I'm done."

"Jesus, look at the face on you."

"Still handsomer than yours."

It may be the oldest comeback in the book, but my delivery must have been particularly convincing, because Espe stands motionless in the middle of the room and broods over it, almost as if he had to agree.

"Oh, I'm kidding," I say.

"I'm not. You look like . . . you know the faces they make when they review movies on TV, and they don't like the movie?"

My brain stalls, I visualize the image, it strikes me as fantastic, then I burst out laughing. And I immediately feel better.

"Espresso?" asks Espe, with perfect timing.

"Well, sure, okay," I reply.

I get my ass up off the Skruvsta, grab my jacket, and we leave.

When we walk into the bar across the street, we run into Giustino Talento as he's putting a liquor glass he's just emptied back down on the counter. He's wearing a distinctly filthy shirt, with a pair of bedroom sandals on his feet, and he's emitting medium-wave frequencies of malaise like a pirate radio station. The resentment that appears on his face when he sees me has an unmistakable hue.

Espe greets him first, with a forced smile.

I limit myself to waving coldly, because the discomfort of our last interaction still lingers.

Giustino responds to Espe but not to me. He crams his head down between his shoulders, walks past us, and leaves.

In the brief instant when he walks by us, I have the impression that his right eye is bruised.

We follow him with our gaze, in embarrassment.

Then we look one another in the eye.

"What did you ever do to him, Vincè?" Espe asks me.

SCHOOL-FAMILY COMMUNICATIONS

I set my alarm clock early enough to show up on time for my appointment with Alfredo's Italian teacher, who called me yesterday evening in my office to ask me to meet with her about the "situation with Alfredo."

Then and there, when she used that expression, I thought I must have misheard her, it seemed so ridiculous; especially because she said it with the kind of slimy courtesy you expect from a government marshal who's in your apartment impounding your living room furniture ("I just need to have a talk with you about the situation with Alfredo, Signore Malinconico, nothing formal, if you could just meet me for an espresso at eight o'clock tomorrow morning, half an hour before class starts, that is if it doesn't interfere with your schedule for the day, of course").

"And just what is this situation?" I asked.

"If I'm suggesting we meet, Signore Malinconico," said Alfredo's Italian teacher, immediately putting on the voice of a high school teacher (because there are certain teachers who the minute you contradict them put on their teacher's voice), "it means that I think it's more appropriate to have a conversation, don't you agree?"

"So what are we doing right now, exchanging faxes?" I replied.

"Well, I meant to say a conversation face-to-face," she amended. "In any case, I'm not at all happy about the tone I'm hearing in our phone conversation," she added, stung by the retort.

"And who the fuck cares," I feel like saying to her. She was starting to make my balls spin like propellers, truth be told.

"Listen to me," I shot back, "did my son steal your pocketbook, by any chance? Has he thrown a classmate out the window? Did he commit obscene acts in the classroom?"

"No, you listen to me, Signore Malinconico . . . " the teacher started reading me the riot act.

"*Counselor* Malinconico," I interrupted.

"All right then, *Counselor* Malinconico, if I took the trouble to call you it's because I'm worried about Alfredo, not because I'm trying to have fun."

"What does fun have to do with it?" I said with scalpel-like obstinacy. "I can't see anything fun about a phone call like this; you call me up and you talk to me about some mysterious situation with my son, as if everybody knows that my son is in the midst of such a notorious situation that there's no need to even say what it is; you act all top-secret and then you talk about it being fun?"

"Listen Counselor, Alfredo came to school again with a bruised face. Do you think that's normal? I don't."

"Exactly what are you trying to insinuate?" I said at that point, raising my voice.

"I'm not insinuating a thing, I'm just doing my job. I have a student who comes to school regularly with a swollen face from being beaten up, and it strikes me as my responsibility to talk to his parents about it," she said.

Whereupon I couldn't think of a thing to say and I just answered, "You're quite right, please forgive me," catching her so completely off guard that she replied, instinctively, "Don't mention it," even though—I'd be willing to bet a sizable sum of money—she was probably yearning to tell me to go jump off a cliff, plunging to my bloody bone-shattering death at the bottom of a jagged ravine, after a long succession of various impacts at different angles and speeds on boulders of all sizes;

but by this point she'd already said "Don't mention it," and she was stuck with her anger and annoyance bottled up inside her, poor thing.

"So . . . are you going to come?" she asked after an extended and demented silence.

"I'm not sure. Look," I answered, "it would be kind of complicated to explain it to you right now, but I'm not sure I see any need for a meeting."

"What do you mean you don't see any need? The need is clear as day."

At this point, I'm about to fly into a rage again, because if there's one thing that sets me off it's when somebody tries to give me lessons in my own field of expertise. "Look, teacher, we're talking about my son here, I don't know if that detail escapes you."

"Listen," the teacher replied, exhausted by the relentless diatribe I seemed incapable of abandoning, "I just don't understand why your wife insisted at such length on having me call you, seeing that you're so uninterested in hearing about this problem."

"And so?" I said, spiteful as a Barbary ape. "My wife! Now, there's a parent who knows how to take on the challenges that her children present . . . Wait a second, did you just say that my wife told you to call me?"

"Why, does that surprise you?"

"And just what do you care if it surprises me or not?" I would have been deeply tempted to say to that dumb cluck, if I hadn't been so completely blown away by the fact that Nives had insisted on involving me in a school conference after my unforgivable cut-and-run from the restaurant; so I agreed to come in for the meeting and we finally put an end to that demented telephone debate, in part because we were both exhausted, I believe.

After which I decided to get inside and stay out of sight

344 · DIEGO DE SILVA

before discovering what else that fucked-up day had in store for me. I made my way home, hugging the walls the whole way.

Along with everything else, just to round out the picture, Pallucca, Maria Vittoria never showed up, and my critical guardian angel just wouldn't let up, and there's nothing more exasperating than having someone on your back saying over and over: "You see? You see? What did I tell you?," especially if that someone is you.

Anyway, I get out of bed on the morning of the meeting with the obsessive thought of Alessandra Persiano playing a Venetian adagio for strings in the background; I turn off the alarm clock before it can ring; I get into the shower and practically fall asleep, I'm in there so long; I put on my bathrobe and drag myself into the kitchen, dripping water on the floor as I go; while I make my morning coffee I turn on the TV and click to a channel with a morning show in which a television show hostess in a miniskirt who's had her mouth redone by a plastic surgeon interviews an orthopedist who looks at her thighs and gives advice on the best way to lift your grocery bags; I sit down on the Stefan closest to the television set, pull the hood of the bathrobe over my head, and start patting my hair dry when the front-door intercom buzzes.

I run to answer, praying silently that it's not Alfredo again. "Hello."

"*Buon giorno*, Counselor. Can I come up for a minute?"

My jaw drops, and my arm, hand, and the intercom receiver with it, so unbelievable is it to me that I'm actually listening to Tricarico's voice.

"Wait a minute, you have the nerve to come ring my doorbell, what's more at my home, and what's more at seven in the morning, after everything you've done?"

"Oh, I know it, Counselor. In fact I wanted to know how it turned out."

"Ah, nothing special, believe me. I just spent two hours trying to explain to the police what happened and they came this close to throwing me in jail. Now that you know how it turned out, would you do me a favor and stop busting my balls from now on for all time *in saecula saeculorum?*"

"Counselor, forgive me, but what was I supposed to do, shouldn't I have defended you?"

I look around, instinctively searching for other human faces that might mirror my helpless astonishment.

"Look, let's just say that you did the right thing," I reply, doing my best to stave off the surge of blood that's inundating my brain, "let's just say that I have no reason to criticize, that your intervention was providential and that in fact I owe you a debt of gratitude. But I don't want you following me around anymore, okay?"

"Sure, but can I come up for a minute?"

"No."

"They arrested Mimmo."

"What did you just say?"

"Mimmo. 'O Burzone. They arrested him last night."

"Come on up."

THE FLEXIBILITY OF THE LABOR MARKET

How can it be that all this is happening? I wonder as I hurry to get dressed before Tricarico gets upstairs. What was the first mistake I made?

I mean, a person ought to know what he's doing, right? But that's not necessarily the way it goes.

I'm deeply upset at the idea that Burzone is back in jail so soon, especially at the thought that I might be to blame for it, in some manner that I can't understand but I darkly fear.

The door.

I welcome Tricarico into the kitchen and I offer him an espresso, as long as we're at it. He seems a little doleful, like someone who hates to have to leave or something like that.

"I'm sorry about what happened at the airport," is the first thing he says, as he takes a seat. "Did you get hurt?"

"Forget about the airport. Tell me what happened with Burzone," I say, pulling out another Stefan and sitting down next to him.

"Maybe they were tapping his phone. Or maybe they were just watching him. The dead body, the one without the hand, was wrapped up in packages in his brother-in-law's car, not far from his house. They caught him with his hands in the trunk, the dick-head."

The memory of the preliminary judge and the ADA walking into the courthouse together surfaces in my mind like a lightning bolt. And it all makes sense.

Including Alessandra Persiano's bafflement when I told her about how quickly Burzone had been released.

I smooth back my hair, which is still wet.

"The case just got a lot more complicated," I point out, already concerned about the coming judicial twists and turns. "As long as all they had was the hand, that was one thing: we could always say that the dog buried it, and who knows where the dog found it, and forget about the rest. But now . . . "

Tricarico looks at me with something approaching compassion.

"You're not going to have to worry about that, Counselor."

"What do you mean?"

"We've already hired another lawyer. That's what I came to tell you."

"Ah," I reply, in the grip of a faint sense of vertigo that passes immediately.

"Valeriani, you ever hear of him?"

"Of course I've heard of him, he's famous."

"Eh," says Tricarico. And he takes a sip of coffee.

I say nothing, mortified at having been flunked and then replaced, however much the news actually comes as a relief.

"Look, just explain one thing," I ask, clearly struggling. "What fault is it of mine if that idiot got arrested again?"

"Oh, no fault of yours. It's just that we figured out why they released him so quickly."

Because by this point it had become clear that the preliminary judge and the ADA were in cahoots to release Burzone so that they could rearrest him later, once he'd provided them with a little extra evidence. Which explains why the ADA hadn't filed a request for the confirmation of detention.

I start scratching myself all over. I'm probably turning red.

"I told you when we started, Counselor, there's no obligation," Tricarico continues. "If you work out, they'll keep you. If you don't work, they'll just hire someone else."

"Ah, right. Thanks for reminding me."

"I knew that you weren't cut out for this kind of work."

"You mean I'm too honest?"

"No. It's just that it's not your thing."

Now I really do turn red. Out of indignation, perhaps.

"Oh, listen, did you just drop by to insult me?"

"Counselor, I only told you what I think, not that what I think is necessarily the truth."

"Of course it's not the truth!"

"Then why are you getting offended?"

"O-o-oh, Jesus Christ! It's impossible to talk to you!"

"Why, what'd I say?"

"Look, here's a great idea: I'll give you back your money, okay? Why on earth would you even pay for a two-bit lawyer like me?"

"Counselor, what on earth does the money have to do with it, who asked you for the money? You did your job. If Mimmo is a shit-head who gets arrested, that's not any fault of yours."

"Okay, listen," I get to my feet, in exasperation, "we've talked enough. Now I have someplace to go."

"Now you're offended."

"That's none of your business. Shall we say goodbye?"

He finally gets to his feet, too.

"*Mamma mia*, you sure are hypersensitive, Counselor."

"How do you know a long word like hypersensitive?"

His eyes seeks out my eyes and stare into them. He's flushing red.

For a few long seconds he reflects on whether he ought to lose his temper or just take the line as a joke.

He leaves me hanging for a while, and then bursts out laughing.

THE FLAVOR OF THE WRONG PLACE

The café Ketty, where I have my appointment with Alf's teacher, is a typical little place of business organized according to its proximity to the neighboring high school—so really, more than a bar, it's a retail outlet offering single-portion pizzas, various fried foods, and pastries with nutella.

In this kind of a bar, if you order an espresso, it's always with a sense of inadequacy. And it's not only because of the smell of fried foods. It's more basic: it's that an espresso really doesn't have anything to do with the kind of café I'm talking about. In the sense that the espresso machine, if you look at it carefully, has the feel of one of those things that they keep around because you never know, it might just come in handy. In fact, the first person to have that twinge of inadequacy when you ask for an espresso is none other than the barista. You can see it from the way he makes an espresso, that he doesn't really have a practiced hand. And then he serves it apologetically. You might be familiar with the blend of coffee, and maybe it's not bad. But then when you taste your espresso, it has that distinctive flavor of the wrong place.

I'm the first to get there and, not knowing what to do with myself while waiting, after randomly punching buttons on my cell phone for a good solid five minutes, I order a flavor-of-the-wrong-place special espresso at the counter and I strike up a friendship with Ketty, the chatterbox who's given her name to the bar. She asks me if I'm the father of a student at the high school across the street, and when I confirm that I am, she demands a rough description of Alf, confident that she'll be able to recognize him from the description, as if I'd come in off the street looking for a scrap of information about his disappearance.

Shortly after we begin sketching out Alf's idenitikit, luckily, Nives shows up, stops at the front door of the café, removes her Safilo Glamour sunglasses, and looks me up and down.

I experience an acceleration of my heartbeat, and I don't know whether it's because of an abiding sense of guilt from having abandoned her in the restaurant or because of how beautiful she is.

Ketty ushers us into a back room, where the walls have been completely defaced by Sharpie graffiti.

We sit there for a while in an unexpectedly intimate silence. Then I make up my mind to say something, even though I still can't bring myself to look her in the face.

"I don't know why I did it, Nives."

"It doesn't matter," she says. But her lips are trembling.

"I can't even say I'm sorry."

"That's not nice."

"I was trying to say that—"

"Come on, cut it out," she breaks in, as if she were scolding me for not undersanding.

Whereupon, obviously, I don't understand. And out of fear of a misstep, I stop talking entirely. Which is I think the reason we broke up.

"I have to tell you something, before Alf's teacher gets here," says Nives.

"I didn't come here to see her," I say.

"Neither did I."

I'm so tempted to kiss her right now. Even though—and I've never been so sure of it—I don't love her anymore.

I look down at the table.

"I've done a lot of thinking in the past few days. And you know something? I don't understand a thing."

"Oh, that strikes me as a good sign," I say.

"Shut up."

"Okay."

She resumes. At first, she's irritated at my interruption, but then she manages to get back to the intonation she started out with.

"I've done everything I could to stay angry at you. I had every reason to feel that way, never to see you again and to reduce our interactions to the minimum necessary for the well-being of our children, but . . . "

"But what?"

"But when you walked out of that restaurant and you didn't come back, I discovered that I didn't give a damn about having a man by my side, if he wasn't you."

For a moment, a single fleeting moment, I melt. Then the material of which I'm composed resolidifies. I feel like crying, goddamn it to hell. And not because I'm happy, but because I don't know what to do with it, at this point. How many thousands of times have I dreamed of this moment? How many nights have I spent watching the Home Shopping Channel, just waiting to hear those words? Would it have taken so much, to say them to me when I needed them? I was here, for the love of God, why couldn't you see me?

"Nives . . . "

"You don't need to say anything."

In fact, I wouldn't know what to say. Luckily, the teacher shows up, out of breath, her car keys in one hand and her purse in the other.

"Excuse me, I'm so mortified. Every morning it's just such a battle to find a parking place."

We stand up and exchange the regulation round of greetings.

Ketty shows up with order pad and pencil. We have barely fifteen minutes to talk about Alf. Currently empty of any thoughts on the matter, Nives and I glance at one another furtively.

"Now then," the teacher begins, "I'm very happy that you could both be here this morning. I've been wanting to talk to you for a whi—"

A cell phone rings. It's mine.

The teacher stiffens and glares at me. Nives seems put out too.

"Sorry," I say, in embarrassment.

I look at the display. There's a phone number, but not one I recognize. I answer.

"Hello? Yes. That's me."

I straighten my back.

"What did you say?"

I get up from the table, in slow motion.

Nives and the teacher follow me with their eyes, uneasily.

I move off. I continue to listen, touching my hair.

"Yes. I'm his lawyer," I say, absolutely convinced of the words that come out of my mouth.

Ketty, at the counter, is preparing a tray to bring to our table.

She meets my disturbed gaze and stops what she's doing.

"I'll be there immediately. No, I'm not far away. Yes. Thank you."

I go back to the table, with a different face.

Nives stands up, frightened.

"Excuse me, I have to go," I say, without haste.

"What's happened, Vincenzo? Who was that on the phone?"

"A murder."

"What?"

"I have to go."

I reach out to shake hands with the teacher.

"Excuse me, I can't stay. I'm sorry."

"Don't worry, Counselor. We'll talk another time."

I feel strangely calm, as if I were starting to glimpse some sense in everything that's happening.

"Vincenzo," says Nives. And she takes my hand. It's nice, the way she does it.

"What?"

"Why are you so upset, who's been murdered?"

"I can't explain it to you now, I have to get going."

She squeezes my hand, hard.

Then she plants a kiss on my lips.

Giustino Talento killed his girlfriend with seven stab wounds. They had an argument in the kitchen, as so often happens.

The kitchen is the most dangerous place to have a fight, because weapons are lurking everywhere.

When the police got there, they found him sitting in the bedroom, a blank expression on his face. He'd actually called the police himself, giving them his name and address. He even took the trouble to give the policeman who answered the call directions to make it easier to find the street door of his apartment house more easily.

Then he washed up, changed his clothes, left the front door open, and sat down to wait for them to come and take him away.

The landing filled up with neighbors, but no one had the courage to go in.

"She didn't want me to eat meals with her," he told the policeman who asked him why he'd done it.

Then he asked for me.

"Are you Counselor Malinconico?" the policeman asks me when I walk into police headquarters.

"Yes. Did I talk with you just a few minutes ago?"

"Yeah, that was me you talked with. Come on."

And he accompanies me into the room next door.

Giustino is sitting in a chair, hands between his legs, in silence, like any ordinary person waiting their turn. For an instant I see him again, sitting at the notarization window, courteous to everyone, with a ready smile.

We walk over to him. The policeman places a hand on his shoulder with a gentleness and delicacy that makes me think: If only this guy was going to be your judge.

"Here's your lawyer, Talento."

He doesn't react.

The policeman says he'll wait outside.

I sit down next to Giustino.

"What have you done?" I say to him.

He looks at me, but I'm not sure that he sees me.

"What happened to you?"

I put a hand on his shoulder too.

"I'm sorry I didn't pay attention to you. I just didn't want to, I didn't feel like it."

Body motionless, gentle eyes wide open. It's like talking to a dog.

I take a deep breath.

"Listen. I'm nothing special, but for now, we're not even trying to win a case. We've already lost. All we need to do is defend ourselves."

He grips both knees with his fingers, probably doing his best to ward off an anxiety attack.

I touch him on the shoulder again.

"I'm happy you called me. We'll get through this, you understand?"

His fingers relax.

He just told me yes, in some way I can't describe.

I leave my details with the policeman. I ask him to call me as soon as the ADA sets a date for the judicial interrogation, any time of the day or night.

Then I head home.

In the street, I think: I hadn't understood a thing.

I'm forty-two years old, two children, I live alone, my wife left me for an architect, I waited and waited for her, now that she wants me back I don't want her; I don't earn much, my career hasn't gone well; and none of this hurts me anymore.

In the front hall, there's a red wheeled suitcase.

I don't own a red wheeled suitcase. Neither do my kids.

I hurry into the bedroom. There's no one there.

I pull open the closet, nothing in there.

In the bathroom.

In the living room.

In the kitchen.

I open the refrigerator, God knows why.

My scanty array of provisions are lined up on the top shelf. On the middle shelf, there's a bottle of prosecco and, next to it, a baking pan full of lasagna covered with plastic wrap. On the plastic wrap is a note stuck on with a piece of scotch tape.

I pick it up.

I'LL BE HOME AT TWO.
DO YOU THINK YOU COULD AT LEAST GET THE BAKING PAN INTO THE OVEN FIFTEEN MINUTES BEFORE I GET THERE?
KISSES,
LATER, ALE

I close the refrigerator door.

I read the note over and over again until Alessandra Persiano's words on the paper have become an incomprehensible scribble.

I lean against the window, clutching that scrap of paper in my fingers as if it were a patron saint prayer card.

Aw, go to hell, I think to myself.

That's what I think.

Those are the words that come to you when you feel happy, an unexpected wave of happiness crashing over you, without warning.

At Last

At last. This is where I can say at last, since we've come to the end.

I'd like to thank Gianfranco Marziano, whose speculations about modernity and the unstoppable neo-oafishness of our miserable times can be found sprinkled throughout this book; Counselor Massimo Ancarola of the bar of Salerno for a pointer in criminal law that would never have occurred to me, and Aldo Vigorito for his gift of an off-the-cuff piece of advice during a reading at which he was accompagnying me on the double bass. Thanks also to Paolo Nori, Hamid Ziarati, and Uncle Flash. And to Dalia, as always.

Now, it hardly seems necessary to point this out, but this is a novel, so the first and last names, the events and circumstances found in this novel have no actual or intended connection with people who happen to share those names and who might happen to have been involved in events and circumstances even remotely resembling those described and recounted.

While we're on the subject, let me take this opportunity to say that there are lots of people you meet every day whose lives would make a good novel. The thing is that you can't just sit down at your desk and write other people's lives. Or at least, that's what I would say, if anyone were ever to ask me.

D. D. S.

Diego De Silva was born in Naples in 1964. He is the author of plays, screenplays, and six novels. *I Hadn't Understood* was a finalist for the Strega Prize, Italy's most prestigious literary award, and winner of the Naples Prize for fiction. His books have been translated into eight languages. He currently lives in Salerno.

EUROPA EDITIONS BACKLIST
(alphabetical by author)

Fiction

Carmine Abate
Between Two Seas • 978-1-933372-40-2 • Territories: World
The Homecoming Party • 978-1-933372-83-9 • Territories: World

Simonetta Agnello Hornby
The Nun • 978-1-60945-062-5 • Territories: World

Milena Agus
From the Land of the Moon • 978-1-60945-001-4 • Ebook • Territories: World (excl. ANZ)

Salwa Al Neimi
The Proof of the Honey • 978-1-933372-68-6 • Ebook • Territories: World (excl. UK)

Jenn Ashworth
A Kind of Intimacy • 978-1-933372-86-0 • Territories: US & Can

Beryl Bainbridge
The Girl in the Polka Dot Dress • 978-1-60945-056-4 • Ebook • Territories: US

Muriel Barbery
The Elegance of the Hedgehog • 978-1-933372-60-0 • Ebook • Territories: World (excl. UK & EU)
Gourmet Rhapsody • 978-1-933372-95-2 • Ebook • Territories: World (excl. UK & EU)

Stefano Benni
Margherita Dolce Vita • 978-1-933372-20-4 • Territories: World
Timeskipper • 978-1-933372-44-0 • Territories: World

Romano Bilenchi
The Chill • 978-1-933372-90-7 • Territories: World

Kazimierz Brandys
Rondo • 978-1-60945-004-5 • Territories: World

Alina Bronsky
Broken Glass Park • 978-1-933372-96-9 • Ebook • Territories: World
The Hottest Dishes of the Tartar Cuisine • 978-1-60945-006-9 • Ebook • Territories: World

Jesse Browner
Everything Happens Today • 978-1-60945-051-9 • Ebook • Territories: World (excl. UK & EU)

Francisco Coloane
Tierra del Fuego • 978-1-933372-63-1 • Ebook • Territories: World

Rebecca Connell
The Art of Losing • 978-1-933372-78-5 • Territories: US

Laurence Cossé
A Novel Bookstore • 978-1-933372-82-2 • Ebook • Territories: World
An Accident in August • 978-1-60945-049-6 • Territories: World (excl. UK)

Diego De Silva
I Hadn't Understood • 978-1-60945-065-6 • Territories: World

Shashi Deshpande
The Dark Holds No Terrors • 978-1-933372-67-9 •
Territories: US

Steve Erickson
Zeroville • 978-1-933372-39-6 • Territories: US & Can
These Dreams of You • 978-1-60945-063-2 • Territories: US & Can

Elena Ferrante
The Days of Abandonment • 978-1-933372-00-6 • Ebook • Territories: World
Troubling Love • 978-1-933372-16-7 • Territories: World
The Lost Daughter • 978-1-933372-42-6 • Territories: World

Linda Ferri
Cecilia • 978-1-933372-87-7 • Territories: World

Damon Galgut
In a Strange Room • 978-1-60945-011-3 • Ebook • Territories: USA

Jane Gardam
Old Filth • 978-1-933372-13-6 • Ebook • Territories: US & Italy
The Queen of the Tambourine • 978-1-933372-36-5 • Ebook • Territories: US
The People on Privilege Hill • 978-1-933372-56-3 • Ebook • Territories: US
The Man in the Wooden Hat • 978-1-933372-89-1 • Ebook • Territories: US
God on the Rocks • 978-1-933372-76-1 • Ebook • Territories: US & Can

Anna Gavalda
French Leave • 978-1-60945-005-2 • Ebook • Territories: US & Can

Katharina Hacker
The Have-Nots • 978-1-933372-41-9 • Territories: World (excl. India)

Patrick Hamilton
Hangover Square • 978-1-933372-06-8 • Territories: US & Can

James Hamilton-Paterson
Cooking with Fernet Branca • 978-1-933372-01-3 • Territories: US
Amazing Disgrace • 978-1-933372-19-8 • Territories: US
Rancid Pansies • 978-1-933372-62-4 • Territories: US

Alfred Hayes
The Girl on the Via Flaminia • 978-1-933372-24-2 • Ebook • Territories: World

Jean-Claude Izzo
The Lost Sailors • 978-1-933372-35-8 • Territories: World
A Sun for the Dying • 978-1-933372-59-4 • Territories: World

Gail Jones
Sorry • 978-1-933372-55-6 • Territories: US & Can

Ioanna Karystiani
The Jasmine Isle • 978-1-933372-10-5 • Territories: World
Swell • 978-1-933372-98-3 • Territories: World

Peter Kocan
Fresh Fields • 978-1-933372-29-7 • Territories: US, EU & Can
The Treatment and the Cure • 978-1-933372-45-7 • Territories: US, EU & Can

Helmut Krausser
Eros • 978-1-933372-58-7 • Territories: World

Amara Lakhous
Clash of Civilizations Over an Elevator in Piazza Vittorio • 978-1-933372-61-7 •
Ebook
Divorce Islamic Style • 978-1-60945-066-3 • Ebook • Territories: World

Lia Levi
The Jewish Husband • 978-1-933372-93-8 • Territories: World

Valerio Massimo Manfredi
The Ides of March • 978-1-933372-99-0 • Territories: US

Leïla Marouane
The Sexual Life of an Islamist in Paris • 978-1-933372-85-3 • Territories: World

Sélim Nassib
I Loved You for Your Voice • 978-1-933372-07-5 • Territories: World
The Palestinian Lover • 978-1-933372-23-5 • Territories: World

Amélie Nothomb
Tokyo Fiancée • 978-1-933372-64-8 • Territories: US & Can
Hygiene and the Assassin • 978-1-933372-77-8 • Ebook • Territories: US & Can

Valeria Parrella
For Grace Received • 978-1-933372-94-5 • Territories: World

Alessandro Piperno
The Worst Intentions • 978-1-933372-33-4 • Territories: World

Lorcan Roche
The Companion • 978-1-933372-84-6 • Territories: World

Boualem Sansal
The German Mujahid • 978-1-933372-92-1 • Ebook • Territories: US & Can

www.europaeditions.com

Eric-Emmanuel Schmitt
The Most Beautiful Book in the World • 978-1-933372-74-7 • Ebook • Territories: World
The Woman with the Bouquet • 978-1-933372-81-5 • Ebook • Territories: US & Can
Concerto to the Memory of an Angel • 978-1-60945-009-0 • Ebook • Territories: US & Can

Audrey Schulman
Three Weeks in December • 978-1-60945-064-9 • Ebook • Territories: US & Can

James Scudamore
Heliopolis • 978-1-933372-73-0 • Ebook • Territories: US

Luis Sepúlveda
The Shadow of What We Were • 978-1-60945-002-1 • Ebook • Territories: World

Paolo Sorrentino
Everybody's Right • 978-1-60945-052-6 • Ebook • Territories: US & Can

Domenico Starnone
First Execution • 978-1-933372-66-2 • Territories: World

Henry Sutton
Get Me out of Here • 978-1-60945-007-6 • Ebook • Territories: US & Can

Chad Taylor
Departure Lounge • 978-1-933372-09-9 • Territories: US, EU & Can

Roma Tearne
Mosquito • 978-1-933372-57-0 • Territories: US & Can
Bone China • 978-1-933372-75-4 • Territories: US

André Carl van der Merwe
Moffie • 978-1-60945-050-2 • Ebook • Territories: World (excl. S. Africa)

Fay Weldon
Chalcot Crescent • 978-1-933372-79-2 • Territories: US

Anne Wiazemsky
My Berlin Child • 978-1-60945-003-8 • Territories: US & Can

Jonathan Yardley
Second Reading • 978-1-60945-008-3 • Ebook • Territories: US & Can

Edwin M. Yoder Jr.
Lions at Lamb House • 978-1-933372-34-1 • Territories: World

Michele Zackheim
Broken Colors • 978-1-933372-37-2 • Territories: World

Alice Zeniter
Take This Man • 978-1-60945-053-3 • Territories: World

Children's Illustrated Fiction

Altan
Here Comes Timpa • 978-1-933372-28-0 • Territories: World (excl. Italy)
Timpa Goes to the Sea • 978-1-933372-32-7 • Territories: World (excl. Italy)
Fairy Tale Timpa • 978-1-933372-38-9 • Territories: World (excl. Italy)

Wolf Erlbruch
The Big Question • 978-1-933372-03-7 • Territories: US & Can
The Miracle of the Bears • 978-1-933372-21-1 • Territories: US & Can
(with **Gioconda Belli**) *The Butterfly Workshop* •
978-1-933372-12-9 • Territories: US & Can

Non-fiction

Alberto Angela
A Day in the Life of Ancient Rome • 978-1-933372-71-6 • Territories: World • History

Helmut Dubiel
Deep In the Brain: Living with Parkinson's Disease •
978-1-933372-70-9 • Ebook • Medicine/Memoir

James Hamilton-Paterson
Seven-Tenths: The Sea and Its Thresholds • 978-1-933372-69-3 • Territories: USA •
Nature/Essays

Daniele Mastrogiacomo
Days of Fear • 978-1-933372-97-6 • Ebook • Territories: World • Current
affairs/Memoir/Afghanistan/Journalism

Valery Panyushkin
Twelve Who Don't Agree • 978-1-60945-010-6 • Ebook • Territories: World •
Current affairs/Memoir/Russia/Journalism

Christa Wolf
One Day a Year: 1960-2000 • 978-1-933372-22-8 • Territories: World •
Memoir/History/20th Century

Tonga Books

Ian Holding
Of Beasts and Beings • 978-1-60945-054-0 • Ebook • Territories: US & Can

Sara Levine
Treasure Island!!! • 978 0 14043 768 3 • Ebook • Territories: World

Alexander Maksik
You Deserve Nothing • 978-1-60945-048-9 • Ebook • Territories: US, Can & EU
(excl. UK)

Crime/Noir

Massimo Carlotto
The Goodbye Kiss • 978-1-933372-05-1 • Ebook • Territories: World
Death's Dark Abyss • 978-1-933372-18-1 • Ebook • Territories: World
The Fugitive • 978-1-933372-25-9 • Ebook • Territories: World
Poisonville • 978-1-933372-91-4 • Ebook • Territories: World
Bandit Love • 978-1-933372-80-8 • Ebook • Territories: World

Giancarlo De Cataldo
The Father and the Foreigner • 978-1-933372-72-3 • Territories: World

www.europaeditions.com

Caryl Férey
Zulu • 978-1-933372-88-4 • Ebook • Territories: World (excl. UK & EU)
Utu • 978-1-60945-055-7 • Ebook • Territories: World (excl. UK & EU)

Alicia Giménez-Bartlett
Dog Day • 978-1-933372-14-3 • Territories: US & Can
Prime Time Suspect • 978-1-933372-31-0 • Territories: US & Can
Death Rites • 978-1-933372-54-9 • Territories: US & Can

Jean-Claude Izzo
Total Chaos • 978-1-933372-04-4 • Territories: US & Can
Chourmo • 978-1-933372-17-4 • Territories: US & Can
Solea • 978-1-933372-30-3 • Territories: US & Can

Matthew F. Jones
Boot Tracks • 978-1-933372-11-2 • Territories: US & Can

Gene Kerrigan
The Midnight Choir • 978-1-933372-26-6 • Territories: US & Can
Little Criminals • 978-1-933372-43-3 • Territories: US & Can

Carlo Lucarelli
Carte Blanche • 978-1-933372-15-0 • Territories: World
The Damned Season • 978-1-933372-27-3 • Territories: World
Via delle Oche • 978-1-933372-53-2 • Territories: World

Edna Mazya
Love Burns • 978-1-933372-08-2 • Territories: World (excl. ANZ)

Yishai Sarid
Limassol • 978-1-60945-000-7 • Ebook • Territories: World (excl. UK, AUS & India)

Joel Stone
The Jerusalem File • 978-1-933372-65-5 • Ebook • Territories: World

Benjamin Tammuz
Minotaur • 978-1-933372-02-0 • Ebook • Territories: World